MW00397398

PRODIGAL

SCATTERED STARS: CONVICTION BOOK 6

Prodigal © 2023 Glynn Stewart

All rights reserved. For information about permission to reproduce selections from this book, contact the publisher at info@faolanspen.com or Faolan's Pen Publishing Inc., 22 King St. S, Suite 300, Waterloo, Ontario N2J 1N8, Canada.

This is a work of fiction. All the characters and events portrayed in this book are fictional, and any resemblance to any persons living or dead is purely coincidental.

This edition published in 2023 by:

Faolan's Pen Publishing Inc.

22 King St. S, Suite 300

Waterloo, Ontario

N2J 1N8 Canada

ISBN-13: 978-1-989674-34-5

A record of this book is available from Library and Archives Canada.

Printed in the United States of America

1 2 3 4 5 6 7 8 9 10

First edition

First printing: April 2023

Illustration by Jeff Brown Graphics

Faolan's Pen Publishing logo is a registered trademark of Faolan's Pen Publishing Inc.

Read more books from Glynn Stewart at faolanspen.com

PRODIGAL

SCATTERED STARS: CONVICTION BOOK 6

GLYNN STEWART

FAOLAN'S PEN PUBLISHING
faolanspen.com

1

Despite Admiral Kira Demirci's best efforts, her boyfriend was still terrible at basketball. The slightly built blonde mercenary dodged around Konrad Bueller on the court, putting her back to her partner to deflect his grab for the ball as she slipped into position and took her shot.

The basket cheerfully dinged her success, and the scoreboard her headware implant was feeding her vision ticked up another.

"Okay, I think I'm done," her boyfriend said with a chuckle. Bueller was roughly twice his girlfriend and boss's sixty-kilogram mass, heavyset and muscular with pale skin and copper hair against her slim build, Mediterranean skin and blonde hair.

"You're not going to try for a second point?" she asked brightly, retrieving the ball from the gymnasium floor and absentmindedly dribbling.

"I think I would need to call it, uh...best of *thirteen*, I think? And then stop you scoring even once." He shook his head at her, still smiling. "I'd love to tell myself that you have a program in your headware or some kind of implant to make you a super basketball player, but..."

"I've been playing this game for over thirty years, Konrad," Kira pointed out. "I've lost count of the ships and planets I've played it on."

Mostly spaceships, in truth. That she was currently in a planet-side gym, with actual dirt underneath the polished wooden floor, was unusual for her. Kira Demirci, after all, ran the Memorial Force mercenary fleet.

Now up to two carriers and three cruisers, plus escorts, her little fleet was actually worthy of the term. Unfortunately, the task before her required...more.

The news had reached Samuels, their current employer and the location of the basketball court, four weeks earlier. Konrad's home-world, Brisingr, had invaded and conquered Kira's homeworld, Apollo.

Interstellar invasion was supposed to be impossible, but Kaiser Reinhardt had managed it.

"Hey," her boyfriend said, putting his hand on her shoulder. "Should take more than the word *planet* to send you down that rabbit hole, love."

Konrad had apparently followed her thoughts perfectly.

"Hell of a job in front of us," she murmured, still bouncing the basketball.

"Yes. And you're not supposed to be thinking about it right now," he told her. "Come on. Let's freshen up. We're meeting the First Minister in an hour, after all."

First Minister Buxton was the leader of Samuels and Memorial Force's employer for a few more months. Kira wasn't going to break contract, after all. Not when Samuels' Defense Command had saved her life from a Brisingr-led ambush only a few weeks earlier, anyway!

THE HOUSE the local government was providing Kira and her people had, until very recently, been the personal residence of the

Brisingr Ambassador. The back and forth between Samuels and Brisingr had been entertaining. For *Kira*, at least.

The government of Samuels—a system founded by Quakers and with pacifism enshrined in their *blood*, let alone their constitution—had done everything to avoid war with their neighbors in the Colossus System except surrender without a fight.

The wrench in the gears had been the Brisingr Kaiserreich supplying the Colossus System with nova warships. That, Kira could probably lay at the feet of the Equilibrium Institute, a think tank turned militant conspiracy from the inner sectors of human space—but then a Brisingr Kaiserreich Navy carrier group had ambushed her ships and tried to kill *her*, specifically.

Buxton and the rest of his government had taken the deployment of BKN warships and the fact that Samuels had been manipulated into putting Kira in position for that ambush *personally*.

So, there was no longer a Brisingr Ambassador to Samuels, and residence and embassy alike had been seized by the Ministries, Samuels' government.

"The First Minister is on their way," an armored mercenary soldier told Kira as she stepped out of the change room in a fresh uniform. "We're coordinating with their security detail."

"Thank you, Corporal," she told the woman.

The First Minister's security detail, like most of Samuels' military personnel, were Gorkhali. Roughly ninety percent of Samuels' population were either Quakers or similarly pacifistic branches of Buddhism. But, from what Kira could tell, when a large contingent of pacifist Buddhists had set out to colonize a planet with other pacifists, several clans of their northern neighbors—also known as *Ghurkas*—had decided to come along to keep them safe.

"What's the Minister's ETA?" Kira asked.

"Roughly two minutes before your scheduled meeting, ser," the mercenary replied.

"Just enough time for Milani to make sure they are who they say they are." Kira chuckled. "Does Em Koch know?"

Jess Koch was Kira's steward: a chef, bodyguard and administrator originally trained to enter the service of the Queen of Redward, the mercenary fleet's current home port. She ran Kira's life with a level of efficiency Kira wouldn't have thought *possible*.

"Of course," the mercenary confirmed.

Kira gave them a nod of thanks and turned to watch as Bueller emerged behind her. The stress of the last couple of years had carved away any of the chubbiness to her partner's body, leaving behind hard-edged muscle and *far* too many stress lines.

Neither of them were young—they hadn't been young when they'd first met, during the *last* war between Apollo and Brisingr, where he'd been a prisoner of war and she'd been one of his captors—but she had to admit that the heavyset man had a definite *look* to him.

And she definitely wasn't biased.

"The First Minister will be here on time," she told Bueller. "Are you ready for the briefing?"

"I'm not sure why *I'm* briefing the First Minister on the status of their ships," her chief engineer said. "But yes, I'm ready." He chuckled. "I spent two hours yesterday on a videoconference with Buxton's husband, getting updates."

"As I understand it, Buxton and Tapadia want an outside perspective on all of the mechanical parts," Kira pointed out. Batsal Tapadia was the man in charge of the spaceborne construction yards run by Samuels-Tata Technologies, one of the largest industrial concerns in the Samuels System.

He was also First Minister Buxton's husband, resulting in the First Minister recusing themselves from a lot of decisions around the new nova-capable defense force Samuels was building.

"Well, I can manage that," Bueller said. "I feel like I spend more time organizing other people's building programs than acting as engineer for our ships."

"Well, the only ships of *ours* currently in Samuels are in the same yards we're briefing the First Minister on," she said. "*Huntress* is due back shortly, but the cruisers are all getting their scratches buffed out."

"That's...*one* description for the hole my old countryfolk put through *Deception*," Bueller said. He shook his head. "'Scratches.'"

FIRST MINISTER BUXTON was one of the largest human beings Kira had ever met. Not *the* largest, but at over two meters tall, they *towered* over the petite mercenary Admiral. Even Bueller, who was far from a small man, looked short as he took his seat across from Buxton.

"Admiral, Commander," Buxton greeted the mercenaries. "I appreciate you making time for me."

"We are still under contract for several more months," Kira reminded them. "While that doesn't necessarily give you *complete* command of our time, you do have some *small* priority."

The First Minister chuckled, glancing aside quickly as Jess Koch emerged from a side door with a tray of drinks. The nervous twitch was new. As someone at least partially responsible for Buxton's security, Kira approved of their increased attention to potential threats.

She still had to feel a moment of regret, though. Buxton was more practical than some of the other Samuels natives who leaned hard into their pacifism, but they'd never seriously been threatened before.

Koch, though, was a known entity—and that she was serving the drinks herself told Kira that the bodyguard-slash-steward already knew this was a confidential meeting.

"I appreciate it nonetheless," Buxton told them. "*Huntress* is due back soon, I understand?"

"Yes." Kira nodded. "She was making a swing back Rimward after her patrol to pick up some new recruits, but she's due today or tomorrow."

"I'll be glad to see her," the First Minister admitted. "I know that we are secure here, but we did just flip off the most powerful state in our astrographic region."

Samuels had maintained the same array of asteroid fortresses and other defenses as any other Rim star system, generally considered impenetrable by a nova-capable force of remotely equivalent technology.

They had *not*, prior to Colossus getting aggressive, maintained a nova-capable force of their own. That was changing now, but they were still understrength for the commitments they'd taken on.

"We did just receive a new update from Brisingr," Buxton continued. "With the full withdrawal of Ambassador Schirmer and her staff, our contact is much reduced."

"You did ban Brisingr ships from the Samuels-Colossus Corridor," Bueller murmured.

The Corridor was what made the two systems rich—and what made them politically and militarily important. In this region of the Rim, there was a roughly thirty-light-year cube of space where Samuels and Colossus were the only places a ship could stop to refuel and discharge static.

And the farthest a nova-drive ship could go without discharging static was about thirty light-years. To pass through the Corridor and pass between the inner and outer regions of this section of the Rim, a ship had to discharge at either Samuels or Colossus.

Or go around, and add at least two weeks to the trip.

"We did, and so far as we know, no Brisingr civilian ships have challenged that," Buxton agreed. "I now have formal notice from the Brisingr Diet that they do not recognize our authority *to* close the Corridor to their shipping, but that's...pretty toothless."

"Right up until they use that as justification to force the Corridor with a battle group," Kira said grimly. "I am much less certain of when the rest of my fleet is going to arrive than of *Huntress*'s return. And Brisingr has recently promoted themselves to a *two*-star-system power."

Those were rare. *Very* rare. In the entire Rim—the region from about a thousand light-years to about fifteen hundred light-years from Sol—Kira was aware of four.

"Which is, of course, why I want to hear Commander Bueller's assessment of our repairs and shipbuilding program," Buxton agreed. He took a glass of water from the tray Koch had delivered, and gestured at Bueller.

"Well?"

The engineer chuckled.

"There's a few moving parts there, I'll admit, but let's take them in turn," he rumbled. "First up, and most immediately critical, the destroyers."

The attempt by the Brisingr Kaiserreich Navy to ambush Kira's mercenaries had ended in the surrender of half a dozen BKN ships to a mixed force of her mercenaries and the Samuels Defense Command.

The joint force had found themselves in possession of two cruisers of ninety-five thousand cubic meters apiece and four destroyers of forty-five thousand cubic meters. There could have been all sorts of arguments over who got what, but Kira had agreed with Buxton that an even split of the cubage was fair—she got the cruisers, and the SDC got the destroyers.

"Two of the D-Twelves had taken relatively light damage and have completed their repairs," Bueller told Buxton. "As I'm sure Mr. Tapadia told you, they are undergoing trials and training right now."

The gendered honorific still felt...rough around the edges to Kira. Outside of Samuels, most of the galaxy had long settled on the neutral "Em" for everyone. In Samuels, though, *marriage* was considered massively important. So, *Mister*, *Missus*, and *Mix* had reemerged in their cultural lexicon, leaving *Em* for unmarried individuals.

"I was told that, yes," Buxton agreed. "But I want *your* assessment, Commander Bueller."

"The D-Twelves are..." Bueller paused thoughtfully. "They're decent ships, First Minister. I don't like the compromises that went into supplying them with heavy guns in single turrets, but that gives them a punch well above what their size would suggest.

"For herding merchants, they're overkill, but they'll definitely do the job. The damage on the first pair is pretty light, so Samuels-Tata fixed them first for two reasons: one, to get ships into service faster, and two, to see what a D-Twelve is *supposed* to look like before someone puts a torpedo into her."

"But they are appropriate to be reactivated?" Buxton asked. "I am uncomfortable enough with commissioning interstellar warships, Commander Bueller; I do not wish to commission ships that are less safe for our people than possible."

"The two that are recommissioning are ready," Bueller confirmed. "The other two..."

He shook his head.

"They are repairable, and I've gone back and forth with your people on how best to do so. I think it's going to take longer than they're hoping—but we are talking three more months instead of eight weeks. They're not particularly large ships as Inner-Rim warships go."

"I believe my husband may have split the difference on the estimates," Buxton said with a chuckle. "*He* told me ten weeks. Minimum."

"For the purposes of the next few weeks, two destroyers backed by *Huntress* should suffice to maintain the blockade," Kira told the First Minister. "More hulls will always be better. Even gunships would be helpful right now, though I understand the logic in only building full-scale warships."

The repairs to the six ex-BKN ships and her own *Deception*—also an ex-Brisingr ship, though by a longer time period—were occupying every yard Samuels had online and would do so at least until the destroyers were online.

She knew that Bueller was using the repairs to make certain that Samuels-Tata and their partners definitely had the skillsets and toolsets necessary to build ships of their own.

"And will our people be ready to build warships from scratch in ten weeks?" Buxton asked.

The First Minister, it seemed, was *also* aware of Bueller's ulterior motive in helping supervise the repairs.

"Yes. Their first pair of destroyers are going to take longer than they think—that's inevitable and normal. But they have everything they need, I think."

"Good. And the other pieces of concern?"

"*Deception* will be back online around the same time as the second pair of D-Twelves," Bueller said, glancing over at Kira. "Eleven weeks, give or take a week, depending on a few factors."

Kira's cruiser had taken some serious hits during the ambush. As the saying went, though, anyone thinking *Deception* had lost the fight should see the other guys.

"The K-Nineties will be a bit longer," the engineer continued. "Sixteen to eighteen weeks." He shrugged. "Basically, the rest of our contract with you, as I understand it."

They were contracted to guard Samuels for another five months —*hopefully* with their entire fleet, which was still somewhere in the Outer Rim. Kira had sent the orders for *Fortitude* and her destroyers to finish up their contract with the Obsidian System months earlier.

Once she had *Fortitude*, *Huntress*, all three cruisers and her dozen destroyers... Well, once Kira had her full mercenary fleet around her, then it would be time to start digging into what had happened at Apollo.

"As we promised, your repairs for those ships will be fully paid for by the Ministries," Buxton assured them. "And Commander Bueller is, I hope, being appropriately compensated for his work with Samuels-Tata?"

"Yes," Bueller agreed. He wasn't going to admit he thought he was being overpaid. Kira had made *sure* of that!

Buxton was about to say something else but paused mid-word as an alert hit the headware implants of all three people in the room.

"Kanchenjunga Fortress is reporting multiple nova emergences on a standard approach," Kira said swiftly, processing the report faster than the civilian First Minister. "Fourteen ships."

"Your assessment, Admiral?" Buxton asked.

"I'm waiting for... There it is." She smiled. "Identity beacons make it *Huntress, Fortitude,* and our destroyer squadrons. I believe we are activating the price-escalator clause, First Minister.

"The rest of my fleet has arrived."

2

Kira flew the shuttle onto *Fortitude*'s flight deck herself. At two hundred meters long, the Crest supercarrier was vastly larger than *Huntress* in every dimension, leaving the Redward-built light carrier looking like a younger sibling as she passed it by.

The two carriers were completely different, but all twelve of the destroyers flying escort on the two capital ships were identical. Kira's Memorial Force had roughly a third of the Redward-built *Parakeet*-class destroyers that had been built to date.

A sign, like *Huntress* herself, of the depth and weight of the mercenary fleet's relationship with its home port. Redward no longer truly needed them, which had led to some tensions over the last couple of years, but the Kingdom of Redward's monarchs and military *mostly* appreciated their mercenary allies.

Even if they still hadn't come up with the hundred-and-twenty-kilocubic carrier she'd been supposed to get at cost. *Huntress* had been partially underwritten by the Kingdom in recognition of that delay, but it still rankled.

Fortitude was bigger than anything Redward would be building for years yet, though. She was bigger than anything Samuels could build—bigger than anything *Brisingr* could build.

She was the latest and greatest from the Royal Crest, a power a few degrees around the Rim that was just as technologically advanced as the Apollo-Brisingr Sector. Even the Crest only had one other ship like her—and Kira had claimed her as payment for an operation that had changed the political balance in that region.

Like so many of the operations Memorial Force had been involved in, the other side had been deeply involved with the Equilibrium Institute. For an organization founded hundreds of light-years away, the Institute seemed to have their fingers in a lot of things in this portion of the Rim.

Kira kept finding them and fighting them. She hadn't known until afterward that the Institute was involved in backing Brisingr and even, from what she now knew, the assassination attempts against Apollo's ace pilots that had driven her into exile. That knowledge turned basically *every* conflict of her adult life into a war against the Institute.

A war that had made her rich, provided her with the most powerful carrier for a hundred light-years in any direction...and made her very, *very* tired.

Even there, aboard a ship crewed and operated by people she'd hired and trusted, Milani didn't allow her to leave the shuttle first. The mercenary ground-force commander probably shouldn't have gone out first themselves, either, but Kira wasn't going to argue that point.

Milani would do as Milani was going to do. Clad from head to toe in powered armor, the mercenary delighted as much in protecting the rest of the mercenary fleet as they did in the red holographic dragon that covered their armor.

Just because they were in charge of security and ground forces for a fleet of *seventeen* interstellar warships wasn't going to change the way Milani approached the world. And that meant that the mercenary in the red dragon armor left the shuttle first.

Kira gave Milani all of thirty seconds to make sure the flight deck of their flagship was clear of unexpected hostiles, then followed them out into the open expanse.

Nova ships were limited in size by the volume that their drives could take with them. That meant that even the largest nova ships—in the Rim, anyway—were relatively small by the standard of any construction that didn't need to go faster than light.

Fortitude's flight deck was probably the single largest open space Kira had ever seen on a nova ship. It was less than twenty meters wide and half that tall, and cut a full sixty percent of the length of the carrier. She'd seen *destroyers* that could be parked on *Fortitude*'s flight deck—though doing so would require moving the nova fighters, the shuttles and all of the equipment used for managing and maintaining those small craft.

But enough of that was pulled to the sides or attached to the roof to make a manual landing on the flight deck possible. Unwise—*Fortitude*'s computers had flown the last minute or so of Kira's approach—but *possible*.

And because the Harrington coils that carried modern spaceships were more contained in their heat release than any reaction thrusters, it had been possible for *Fortitude*'s Captain to be waiting less than half a dozen meters from the shuttle, grinning from ear to ear as she waited for Kira and Konrad Bueller to step off the small spacecraft.

"Welcome back, Admiral," Kavitha Zoric told her boss.

"Welcome to Samuels, Captain," Kira replied. "How was Obsidian?"

"A brush war, as we figured," Zoric said. "Shall we discuss in my office? My impression from Captain Davidović is that you've found some surprises for us that she didn't want to tell me about in advance!"

Marija Davidović commanded *Huntress*. Apparently, she'd felt that the whole "we're going to go take the majority shareholder's homeworld back by force" thing was something she should leave the shareholders to sort out between themselves.

Kira smiled thinly.

"I hope you have decent tea," she told Zoric. "Because I don't think anyone in this star system does!"

WHILE EVERY SHIP in Memorial Force was well stocked with good coffee—it was Redward's main export product, and Kira had been given access to the royal family's own product—her continued exposure to the overbrewed mountain tea the Gorkhali had brought with them to Bennet had left Kira craving decent tea.

Fortunately, her dark-haired second-in-command *did*, in fact, have decent tea. Reading the label as the leaves steeped, Kira saw that it was a genetically engineered blend of green and white teas put together to thrive in Obsidian's particular soil chemistry.

"Did they engineer it for taste, too?" Kira asked with a chuckle.

"I have no idea, but I like it," Zoric admitted. "Not quite as much as some of the coffee from Redward, but it makes a nice change."

The Captain's office on *Fortitude* rivaled some entire flag bridges Kira had seen for space. The Admiral's spaces, her own home when the fleet was together, were similarly ridiculous to her gaze—though, of course, the entire "flag deck," bridge, offices, quarters and all, would probably fit inside the ballroom of the house she'd been using on Bennet.

And the former Brisingr Ambassador's mansion wasn't *that* excessive, really.

"It does," Kira agreed, taking in the gentle smell. "Unfortunately, the locals in Samuels appear to have imported the darkest and bitterest of black teas—and then decided that it must be steeped for no less than an hour before serving."

"Ah. So, a concentrated caffeine-delivery system pretending to be a beverage?" Zoric asked. "I've encountered coffee of that style, if not tea."

Kira took a careful sip of the tea and sighed in relief when it tasted as good as it smelled.

"Basically." She slid a cup over to both Bueller and Zoric. Milani, for their part, had declined as expected. Kira *had* seen them drink—through a straw hooked up to a port on their armor—but only cold beverages.

She had never seen Milani out of their armor, and she suspected no one except the mercenary's doctor had in at least a decade. And given the armor's ability to provide bioscan readouts, she wasn't entirely sure any of Memorial Force's *doctors* had seen the merc unarmored.

"So. Davidović said shit had gone down here, beyond just the stuff she *did* brief me on," Zoric said. "I am informed we've picked up another pair of Brisingr hand-me-downs?"

"K-Ninety-class cruisers," Bueller confirmed. "*Deception*'s newer sisters. Heavy cruisers, not major capital ships, but modern and capable units."

"By Rim standards," Zoric pointed out.

Kira wasn't entirely sure where Kavitha Zoric came from originally. She did know that the other woman had joined *Conviction*—the mercenary carrier that Kira had fled to Redward to sign onto originally—while she'd been in the Fringe. Occasionally, she had hints that the woman had come from even farther toward Earth than John Estanza, *Conviction*'s original CO.

John Estanza, like Kira's old boss Jay Moranis, had once been a member of Cobra Squadron, a legendary fighter wing that had turned out to be Equilibrium Institute operatives. When Estanza and Moranis and a few others had realized the scope and scale of the Institute's failures, they'd "gone rogue."

To Kira's knowledge, all of the original Cobras were now dead. The Institute had assembled a *new* Cobra Squadron to replace them —which had collided with *Conviction* and what had become Memorial Force afterward.

That Cobra Squadron had been equipped with ships from the

Fringe, the systems closer to Earth than the Rim. The Fringe spread from seven hundred light-years from Sol to a thousand light-years and had a generally higher level of technology than the Rim. It was a decent rule of thumb that for every ten light-years a system was from Earth, their military technology fell about a year and a half behind.

So, on average, Fringe ships and weapon systems were about thirty years ahead of their equivalents in the Rim—and the ships and systems available to the Solar Federation, anchored on Sol itself, were basically mythology out there.

"Rim standards are the only ones we need to worry about," Kira said softly. "If we can go toe-to-toe with Brisingr or the Royal Crest, we're as well equipped as any mercenary force out here can be."

"The only reason we can go up against the BKN or the Navy of the Royal Crest is because we stole the NRC's latest fighter designs with this ship," Zoric said bluntly. "*Fortitude* is our only truly modern ship, even by local standards, and even *she* would be a back-line unit in the Fringe."

"We are not fighting in the Fringe, thank all deities," Kira replied. "But your point is taken. *Harbinger* and *Prodigal*, once online, will bring us up to five capital ships and a decent heavy-carrier group.

"A fleet by Outer Rim standards...but we're in the Inner Rim now, so a carrier group."

There was a long silence as Zoric considered that.

"The contract has us standing guard over Samuels for the next twenty weeks or so," she observed. "After that, I think I was assuming that we would fall back to Redward to rest and refit while we considered our next offers of employment.

"But if you're planning around the Inner Rim...we're staying here or going deeper. And the names you've given those cruisers make me think this has something to do with *Apollo*."

Kavitha Zoric, Kira reflected, was very, *very* smart.

"We're going to need to call a shareholder meeting in the very near future," Kira told her second-in-command. "We're not breaking contract with Samuels, of course, but Memorial Force's next contract is already lined up.

"*I* will be paying us."

Zoric nodded slowly.

"What happened?"

"Brisingr took Apollo."

The carrier Captain exhaled a surprised sigh and leaned back in her chair. She glanced at Milani and Bueller, clearly checking that Kira wasn't playing games with her.

"I want to say that's impossible, but clearly I would be wrong," she observed. "And while I'm not sure Milani has seen Apollo's fixed defenses, *I* have. I know you have. And I'm sure Konrad, when he was a BKN officer, was briefed on them.

"So...given that, for example, the fortress over *there*"—Zoric waved at a wall, presumably in the vague direction of the nearest of Bennet's orbital forts—"carries a *thousand* heavy plasma guns to the average Rim battlecruiser's *thirty* and Apollo had more and bigger fortresses than the Samuels System...how in broken stars did the Brisingr Kaiserreich Navy manage *that*?"

"I'm not sure it's fair to say that the BKN did," Bueller observed softly. "From what we have learned from the news and...other sources, the *Shadows* did."

A lot of Kira's detailed information came from a contact with Solar Federation Intelligence. Captain Zamorano had no business, so far as she knew, getting involved in local conflicts at *all*, but he'd owed her a favor.

So far as she knew, Captain Zamorano and his ship were the *only* SolFed Intelligence asset in this section of the Rim. And, she suspected, potentially the same portion of the *Fringe*.

"The Brisingr Shadows are...a bunch of assassins and covert operators," Zoric observed. "They're not even Kaiserreich Intelligence. They're—"

"Kaiser Reinhardt's personal murderers," Bueller said bluntly. "They don't have a good reputation on Brisingr, either. Back during the war, the BKN basically regarded them as an unfortunate tumor growing out of Special Operations Command and National Intelligence."

He shook his head.

"As I understand it, the Shadows have completely absorbed SOC, and I'm not sure how well BNI is doing, but the Shadows answer to Reinhardt. Not the Diet and not the BKN."

"Always a great thing for your constitutional monarch to have their own personal guild of assassins," Milani added dryly.

"Reinhardt has been Kaiser for forty-three years," Bueller observed. "He's had a lot of time to do things no Kaiser should have managed to get away with."

"And he also, from what I can tell, spent those decades laying the groundwork for this exact moment," Kira told her subordinates and friends. "Sending the Shadows after the aces of the war was, in hindsight, a test."

That assassination campaign had sent her and a slew of other Apollo System Defense Force pilots into exile. Most of them were coming back with her, and Kaiser Reinhardt Wernher was going to regret unleashing them.

"So, he spent four decades preparing for this," Zoric said quietly. "With the entire star fleet of a major regional power and a specialty corps of assassins and covert operators. And...what, exactly, are we going to do about it?"

"I'm working on details," Kira admitted. "And we've got potential allies I need to get in touch with. But...one way or another, I'm going home, Kavitha. And I am kicking Reinhardt's collection of jack-booted thugs all the way from here to *Earth* if that's what it takes to retake my homeworld."

3

THE MAIN DIFFERENCE BETWEEN A "COMMAND MEETING" and a "shareholders meeting" was that Konrad Bueller and Captain Davidović weren't present. Kira held fifty-one percent of the shares in the fleet, with the other forty-nine percent split between her old Memorial pilots and the original senior officers of *Conviction*.

Kavitha Zoric had been the senior surviving officer of John Estanza's mercenary force, so she held twenty percent of the combined company. Akuchi Mwangi—now *Deception*'s Captain—Angel Waldroup—originally *Conviction*'s flight deck chief and now *Fortitude*'s—and Ruben "Gizmo" Hersch—the senior survivor of Estanza's fighter pilots and now second-in-command of *Fortitude*'s group—all held two percent apiece.

Combined with Caiden McCaig—formerly *Conviction*'s groundforces commander and now the senior destroyer CO—and his three percent, those five former *Conviction* officers held twenty-nine percent of the company. They sat along one side of the table aboard *Fortitude*, a study in contrasts from McCaig's immense blond bulk to Mwangi's gaunt black frame.

The other side of the table was the other four survivors of Kira's old Apollo System Defense Force fighter unit, the 303 Nova Combat Group. *Deception*'s Commander, Nova Group, Mel "Nightmare" Cartman, was Kira's oldest friend and one of her strong right hands. *Huntress*'s CNG, Abdullah "Scimitar" Colombera, had spent most of his career getting into trouble alongside Evgenia "Socrates" Michel— and losing her legs and taking command of a nova destroyer hadn't slowed Michel down.

Those three each held four percent of the company, twelve percent between them.

The last eight percent was held by *Fortitude*'s CNG, Dinesha "Dawnlord" Patel. Patel had inherited the four percent held by his boyfriend, Joseph "Longknife" Hoffman , when Hoffman had died against the Equilibrium Institute's patsies in the Syntactic Cluster.

Five former *Conviction* officers lined one side of the conference table. Four former Apollo officers lined the other, and Kira sat at the head, surveying them all.

The table itself was a symbol. It had taken Kira more effort to source the piece of furniture than she'd thought, but everyone she'd talked to had moved stars and worlds to make it happen. The slab of high-density hull alloy was designed to act as the inner layer of a three-tier armor system able to stop plasma bolts.

And it was the single largest fragment left of the outer armor of the escort carrier *Conviction*. Finding a piece even that large of Estanza's ship had taken *days* of searching at the deep-space trade-route stop where she'd rammed an Equilibrium carrier.

But they'd found it, and a team of artisans and metalworkers had spent *months* turning the piece of warship-grade armor into a conference table four meters long and two wide. Small holographic projectors had been concealed in the surface to give it modern functionality, but the only visible addition had been a carefully enameled side profile of the old carrier.

Conviction had never been a pretty ship, but no other emblem made sense to Kira for this room.

"So, you want to take our entire fleet—the one we've spent years building up together—and charge off on a damn fool crusade to liberate your homeworld?" Caiden McCaig rumbled. With his size and breadth, Kira didn't think the man was *capable* of speaking except in geological movements.

"Basically," Kira confirmed. "I have contacts in the region, obviously. My information is that the main strength of the ASDF carrier fleet *did* manage to escape. I believe I can make contact with them. I also think that, faced with this kind of provocation, the old Friends of Apollo may yet decide to fight with us."

Michel chuckled bitterly, the ex-nova-fighter pilot smacking her metal leg hard.

"Don't let the name fool anyone who isn't from Apollo," she told the others. "To be a Friend of Apollo meant accepting some ridiculously imbalanced trade treaties. Our dominance of the region was by trade and treaty, not by starship and nova fighter, but it was no less real. And no more welcome."

"I'm surprised the Equilibrium Institute even got involved in the Apollo-Brisingr Sector," Zoric admitted. "It seems, from the outside at least, that Apollo had the area locked down in the way they prefer."

"Apollo was not a military hegemony," Kira pointed out. "That meant, by Equilibrium standards, that we—they—were vulnerable to exactly what happened: a militaristic neighbor moving in and proving capable of defeating us in open battle.

"It was a *hegemony*, yes, but it wasn't one that would sustain local *equilibrium*." She used the Institute's preferred language with a carefully measured dose of acid. "That the Institute appears to have helped fund Brisingr's rise to power with money and technology, of course, was them taking action to create a proper stabilizing force in the region."

There was a long silence.

"I suppose the inherent irony and hypocrisy of that just washed right over their heads," Angel Waldroup finally growled. She was a broad-shouldered woman with a deep voice—a voice trained to project across a flight deck in the middle of a battle.

"They are, at least, consistent in their methods and their reasoning," Kira said. "John Estanza told me they got their Seldonian calculations wrong. I don't pretend to understand the math behind psychohistory, but apparently the Institute regularly recalculates Seldonian projections in their area of operations.

"According to Estanza, a psychohistorian he gave their numbers to said they were fundamentally flawed," she concluded. "As I understand it, Seldonian math is inherently non-definitive. To produce *any* kind of specificity in the results, placeholder assumptions are required.

"And the Institute has taken their assumptions as fact."

"And are carrying out an empirical experiment on a massive scale," Cartman added. "We've fought the bastards in three different places now. I don't see a reason to stop now—and I, for one, would very much like to go home."

"I don't know if I'm that attached to Apollo, these days," Patel told them. "But I'm still not willing to stand by as Brisingr conquers it."

"It's not really a vote on whether we're going," Kira noted, laying her hands on the table and glancing around her people. "I am offering a contract with Memorial Force from my own resources. I, obviously, will draw no profit from the contract, but we will structure it so the rest of the shareholders receive their normal margin."

"Or..." Zoric glanced around the rest of the room. "Minority shareholder vote," *Fortitude*'s Captain said formally.

"I propose that Memorial Force, as an organization, takes on this campaign," she continued. "No margin, funded from the company's cash reserves until those drop to a level sufficient to fund roughly three months of operations.

"At that point, we will need to find work to keep the company afloat, but I believe we have the resources on hand for at least a year of full-tempo operations."

Kira swallowed.

"I can't ask that of you," she pointed out.

"I second the motion," Cartman said, ignoring Kira. "I don't think any of the Apollons could put it forward, but I definitely second it."

Every single person in the room had modern headware, and the vote was taking place electronically even as Cartman was pointing out her conflict of interest.

"Forty-nine percent of shareholders are in agreement, Admiral Demirci," Zoric told Kira. "I *suppose*, as majority shareholder, that you could override us."

Kira bowed her head.

"Thank you," she whispered. "It's...good to have friends, I suppose."

"I hope you also have a *plan*," Zoric said. "I feel like you owe it to the shareholders of Memorial Force, at least, to tell us everything."

"Okay."

KIRA LAID it out as cleanly as she could. They had a contract in place to protect Samuels for a few more months, which provided them with a financial and time cushion during which they could scout out the situation and make the connections they needed.

A lot of that was going to depend on Captain Zamorano, though, and she could see the concern on Kavitha Zoric's face.

"We'd kept the existence of our SolFed connection pretty quiet," Zoric told the other owners. "Bueller and Demirci made it while we were operating in Crest, and the Admiral briefed *me* as the primary minority shareholder.

"We've been, for those curious, funneling basic news reporting and analysis back to Captain Zamorano since our operation to retrieve *Fortitude*. We have a relationship with him, but I worry about the overall position of SolFed Intelligence."

"I'm still trying to swallow the fact that we're working with intelligence operatives from *Terra*," Michel said bluntly. "What the fuck is SolFed Intel even *doing* out here?"

"Keeping an eye on things," Kira replied. "But, from what Captain Zamorano has told me, he and his ship are basically SolFed's *only* assets in a large wedge of the Rim."

"Which brings me to my concern," Zoric said quietly. "He has a massive number of demands on his time and is subject to higher authority. Higher authority that likely doesn't want him to draw attention to his existence.

"How far can he go before he has to stop? And are we going to get any warning if our Terran friend suddenly needs to go dark because something else grabbed him or because his superiors told him to shape up?"

"We don't know," Kira admitted. "But we also aren't dependent on the Captain, either. Right now, he is supposed to be laying groundwork for us to make contact with Colonel Killinger, but he provided me with the information on the digital dead drop he has for communicating with Killinger."

"So, if he ghosts us, you think we can make contact with the necessary players ourselves?" McCaig asked.

Kira glanced at the Apollon side of the table and smiled.

"My impression, from the information I have already seen, is that Colonel Killinger is likely to attempt to make contact with *us* if we move into the region and begin operating against the Kaiserreich," she told her people. "Captain Zamorano is only in contact with the Colonel thanks to a letter of introduction I provided."

"I'm still unsure about Killinger being *alive*, let alone having enough ships and people to make a solid stand against Brisingr," Cartman noted. "I think Kira and I are the only ones who've ever met him. And I thought he was dead."

"That was apparently intentional on his part. Like us, Killinger found himself on the list of targets our government okayed the Shadows going after," Kira reminded Cartman.

The irony to the situation wasn't lost on her. She wouldn't have lifted a finger to save the Council of Principals, the leadership of Apollo's "democratic oligarchy" government. But with the entire planet now under Kaiserreich occupation, she would come to the rescue of the *rest* of her people.

And the very people the Council had betrayed to Brisingr as part of their peace deal would be the salvation of the planet.

"So, he faked his death and, what, stole a few fighters like we did?" Cartman asked. "I'm not sure how that converts into him being a player in what happens now."

"I don't know the details," Kira admitted. "But what I've been told is that he either cut a deal for or outright *stole* a number of capital ships from the Friends when they found themselves under Brisingr's 'protection.'"

"Since the Apollo-Brisingr Agreement on Nova Lane Security limited how much cubage of nova ships the other systems could have, most of the people Apollo betrayed had a choice between decommissioning a good chunk of their fleets or trying to fight Brisingr without Apollo." Colombera just sounded *tired* as he explained the mess to the others.

"Apollo had betrayed them, and without the ASDF, our allies didn't have the ships or morale to go up against Brisingr on their own."

"So, a bunch of ships that were officially scrapped are now flying for Killinger," Cartman concluded. "There had to have been someone better."

"I suspect that anyone else with the connections and the rep to make those deals went either Coreward or Rimward, like us," Kira told Cartman. "Killinger was—*is*, I hope—good. I know he rubbed some people the wrong way, but the Three-Oh-Nine racked up some of the best kill ratios in the war.

"And the very things that rubbed you and me the wrong way probably helped him build connections with the Friends."

She let that hang unspoken. Killinger, in her brief encounter with him, had struck her as more of a uniformed politician than a real combat pilot—but the record of the 309 Nova Combat Group said differently.

"As for the fleet," Patel said quietly. "Anybody from Major on up knew the dark-point fallbacks, didn't they?"

He was looking at Kira—who, unlike anybody else in the room, had been an Apollo System Defense Force Major before. She'd been a squadron commander, one of four in the 303 Nova Combat Group.

She nodded at his explanation.

"Sure as stars shine," she said quietly. "There were six dark-route points around Apollo. Given everything that went down, I suspect that Admiral Michelakis fell back to a tertiary location."

Admiral Fevronia Michelakis was the flag officer that Kira had been told had extracted the carriers from the mess of betrayal, invasion and battle that that had been the invasion of Apollo.

"I gave Zamorano the location of every dark stop I thought she'd have headed to," she noted. "He's supposed to make contact with her, but if he fails or ghosts us, the next step is for *me* to head into the Sector to make that link."

While novaing toward a star was relatively straightforward due to the star's gravity overwhelming the space-time fabric, a nova drive had a maximum range of six light-years for a single nova. Novaing into deep space required excruciatingly detailed charts of every gravitational impact of the location.

The answer, traditionally, was the trade-route stop. Fixed locations every ship passed through—and that every ship passing through scanned for that gravitational data changing. A group of corporate entities spread across the three-thousand-light-year sphere of civilized—or, more accurately, *mapped*—space bought that information from each ship's captain when they entered their next system.

Massive updates flew around the galaxy at the speed of shipping, making the standard trade routes accessible to everyone for a nominal fee that made the companies involved unimaginably vast sums of money.

But since militaries didn't want their enemies to know where they were novaing to, almost every star system kept a map of "dark stops"—fully mapped nearby locations that weren't on the civilian charts.

Kira's copy of Apollo's dark-point map was badly out of date. But while the age made novaing to the points less safe than it should be, it wouldn't be dangerous.

Probably.

"We are all aware that *everything* about the contract with Samuels was rigged up to lure you, *specifically*, into a trap, yes?" Cartman asked slowly. "They played Samuels into hiring you, they played Colossus into starting the war..."

"The question, of course, is whether that was Brisingr on their own or whether the Institute was involved," Kira replied.

"No, that's irrelevant to the point, I think," Zoric told her. "The point Nightmare is making is that if you go wandering around the Apollo-Brisingr Sector by, say, regular civilian transport, you will end up dead."

"I wasn't planning on buying a passenger ticket home, if that's what you mean," Kira said.

"No," Zoric agreed. "But I think we all, as shareholders, can agree that you shouldn't be going anywhere within the BKN's operational radius with less than a damn *carrier group*."

"That is overkill," Kira replied.

"Given that the last time Brisingr had a shot at you, *they* came up with a carrier group, I'm not sure it is," Cartman told her. "Right now, the only force I'd feel comfortable letting you swan around our home systems with would be *Fortitude* herself, who is bound by contract to Samuels."

"All right, all right," Kira conceded. "I'll wait until we have the cruisers and our contract with Samuels is wrapping up. By then, we'll have a lot more information through assorted channels."

Four months would give them time to prep and plan. And it wasn't like she figured she could pull off in four months what had taken Kaiser Reinhardt four *decades*.

If she was going to retake her home system, she needed information, people, guns and allies. All of that was going to take time.

4

NONE of the news that was coming in from back home was good. No one in the Rim had ever invaded a planet before, and Brisingr was apparently working out military occupation from first principles again.

The only thing Kira was certain of as she went through the news from home was that a lot of people were dying. Not just on Apollo, either. The BKN had become far quicker to react violently to actions by the systems of the Brisingr Trade Route Security Zone, their nondescriptly named tributary empire.

The informal protectorates with their limited fleets were no match for the BKN, but Kira had to suspect that the BKN was following an age-old theory: that the best way to avoid spilling an ocean of blood was to be demonstrably willing to spill a lake of it at a moment's notice.

There were a lot of counterarguments to that point, though the metaphor that came to mind for her was the parable about the draftees who realized that the penalties for being late and for rebelling were the same...and they were already late.

There were, equally, a lot of reasons why the Admiral of Memorial Force shouldn't be flying an interceptor out with the rest of the fighters for an exercise. Still, she needed to keep her hand in, and the Admiral's clever ideas were often useful for training.

Right now, she had *Huntress*'s ten squadrons of heavy fighters and interceptors spread out behind her in a parade-ground formation, while Nightmare had her twenty planes from *Deception* and Patel brought up the hundred and twenty nova fighters from *Fortitude*.

They hadn't had many opportunities before Samuel to exercise the entire fighter force as one entity. The bombers weren't present today, though their pilots were going through an array of virtual exercises aboard the carriers.

"All right, everyone," Kira said, a headware command opening the channel to the two hundred starfighters around her. "We have to arrange things pretty carefully to get chances for exercises like this, and Captain Michel will be very grumpy if we don't make good use of the time her destroyers are putting in!"

They weren't *officially* all Michel's destroyers yet, but she'd lost—or won, Kira wasn't entirely sure—the rock-paper-scissors for who took command of the destroyer squadron and who got command of a cruiser.

Captain Michel would officially become *Commodore* Michel shortly. Zoric and McCaig would also get the same title, commanding the carriers and cruisers respectively, with Patel becoming Fleet CNG.

They'd never *needed* a Fleet-level Commander, Nova Group, before. Deception's three squadrons had just vanished into *Fortitude*'s twenty-five. But *Huntress* brought twelve more squadrons, bringing them up to over *two hundred* fighters and bombers.

Someone had to wear the big hat, and that someone was Dawnlord—if, for no other reason, because he was the third-largest shareholder in the company.

"Now, Dawnlord and I have spent a great deal of time working through what we're going to be doing today," Kira told her people.

"We'll be operating with simulated jammers for most of this. If I see a *real* multiphasic jammer turn on today, we'll be having some remedial training on Crest-style fighter controls!"

Maybe a quarter of her pilots had ever flown with any other style of controls, so it was unlikely that was going to be the problem.

On the other hand, a multiphasic jammer rendered a light-second-wide bubble of space basically impenetrable to any scanner more complicated than a medium-resolution digital camera. The fighters' combined computer network could easily simulate that effect while also making certain that there were no collisions or other accidents.

An *actual* jammer would shut down that network, disable the entire training simulation and create no end of chaos. It was exactly the type of chaos nova-fighter pilots thrived in, but Kira preferred to have control over whether it existed.

"A course should now be showing up on everyone's systems," Kira informed them. "We're opening with a pretty standard nova-and-attack. Scenario is a BKN carrier battle group that will look familiar to *Huntress*'s people.

"We will nova one light-minute, carry out a standard sixty-second firing pass in simulated jamming against simulated targets, then reverse nova and regroup here for debriefing."

And because they weren't firing actual plasma bolts, they could carry out more of those firing passes than Kira could ever ask of them in a real battle. Not *many* more—the main overall fuel drain was the novas themselves, even at only one light-minute a time—but enough to push her people's endurance.

Which was why she didn't want a real jammer running.

"All pilots...*nova and attack!*"

KIRA JOINED each of the four exercises she put her people through, leading the Wolverine interceptors as they practiced the sweeping cutout maneuvers they would use to separate interceptors from capital ships—or bombers from their own protectors!

While the Wolverines carried a single torpedo apiece, they weren't really intended to go after capital ships. Their maneuverability suffered when they carried a torpedo—though by less than the Apollon Hoplite-IV she'd flown in the war.

Their job was to draw enemy interceptors away to allow bombers through—or to take down bombers coming at their own ships. The Hussar-7 heavy fighters could back them up in both roles, though they were notably less maneuverable to pay for their dual torpedoes and heavier guns.

The bombers, present today only as virtual simulacra, were the least maneuverable of all. At least Crest Wildcat-4s *did* have guns. Apollon Peltast bombers, at least in the versions Kira had flown escort for, had *only* carried their half dozen torpedoes.

"All right, folks," Kira told the group, checking in silently with Dawnlord. "We've run through attack scenarios repeatedly now, and you all seem to be doing decently." She smiled, knowing it would carry through the secondary channels of the com network.

"I and your squadron and flight group leaders will, of course, have critiques and adjustments we'll want to make, but no one here has fallen too far short of my demanding standards."

When Kira had first joined *Conviction*'s mercenary fighter group, years earlier, she'd been horrified by the lack of training in important areas. She knew, now, that those pilots had been just as capable in a fight as hers—but she still felt that they had possessed too little training for emergencies and noncombat complications.

The survivors of those pilots now commanded squadrons for her, which brought her to the final part of today. No set of exercises was ever complete without a proper mind-screw closing scenario.

"For the next and final exercise," she continued on the main network, silently reaching out through her headware to her senior officers and veteran pilots as she told them what was coming, "we're going to do a live-space scenario with simulated fire and jamming against live targets.

"This is a command-breakdown scenario," Kira told her people. "All squadron and group commanders are now the Op Force. The *rest* of you... Well. Good luck.

"Nova and attack!"

The only concession she made to her poor junior pilots was that the two groups novaed to locations about fifty thousand kilometers apart—rather than opening the dogfight with the senior pilots in the middle of their squadrons!

Otherwise, she figured five to one was about the right odds for this kind of game.

5

"Officers, I give you Memorial Force!"

Ionut Ayodele was a Redward native, a slim Black man who had been selected by the destroyer COs as the fleet's third cruiser commander. A shareholder, McCaig, had taken command of *Prodigal*, and another shareholder, Michel, now commanded the entire destroyer squadron.

They'd asked the remaining ten destroyer captains to select one of their own to take on the second new cruiser. Ayodele had been the only dissenting vote in selecting Ayodele.

He still looked perpetually nervous as he stood in *Deception*'s mess and held up the wine glass in the toast.

"Memorial Force," Kira chorused back with the rest. She tapped her own glass to Ayodele's as she rose, giving the younger man a firm nod.

She knew he was neither as young nor as nervous as he appeared, but it was hard *not* to act as if he needed assurances.

"We've come a long way, everyone, from a battered old carrier commanded by an alcoholic with an understrength fighter group—

and a bunch of exiled Apollon pilots who didn't have a *damn* clue what to do with themselves that far out in the Rim."

The group chuckled. It was far from a small crowd—though it was "just" the ship captains and the flight group commanders. Each carrier had three "flight groups," each based around one type of starfighter. Plus the CNGs, Kira and Konrad, that brought the total up to twenty-eight.

All three of her Commodores also commanded their own ships, which kept the total down—and they hadn't yet selected CNGs for the two new cruisers, even if she had Captains for them.

"Today, we got our oldest ship back," she reminded them. "*Deception*'s been worked hard, and she's taken a few solid blows over the years, but she's still got our backs. I'd love to still have *Conviction*—hell, I'd love to still have Estanza and have *him* in charge of this mess!"

"Nobody in this room thinks that you *actually* want someone else in charge," Bueller told her, his chuckle reverberating warmly down her spine as always. "But these days, even *I* count as an old hand around here."

The Brisingr and Equilibrium defector was the reason they even *had Deception*. He'd been the engineer on the ship when she'd been an Equilibrium asset, and when the Institute had pushed hard enough to break his idealized view of their cause, he'd betrayed them and delivered the ship into Kira's hands.

"We've come a long, long, way," Zoric agreed. *She'd* started, Kira remembered, as *Conviction*'s executive officer—effectively running the ship until Equilibrium's interference in Redward had dragged John Estanza out of the bottle.

"We've pulled a few systems along with us," Mwangi observed. *Deception*'s captain was thoughtful. "Redward had, what, a single sixty-kilocubic cruiser when we showed up? Now they have a carrier fleet of their own and don't need us anymore."

"That's what lets us be here, backing up Samuels while they set up to be able to defend themselves," Kira replied. "Four destroyers isn't much, but it's four destroyers they didn't have six months ago."

The locals had put the time repairing the four D12s and *Deception* to good use, too. *Deception* had barely made it out of the building slip before the first prefabricated sections of Samuels' first *Vishnu*-class cruiser had arrived.

Four *Vulpine*-class destroyers were being laid down at the same time—and a second set of forty-five- and hundred-kilocubic building slips were under construction as well. And in five weeks, when *Harbinger* and *Prodigal* finally cleared their slips, the locals would be up to *five* sites suited for building hundred-kilocubic ships.

Samuels didn't want to fight anybody, but they also had *no* intention of being pushed around. Kira regretted the need—but she figured they were going about it as quickly as they could.

"We'll be adding *Deception* to the destroyer patrols," she told them. "Keeping our eyes and ears open to see what comes our way. So far, the Kaiserreich's civilians haven't pushed the blockade and the BKN hasn't attempted to breach it.

"My gut feeling is that they don't have the forces available. Their Security Zone is being turbulent, and they have a lot of resources tied down securing Apollo."

"And our contacts?" Zoric asked.

This was a command meeting, not a shareholder meeting. There were still some subjects that were kept quiet, some details that weren't shared. But everyone knew they were going after Brisingr, and everyone knew that Kira had feelers out into her old home sector.

"A few messages," Kira told them. Zoric knew most of this. "We've got a pretty good idea, at this point, of how much of Apollo's System Defense Force escaped from the invasion.

"The more I hear about the attack, the more I'm surprised they got *anything* out," she warned. "But it looks like Michelakis got all six of the new fleet carriers out and maybe twelve light carriers. Not sure which ones, but eighteen carriers make for well over a million and a half cubic meters of capital ships."

Apollo's *new fleet carriers* were smaller than *Fortitude*, but they were still a hundred and forty thousand cubic meters apiece. The light carriers were half that, but a dozen of them and six fleet carriers was still a *lot* of fleet.

"The *problem* is that it sounds like she might not have got much else out," Kira admitted. "The BKN hasn't released official numbers, but a few of the systems in the Zone have news media that doesn't listen when people tell them to shut up."

She grinned.

"That was a pain in the ass during the war, but it's damn useful right now. But..." Her smile turned bitter. "If the numbers the newsies are estimating are correct, the BKN captured or destroyed *every* battlecruiser the ASDF had."

"And while Apollo snuck in that Brisingr had to allow the systems at least half a million cubic meters of nova fleets, well..." Bueller shook his head. "Kaiser Reinhardt turned that into *exactly* half a million cubics. I don't think many of the systems in the Security Zone were wasting any of those five hundred kilocubics on battlecruisers and fleet carriers, not when they needed corvettes and cruisers for trade protection."

"In theory, of course, the BKN is providing that protection," Zoric noted. "I'm guessing no one is trusting your people to do that?"

"The BKN *should* be providing that protection," Bueller said. "We certainly were before I retired. But even if the BKN is *doing* what's been promised, I don't think anyone in the Zone trusts them for it yet.

"Everyone in the Zone *does* know, however, that the Kaiserreich will come down like a ton of bricks if anyone tries to stand up to them." He didn't sound particularly happy at the thought. Then again, neither was Kira.

"So, why have capital ships when they're obvious and the BKN will only let you have five—when you can build a dozen heavy destroyers for the same cubage, and they'll do what you actually *need* better?"

"As long as the Kaiserreich is successfully enforcing the half-million limit on the Security Zone, none of those systems can afford to maintain more than, say, a single heavy cruiser or carrier as a presence ship," Kira concluded. "Most, if we're being honest, probably have at least two ships in the eighty-to-hundred-twenty range hidden somewhere in their star system—but we can assume that Brisingr is keeping a very careful eye on everyone's big units."

"When do *we* start poking into things?" Michel asked. "Now that we've got *Deception* to fill up the back line, I figure we can probably split off two or three of the destroyers to go 'job-hunting' in the Sector."

"We will need to step carefully, Socrates," Kira warned. "Remember that Memorial Fleet's destroyers alone make up a good chunk of what's allowed to any single star system under the Agreement.

"Our strength *before* we picked up our latest additions already exceeded the half-million-cubic-meter line. Hunting for work is all well and good, but I suspect that Brisingr would turn a dark eye on major mercenary forces even *without* all of us old Apollons in the command crew!"

"Still, getting our own information is a good idea," Zoric said. "I like the Commodore's plan."

"So do I," Kira said. "But we can't send you, Socrates. Two detachments, two ships apiece. And"—she held up a finger and surveyed her destroyer captains—"at the first sign of real trouble, you *run*.

"We will fight the BKN on our terms and our time. Not one second sooner and never on their terms if we can possibly avoid it!"

6

FORTITUDE's flag bridge put the facilities on *Deception* to shame. *Deception*'s squadron-command infrastructure was more modern than *Huntress*'s, but neither the Brisingr-built cruiser nor the Redward-built light carrier were designed to be a flagship.

The Crest-built carrier had been intended to be *the* flagship for the Navy of the Royal Crest. The flag bridge might have the same space restrictions as anything else on a nova ship, but it was still almost two hundred cubic meters dedicated purely to providing information and communications for an Admiral.

In battle, once the multiphasic jammers went up, command-and-control loops notoriously went to complete hell. Communications were even more badly affected than sensors, and the only methods that worked required near-perfect knowledge of the recipient's location.

Something you didn't *want* to be easy to find. Any communication that could pierce multiphasic jamming was different from a *weapon* that could do the same only in power level.

But until *Fortitude* herself fired off her jammers or entered the primary battlespace, her Admiral would have the best information of what was going on in whatever star system surrounded her. Automatic downloads from the nova fighters as they flew around her, novaing into and out of combat, plus links to the cruisers and the escorts, plus—there in Samuels, at least—links to the planetary defense network.

Admiral Mahinder Bachchan, from her command facility on the fortresses above Bennet, probably had a slightly better view of the Samuels System than Kira did. *Probably*.

Fortitude's own sensors, after all, were notably higher-quality than those on the asteroid forts. The sheer scale of the forts' scanners, though, made up much of the difference. Kanchenjunga Fortress had passive radio telescopes wider than *Fortitude* was long, after all.

"Ser, you'll want to check this out."

The flag bridge used holograms and links to the crew's headware to appear larger than it was—*and* to appear that the various stations were hanging in deep space. Kira's headware made sure that the illusion wasn't confusing, but it gave her a perfect view of the space just around *Fortitude*.

"What am I looking for, Jacen?" she asked.

Jacen Ronaldo had been the assistant coms officer aboard *Deception* for a long time. Now that Kira was actually using *Fortitude* as a flagship, for now, at least, he'd become one of the handful of officers making up her staff.

As flag communications officer, he wouldn't have been managing sensors in a combat situation, but he was capable of handling the small team of techs running the flag bridge while Isidora Soler, Kira's chief of staff and formerly *Deception*'s tactical officer, was off-shift.

"New ship just novaed in. Course report says she's from out-Rim...but she's flying Apollo diplomatic codes."

"Apollo codes?" Kira murmured. "Highlight her."

Ronaldo had finished doing so before Kira even asked, a pulsing mental halo appearing around the newcomer.

At first glance, the ship was an ordinary tramp freighter. Twenty-five kilocubics put her on the small side for that, even in the Rim, but stars knew there were enough *ten*-kilocubic ships floating around, running small cargos.

A ten-kilocubic ship might only have three or four thousand cubic meters of space—enough for maybe sixteen of the standard ten-meter-unit containers—but every star system could build the basic Ten-X class one nova drive, a thousand-cubic-meter installation that could take ten times its own volume into a nova.

The ten-thousand-cubic-meter starship was easy to build and dirt cheap. Twenty-five kilocubics was still easy and cheap—though in Kira's experience, most merchants went for either ten thousand cubics to save money or the largest ship they could buy, to *make* money.

"Any information beyond the diplo codes?" Kira asked. She was pulling the key data available on the ship as she spoke. Unarmed. Registered to Denzel. She'd had problems with the Denzel System's military blockading her on her way to Samuels, but they were *mostly* a reasonably civilized place.

"No messages or unusual transmissions, ser," Ronaldo told her. "They're en route to discharge at Haven."

That meant their information was about two hours out of date. Haven was the closer of the system's two gas giants, Haven and Sanctuary, but it was still two light-hours away at that moment.

Discharging tachyon and electromagnetic static would take the ship most of a day, which gave her options.

"I think..." She trailed off, studying the information on the distant ship. "Let's send a pinnace out as a courier," she decided aloud. "And invite whoever is ballsy enough to head toward Apollo flying our diplomatic codes aboard *Fortitude* for dinner.

"I suspect we're going to want to chat."

NOVA PINNACES, like nova fighters, were small craft equipped with the much-smaller class two nova drives. The class two drives were capable of the same six-light-year jump as a class one drive but took far longer to cool down from it. However, they were much *faster* to cool down from a shorter jump.

If Kira had taken *Fortitude* out to Haven, for example, the two-light-hour jump would have required almost twenty minutes of cooldown on the part of the carrier.

For the five-hundred-cubic-meter pinnace, on the other hand, each leg of the journey only required *six* minutes of cooldown. That allowed the pinnace to return, with a passenger, less than an hour after Kira had sent them out.

She hadn't gone so far as to pull together a formal greeting party, but she was on the flight deck herself. Konrad Bueller stood to her left and Milani to her right, the dragon-armored officer silently coordinating at least a dozen visible and concealed ground troopers to provide security.

Kira was surprised, however, to *recognize* the two-and-a-bit-meter-tall man with the graying hair and the immense arms who emerged from the shuttle. Angelos Argyris was the trade attaché for the Mowat System, where her two-ship task group had discharged static on their way to Samuels.

He'd given her useful intelligence on the situation in the Samuels-Colossus Corridor, information that had helped her pull a win out of the mess.

"Admiral Demirci," he greeted her with a smile. "I'd hoped to find you still in Samuels, but I knew I couldn't count on it." He glanced over at where Milani loomed and raised a wine-bottle-sized box.

"I assume Commander Milani will want to scan my gift before you open it, but it is just retsina."

Her enthusiasm for being offered her homeworld's unusual fortified wine had apparently been less concealed than Kira had thought.

"A bottle of retsina would help get you in the door, Em Argyris," Kira said with a chuckle. "But, to be honest, the situation would require us to speak anyway. My steward has put together a meal for us to talk over, if you'd care to join me?"

"As I understand it, my ship will be here for another ten hours no matter what," Argyris told her. "I expect the conversation over dinner to be much more scintillating than watching the weather on Haven!"

ZORIC JOINED THEM FOR DINNER, the Commodore in charge of Kira's carriers appearing more amused than anything else when offered a glass of retsina.

"I have *tasted* Apollo's retsina," she replied, shaking her head. "I have also tasted other planets' retsina. Apollo's is better but, uh, I'll stick to beer."

Bueller chuckled and slid a bottle across to Zoric. "I'm of similar opinions myself," he admitted.

"More for the trade attaché and me, then," Kira replied, passing a second glass over to Argyris.

"Not a trade attaché anymore, I'm afraid," the big man told her. "Not entirely sure what I am, to be honest."

"So, you've definitely heard the news from home," Kira observed.

Koch appeared as she was speaking, serving out plates with the latest attempt at a local Samuels dish. Kira was reasonably sure that *something* had happened to Samuels' lentil population, as, in her opinion, a stew of spiced lentils had no business being edible, let alone good.

"I have," Argyris said. "I've been in touch with a number of other systems and we're all, I suppose, dealing with the realities of being suddenly unemployed."

"No orders or communication from the Council, I take it," Bueller said. "I might have expected a more-planned response from the Kaiserreich, but... I feel like only a few people knew this was coming before it happened."

"They tested some of the theories in advance," Kira observed. "Hence the attack on Corosec."

Corosec had been an out-system possession of Apollo, basically wholly owned by the corporations and oligarchs of Kira's homeworld. It had been protected by a proper asteroid fortress—which someone, presumably Brisingr, had sabotaged to allow the system to be robbed blind.

"No orders, no updates, just silence since the invasion," Argyris confirmed. "Those of us this far out from home have always kept an informal communication network going through the assorted merchant ships and friendlies, but we weren't really set up for this."

"And now you're heading home to...what? See if Brisingr will give you instructions?" Zoric asked acidly.

"Hardly." The big diplomatic grimaced. "I've acquired a few sets of identity codes from...*friends* in the Mowat System that should allow me to move quietly through Brisingr's controlled space. I was only running Apollon codes here in the hopes that the locals would put me in touch with you."

"That seems to have worked out for you," Kira conceded. "So, what *are* you planning on doing while not being noticed?"

"The communications loop between remote offices and Apollo is too long for us to be able to really draw on homeworld accounts," Argyris noted. "All of us have extensive cash reserves—often well out of proportion to our actual budgets, because... Well, have you ever met a bureaucrat who'd *admit* they didn't spend all of last year's transfer?

"And since we only got money from home once a year, we were encouraged to include contingencies and build up cash reserves." He shrugged. "We also generally collect a moderate sum in fees and licenses on behalf of the home government, which is rarely enough for us to be required to send it home rather than roll it into those accounts.

"There is a *lot* of money floating around the Mid Rim that techni-cally belongs to the Council of Principals, and it's under the immediate control of diplomats and trade attachés and, well, people like me."

"Most of which is already quietly disappearing, one assumes," Bueller murmured.

"Some, I'm sure," Argyris conceded. "I will admit my own surprise at the level of patriotism and determination I found among my fellows when I started reaching out. While a collection of bureaucrats and diplomats hardly constitute anything resembling a government in exile, we have begun to assemble resources to hopefully intervene back home.

"My part in all of this was to start making contacts in the Security Zone while several others start sounding out mercenary forces in the Outer Rim," he told them. "We were also hoping that, since I *had* met Admiral Demirci and seemed to have made a positive impression, I would run into Memorial Force on my way home.

"We would like to contract you to take part in a campaign to liberate Apollo."

Kira glanced over at Zoric and watched her second-in-command womanfully resist rolling her eyes. Shaking her head at Zoric, Kira chuckled and sighed.

"Em Argyris...it is not, apparently, only amongst diplomats that we find a surprising degree of 'patriotism and determination,'" she told him. "I am not going to turn down your money, but we are already in the process of launching a campaign against the Kaiserreich to retake Apollo."

"Huh." Argyris leaned back in his chair and considered the pale liquid in his glass. "I had hoped, but I still expected to have to put much of our funds into paying you."

"I have already pledged my own financial reserves to operate Memorial Force against the Kaiserreich once our contract with Samuels expires," Kira told him. She *didn't* admit that Memorial Force was planning on operating out of the corporate reserves as well.

She was going back to Apollo on her own, one way or another, but she was still a mercenary. And she owed her people fair coin for their efforts, too.

"But if you are prepared to put up Apollo's drachmae to cover our costs, that will extend our potential operating window," she noted. "Potentially...well." She sighed. "There is a limit, Em Argyris, to the time period in which it is remotely feasible for us to pull off anything."

"My little coalition of trade offices and embassies already decided we wanted to hire you," Argyris said. "A costs-only or minimal-costs-plus contract would be more than we'd dared hope for."

He paused.

"I'll admit, Admiral, I'm an economics analyst, not a fleet officer. I don't necessarily follow why there would be a time limit."

"Kaiser Reinhardt and his Shadows spent, so far as we can tell, his *entire reign* laying the groundwork for the operation that took Apollo," Bueller said softly, his Brisingr accent more pronounced than usual. "We do not have four decades to build up a fifth column to undermine and betray our target."

"I would hope we can call on local allies with less effort than a foreign invader," Argyris replied.

"Potentially, yes," Kira said. "But...by treachery, sabotage and direct assault, the invasion destroyed or disabled functionally the entirety of Apollo's fixed defenses.

"One of the key pieces of intelligence I *don't* have yet is how many of the orbital forts are left. But it is a fraction of what the ASDF had in place before. That weakness, Em Argyris, is our window of opportunity."

Argyris was no fleet officer, but he was, as he said, an economist. She could see the math running behind his eyes, and then he sighed.

"Asteroid forts are generally a *cost is no object* kind of project," he observed. "Assuming the collaborator government and Brisingr are aware of the weakness, they will be limited more by the physical ability to hollow out and reposition the necessary asteroids than funding.

"Twelve months."

That was a very definitive timeline and Kira gave him a questioning look.

"Our government maintained the ability, partially as an economic stimulus program, to rework four asteroids at a time," he told her. "From the numbers I have on file, they take about four months to work through an asteroid, after which it would be passed on to standard construction and armaments installation.

"Installation can probably be rushed, and I don't think it would take more than four months to set up a second set of four yards," he continued. "So, four fortress hulls, basically, after four months. Those are already done. Probably not armed and in service yet, but the hulls exist.

"So, eight more are probably under construction right now. As, I would guess, are another set of the asteroid-refit facilities. So, at eight months, eight more fortress hulls will be available. At twelve months, *twelve* more—a total of twenty-four stations."

Argyris tapped his forehead absently, pointing out that he was drawing on the information stored in his headware implants.

"Fitting out a fortress could take anywhere from two weeks to ten months, depending on how much of the systems they prefabricated," Bueller told them. "Probably around a month. So, the first four either are online or will be coming online in the near future. Then eight in four months. Twelve more four months after that."

"Twenty-four fortresses ten to twelve months from now," Argyris agreed. "That's more than are present in this star system, hence my assumption that such a formation would render liberation effectively impossible."

"Thank you, Em Argyris," Kira said. "That tracks and gives us a rather distinct time limit, doesn't it?"

She grimaced.

"I can vaguely see ways I might overcome half a dozen forts," she admitted. "Given the resources, anyway. Twelve plus whatever survived the invasion...would need a lot more resources but might be doable.

"But once they've added twenty-four new forts to whatever they captured, Apollo returns to being as impregnable as any star system."

The dinner table was silent as everyone studied their drinks.

"We are agreed, in principle at least, that my coalition will help fund your operations," Argyris told them. "How else can we help?"

"Honestly...even more than money, I need diplomats," Kira told him. "The Friends of Apollo, Em Argyris, are now the Brisingr Trade Route Security Zone. Our middlingly-benign-but-still-exploitative network has been replaced with an explicit tributary protectorate.

"The systems of the Zone play by Brisingr's rules, or they find themselves cut off from the rest of the galaxy. But they have money, spacers, pilots, fighters and ships." Kira smiled. "I need all of those. I need your coalition, Em Argyris, to speak to our old allies and convince them to help us.

"This will not be an easy task," she warned before the big man could speak. "We utterly betrayed them, completely failing in our end of a clearly unbalanced deal. We withdrew our fleets and we left them to Brisingr's mercy.

"We will need to convince our one-time allies that they will not be betrayed again. That a new Apollo will be first among equals at worst. We will need to convince the people we abandoned not to abandon us."

"That is a hell of a job," Argyris admitted. "I don't know if any of the ambassadors I've managed to keep contact with are that silver-tongued, but...that's what we were going to try anyway. An alliance of our old friends may be the difference between victory and defeat.

"But the Council of Principals definitely shot us in both feet on saving those friendships."

"You talk to our friends, Em Argyris, and I'll dig up what's left of our fleet and *talk* to our enemies," Kira told him with a chuckle. "And we'll see what we can pull off before everything goes to hell.

"We'll give you contact information for the destroyers and rented freighters we're starting to set up communications networks with," she continued. "So long as we work in concert, both diplomatic and military actions can lead us toward the goal."

She was about to mention something about *intelligence* operations as well when her headware received a silent alert from Ronaldo.

Baile Fantasma *has entered the system,* her coms officer informed her. *Captain Zamorano's ship is on approach to Bennet orbit. Should I arrange a meeting?*

7

THEY ENDED up meeting on Kanchenjunga Fortress for breakfast. There was a decent-sized civilian concourse on the station, which served a secondary purpose as the counterweight for Bennet's primary orbital elevator. Kira had been in the system long enough to have located a decent breakfast place aboard the battle station.

Her standard of decent was "doesn't muck up toast and eggs." Which, in her opinion, *should* be a low bar to clear, but she'd definitely eaten at places that had managed it.

Thanks to Milani, Kira knew when Zamorano was arriving several minutes before the Hispanic Terran spy stepped into the diner. She might have *looked* like she was obliviously drinking her coffee on her own, but she had half a dozen mercenaries scattered through the surrounding area under Milani's command.

Milani hadn't given her a choice in the matter.

"Captain," she greeted Zamorano, waving him over. "I took the liberty of ordering food for us both. Toast and eggs, sunny side up?"

Zamorano chuckled, stroking his strangely scraggly beard as he took a seat. There was no way the man didn't have the tools and skills to properly maintain his graying facial hair—not least because he kept his scalp trimmed close and dyed pitch-black.

"It'll do," he conceded. "It's not proper huevos rancheros, but this isn't the right planet to find that!"

Kira wasn't even certain what "proper huevos rancheros" would be. Her implant told her that the *words* meant "ranch-style eggs." That just didn't tell her anything useful without further searching, which she didn't have time for.

Zamorano accepted a coffee from the artificial-stupid robowaiter and studied Kira over it.

"Is this diner secure?" he asked.

"The robot dumps all audio it doesn't need for orders after fifteen seconds and is checked by SDC security every six hours," Kira told him. "SDC security also sweeps the space for bugs when they're in to check the bot.

"The owner is a forty-year veteran of the Samuels Defense Command and mostly hires disabled vets for her staff. They are security-cleared by the SDC Admiralty on a monthly basis."

She smiled.

"Secure enough?"

"I take it breakfast meetings are a common thing here?"

"This is the closest restaurant to the main SDC command offices," she pointed out. "It's very much in Samuels' interests to make sure this space is secure. And they like me enough that I get the deluxe package."

"Jammer and white-noise generator under the table?" Zamorano asked.

"Bingo. Now. How was your trip?"

Zamorano waited as he saw another robowaiter trundle over to them and serve up their breakfasts. From his expression, he at least understood what Kira liked about the place!

The "toast" was three thick slices of handmade sourdough bread toasted to golden brown, accompanied by four full eggs. The diner skimped on neither quality nor quantity of food—though combined with the security arrangements, it was not as cheap as the place looked from the outside.

"My trip was an exercise in discovering the problems of being an outsider when things go to shit," Zamorano finally told her. "I had a lot of connections and links and dead drops arranged with assorted movers and shakers in the shadows before the invasion.

"But Apollo fell. And now a lot of contacts have gone dark or outright told me they can't talk anymore." He shook his head. "I've learned quite a bit but not as much as I'd like."

"Colonel Killinger?" Kira asked.

"Alive, active, in command of an unknown number of capital ships," Zamorano said quickly. "Calling himself an Admiral these days, to anyone who knows he's still around. He's keeping his head down, but his people are at least checking the dead drops."

"You made contact?"

"We're trading messages, but he wasn't willing to meet me," the spy admitted. "I'll admit that I'm circumspect about who I am and the role I play, but even my official gunrunner cover should have caught his interest."

"Damn," Kira murmured.

"All is far from lost there," Zamorano told her. "Killinger wouldn't meet *me*, but I name-dropped a certain Apollon exile as someone I could put him in contact with. *That*, I shall note, got me my first live conversation with anyone from his organization.

"Suitably filtered and anonymized on both sides...but I have a meeting arranged for you."

"Thank gods," Kira said. "I still need a week before I can leave Samuels, though," she warned. "What's the timeline you promised?"

"Pretty open. I figured you weren't moving until *Harbinger* and *Prodigal* are online," he said.

"Exactly. Seems like they may move through the Security Zone while drawing less attention," Kira admitted. The plan was to also bring *Huntress* along, but the light carrier would hopefully fade into the background next to two modern BKN cruisers.

If people assumed the cruisers were in their original owners' hands, well, they weren't going to ask questions about the third ship with them.

"You're to make contact in the Hera System," he told her. "From there, Killinger's people will tell you where to go." He smiled thinly. "Which is the Faaselesitila System."

That took Kira a moment to locate. Named *Loneliness* in Samoan, it wasn't a system that she consciously knew anything about without referencing her implants.

"Brown dwarf star, ten light-years from Hera," she noted. "There is nothing there."

"Except a bunch of rock not really worth mining and a gas giant that serves as a discharge point...and Killinger's fleet." Zamorano shrugged. "That took me quite a bit of effort to source, so you're *probably* best off following instructions and hitting the contact point in Hera."

"Fair enough. We'll make that the plan," Kira promised. "What about Michelakis?"

"Less clear," he admitted. "She got out of Apollo with a *lot* of firepower. Which means the BKN has spent the last few months chasing her away from anywhere they could locate her. The Kaiserreich pretty clearly knew more of the ASDF's fallback dark stops than anyone expected."

"Or got their hands on the records on Apollo," Kira said. "I doubt anyone really believed in their contingency data-security plans for invasion. If they even *had* them."

"Most militaries and intelligence agencies do have them," the Terran told her. "But I have never met anyone, in any star system, *anywhere*, who actually expected to need them. Except, I suppose, for people who share star systems with their enemies."

Kira snorted. She'd seen...three systems like that in her life, where nova ships were a neat toy compared to the massive arrays of in-system monitors the factions waved at each other.

She'd been instrumental in one of those systems combining into a single national entity. Ypres, the gateway to the Syntactic Cluster, was now a key member of the Free Trade Zone tying that group of stars together.

"So, Michelakis may not be a factor after all?" she asked. "If she's been harried that hard..."

"Her fleet has been harried, pursued and repeatedly engaged—but she is *definitely* still out there," Zamorano told her. "She's definitely still sourcing supplies, and I have feelers out into those channels.

"I have not successfully made contact, and I can't confirm what's left of the fleet she extracted from Apollo," he admitted. "Give me time, and I should be able to establish that link and get the two of you in the same room for a chat."

Kira sighed and nodded.

"There's a time limit in play, Tomas," she warned. "Both in how long I can afford to operate Memorial Force and in how long it will take Brisingr to restore the defenses they wrecked."

"I know," Zamorano said. "Give me time," he repeated. "I have a few irons in the fire to help with the costs. I have a discretionary budget that will cover a bit, but authorization from on high would let me basically write you a blank check."

Kira took a moment to finish a slice of toast as she processed that.

"Why would...your superiors"—even in a secure space on the SDC fortress, she wasn't going to say who Zamorano worked for—"put up that kind of money?"

"Because the Equilibrium Institute has made themselves our problem," Zamorano said bluntly. "Thanks to your information supplied since our previous encounter, the reports we'd been sending about their activities reached a *long*-overdue critical mass."

"Given some of what I know they got up to with Cobra Squadron twenty, thirty years ago..." Kira shook her head.

"You know who my superiors are," he reminded her. "It takes a lot to get them to *notice* something is going on. Let alone to decide it's something we should act on. Yes, we probably should have decided they were organization non grata forty years ago, but here we are."

"You're authorized to move against them?" she asked.

"Not truly; it's a mess still," he admitted. "But I am *permitted* to act. So long as I keep it under wraps and, well, act through proxies and allies." He indicated her with a piece of toast.

"I'm glad to know that I have value, if only as a shield for your own involvement," Kira noted wryly.

Zamorano chuckled.

"I did mention that Killinger all but *refused* to speak to me but ran roughshod all over his own security protocols to arrange a meeting with you, yes?" he noted. "Plus, the whole *battle fleet* is a small contributor to resolving the situation."

She nodded as she finished her toast.

"So, your superiors are content to let you run around acting as our lead spy so long as you don't act directly against their interests?"

"And our interests out here... Well, the only reason I'm out here is to keep us informed," he reminded her. "We *have* no real interests out here. I am hoping to get the budget to keep our organization non grata under control, but for now...I am allowed to provide you support in terms of information and contacts.

"So long as I don't draw too much attention to myself, that is."

"I appreciate the efforts you've put in on our behalf," Kira told him. "Next steps, as I see them, are that I take the battle group my people insist I fly into Brisingr space with to the Hera System and touch base with an old friend—and you keep digging on Michelakis?"

"That's about what I see as well."

He made a small hand gesture, and a file-transfer request appeared in her headware.

"Information on the contact in Hera is in the file, plus what I know about Killinger's base in Faaselesitila," he told her.

"Thank you," she said. "Is there anything else I should know before we part ways?"

He smiled.

"There is one thing. That stays between us, for the moment at least. I'm not certain enough of it yet to want even your officers to know."

Kira gave him a questioning look as she leaned back and cradled her coffee.

"Okay, color me intrigued," she admitted.

"I also have contacts on Brisingr," he told her. "I'm choosing a side in this mess, yes, but I'd prefer to keep the realization of that very, *very* limited. My job is to maintain channels of information flowing back to my superiors from *everywhere*, Admiral.

"I can't burn bridges, not unless it's absolutely necessary. So, while I am getting information from Brisingr, I'm not going to be passing much of it along to you."

"That's fair," Kira conceded. "But it sounds like you have something you *are* passing along."

He nodded.

"Reinhardt took *everyone* by surprise with the attack on Apollo," he told her. "I'm not entirely sure *how* he got three-quarters of his active nova fleet and three hundred thousand Weltraumsoldats into position for the assault without the Diet and a good chunk of his *military high command* not realizing, but he did it."

Even the *thought* took Kira's breath away.

"Do they even *have* enough Weltraumsoldats to make that possible?" she asked. *Space Soldiers* in English, the Weltraumsoldats were the equivalent to Redward Royal Army Marines or Apollon Hoplite troopers.

"Last I checked, the Kaiserreich had about one point two million Weltraumsoldats and another five million in the Planetarewehr. The latter aren't supposed to leave the system."

"Is that changing?" Kira murmured.

"A special act is before the Diet to authorize them to deploy a hundred divisions—two and a half million soldiers, give or take—of the Planetarewehr to Apollo," Zamorano told her. "Which is controversial, from what I can tell.

"The Diet is torn on the invasion. By and large, they're coming down on the Kaiser's side—but victory always has many friends."

Kira took a second to chew on that phrasing.

"You think Reinhardt's support is more fragile than it might look? So long as he's the winner, the conqueror of Apollo and the founder of the Security Zone, Brisingr's government and people fall in line behind him. But if he falters, if he loses...the *means* to his ends start getting examined."

"I *suspect* there is already a solid contingent that doesn't feel Reinhardt's ends have justified his means," Zamorano said. "But so long as he is victorious, no one will rock the boat too heavily.

"But if you succeed in liberating Apollo...we may find the Kaiser-reich and the Diet more willing to negotiate peace than we expect."

"Or the losses inherent in that process may turn this into a blood feud that will not end in our lifetimes," Kira suggested.

The Terran grimaced.

"I have to hope that we can find a better solution than that," he admitted. "Because, bluntly, Demirci...if I can't see a way that liberating Apollo will lead to *less* war and *less* death, I might have to concede that the Institute has a point."

"From where I sit, it almost doesn't matter," Kira warned. "I'm in this for the freedom of my people. I'd *like* to think that we can build a better peace afterward, but I will not leave my world, my people—my *family*—conquered."

While she had often argued with her brother and his wife over their determined lack of interest in the municipal politics of their tiny village and the county around it, let alone Apollo's interstellar position and relations, she hoped that disinterest was keeping their heads down.

Kira's sister-in-law hated her guts, but Kira's brother loved the woman for some reason. And even Kira had to admit that a shepherd was better served staying on good terms with the nurse he'd married than the naval officer sister he rarely saw.

She couldn't do much to influence what happened to her brother or his wife. But she didn't have it in her to *forget* that her solitary sibling lived in the hills above the city of New Athens. His focus might be on his sheep, like their father's focus before him, but he would almost certainly have seen the assault forces land.

He was safe. He wasn't the type of person who would get involved in politics or resistance or anything so foolish.

Kira hoped.

8

IT WAS both a relief and terrifying for things to finally be moving. Kira stood on *Prodigal*'s flag bridge—smaller than *Fortitude*'s but still designed around the same idea of an illusory bubble of vacuum—and watched her new Recon Group move away from the planet.

"McCaig, Ayodele, Davidović," she addressed the air, her headware automatically linking in the captains of *Prodigal*, *Harbinger*, and *Huntress* as she spoke.

"Anything to report? I know the cruisers didn't get the workup any of us would prefer, but we need ships here and we need recon. But if you've got any concerns, now is the time."

"I'm a touch thrown by not having a single pilot aboard who flew from *Conviction*," McCaig admitted. "I know the cruisers are our last priority for fighter crews, but even my CNG was recruited after Memorial Force was created."

"It's the same on *Harbinger*," Ayodele agreed. "Though, to be fair, it doesn't bother *me* as much."

Ayodele, after all, had *also* been recruited after the loss of *Conviction*. One of the few people Kira knew who was even shorter than her, he had come highly recommended from the Redward Royal

Fleet—he'd started as tactical officer on their first *Parakeet*-class destroyer, risen to command a *Parakeet* of his own and now to command their third cruiser.

"When we lost *Conviction*, Captain Estanza got almost everyone off," Kira noted. "But our only other ship was *Deception*. We picked up transports and carriers and destroyers and now more cruisers, but in a very real sense, Memorial Force started with just one ship."

Redward had provided them with a converted freighter, a so-called "junk carrier," within weeks. But they'd *started* with just Mwangi's ship.

"That's fair," McCaig allowed. "But other than a vague sense of my age and impending mortality, *Prodigal* is entirely functional."

"I lack even the sense of mortality," Ayodele said. "I have the occasional fear that you'll realize I shouldn't be commanding a cruiser, but my competence at the job is convincing even to me!"

Kira chuckled and turned a mental glance on Davidović.

"Marija?" she asked.

"*Huntress* had anything less than perfect about her fixed after the battle here," the light carrier's CO told her. "I have zero concerns about my ship, ser."

"Well, that tells me I'm correct in having zero concerns about any of the ships," Kira said. "Everyone has the course?"

"Nova to the trade route, four novas to get out of the Corridor, nova to the Prasináda System to discharge," Ayodele reeled off. "From there, nova back to the trade routes and three more jumps to the Hera System."

"Are we going to have issues discharging in Prasináda?" McCaig asked.

"So long as we don't go near the planet, my fellow Greeks are likely to genteelly ignore us," Kira said. "We pay for discharge rights and fuel like anyone else. The Prasinádans aren't going to argue with cruisers, even when they realize we're not *actually* Brisingr ships."

She smiled thinly.

"I have the sneaking suspicion that few in the Security Zone are going to be eager to help Brisingr out."

Kira felt more than saw her captains' nods.

"All ships nova in ten minutes from my mark. Mark."

―――――――

THE LIVE LINK to the ship commanders dropped away, and Kira watched the three ships form up as they blazed away from Bennet. Their formation was an inverted triangle, with the two K-90-class cruisers in front and *Huntress* behind and in the middle.

A six-ship squadron of Wolverines from *Huntress* had been running a Carrier Aerospace Patrol, but they fell back on the carrier as the countdown to nova ticked away.

They'd alternate which squadron was flying the CAP and probably increase the size as they entered the Security Zone. Each of her cruisers had two squadrons of interceptors, a squadron of heavy fighters, and two bombers—nothing star-shaking but a solid addition to *Huntress's* six squadrons each of interceptors and heavy fighters and two squadrons of bombers.

Sixty interceptors, forty-eight heavy fighters, and sixteen bombers. Wars had been fought with fewer nova fighters than that, even ignoring the firepower of the two modern cruisers providing the bulk of the Recon Group.

Hell, *Kira* had fought wars with less firepower than her current reconnaissance-in-force. When she'd arrived in the Syntactic Cluster, the six Apollon interceptors she'd smuggled out with her had been twenty percent of *all* the nova fighters in the *cluster*.

Six novas to the Prasináda System. A twenty-hour cooldown between each one meant it would be a hundred hours before they reached their destination, where they would need to trail cables through the magnetosphere of a planet for at least twenty-four hours before continuing on their way.

But...by the last nova along the trade route, she would be in the area that Apollo had regarded as its *personal* frontier and extreme operations range. Regardless of how the line was drawn, once they left the Samuels-Colossus Corridor, they were in the Apollo-Brisingr Sector.

From Prasináda to Apollo was a single set of novas. Twenty-five light-years. From Apollo to Brisingr was thirty-two light-years. Once she left the Corridor, Kira was in theoretical striking range of her enemy.

Everything was about to change—and as she considered the distances, the universe flickered around her. A pulse of tachyon energy and Cherenkov radiation rippled across her holographic bubble, and the Samuels System was gone.

9

THEIR FIRST POTENTIAL difficulty arose exactly when Kira was anticipating. They emerged from their jump into the mapped nova point four and a bit light-years from Prasináda to find a security patrol waiting.

Since Kira had been anticipating trouble, she was back on *Prodigal*'s flag bridge and accessing all of the sensor feeds as everything came online post-nova.

"Soler?" she addressed her operations officer as the identity beacons processed through the computers. "I'm going to guess those destroyers are not random."

The SDC and Memorial Force were keeping a destroyer force in place across most of the mapped entry points for the Corridor. It made sense for Brisingr to keep an offsetting force in play.

"Three warships," Soler confirmed. "Beacons make them BKN Seventeenth Destroyer Flotilla—which means they've got nine friends around somewhere."

"And probably a CVL," Kira noted. A light carrier—like *Huntress*, with sixty to eighty fighters—would make a solid backup. Three destroyers could deal with most difficult civilians and gave the picket the ability to keep two ships on station while sending the third for backup against a more serious threat.

"Most likely, they've divided the flotilla by division," she continued. "Three divisions rotating through the trade routes out of the Corridor. Fourth guarding the carrier, probably in...Prasináda."

"They're a bit over a light-hour away, ser," Soler told her. "I make it one D-Twelve destroyer with a pair of D-Eleven-Ds."

The D11-class destroyer had been the new shininess at the end of the war, but Brisingr iterated quickly on destroyer designs. The D11D was, from what Kira understood, the final evolution of the design: a thirty-eight kilocubic ship with seven single turrets carrying destroyer-grade plasma cannon.

The D12 was the *current* new shininess, four of which had ended up in the hands of the Samuels Defense Command. They traded one fewer turret and an extra forty-five hundred cubic meters to bring their guns up to what, prior to the D12, had been regarded as *cruiser*-grade in the Sector.

Like *Prodigal* herself, all of the Brisingr ships were boxy things with sharp angles and few curves. Apollon ships—and Crest ships, like *Fortitude*—were built with rounded edges and gentle angles to avoid dead space. Any given Brisingr ship, in Kira's experience, lost about three-quarters of a percent of their nova-capable volume to dead space of minimal use.

The result of the war between Apollo and Brisingr, however, suggested the value of having twenty-one ships that were ninety-nine percent as effective as your enemy's *twenty*. The sharp angles, straight edges and blocky designs lent themselves to ever-so-measurably easier construction.

"Let me know when they send the junior captain for backup," Kira told Soler. Either of her two cruisers could take on the entire opposing destroyer division. *Huntress*'s full fighter group would be complete overkill.

"If they're in Prasináda, is that going to be a problem for us?" Bueller asked. Kira's boyfriend was sitting at the console for the squadron engineer, a role she supposed he was filling. There hadn't been much formal discussion about his coming along.

"It might be," Kira conceded. "I'm figuring that Prasináda is going to lean on the tradition of neutral ports. They don't give a shit about *us*, but it's a point of principle and privilege for them to be able to order the BKN to not start fights in their space.

"Plus, unless everyone is tiptoeing even more softly than I expect, there are going to be a stack of monitors *just* out of range of the BKN carrier," she noted. "The Security Zone is pretty hard to argue with—with Apollo no longer a factor, nobody else in the Sector has the numbers to stand up to the BKN blockading their system.

"But even with the Fall of Apollo, I doubt anyone is expecting to see Weltraumsoldats in *their* capital city. They will maintain the privileges of their sovereignty."

"Probably all the harder for the degree to which Brisingr is grinding away at said sovereignty," Bueller replied.

"Exactly." Kira eyed the distant destroyers. It would be an hour or so before their sensors saw the Recon Group—but it would be an hour after *that* before she saw what they did. Unless...

"Scimitar," she said aloud. A moment later, she felt the link establish between her and *Huntress* Commander, Nova Group.

"Basketball," Colombera greeted her, using her old callsign. "What do you need?"

"Trade-route patrol," she told him. "We've got a Brisingr destroyer division I want to keep a closer eye on, so let's get fighters in close enough to give us faster data. We'll set up for the standard anti-piracy patrol pattern, keep fighters cycling around the trade-route stop—keep an eye on *everyone*."

"Can do, ser. What's our story if they challenge?"

"McCaig, Davidović, Ayodele." Kira pulled the three captains in before she continued. "The story is that we're under contract with Samuels to do extended anti-piracy patrol out into the edges of the Security Zone...just in case, you know."

"If we were doing that, we'd still need to discharge at Prasináda,"

Davidović noted. "That covers us through their perimeter—but they'll realize that we didn't go back."

"I'm fine with that," she told the Recon Group's senior officers. "I'll avoid fights where I can, but I have no issue punching a hole through any barrier Brisingr puts in our way.

"But once we're clear of Prasináda, we're out of the area where they're most actively patrolling. We clear the border area, and the fact that we're flying K-Nineties will clear away any non-BKN trouble!"

"I'll have the first squadron up in sixty seconds," Scimitar told them. "Pulling one squadron of Wolverines and Hussars from all three ships. Six squadrons will give us a solid sweep of the trade route while hanging on to a full strike to ruin their day if they do pick a fight."

"Make it happen, CNG," Kira ordered. "Everyone, stay on your toes. Bring the ships to readiness two. Battle stations aren't needed yet, but I want everyone ready for if the BKN pulls a fast one and dumps a carrier and a fighter strike on top of us."

Part of Kira's job, after all, was to consider how she'd ruin the Recon Group's day as efficiently as possible—and if *she'd* been in the BKN's carrier group CO's boots, she'd be sending her "challenge" via a single interceptor.

One followed a minute or so later by a full-deck strike from the carrier itself.

FIGHTERS FLICKERED in and out of existence, reports automatically downloading back to the flag deck and filling in their view of the well-mapped piece of empty space. There were dozens of freighters, ranging from the ubiquitous ten-kilocubic tramps up to a massive hundred-and-twenty-kilocubic fast packet out of the Syndicated Republic of Bowden in the Fringe.

Bowden's corporations almost certainly had even bigger ships operating in their own space, but it was rare enough for a Fringe ship to be over a hundred light-years out into the Rim. No one was going to be foolish enough to send a *freighter* out into space where she was bigger than local warships.

Captains and shipowners that foolish tended to suffer from unfortunate accidents that resulted in their more-advanced nova drives being strangely intact when the local military forces salvaged them. There were a few reasons why military technology declined as one got farther from Earth—and the biggest was that few nations saw it as in their interests to upgrade potential rivals' technology.

For now, the Syndicates' ship was ignoring the careful dance of half a dozen warships. Her captain was probably secure in the knowledge that no one wanted to draw the Syndicated Republic's attention out there. Bowden didn't have a pleasant reputation, after all.

"Ser, *Harbinger*-Alpha-One just novaed back and is uploading a message from the BKN detachment," Ronaldo reported. "Fregattenkapitän Carolus Riker, commanding."

"Put it on the display," Kira ordered.

The image of a stocky middle-aged man in the black-and-gold uniform of the Brisingr Kaiserreich Navy appeared in front of her, part of the holographic bubble changing into a screen.

Fregattenkapitän Riker—a Captain too senior to command a destroyer, so presumably the division CO—had the red-tinged look of a man who spent a lot of time studying the bottom of a glass of alcohol. He also, though, looked surprisingly determined in the face of overwhelming force.

"Memorial Force commander," he said calmly. That was probably intended to be rude, though given that Kira wasn't officially aboard any of the Recon Group's warships, she wasn't going to get a *polite* greeting regardless.

But Riker would have been told Davidović was in command.

"I must register, in the strongest terms possible, a formal protest against your presence and actions here," Riker continued. "I recognize the reality that I am not capable of retrieving the warships you have stolen from my nation, but you have no authority to operate in this trade-route stop.

"No sovereignty of your employer, the Samuels System, stretches this far. This area is part of the Brisingr Trade Route Security Zone. Operations by mercenary warships in the Security Zone are forbidden.

"The presence of *any* warships, domestic or contract, from the Samuels System is unwelcome. If you do not recall your fighters, it will be regarded as an act of war by Samuels.

"I doubt your employers have authorized you to start a war, mercenary. Recall your fighters and stay the hell away from my ships, or we will respond with force."

Kira smiled.

"Perfection," she said aloud. "Davidović?"

"He's being all rude and authoritarian, isn't he?" the carrier Captain replied. "I guess since I'm supposedly in charge, you want me to talk to him?"

"Yep," Kira confirmed. "He has conveniently played directly into our hands. I want you to offer him a 'reasonable compromise.' We will withdraw our fighters and carry his protest back to the Samuels System, but we need official permission to discharge in Prasináda and promise of safe conduct while we're there."

She smiled.

"They'll figure out we played them pretty quickly after we leave Prasináda, but that's not our problem."

If anything, she was doing Fregattenkapitän Riker a favor. She didn't think she could take out his three ships without any casualties, and she didn't want to deal with a BKN carrier flight group in Prasináda, however "light" said carrier was. There was no doubt in her mind of the end result of her Recon Group clashing with either force.

Their deception was entirely unnecessary, but it might get Kira through *two* encounters with the Kaiserreich Navy without killing anyone.

EVEN SENDING nova fighters back and forth as couriers, communicating across a light-hour wasn't instantaneous. It took almost half an hour for Fregattenkapitän Riker's response to arrive.

Part of that had probably been Riker waiting to see if they were actually recalling their fighters—which neither Kira, Scimitar, nor Davidović had seen a point in delaying.

Riker didn't look like the stick up his ass or his need for a drink had decreased in size since the last message. He was glaring at the pickups, his shoulders rigidly back in the holographic image.

"I would *like* to tell you to drag your stolen ships back to Samuels and never show yourselves around here again," he growled. "But I recognize the impracticality of that request. You will need to discharge static and Prasináda is the only system I can see you reaching.

"Against my better judgment, I will provide authorization for you to discharge static in that system once I have confirmed you have withdrawn all of your fighters," he continued. "Kapitän der Weltraum Greta Fried will keep a very close eye on you while you are in Prasináda.

"You are *not* authorized to deploy nova fighters or do anything *except* discharge static, and the Kapitän der Weltraum will make certain you do not. There will be no second warning, Memorial Force.

"If you enter the Security Zone again, we *will* be coming for our ships."

The recording ended, and Kira laughed aloud and glanced over at Bueller.

"Does he really think that even the full carrier group could recapture the K-Nineties?" she asked.

"No," the Brisingr native told her, eyeing where his countryman had been standing. "But I suspect that the BKN figured we wouldn't have the audacity to actually sail the K-Nineties into the Security Zone.

"He doesn't have orders to retake the ships, and even Kapitän der Weltraum Fried is likely heavily outgunned by the Recon Group alone—but believe me, Kira, if Fried or Riker thought they could take us, they'd try.

"We stole their ships and we are waving that fact under their noses." He shrugged. "I agreed with the logic of using them for this, especially since *Deception* would be just as bad in a lot of ways.

"But we are...*irritating.*"

"I can live with being irritating to the BKN," Kira noted. "Especially since once we're past Prasináda, I don't expect them to be quite as thick on the ground."

"They will be patrolling," Bueller warned. "And in force. Otherwise, the Security Zone is meaningless."

"I know. But here is where they had positioned scouts and reinforcements who were looking for us," she pointed out. "We'll make this work, Konrad. And if all we pull off is just to avoid one or two skirmishes by bullshitting them, well..."

"Bullshit is free," her engineer conceded.

10

For all that Apollo and Brisingr were separated by almost the maximum distance that a ship could travel without discharging, it was clear that Kira and her Brisingr counterparts had very much learned their tactics and planning from the same schools of thought.

As her three ships slowly descended into the upper reaches of Prasináda's gas giant, Megálo Mov, she could see that her estimate of the patrol deployment had been bang on. Another trio of destroyers—a D_{12} and two $D_{11}Ds$, the same division structure as at the trade-route stop—hung in high orbit, providing overhead watch for the N_{48} light carrier *actually* securing the system.

Two ten-ship squadrons of Weltraumpanzer-Fünfs, modern heavy fighters, supported the three destroyers. That was roughly a quarter of the fighters aboard the sixty-kilocubic carrier, which was more than *she'd* have let them put up if she were the Prasinádans.

Still, as she listened in on the conversation between Davidović and the local traffic controllers, she did count six asteroid fortresses positioned to cover the gas giant. Megálo Mov—*Big Purple* in the Greek Kira shared with the locals—was relatively small as gas giants went, but she was the only gas giant the locals had.

The fortresses had their own nova fighters out and patrolling the planetary system to watch the ships discharging and make sure the visitors paid their fees. A veritable swarm of local sublight craft, ranging from gaudily painted shuttles offering the oldest services in the universe to mobile repair ships capable of taking on damaged battlecruisers, drifted through the orbitals.

"Any word from our Brisingr friends?" Kira asked Ronaldo.

"Nothing so far," her coms officer reported. "The destroyers are *definitely* aware of us. They've adjusted their orbit to put themselves on the far side of one of the local forts in about ten minutes."

"They're figuring we might pick a fight with *them* but we have no grief with the Prasinádans," Kira guessed. "Which would be correct."

A chime in her headware told her Davidović had opened a link.

"No problems with the locals," *Huntress*'s Captain told her. "Well, I think they jacked discharge fees over even warship rates to make up for any potential trouble, but they didn't *tell* me that."

"I'd expect no less," Kira said. "Though we aren't going to cause any trouble. How long until we're out of here?"

"Megálo Mov isn't big enough for a minimum-time discharge without us getting closer in than we probably want to get with a BKN carrier group on our asses," Davidović pointed out. "How deep we get into the magnetosphere is your call, boss, but for anything less than thirty hours, we're into a zone where novaing gets dangerous."

Kira regarded the green-and-purple gas giant with scant favor. She hadn't considered that aspect when putting together her time-line. Normally, getting a twenty-four-hour discharge at a gas giant was easy. At a habitable planet, discharge was more usually in the thirty- to thirty-six-hour range—less than it could be, as one of the key characteristics of a planet humans could live on was a strong magne-tosphere, but still more than gas giants.

"Let's stick where we can run for the hills at a moment's notice," she told Davidović. "I'm not going to trust this Kapitän der Weltraum Greta Fried for one damn second, even *with* her subordinate's promise of safe passage."

A new set of icons flickered into existence around the Brisingr carrier, and Kira grimaced.

"I don't suppose the locals authorized *us* putting up a fighter patrol?" she asked.

Davidović laughed acidly.

"*We're* under neutral-port rules," she told Kira. "No fighters. No charged plasma capacitors. No sudden movements."

"Whereas our friend Fried just put up a bomber flight with interceptor escorts," Kira said grimly. "Let's make sure we have eyes on every one of her fighters and ships at all times. If that bomber strike so much as *twitches* toward us, we scramble and apologize to the locals *after* we've blown Fried to debs and lost dreams!"

TO EVERYONE'S UNSPOKEN RELIEF, the four-bomber strike continued to orbit Fried's carrier. The Recon Group could easily take down the strike if the BKN actually launched it—but it was a pointed reminder that Fried could flout standard neutral-port rules and the mercenaries couldn't.

"Somehow, I doubt the locals are particularly happy with her having a ready anti-shipping strike just sitting there, ready to go," Bueller observed. "*I'm* not happy, but that's because I was hoping you'd get some sleep in the next thirty-odd hours."

Kira chuckled at her boyfriend.

"Give it another dozen or so hours without anything exploding, and I'll think about it," she told him. "For now, though, I want to keep an eye on things."

"Kira, if I had a *problem*, I'd have said so," he replied with a chuckle of his own. "I'm just observing the downsides of our opponent's choices."

"It doesn't help that I can't just call up Fried and hash it out like adults," Kira told him. Her flag staff was busy with their own tasks, leaving the conversation between the Admiral and the task-group senior engineer—who happened to be the Admiral's boyfriend—to them.

"Once the BKN realizes that *you* are here, all the evidence we have says that they're going to come for the Recon Group hard," Bueller reminded her. "Both Reinhardt and the Institute seem to have an itch between their shoulder blades when it comes to you."

"At this point, Konrad, I'm not sure if there *is* a distinction here between Reinhardt and the Institute," she said. "He's either a sufficiently valuable asset or sufficiently powerful *member* of the Institute that their goals in this region appear to be entirely aligned."

"Would be interesting to see if we could *dis*-align them," Bueller noted. "But I don't see a way to do that."

"You'd know better than I would, but I suspect we're more likely to separate the Kaiserreich from the Institute than we are to separate Kaiser Reinhardt," Kira said. "Most likely by Reinhardt having some kind of unfortunate accident."

Konrad Bueller shivered and shook his head at her.

"I see the appeal," he admitted. "But it still goes against the grain to *hope* for my head of state to fall off a balcony!"

"Prior to living on Redward, I never had a singular head of state," Kira told him. "And, well, the Council of Principals long ago erased any warm, fuzzy feelings I had for them."

Both Apollo's ten-Councilor executive and two-hundred-representative legislature were elected—but Apollo was a constitutional *oligarchy*, which limited the planetary franchise to those in the top income-tax bracket.

The constitution laid out exactly what that "top income-tax bracket" had to entail—and that modifying the *constitution* required a planetwide plebiscite. With municipal politics having a universal franchise and the judicial system being primarily answerable to the municipal level of government, Kira had grown up thinking it was a well-balanced system.

Then, of course, her planetary oligarchs had thrown *her* to the wolves to end a war that was costing them too much money. That key members of the Council and the legislature had to have participated in betraying her planet to Brisingr hadn't *helped* her opinion of them!

"That's fair," he told her. "But I grew up in Brisingr high society, where at least lip service was paid to the concept of personal loyalty to the Kaiser."

Kira had been surprised to discover a while back that Konrad was, as a contact had put it, one of "*those* Buellers"—a member of one of the six Alteste Families whose bloodlines, by some arcane rules she couldn't decipher, had the right to stand for election as Kaiser when the previous ruler died or retired.

Given that Alteste Families had over nineteen hundred living members in the right age bracket, *he* hadn't thought that was important enough to mention—but he'd come from a higher tier of his society than Kira did of hers.

Her parents had been shepherds, after all.

"From what I understand, assassinating Reinhardt wouldn't change much," Kira told him with an intentionally flippant chuckle. "Not until we kick the ass of his little 'special operation,' anyway."

Bueller was shaking his head at her when Ronaldo coughed to interrupt.

"Ser, it appears Kapitän der Weltraum Fried is attempting to establish a communication link with Captain Davidović," he reported. "Your orders?"

A silent chime advised of Davidović's own presence in the conversation.

"Marija, talk to the woman," Kira told her. "I'll listen in and drop you text if I think we need to challenge something specific.

"You know the story and you know where we're at. We don't want to fight her, and we *definitely* don't want to violate Prasinádan neutrality—but Scimitar's people will chew up that carrier like a toy if we have to!"

11

IF THERE WAS a stereotypical Brisingr citizen, it was a stocky individual of Germanic extraction with blond or brown hair. Kira had known dozens in that mold—including both Konrad Bueller and Fregattenkapitän Carolus Riker.

Kapitän der Weltraum Greta Fried had the Germanic *name* common to citizens of the Kaiserreich, but she looked nothing like the image the name implied. She was a willowy woman with dark skin, sharp features, and obsidian-black hair pulled back into a severe bun.

Her eyes were as dark as her hair, and nothing in the flat glare the holographic image was showing suggested that Fried was a millimeter less sharp than she appeared.

"Kapitän Davidović," Fried greeted Kira's subordinate—also showing up in the flag bridge as a full-height hologram, the two dark-colored women glaring at each other.

Kira wasn't sure if the use of the German title, generally restricted to BKN officers, was a compliment or a slight. Either way, she suspected it was very carefully calculated on Fried's part.

"Kapitän der Weltraum Fried," Davidović replied. "I believe my people already forwarded Fregattenkapitän Riker's promise of safe passage? We have agreed to carry the *request* that Samuels' forces refrain from active patrols in the Security Zone back to our employer, but my ships must still discharge static before we leave."

"*Your* ships?" Fried replied. "I only see one ship that belongs to you, Kapitän Davidović. Two of the vessels you are claiming to command are warships of the Brisingr Navy. While *Huntress* may discharge and leave, as promised, *K-Ninety-Two-E* and *K-Ninety-One-A* will be turned over to myself.

"I will not condone your theft nor permit it to continue."

"I see." Davidović smiled. "Do the Prasinádan authorities agree with your assessment of the situation? Because your *suggestion* is a violation of the normal rules for neutral ports.

"And if Prasináda is not *neutral*, then the only thing keeping you alive is no longer in play."

Kira hadn't even managed to put her thoughts together to send Davidović instructions—and clearly, she didn't need to.

"This system is part of the Brisingr Trade Route Security Zone," Fried snapped. "Prasinádan authorities understand the requirement for our units to operate in this system to maintain the security of the trade routes we guarantor.

"I am not *intimidated* by your little mercenary fleet. You will surrender the ships you have stolen from the Kaiserreich or we will destroy them. And you."

"I see." Davidović's smile made *Kira* want to recoil in fear, and it wasn't even directed at her. "I am checking our datawork with the Prasinádan traffic controller and I'm not seeing anything in there about any authority delegated to the Brisingr Kaiserreich Navy.

"The corollary to my keeping my guns safed and my fighters landed in a neutral system, Kapitän der Weltraum, is an obligation on said neutral system to provide the security I am yielding," she continued. "We are all in range of the guns of Megálo Mov Orbital Defense Command.

"I will, of course, inform them of your threats," the carrier captain continued. "I will *not*, of course, be turning my ships over to you. And as I will inform MMODC, any aggressive action towards my flotilla will be met with overwhelming force.

"You have three destroyers and a sixty-kilocubic carrier, Kapitän Fried. My carrier is bigger than yours, and either of my cruisers can take all of your destroyers. I have no desire to start a fight here—but if *you* start one, I can guarantee you won't be the one finishing it."

Kira leaned back in her seat and grinned. Marija Davidović was a former Redward Royal Fleet officer, but Kira had clearly managed to do enough shaping along the way that the younger woman was saying *exactly* what Kira would have.

"You *dare* threaten me?" Fried demanded.

"I am not threatening anyone," *Huntress*'s Captain replied. "I am advising you of possible consequences should you engage in precipitous actions, so that you can appropriately plan your next steps."

"If you threaten my people, I will destroy you," the BKN officer snarled.

"Likewise, Kapitän der Weltraum," Davidović said. "So long as neither of us does anything rash, I believe we will all have a nice quiet day or two while my ships discharge, and then we will return to Samuels.

"That seems like a much better result for everyone to me, don't you agree?"

There was a long silence—and then Kapitän der Weltraum Greta Fried cut the connection.

"I don't think she likes you, Marija," Kira told her Captain. "I, on the other hand, am impressed. How do you think she'll jump?"

Now that the Brisingr officer was gone and Davidović was only connected to Kira, the captain slumped in on herself and exhaled a long, shaky sigh.

"I *think* she'll stay put," she admitted. "But I also think I'm going to have Scimitar prep our own bomber strike and keep them warmed up on the deck for the next little bit."

"Not a bad plan," Kira agreed. "You did good, Captain. Do me one small favor?"

"Ser?"

"Make sure our people *do* advise the Prasinádans about her threats," she told her subordinate. "Because under the traditions of neutral-port rules, by asking us to keep ourselves peace-bonded, they *are* taking on responsibility for our protection.

"And *nobody* is going to pick a fight with an orbital fort when all they've got is a CVL and some destroyers!"

12

HERA WASN'T much of a star system by most standards. A billion and a half souls lived on Eleutheria, a chilly world with vast ice caps and an average temperature barely above the freezing point of water. A single gas giant, Eris, provided fuel and discharge for ships passing through, but the lack of asteroid belts impeded the development of major spaceborne industry.

That, plus its distance from Apollo and Brisingr alike, had kept the system at the bottom of the tier for the economic benefits of first being Friends of Apollo and now of the Security Zone. Hera was far enough from any other centers of military or economic power to leave their trade vulnerable.

Still, after the delicate dance of getting through Prasináda without starting a war and the spark of worry every time they'd seen a warship on the trade route out to Hera, Kira was glad to see the system.

"Local control isn't giving us any difficulty," Ronaldo reported. "They are requesting that we keep the warships in high orbit, no closer than thirty thousand kilometers."

"In easy firing range of the forts," Kira guessed. "What are we seeing for nova forces, Soler?"

"Looks like hangars on the asteroid forts for fighters, and I'm seeing low-orbit facilities that could be class two drive factories," the operations officer told her. "They've definitely got nova fighters, but I'm not seeing *any* warships—not even monitors."

"Huh." Kira double-checked Soler's information as the sensor data fed into the holographic bubble around her. No warships at all, neither Heran nor Brisingr. Six decently sized asteroid forts hung around the planet, each of them acting as a counterweight to an equatorial orbital elevator, and there were a handful of fighters poking around on security patrols, but nothing bigger than five hundred cubic meters.

The fighters were big enough that they were probably nova fighters, not sublight planes, but they were *it* for mobile defenses.

"It's funny," Kira murmured. "When I arrived in Redward, they were unquestionably technologically behind these people...but for all that, I think Hera might actually have been poorer even then."

"We are also drawing a lot of attention, ser," Soler pointed out. "The Recon Group has more nova capital ships than this *system*."

"I know," Kira said. It hadn't been *her* decision to bring an entire carrier group along, after all. "But coming in aboard a pinnace, for example, would have ruined the whole point of *bringing* the Recon Group."

"I understand the logic, ser, but I wonder if drawing attention to us—to *you*—is really the best answer," her ops officer said.

"I don't think we were going to be able to avoid the Shadows' attention, no matter what we did," Kira replied. "Given that we can't avoid small-scale threats, the best solution we could see was to make sure that Brisingr *needed* a large-scale threat."

The Recon Group could handle anything short of a battlecruiser division or a proper fleet-carrier group. Reinhardt and the Institute had demonstrated that they *would* send forces of that magnitude after Kira, but they weren't quickly mobilized. So long as Kira kept her force moving and kept Brisingr guessing as to where they were, she *should* be able to outrun any force she couldn't fight.

"For now, we need to locate a bar," she told Soler. "The Jacobite Dream. Should be in the capital city somewhere."

"That sounds significantly less Greek than most of the other names I've heard in this system," Soler observed.

"The system and its planets were named by the same Greek-speaking survey crew that surveyed Apollo," Kira said. "And the system was colonized by mostly Greek speakers, also like Apollo. But not everybody on any given planet speaks the main tongue.

"And so far as I can tell, the Scottish ended up *everywhere*."

THE LOCALS, quite sensibly, required that shuttles landed and took off from proper shuttleports with appropriate landing pads. There were a number of reasons for that, but Kira wasn't surprised to find several uniformed system-security officers accompanying an official in a black toga.

Kira found the garment laughable, but she supposed everyone had their own logic for formal wear. There were arguments that the standard cut of military uniforms was utterly archaic, after all.

"Who is in charge here?" the togaed woman asked harshly, first in Greek and then in English.

"I am," Kira replied in the first language. She didn't even need a translator soft to speak Greek, though she could have loaded one. In her experience, despite the integration of headware, it was easy to tell the difference between someone using a soft and someone who'd actually learned the language.

"I see. I am Administrator Siana Romilly," the local official told her. The woman's pale skin and reddish-blonde hair contrasted poorly against the formal toga, making her look even paler and almost washed out.

"I need you to clarify your purpose on Eleutheria, please."

Romilly's demeanor flickered as Milani emerged from the shuttle behind Kira, gesturing their commandos to spread out and secure the area as Kira spoke to the official.

"Shore leave," Kira told the local. "We weren't advised that there would be any particular restrictions on that."

"Power armor is not permitted for civilian ownership on Eleutheria," Romilly said after a moment. "Your people must return the armor to your shuttle or it will be confiscated."

Milani was the only one in full body armor, and Kira smiled slightly as she flicked the local a file.

"That isn't power armor, Administrator," she told Romilly. "It's a medical prosthesis. I've transferred you a letter from Commander Milani's doctor."

Even Kira didn't know what the armor was a prosthesis *for*, but she suspected it was for Milani's gender. It was possible, she supposed, that Milani was missing a limb or two underneath the armor—but there were other solutions for missing limbs.

"I...see," the woman replied, still half-glaring at Milani. The holographic dragon flickering across the mercenary's armor aligned itself to meet the local's gaze and grin at her.

Romilly seemed to mentally shake herself, then returned her focus to Kira.

"Eleutheria maintains restrictions on most weapons and military systems," she said primly. "Only low-power stunners are permitted for civilian ownership. We do *not* recognize mercenaries as non-civilian for that purpose.

"While we cannot, in practicality, restrict you from ownership of weapons and warships in the star system, you are not permitted to bring such onto the planetary surface."

Kira spread her hands. She wore a sheepskin leather jacket over her dark teal uniform, a gift from her parents that had been reinforced with energy-dispersing webs and an integrated shoulder holster.

It took a conscious effort to open the jacket sufficiently to allow the contents of the holster to be seen, but it made it clear she was only carrying a stunner. Restrictions on blasters were common enough, after all, that she'd *checked*.

"All of my people are carrying stunners only," she assured Romilly. The commandos were also wearing low-profile body armor just as capable and notably more covering than her jacket, but she wasn't drawing attention to that.

"Fine. I'm transferring you a primer on key Eleutherian law," Romilly told her. A file-transfer request pinged on Kira's headware. "There are no special allowances for foreigners. Your headware identity beacons must be transmitting at all times.

"Is this understood...Em Riker?"

Kira's personal identification beacon was currently giving her name as Kira Riker, without military rank or identifiers at all. She'd taken her insignia off her uniform as well—though she recognized that the presence of her escort made the deception at least partially obvious.

"It is," she assured Romilly. "I will make certain my people behave, Em Romilly. We are not here to cause trouble."

"Right." The official studied them for a few long, silent minutes.

"Welcome to Eleutheria, Em Riker."

13

IN THE END, it took them longer to rent enough vehicles to transport Milani and their team than it had taken to convince Romilly they weren't going to cause trouble. Milani and one other commando traveled with Kira, while four other vehicles with three mercenaries apiece started in a convoy.

By the time they reached the Jacobite Dream, those vehicles had separated so as not to be obviously traveling in escort. When Milani handed their car over to an automated vehicle-storage facility that whisked the rental away with robot arms, the other cars weren't in sight.

Kira's headware was telling her exactly where her escorts were, though, and she knew that half a dozen more mercenaries were now concealed in the passers-by walking down the street.

The Jacobite Dream was in a "main street"–style commercial district, with two sets of restaurants and stores facing each other across a pedestrian-only street. The facades were clearly intended to evoke a medieval British town—though Kira knew enough ancient history to recognize just how poor a job had been done.

Still, the stores and restaurants seemed popular enough. The

Dream was quieter than most of the others, though its dark wood front and tinted windows were probably closer to the overall façade's intent than most of the other storefronts.

Walking in, her two escorts in tow, Kira found the entire place was intentionally dimly lit. She suspected the faux oil lamps on the walls could easily be turned up to light the place up completely, but at that moment, everything about the restaurant felt...muffled.

There was a burble of conversation in the background that she swiftly realized didn't match the sparsely occupied booths—there were no freestanding tables, only four rows of high-backed seating booths.

The white-noise generators had been well concealed, but they rendered it impossible to clearly pick out any conversation more than a meter away. For a moment, Kira wasn't sure if there would be a human or holographic host.

The answer, it turned out, was neither. A handshake request appeared in her headware. Accepting it, a virtual icon appeared on her screen, directing her to a booth with space for six.

"Interesting place," Milani murmured.

"Named for a rebellion that failed," Kira whispered back. "I guess the hope is to avoid that happening again."

Her bodyguard chuckled as they took a seat across from her. The other mercenary took the outer seat of the bench Kira took, blocking any approach.

"So, what now?" Milani asked.

"We order drinks and appetizers, and I put a specific note in the requests to the kitchen," Kira told them. "And then we wait and see."

AN ARTIFICIAL STUPID delivered their drinks silently a few minutes after they ordered them. Milani's drink was the only thing they'd be consuming, and they'd gone for a thick shake of some kind that smelled of so much sugar, Kira could taste it from across the table.

The mercenary tried to be subtle about dropping a sensor probe into the drink before touching it, but Kira knew their habits. They'd make sure the creamy, overly sweet beverage was entirely safe before they let it into their suit.

For herself and the other merc, a plate of vat-grown chicken wings joined a couple of glasses of water and two cups of coffee that smelled surprisingly acceptable.

Kira took a wing and nibbled on it, wondering how long it was going to take before the message she'd sent brought an actual human —the restaurant was very clearly set up to involve few, if any, humans in its regular operations.

She'd just finished the wing and was wiping her fingers clean when a shaven-headed man of indeterminate age slid into the seat next to Milani.

"And how are you all enjoying your lunch and drinks this afternoon?" the stranger asked. "I'm the manager of the Jacobite Dream, Bonnie."

Kira couldn't help but raise a questioning eyebrow.

"As in Bonnie Prince Charlie?" she asked.

Bonnie laughed and grinned, some stress and lines relaxing from his face. He could still have been anywhere from thirty to a hundred, depending on his access to cosmetic and anagathic procedures.

"My parents, stars rest their souls, looked at their family name of Prince and proceeded to put *Bonito* on my birth certificate," he observed. "I don't think anyone called me anything except Bonnie Prince in my entire life!

"My first husband was an ancient history professor and pointed out the Bonnie Prince Charlie reference, and I went down a rabbit hole of Old Earth facts. So, when I founded my restaurant, Jacobite Dream it was."

"I don't actually know enough about the Jacobite Rebellions to really guess if they were fighting for a just cause," Kira observed.

"Let's just say it's...still contentious," Bonnie Prince told her. "But as I asked, how is the food?"

"The wings are fine," Kira said. "I'm more impressed by the security arrangements, though. I'm guessing even the other booths can't hear anything? Does Eleutheria really find itself needing this kind of place?"

Prince leaned back and pressed his fingertips together, studying her.

"Apollon?" he asked.

"Yeah."

"Let's just say your experiment with constitutional oligarchy worked out better than what happens when oligarchs take over a democracy and *don't* have a constitution to limit them," Prince told her. "And I'm only comfortable saying *that* much because this restaurant neatly covers me against surveillance."

Kira nodded politely. Her own briefings on Hera when the system had been one of Apollo's "Friends" hadn't said anything of the sort, but the focus had very much been on the system's capabilities and their relations with Apollo.

Then, Hera had possessed a small flotilla of Apollon-built nova warships backed by homebuilt fighters and bombers. The ASDF had been unimpressed with Hera Security Service's nova fighters, but they were at least building their own.

Either those ships were gone now or the HSS kept their warships well away from anywhere they expected to see strangers. That spoke to an *interesting* position vis-à-vis the Security Zone and its BKN enforcers.

"Captive voting blocs and control of candidates who can run?" she guessed. "Not a single-party state, as I understand it, but not much difference between the two?"

"Tale as old as time, from what I can tell," Prince conceded. "Seems like the Purples and the Yellows agree on nothing except that things shouldn't change in a way that undercuts their authority." He shrugged. "It could be worse, I suppose. We get what we need from our government, most of the time; we just don't get much say in it.

"Doesn't leave one feeling it's much of a democracy."

"I've spent the last few years in an outright monarchy that felt more democratic than that," Kira replied with a chuckle. "But I suppose the discussion of what worlds *are* versus what worlds should *be* is related to why I'm here."

Prince studied her over his steepled hands, waiting silently.

"I'm *told* the code words I attached to the order should have told you why I'm here," she noted. "But let's be clear: I am here because you are supposed to be able to tell me where to find Henry Killinger."

The restaurant manager nodded and sighed.

"That is what the codes you included say, yes," he agreed. "You understand, of course, that it's not as simple as *produce code word, get instructions.* The Admiral may be our last best hope of a free sector and a better future. It's my job to make sure no one gets to him who is going to be trouble."

"He knows me," Kira said. "I served with him in the war, Em Prince. If he gave you any names that were good to let through, I suspect *Kira Demirci* was on that list."

"You belong to the cruisers up high, don't you?" Prince asked, not addressing her point.

"Something like that," she agreed. "Not sure I really need to tell you all of the bits and details, Em Prince. Either Killinger told you to tell me how to find him, or you need to make your own call. But I'm not his enemy. We're here to fight the same damn war he's already fighting—against Brisingr, for the freedom of Apollo and the rest of the sector."

"Words are easy," Prince said softly. "But you have to have jumped through a lot of hoops to be sitting here with the code words you brought, Em Demirci. I am the last filter, the person whose job it is to say *no* and to take the fall. Even if you are on the list I was given, I still have to decide whether I think we can trust you.

"And whether it's worth it for us to trust you."

"There are three capital ships in orbit of Eleutheria that suggest it'll be worth it," Kira replied.

"And you are on his list," Prince acknowledged. A datachip appeared on the table. "Coordinates and codes, Admiral Demirci. I hope I won't regret this."

"You won't," she promised.

Or, at least, if Prince *did* end up regretting letting Kira meet Killinger, the fault was probably going to be Killinger's.

14

"So, what have we got?" McCaig asked.

All of the senior officers of the Recon Group were present at the meeting, though everyone not aboard *Prodigal* were holograms linked in remotely.

Kira tossed a map of the Apollo-Brisingr Sector up above the table. The three-dimensional image rotated for a moment, then zoomed in on the Hera System.

"We're at Hera," she said, unnecessarily. "Basically, the ass end of the A-B Sector. I'd have to check, but I don't think Brisingr even bothered to blockade Hera during the war. It was too far away, at the limits of their logistics ability."

"From what I remember, BKN Command assumed that Hera would fall into our hands if we brought the ASDF down," Bueller pointed out. "Correctly, it appears. I'm assuming they patrol here occasionally, or they can't justify claiming it as part of the Security Zone with the attendant fees to the system government."

"Which leads me to the conclusion, I have to note, that the BKN has to have convinced *somebody* to let them set up a logistics base somewhere closer to here than Brisingr," Kira said. "They could theoretically be operating out of Apollo now, but the Security Zone predates the invasion."

"It's been damn quiet if so," McCaig observed. "I've been watching the data we bring in and the news reports, and I haven't seen any mention of a Brisingr base outside their system. They might just be running long patrols and discharging where they need to."

"No, the Admiral's right," Bueller said. "The BKN wouldn't want to be sending patrols more than one full discharge cycle from a significant base, someplace they can fall back to for anything they need.

"Six jumps out, discharge, six jumps back. Their doctrine puts that as the maximum range for regular ops. Long-distance *strikes*, sure, but they won't do regular patrols more than thirty-ish light-years."

"And Hera is forty-five light-years from Brisingr," Kira added. "So, there is a base somewhere along the way."

"Corosec?" McCaig suggested. "It's in the right place."

"No. Like I said, the base was in place before the invasion, and Corosec was Apollon territory," Kira said. "That's a problem for later, though. Right now, what matters to us is Faaselesitila."

The system, a bit less than ten light-years from Hera—back toward the Samuels-Colossus Corridor, putting it even farther away from Apollo or Brisingr than Hera—highlighted on the screen.

"Specifically, Faaselesitila Five," she continued. "A super-Jovian gas giant orbiting well over a light-day from the star. Massive collection of rings, moons, everything you might want for gravity sources, fuel supplies and raw materials.

"Of course, Faaselesitila also has three big asteroid belts to add to those raw materials. If the system had anything remotely inhabitable, it would be a treasure trove."

"As it is, I imagine Hera keeps making noises about using it as a resource-extraction site," Bueller said. "But everyone always underestimates the difficulty and expense of doing that. It's why the Costar Clans ever existed in the Syntactic Cluster."

The Costar Clans had been a recurring problem for the Syntactic Cluster's key powers, the leftovers of repeated attempts to colonize marginalized systems that had made their living by robbing everyone else's shipping. Kira and the rest of what had become Memorial Force had been instrumental in Redward's massive investment, both military and economic, in taking control of the Clans' systems and hopefully offering them a better option.

"And there's a lot of evidence that even with the frankly grotesque way Apollo's corporations handled Corosec, the entire extrasolar colony project barely broke even," Kira said, nodding.

"So, right now, there is officially no one in Faaselesitila," she continued. "In reality, as our sources told us before we even left Samuels, it appears that Admiral Killinger has set up a fleet base in the moons of Faaselesitila V.

"Our information from Prince doesn't include any information on what Killinger's strength is. We know he has enough hulls to have engaged in some moderately successful piracy on Brisingr traffic around the edges of the Security Zone, but we have no detailed information on the strength of his fleet."

"But we know where he is and how to say hello?" Davidović asked.

"We have contact frequencies and an approach vector," Kira confirmed. "Reading between the lines of what we have been given, Killinger's people have spent a good chunk of time seeding the outer rings and moons with plasma mines.

"Anyone who comes in on the wrong vector and isn't transmitting the right codes on the right frequencies, well..."

"Boom," Scimitar concluded, *Huntress*'s CNG looking thoughtful. "Basically refitted torpedoes, right?"

The torpedoes carried by a nova fighter had roughly four seconds of actual flight time, mostly intended to get them clear of the launching fighter before their warheads detonated. They used a magnetically focused fusion warhead to convert most of their mass to superheated plasma—a single-shot duplication of a larger warship's plasma cannon.

A plasma mine might not even bother with the minimal engines. It would simply point itself at its target and fire—and be all but undetectable until it was too late!

"That would be my assumption," Kira agreed. "Though I think Apollo had a fabricator schematic for a specialized mine, and Killinger should have access to that database."

"With the resources in Faaselesitila, he can build a lot of things, given a capital-ship fabricator," Bueller said. "Given the labor pool and the time, he could take those fabricators and build up to full-on shipyards."

"I'm not sure how complete the database on a capital ship would be on large-scale military technology," Kira admitted. "Nova drives are a lovely mix of needing gravity and microgravity to complete, so I don't know if he'd have the fabricator schematics for those aboard ship."

Class one nova drives needed about a third of their components constructed in gravity to work properly—and real gravity, too. Neither artificial-gravity systems nor centripetal pseudogravity or thrust pseudogravity worked.

And while part of the components needed to be manufactured in microgravity, the *ships* tended to be built in orbit, which made that part relatively simple.

Most artificial-gravity systems—including the Harrington-coil reactionless drives—had key pieces that needed to be assembled in microgravity. Once a planet had managed to begin manufacture of them, though, surface-to-orbit transfer and vice versa became straightforward.

The real trick, as Kira understood it, was that the more complex a nova drive became, the more specific the manufacturing requirements. Larger and more powerful class ones had narrower windows for the gravity they could be built in—and class two drives, the smaller units with the steeper cooldown curve used by starfighters, were even more specific still.

"How long has he been at this?" McCaig asked. "If he's been out there since your war ended, he might have built himself a whole industrial base."

"There's a lot of questions around what he might have," Kira noted. "All we *know*, for sure, is that he has at least some Apollon ships and some ships acquired as our Friends were being forced to downsize.

"Remember that the Friends, between the twelve of them, had around ten *million* cubic meters of nova ships at the end of the war—and Brisingr's Security Zone rules cut them down to five hundred thousand apiece.

"Now, some of those ships almost certainly went into asteroid-miner ore bins or something similar, and I imagine the Shadows were paying enough attention that most of them actually *did* get scrapped, but..."

She shrugged.

"Four million cubics of warships ended up hidden or scrapped. I know most of the Friends wanted to keep up their hull numbers, so they often only held on to a single fleet carrier or battlecruiser—but the hundred-kilocubic-plus ships were the ones the Shadows were watching.

"I'm *guessing* he's mostly got smaller cruisers. We'll find out soon enough, though, so I'm not sure there's any point guessing."

Kira gestured at the hologram in the middle of the meeting.

"Barring any new information or intuitions, I see no reason not to be on our way. Anyone?"

15

IN THEORY, the journey to Faaselesitila could have been made in two novas. The uninhabited system was less than ten light-years from Hera, after all. Unfortunately, the mapped nova points around Hera weren't laid out to allow easy travel to a system no one went to.

That meant the Recon Group had to make a jump to a trade route, a jump *along* the trade route—in the rough direction of the sector around the Crest, where Kira was officially persona non grata even if the royal family were *personally* indebted to her—and only then jump to their actual destination.

And it was the second system where their luck in avoiding major BKN formations finally ran out.

"Someone, I suspect, is starting to narrow down Killinger's location," Soler suggested. "Unless anyone else can think of a reason for a carrier group to be out here?"

"The Crest just kicked the Equilibrium Institute to the curb a bit over a year ago," Kira noted as she took in the scan data. "And now they're working on some *serious* regional politics and reform."

Thanks to their military and financial power, the Kingdom of the Crest had imposed a more explicit control-and-tribute system over its surrounding systems than many of the hegemons the Equilibrium Institute had propped up. Now, with the Institute out of the way, the Crown Zharang was working to convert that empire into an explicit co-equal federal union.

"The type of reforms that will make the Institute nervous," Bueller agreed with a chuckle. "Which means they'll make Reinhardt nervous, so far as I can tell."

"So, they're watching the main approaches from the Crest." Kira shrugged. "And the Crest Sector sends a lot of shipping this way, too, which means they don't have to *say* that's why they're doing it."

A timer was ticking down in the corner of her vision—marking the handful of minutes before the Brisingr L75 fast carrier knew they were in the trade-route zone. The L75 wasn't a full fleet carrier, but it was definitely more than Kira really wanted to tangle with without preparation.

Eighty-five kilocubics, eight starfighter squadrons, six heavy guns. She was small but still a modern ship, fast enough sublight to leave behind anything her fighters couldn't handle. The four D11D destroyers and the two I60 cruisers backing her up were just the icing on the cake.

The I60s were counterparts to the L75, modern versions of the obsolete I50s the BKN had given Colossus to blockade Samuels. Sixty-kilocubic ships with dual-turreted heavy guns and a single squadron of fighters aboard, they weren't up to the weight of the K-90s of Kira's Recon Group, but they were effective ships for their size.

And she would very much have preferred that they be effective somewhere else.

"Admiral, your orders?" McCaig asked. "They've got the firepower to be a real problem."

"Hold one moment," Kira told him. "Linking in the other COs."

Ayodele, Davidović and Scimitar were on the link a few seconds later. All of them had clearly been waiting for this conversation.

"Scimitar, can we take them without risking the capital ships?" Kira asked bluntly.

"Easily," Colombera confirmed. "It'll be another five minutes before our arrival light reaches them. We can get the bomber squadrons into space with escorts in three and, unless they've moved an unusual amount in the last fifteen minutes, jump them before they even know we're here.

"They're BKN, so they won't go without a fight, but they'll never really know what hit them."

Kira nodded. She'd drawn the same conclusion herself. She had over a hundred fighters between the cruisers and the carrier. The Brisingr ships had exactly a hundred, but given the advantage of surprise, her fighter group could wipe the capital ships out. Probably before the carrier managed to launch more than the patrols she currently had up.

Except...

"How many of their fighters are deployed?" she asked. "That we can see, at least?"

Speed-of-light delays were a problem, especially when dealing with nova fighters whose entire *purpose* was to be tactically faster than light.

"Two squadrons as a CAP," Ayodele reported first. "Scans suggest Weltraumfuchs-Sechs interceptors. Two more squadrons split into two-ship flights, scattered across the trade-route stop. Weltraumpanzer-Vier heavy fighters."

"Standard L-Seventy-Five complement would be three squadrons of interceptors, three squadrons of heavy fighters and two squadrons of bombers," Bueller reminded them all. "Cruisers will carry Weltraumpanzers by default. The BKN regard the heavies as the most versatile fighters."

Kira could see the argument—a heavy fighter could both tangle with other nova fighters and deliver torpedo strikes—but she wasn't sure that having the most *versatile* fighter was actually what a cruiser needed.

Her own cruisers carried all *three* types of nova fighter, but they had two squadrons of interceptors and only one two-plane flight of bombers. A cruiser's mission was to fight the enemy—which meant the main purpose of a cruiser's organic fighter complement was to keep everybody *else's* fighters out of the brawl.

"So, forty fighters in space, with twenty bombers and forty more fighters on the ships," Kira concluded. "Plus the destroyers and the cruisers."

The carrier herself wasn't really a threat once her fighters were deployed. She was more of one than, say, *Huntress* herself—the L75 had six heavy guns to *Huntress's* two—but either of the K-90s in Kira's force had *fourteen* similar guns.

"We can take them down before they can launch anything," Colombera confirmed. "Just give the word. The fighters in space are cleanup after that."

"And how many *civilian* ships are present at the nova stop, people?" she asked.

"Eighteen," Davidović told her. "Two are Brisingr-flagged. Rest is a mixed bunch—no real groups or shared origins."

"So, no matter *what* happens, the news will spread," Kira stated. "We could justify seizing the two Brisingr ships, but that's it."

She supposed they could kill *everyone*, but that wasn't even an option she'd say aloud, let alone consider.

"The correct *tactical* decision is to launch now," she conceded, hating where her brain was going. "But the *strategic* consequences of firing first, without warning, with no employer in a formal state of war with the Kaiserreich…"

"Politics," McCaig said darkly. "We need everyone to see us as the good guys."

"Hell, we need the BKN to think they can safely *ignore* us if we're not actively engaging them," Bueller replied. "Not all of my countryfolk are going to be entirely in line behind Reinhardt on this. And while the Kaiserreich frowns on mercenaries, their policy is to bar them being *hired* inside their zone of influence.

"Not to attack them on sight."

"So, we need to be clearly and visibly non-hostile right up until they send up the rocket," Kira concluded. "We have a CAP up. Triple it."

That would bring them up to nine squadrons, fifty-four fighters. It wasn't a *peaceful* gesture, but so long as they stayed around the Recon Group, it wasn't an *aggressive* one, either.

"Permission to prep the rest of the fighters for a full-deck strike?" Scimitar asked after a second.

"Granted. We're playing the appearance game right now, people. We need to *look* like we're not picking a fight here." Kira smiled thinly.

"And who knows? Maybe the BKN commander will learn to sing?"

16

KIRA's vain hope that whichever Flottillenadmiral was in command of the carrier group would be taking opera lessons were shattered in short order.

She'd taken the gesture of starting the Recon Group moving *away* from the Brisingr ships, with their Carrier Aerospace Patrol held in relatively tightly. She had over fifty fighters in space, but keeping them close also limited her ability to keep an eye on her enemy.

It was a carefully calculated risk. All joking aside, she *knew* that the Flottillenadmiral was going to attack. But she also knew that the dividends of letting the BKN fire the first actual shots of her war with them would be worth it in the long run.

If they survived—which was *why* she had nine squadrons in space. "Scimitar" Colombera had learned his job from Kira, and the interceptors and heavy fighters formed a three-dimensional star around the three starships, "spikes" of starfighters extending out into the most likely zones for the enemy's arrival.

"I really feel like we should have someone watching them," Soler murmured.

"Not much point," Kira replied. "They saw the light from our arrival forty seconds ago. If they're scrambling, they'll have a strike up in about three minutes."

She shrugged.

"They'll be here in five minutes. We're ready for them."

"And if they don't show up on time?"

"Nineteen hours until we can nova," Kira replied. "If they want to avoid a fight, I'm not going to chase them for one. But they may *try* to talk first."

She couldn't think of anything the Brisingr Flottillenadmiral could say to avoid a fight. The enemy officer either had orders to attack Kira's people...or they didn't, but they still likely knew she was on the Kaiser's hit list.

"Fighters are ready on the decks," Soler said quietly.

"All capacitors are charged, all guns are live, all engines and defenses test green," Bueller added. "We are ready. Doesn't mean this is going to be any fun, but we are ready."

Kira nodded, watching her headware timer countdown.

"Order all units to stand by multiphasic jammers and prepare for evasive maneuvers," she said calmly. "They will be here momentarily."

Whatever else the Brisingr Kaiserreich Navy was, she couldn't dispute their efficiency or their punctuality. The energy flares of arriving nova ships blazed into existence ten seconds before she'd expected them, dozens of tiny sparks in the void announcing the arrival of the enemy.

And less than half a second later, the sensor screens turned to hash as the emerging fighters activated their multiphasic jammers— and so did the Recon Group!

ONE THING KIRA had learned about the chaos of battle was that she had *far* preferred being in a nova fighter during it. In a fighter, the universe shrank down to what you could see and identify with your own eyes and optical scanners. Anything more complicated was lost in the mess of multiphasic jamming, with even communication to your squadron-mates swiftly lost.

The commander of a nova-fighter squadron lost control of their wing almost immediately, leaving the main success of the mission up to the training and planning—but they *also* had their own contribution, often being the most experienced and skilled pilot in their squadron.

An Admiral had no such direct action. Once the multiphasic jammers activated, Kira almost immediately lost contact with her starfighters. The data connections to *Huntress* and *Harbinger* dropped too, though they were quickly reestablished via laser tight-beam connections.

They lost a lot of bandwidth to the necessary double checks, but Kira was at least in contact with the Recon Group's two capital ships. Coordinating the optical sensors of the three ships even gave her a rough idea of what was going on in the chaos around her.

But only a rough idea. The success of her plan was now utterly dependent on the pilots of her fighters and the gunners aboard her capital ships.

"*Huntress*'s strike is up," Soler told her. "I'm still analyzing the incoming, but it's definitely not their full force. Probing strike."

Kira nodded, watching the icons on her screen. Each of them was a fuzzy probability zone, and her headware instantly filled the information in as she glanced at each potential target.

"All heavies," she told her staff. "Which means they're holding back the interceptors to protect their own ships—and that the bombers are going to try to sneak up on us."

The Brisingr force was badly outnumbered by Kira's defenders, no matter what games they were playing, but she suspected that was the *point*.

"Try to get a message through to the fighters," she told Ronaldo. "They're trying to unbalance our formation, clear a side of the Recon Group for their bombers to make a reciprocal strike."

"Scimitar's full-deck strike is heading toward the likely emergence zone for that, ser," Soler reported. "He had the same thought."

Of course he had.

"McCaig, Ayodele, let's make sure there's a cruiser along each likely approach vector," Kira told her captains, nodding her understanding to Soler. Their formation made that straightforward enough —but even as she gave the order, the heavy fighters vanished back into nova.

Sixty seconds. The minimum cooldown of a class two nova drive, and the usual length of any nova-fighter strike.

"We've got a likely line on their orchestration point," Soler reported. "Orders?"

"Hold jamming, hold position," Kira replied. "Expect a ninety-degree vector for the next strike by the fighters, with...two bomber strikes coming in on opposing perpendicular vectors to the fighters."

"Dividing their forces is risky," Soler noted.

"But it's what the BKN will do," Bueller said. "The Flottillenadmiral doesn't think they can take us toe-to-toe without bringing up their capital ships, and they'll want to soften us up first. They'll use vectors and timing to try to draw our main strength out of position so they can get bombers in."

"I suppose they might have changed their doctrine since the war," Kira murmured. "But keeping our formation spread out helps, no matter what."

With the enemy currently out of the battlespace, they had intermittent contact with the fighters. Mostly quick burst transmissions each way.

"Scimitar is requesting permission to launch a counterstrike," Ronaldo passed on. "He figures if he takes the bombers and three squadrons of Hussars, that'll leave enough to cover the capital ships."

Kira's eyeball estimate was that the Brisingr force had brought four squadrons to the first strike—forty heavy fighters—and lost about a quarter of them.

That left the enemy with seventy fighters and twenty bombers, where she had sixteen bombers and over ninety fighters left. She wasn't sure of her losses, but they were lighter than the BKN's.

Taking eighteen of their Hussar-Sevens, the Memorials' heavy fighters, would still leave the fighter edge with her—plus, the BKN had to be holding some fighters back for their own security.

But for the first time in her career, Kira was commanding a true carrier duel at a distance that let her take the time to think. She could work through the same math as Scimitar and see his logic—but she could also see the need to hold everything back to protect *her* carrier.

This wasn't even tactical versus strategic. This was defense versus offense, and there were arguments both ways.

"Permission granted," she told Ronaldo before the weight of her new role overwhelmed the instincts from her *old* one. If nothing else, pressing the enemy carrier group would give *their* fighters something to worry about.

It took a good fifteen seconds for the message and orders to percolate out through the sporadic links between the nova fighters. Only the fact that the enemy wasn't immediately present allowed even remotely reliable communications between the fighters.

Once the message had been passed, thirty-four of her small attack ships vanished. There were still seventy-some interceptors and heavy fighters spinning around her three capital ships like the spokes of a wagon wheel, with *Huntress* at the center and the two heavy cruisers rotating around her more slowly.

"Nova signatures," Soler reported. "Looks like they found some more fighters; I make it fifty planes, plus/minus half a dozen."

"Risky," Kira whispered to herself. "That's leaving either their bombers on their own or their capital ships on their own."

Though the BKN Flottillenadmiral might think their destroyers were enough protection. They might even be right.

"Move the cruisers to the perpendicular vectors," she ordered again. "That's where the bombers are going to come from."

It felt strange to pull the capital ships *out* of the main visible threat, but Kira wasn't actually *worried* about the mix of heavy fighters and interceptors swirling toward their counterparts. If any of them got through to torpedo range, it would hurt—but there were as many fighters blocking the Brisingr planes as the BKN strike had brought.

But the seemingly "main" strike was the distraction. She knew it in her bones, and she watched as two of her interceptor squadrons fell back on the cruisers as they maneuvered. Mostly likely, those were from the Wolverines that flew off each of the heavy warships, and *this* was their intended role.

"Contact!" Soler snapped. "Danger close—fifty thousand klicks!"

Not quite where Kira had expected them but definitely in the zone she'd allocated for *Prodigal*. The bombers were coming in at ninety degrees from the original fighter strike, pushing their nova dangerously close in and moving in fast on *Huntress*.

Except *Prodigal* and six Wolverines were in their way. The bombers' torpedoes couldn't hit the cruiser at this range—but *her* guns could hit *them*. In theory, at least.

"I make it ten bombers, five interceptors," Soler reported. She coughed. "Make that eight bombers."

Prodigal's main heavy guns weren't really designed to hit nova fighters. Reliably hitting nova fighters took rapid-firing guns at ten thousand kilometers or less—guns which *Prodigal* had in generous supply but wasn't using at that moment.

Plasma torpedoes had an effective reliable range of about fifteen thousand kilometers. The preferred approach to a bomber with torpedoes was to put an interceptor or other fighter, carrying said rapid-firing guns, in the bomber's path.

The other option was to use a capital ship's main guns, with an effective range of over *fifty* thousand kilometers, to walk fire across their approach zone. It wasn't reliable and it was overkill—but Caiden McCaig's gunners had just put rounds sufficient to vaporize ten-kilocubic gunships into five-hundred-*cubic* bombers.

They'd fired over a dozen shots to score two hits, but that was two hits *more* than Kira had expected at maximum range.

"Well done, Captain," Kira told McCaig. "Now fight your ship."

Those six interceptors might have been able to handle the bomber strike on their own, given more distance to work with. Backed up by a cruiser filling space with fusing hellfire, the bomber crews were left with the decision every escort tried to force on a bomber strike: go for the main target or fire on the escort in your way.

Huntress was in every respect a less survivable ship than *Prodigal* —built smaller, cheaper and cruder by an inferior tech base—but without her, they had no way to move all of their fighters.

"Bomber range...now," Soler reported.

Five more bombers had died getting that close. An eighth fighter caught a burst from one of the Wolverines *as* she released her torpedoes, her own death throes taking her munitions with her.

The last two launched their torpedoes and fled into the violet flash of novas. They left twelve one-shot plasma cannon behind— running straight and true for Kira's flagship.

She felt her stomach lurch into her chest as McCaig pushed the limits of the compensators and Harrington coils to twist the cruiser out of the way of the torpedoes. Determined bomber pilots might have stuck it out in the battlespace for a few more seconds until the torpedoes converted, and the flight of the BKN crews gave them a tiny window in which to escape.

The lurch of Kira's stomach turned into a wave of electromagnetic energy that lifted her hair and sent tingles down her arms. She knew *that* feeling—from much closer exposure to much smaller weapons!

"Report!" she snapped.

"They lost their nerve and blinked," McCaig said calmly. "Without them guiding the birds, we evaded ten of them. Armor held. No casualties, but I could use a few hours with a handy asteroid."

Kira exhaled a sigh of relief and checked in on the rest of the battle. *Harbinger* was dancing with her own wing of bombers, but the extra few seconds the BKN had hoped would confuse the mercenary force turned in *Harbinger*'s favor.

None of those bombers launched, their nerve breaking and the last three fleeing back into nova before they fired.

"I think the BKN might have forgotten what it means to face a peer opponent," she murmured, running her attention across the reports. "Hold the jammers up and prep search-and-rescue teams.

"We've shattered their bomber force, but that doesn't mean this is over!"

17

THE INITIAL MELEE around the Recon Group had taken just under
ten minutes. Even without the jammers live, they wouldn't have seen
anything from the BKN carrier force in that window.

Five minutes after the bomber strike had disintegrated, a new
wave of nova emergences marked the return of their own long-range
strike.

Thirty-four starfighters and bombers had jumped away to attack
the enemy flotilla. Thirty-two returned, which was better than Kira
had dared to hope.

It was still two bombers missing and six of her people who were
going to be, at best, prisoners of war.

"Get an identity confirmation on those ships," Kira ordered. The
numbers and formation were right, as was the timing, but multiphasic
jamming made even standard identity beacons useless.

"Nova fighters are pinging *Huntress* with tightbeams," Ronaldo
told her. "We're getting confirmations relayed." He paused. "We lost
two bombers from *Huntress*'s Avalanche flight group. Swordheart
reports that at least one of the crew pods managed to eject."

Shun "Swordheart" Asjes commanded *Huntress*'s Avalanche

flight group, consisting of her two six-ship squadrons of Wildcat-Four bombers. He'd been one of the pilots Kira had borrowed in their earliest days to fly one of her fighters.

Like most of the survivors of those first wings, he'd risen swiftly as the organization had transformed and expanded.

"How's our S&R proceeding?" Kira asked. It was a careful balancing act to walk. The search-and-rescue shuttles were vulnerable to enemy fire—though everyone would *try* not to shoot at them, identifying them in the mess of jamming would be difficult.

More dangerous overall, though, was the need for windows with deactivated jamming for the shuttles to locate their objectives. The windows only lasted fifteen seconds, but the Recon Group was at its most vulnerable in those moments.

Modern targeting systems were designed to hit enemies through the chaos of multiphasic jamming. *Without* said jamming, the effective range of plasma cannon dramatically expanded.

"We've picked up all of our people we can find," Soler reported. "And about thirty pods from the BKN planes. Using the pods themselves as cells for the moment, but they're linked in to our air and power."

Kira nodded her understanding. The escape pods from starfighters were designed to keep the crews alive for up to a week, but hooking them up to a capital ship's systems extended that indefinitely.

They made for uncomfortable but safe prisoner-containment facilities and, if necessary, could be ejected *back* into space to be retrieved by their own people.

"And drive pods?" she asked. The class two drives were difficult enough to manufacture, even for the most advanced economies in the Rim, that the drive cores were usually also rigged to eject under the same parameters as the crew pods.

Neither were perfect. Memorial Force had taken out somewhere around fifty or sixty Brisingr nova fighters and bombers and only retrieved thirty escape pods, after all.

"Including ours and theirs, forty-three," Soler told her. "S&R thinks there may still be some escape pods. They're coordinating and narrowing down their search patterns with each clear window."

"Understood. Do we have a report from Asjes?"

Swordheart would have taken control of the bomber strike, since the purpose of the three squadrons of interceptors was to get his people close enough to fire their torps.

"Burst transmission coming in from *Huntress*," Ronaldo told her a few seconds later. "Bombers are coming in to land and rearm. I'm relaying Swordheart's update to you."

Kira nodded, accepting the file transfer and activating the video. The soft-cheeked image of the bomber commander appeared in front of her, blue eyes grim despite the usual cheerful cast of his face.

There wasn't much *other* than Asjes' face visible in the video. He was wearing his flight suit and had popped open his faceplate to make the video clearer.

"Admiral, bomber strike reporting in. Enemy had held back a single ten-ship squadron of interceptors to protect their capital ships. Destroyers were clearly expected to do the bulk of the work, as they had jammers up and maneuvered to intercept us.

"Took out all ten fighters and two destroyers, then tagged the carrier and one of the cruisers." Swordheart shrugged. "Carrier and cruiser were intact when we novaed out, but each took at least two hits.

"I lost two bombers," he concluded grimly. "One definitely ejected the crew pod. The other...I am not certain, but I don't believe so.

"Proceeding aboard *Huntress* to rearm and prepare for another strike. On your order, Admiral."

Kira exhaled a sigh as she considered the situation. She was down a dozen fighters including those bombers, with three flight crew likely in enemy hands. Most of her losses around the Recon Group were interceptors, which meant she had less than ten casualties so far.

Versus the BKN group which had lost over fifty fighters and

bombers, with at least forty dead even with the pods her people had pulled aboard, *plus* two destroyers with a likely crew of around a hundred and fifty each.

The Kaiserreich force had lost a lot more people and firepower than she had—and the firepower balance had already been in her favor.

And the strategic imperative that said she had to let them take the first swing did *not* mean she had to let them go.

"Get me a link to Scimitar," she ordered. "Live. Even if he has to hide under *Prodigal*'s skirts to manage it."

"Yes, ser."

THE PROBLEM WASN'T ESTABLISHING a tightbeam link with Colombera's Wolverine. The *risk* was that Colombera had to remain nearly still relative to the cruiser while they were having the conversation, and that put the Recon Group's Commander, Nova Group, at risk if the enemy returned.

Which meant that Scimitar did one better than what Kira had suggested. His fighter was actually *landed* aboard *Prodigal* as he established a direct link with her, taking advantage of the momentary pause to refuel his interceptor.

"We're down two Wildcats, six Hussars and four Wolverines," he told her as soon as the channel opened. "I know we're flying Crest's best, which puts our birds ahead of the BKN's but...this is *not* Brisingr's A-team."

"I didn't expect it to be," Kira replied. "Their A-team is on the fleet carriers—and the fleet carriers are at Apollo. Most likely the squadron leaders are veterans of the war, but the rank-and-file pilots have probably only flown against pirates.

"They're well trained, but they hadn't seen the elephant before today."

"And they paid for it. The flip side of that, ser, is that the ones they have left are the better ones," Scimitar warned. "They might try something clever—but we've gone from having a dozen fighters more than them to having *twice* as many fighters as them.

"Asjes's report says their destroyer skippers *do* know what they're doing. We can take the carrier, Admiral, but it'll either take time while we peel off their destroyers—or we'll lose more people than we can spare."

"We might have lost less than the BKN so far today, but they have reinforcements to hand," Kira noted. "We don't. I don't want to risk further losses—but I also don't want them to think we'll just let them waltz away, either!"

There was a long pause—only a few seconds, really, but with both of them fully sunk into their headware, it felt longer.

"Recommendations, CNG?" she finally asked. "I don't want to take more losses than we have to, but outside of that, I *do* want to crush these idiots."

"We're here for another eighteen hours, ser," Colombera pointed out. "They might be able to run, but we can't. It sounds like we're not going to lock down and porcupine so long as they leave us alone, and if we want to take them slow and careful, we start by hitting their destroyers."

"And if they stick out the fight—or have too much cooldown left on their drives to run—we finish it," Kira concluded. "I like it, CNG. Prep a plan; distribute to the pilots.

"Diplomacy and politics meant we couldn't start this—but they *did*, so let's damn well finish it!"

REARMING THE BOMBERS TOOK TIME, time in which Memorial Force had to keep the multiphasic jammers up and scan the system during carefully scheduled windows.

A handful of the interceptors were cycling across the system to provide the Recon Group with more up-to-date information on the state of the BKN battle group, which meant Kira knew that they were doing basically the same thing her people were.

The carrier might have been damaged, but her engines seemed to be fully online. The BKN ships were concealed in a bubble of jamming, but that only meant that the nova fighters couldn't locate individual ships.

The jamming bubble itself made it easy to know roughly where the Brisingr *fleet* was. And to tell that they were now heading toward the Recon Group at full power.

"They'll get to us before we can nova," Soler warned. "They're about sixteen hours away. They bring that many destroyers to the party, and the cruisers might be challenged."

The ops officer paused.

"We can open the distance ourselves," she observed. "They have a speed edge over *Huntress*, but we might buy enough time to nova."

"No, Commander Soler, we're not running," Kira replied softly. "Time to rearm the bombers?"

"Five more minutes."

Kira nodded. They'd been able to see their attack on the Brisingr task group in direct light a few minutes earlier—though even that had been relayed to the capital ships in the open windows from drones outside the jamming bubble.

This was the most awkward part of a space battle. Neither side could afford to lower their jammers—accurate sensor data could allow the bombers to emerge practically on top of a starship and fire immediately. With the jammers live, the nova fighters needed to come in from a distance, giving more time for the defenders to intercept.

But jammers screwed up long-range sensors just as thoroughly as short-range sensors. Being in the bubble left *Prodigal* half-blind.

"CAP is up," Kira stated, hoping that no one would contradict her. Even her own fighters were in intermittent contact, but she could see the cycling wheel of Scimitar's interceptors and heavy fighters as they guarded the capital ships.

"They don't have enough bombers left for a real strike," Soler pointed out.

"They don't have enough bombers left for a *concentrated frontal strike*," Kira corrected. "Five is enough to give us a hell of a headache if they pull off the right tricks—and while their pilots might be green, the BKN is most definitely not.

"Someone over there knows the drill, and they will do their damnedest to make it work."

She and Colombera also knew the drill, though, which meant she had faith in her CNG to make sure the CAP was ready—and to press home their own attack.

"Emergence!"

Multiple emergences, Kira noted. Eight different collections of signatures appeared across her screens, forming a near-perfect sphere a hundred thousand kilometers across. The englobing attack was centered, roughly, on the same point as the jamming bubble.

With just *one* attack vector, the odds were that you'd be off by dozens of thousands of kilometers. With eight different attack wings, however, the trick meant that at least a third of them would be *closer* to their targets by that same error margin.

The risk, of course, was that they were throwing wings of less than half a dozen fighters in on their own. Eight attack wings had thirty-five fighters between them—most of the remaining Brisingr planes and almost certainly *all* of their bombers.

"Contacts close," Soler warned. "Two wings within fifty thousand klicks of *Prodigal*, one within fifty thousand of *Huntress*, one within fifty thousand of *Harbinger*."

The cruiser shivered gently around Kira as McCaig's people once again opened up with the main guns. Slow to aim and inarguably overkill when they hit, they were the only things aboard the cruiser with a real chance of hitting at maximum range.

The secondary guns opened up as well, but they lacked the power to do real damage, even against fighters, at torpedo range.

But the CAP was already there, entire squadrons of Wolverines diving in on the closer enemy forces. Kira watched, silently, as her people set to work—and her life depended on other people again.

"We can't identify the bombers," Soler warned. "Not sure how they're managing it, but we do not have optical identifiers. Only five of those groups should have a bomber, but I can't tell you which ones."

"So, we assume they all have one and shoot them down."

The closest wing to *Prodigal*, four fighters strong, found itself tangling with a squadron of Wolverines. The way they immediately broke apart to dogfight told Kira there were no bombers there.

But they were tying up a defensive squadron as more fighters dove toward Kira's flagship. One attack force vanished from the screen. Another. A third. Kira's trained eye told her that two of the Brisingr wings were too far away; they were almost guaranteed to nova out before firing.

A fourth wing died. All of the initial danger-close wings were gone, though the wing of interceptors was doing a surprisingly good job of tangling up the defenders on their vector.

Too good. A three-ship wing of fighters dove through the chaos that first wing had engendered, pushing *Prodigal* at maximum thrust.

Kira opened her mouth to bark an order—but McCaig had already seen the threat. The cruiser heeled over ninety degrees in space, opening the distance from the oncoming presumed bomber and opening fire, focusing all of her guns.

"Torps on the screen!" Soler snapped. They hadn't been fast enough. "They're sticking with them. *Brace!*"

The heavy cruiser lurched underneath Kira as four of the six torpedoes converted to plasma that hammered into *Prodigal*.

Then silence.

"Report, Captain," Kira told McCaig.

"We are still here, ser," the big man replied. "We have hull breaches on multiple decks, but all combat systems remain online." He paused. "It...will be a few minutes before we can retrieve our own fighters. The flight-deck doors appear to have been badly damaged.

"Understood. Keep me informed," Kira ordered.

She glanced over at Bueller.

"Brisingr builds solid ships," she conceded. "We're still here."

"I'm linking into shipboard damage control," he told her. "I'll support as I can."

She nodded her thanks and turned her focus back to the fighter reports. The last of the bombers was finally plunging back into space. It took a few more seconds for the formation to shake out, with the fourteen surviving bombers picking up four squadrons of escorts this time, and then they vanished into the flash of novas.

"Let's see how you like it," she said softly.

THE TWO CARRIER groups were still far enough apart that the nova fighters couldn't jump straight from one to the other—not without needing to spend more than a minute in drive cooldown, and no experienced nova-fighter pilot wanted to enter combat with more cooldown on their drive than they absolutely needed.

Thanks to her cycle of interceptors jumping back and forth to keep Kira updated on the approach of the Brisingr battle group, she was able to watch the attack go in with only about a quarter of the delay that lightspeed sensors would have given her.

As much as anything, Kira was watching for signs of problems, shortcomings they'd have to make up in training. Her pilots were veterans, most of them having flown in at least one Outer Rim brush war with Memorial Force.

But outside of the Syntactic Cluster and a few other bootstrapping sectors, the Outer Rim still didn't have a lot of places manufacturing class two nova drives. Which meant that fighters were scarce on the ground, and a lot of Memorial Force's operations had been against people *without* nova fighters to counter them—and, more importantly in some ways, people without experience in countering nova fighters.

This task group was clearly green, probably freshly assembled out of new ships with new crews, but they had the doctrine and the tech to go toe-to-toe with Kira's pilots in a way they'd rarely faced before.

Whoever was commanding the destroyer screen had clearly guessed what the strike's intent was—but there was only so much the escort ships could *do* to protect themselves without exposing the very ships they were escorting.

Scimitar and his fighters cut through the handful of remaining enemy fighters, closing to the edge of torpedo range and then unleashing a devastating barrage. Between the escorts and the bombers themselves, each of the destroyers found themselves on the receiving end of over fifty torpedoes.

At maximum range, with the bombers and their fighters vanishing before the Brisingr ships could inflict a single loss on the strike, accuracy sucked. But twelve torpedoes on *Prodigal* at only slightly shorter range had scored two hits.

Fifty torpedoes at full range scored half a dozen—and it was a tough and lucky destroyer that could survive *two* torpedo hits.

"Clean sweep on the destroyers," Soler reported aloud. "Wait...I have nova flares! They're running!"

Kira nodded, swallowing a sigh of mixed relief and disappointment as the remaining BKN ships vanished from her displays.

"Let's make sure we relocate them if they're still in the trade-route stop," she ordered. "But they novaed, what, five minutes ago? We'd have seen them by now if they were coming for us."

And she doubted that the Flottillenadmiral wanted to match two sixty-kilocubic cruisers against two *ninety-five*-kilocubic cruisers. *Prodigal* might be battered, but her people had hit one of the 160s, too.

"I think we're clear," she said aloud. "Drop the jammers and let's get a sweep going to make sure of that.

"If nothing else, I don't want the BKN watching us jump to Faaselesitila!"

18

"WELL, this definitely looks like it's going to have some nice rocks for us to get cozy with."

Kira chuckled at Bueller's observation as the Recon Group settled back into formation after their nova. Faaselesitila V was a massive blot on their scanners, almost a full light-second across and larger, if neither heavier nor hotter, than the star Faaselesitila itself.

Over two dozen moons, rings, and captured asteroids spilled out from the super-Jovian gas giant, marking a planetary system over a hundred million kilometers across. The mass of a couple of Earthlike worlds was broken up into pieces and circling the huge planet.

As her boyfriend observed, they'd have no problem finding the raw materials needed to fix up *Prodigal*'s armor and replace their lost fighters. They had the parts they couldn't manufacture in storage, which meant even starfighters could be fabricated by the ships' onboard systems.

"The problem, Konrad, is that our information suggests that those rocks are hiding a lot of things that go *boom*," Kira pointed out. "We are on a very specific vector. Once we're *talking* to people, I'm sure we'll be able to borrow a few hundred tons of nickel-iron, but right now..."

"Leaving the path will probably hurt," he agreed.

Harbinger, the more intact of the two cruisers, led the way along the course they'd been given. *Huntress* followed the first cruiser, with *Prodigal* bringing up the rear. Damaged or not, the heavy cruiser was still fully combat-capable.

Kira's flagship was more vulnerable than she'd like, with large swathes of reactive armor expended and chunks of the underlying energy-dispersal webs burnt out, but her guns, sensors and jammers were operational.

"No response to our transmissions," Ronaldo reported.

"Soler, any sign of our soon-to-be friends?" Kira asked.

"I can see why they picked Faaselesitila V for a hiding place, but we haven't found them yet," Soler replied. "I'm...not entirely sure, but I think there's a series of natural fission chain reactions going on in one of the middle rings. None of the individual sites are huge, but overall, we've got a couple of gigawatts of waste radiation getting spread through the entire planetary system.

"It makes picking out *anything* hard—and from the radiation signatures on the other bodies, it's been going for a few thousand years."

"At least," Bueller said. "I'm familiar with the theory and some of the sites we've seen during the diaspora, but the vast majority of them have been *former* natural reactors. Takes pretty unusual geologic formations to get one running at all, and they usually run out of fuel after a hundred thousand years or so."

"Well, right now, I don't overly care how long it's been running," Kira admitted. "I care that it's fussing our sensors right now. It's no multiphasic jammer, but it's still a pain."

"We're entering the outer limits of the planetary system now," Soler warned. "Watching for any contacts."

"We don't have a lot of information on when we'll be contacted," Kira said, making sure the ship COs were on the channel. "We proceed along the course we were given until we're contacted or we look like we're going to hit something."

"If it looked like that course was going to hit something, I'd have mentioned it by now," McCaig rumbled. "But it is going to be an unusually crowded bit of space."

"All things are relative. I'm sure we can manage not to hit anything."

"Crowded" in space, after all, still left hundred-kilometer gaps between chunks of rock and ice large enough to be any kind of threat to the starships.

MINUTES TURNED to hours as they crept their way through the debris field above Faaselesitila V. There were clearer sections around the poles, as usual, but their course wasn't taking them into those areas.

"The course we're following is clearer than I'd expect," McCaig warned around the end of the second hour. "It wouldn't be obvious from outside, but I think someone is actively keeping a corridor clear."

"Would make sense," Soler said. "And while I haven't seen any actual ships out here, I've got partial locks on at least a few hundred mines along the way. Which means I've missed, well, a few thousand."

If the mines were even half as stealthy as Kira expected, there were at least a dozen they'd missed for every one her people had picked up. She wouldn't have wanted to fight her way into this mess, though she could think of a few ways to render the defenses less dangerous.

"The course we've got appears to be bringing us into the orbital path of V-Four," McCaig said. "Four-thousand-kilometer radius. Toxic atmosphere, surface temperatures around a hundred Kelvin.

It's a good-sized planetoid, well inside our radioactive ring and close enough to allow easy skimming of the gas giant.

"We're going to come in about thirty degrees behind the moon on her current orbit, but..."

"The course terminates in her orbital path," Kira finished. "Barring any new instructions, we'll turn to catch up to V-Four at that point."

They were getting close to the end of their course, and other than the mines, they hadn't seen a single sign that they weren't alone in the orbitals of Faaselesitila V.

The hair on the back of Kira's neck strongly suggested they were being watched. She scanned the nearest moon—V-Six, a decently sized rock, if far smaller than Four. If she was going to ambush anyone...

"McCaig, do me a favor," she said softly. "Pulse V-Six please, maximum scanner strength. Everything we've got."

Prodigal adjusted slightly in space, keeping to her course as she aligned the transmitters for her sensor array on the five-thousand-kilometer-wide moon. Energy signatures flickered across Kira's datafeeds as the heavy cruiser's scanners went fully active on a targeted cone.

"Contact!" Soler snapped. "Large contact, coming around Six's horizon! Estimate one hundred–plus kilocubics."

"Clever," Kira murmured. "But not clever enough. All ships to battle stations; stand by jammers. Get me an ID on that ship, people."

The unknown capital ship wasn't alone, she saw. The strangers had taken their time assembling their welcoming committee and had cut their acceleration before they passed out of V-Six's shadow.

One hundred-plus-kilocubic signature that Kira was still waiting for a closer analysis of. Six smaller signatures, somewhere between fifty and eighty kilocubics.

"We've got a tentative on the battlecruiser," Soler said after a few moments. "One hundred twenty-five kilocubics, *Sun Arrow*–class. Escorts appear to be a mix of lighter cruisers—four of the six are almost certainly Apollon designs."

"*Sun Arrow?*" Kira asked. "That was Apollo's last wartime production battlecruiser." She'd watched *Sun Arrow* herself, the nameship of the class, be battered into uselessness in one of the last battles of the war.

But there had been two other *Sun Arrow*–class ships in commission when she'd left Apollo. *Lightning Spear* and *Oceanic Trident* might not have been the last of their class built, but they were the two she knew of.

"Is she flying any kind of beacon?" Kira continued.

"Negative; none of them are transmitting beacons," Soler replied. "They know we've spotted them, ser. I'm detecting nova-fighter launches. Hoplites and Phalanxes, ser."

Interceptors and fighter-bombers, all Apollon types.

"Ronaldo, pulse the signal we were given," Kira ordered. "Scimitar, get a defensive perimeter up."

She had barely given the order before the first squadron of Wolverine interceptors blazed off *Huntress*'s flight deck.

"Defensive formations," she reiterated. "No jammers, no aggressive maneuvers. We can take these guys, but let's not start a fight we don't need."

It spoke to the sheer size of Faaselesitila V's planetary system that the strangers were outside weapons range as they emerged from an orbiting moon. They'd likely hoped for their emission control to get them across the twenty thousand kilometers or so to be in heavy-gun range.

"Signal pulse," Ronaldo said. "Holding for... We have a response, ser!"

"Unknown vessel beacons coming online," Soler added. "Lead ship is *Oceanic Trident*, ser!"

"Understood. Give me a link, Ronaldo," Kira ordered. "Time is a quarter-second?"

"About that."

"Thanks. Let's see what our new acquaintances have to say about being friends."

THE SIX YEARS since Kira had last seen him had not been kind to Henry Killinger, but she still recognized the man who appeared in her headware visual feed. He had the type of broad-shouldered build that carried excess bulk well, and he'd covered a barrel of muscle with a layer of fat as a starfighter pilot.

He'd lost most of both since, leaving him looking gaunt and almost sick. Somewhere along the way, he'd lost an eye and a good chunk of his face. The surgeon who'd fixed him up had been...*competent*, but the artificial eye wasn't properly matched to the replacement skin, and the synthetic tissue sagged noticeably inward compared to his natural flesh.

"Admiral Henry Killinger," Kira greeted him. Battered and bruised or not, this was definitely the man she'd come to see.

"I am Admiral Kira Demirci, commanding officer and primary shareholder of the Memorial Force mercenary fleet. Mutual friends and contacts have put quite a bit of effort—and *risk*—into putting us in touch."

She waited through the notable pause as their messages flitted around at the speed of light, watching Killinger's face for some sign of his reaction.

Whatever else his surgeon had saved, he'd still lost the eye, and it looked like the new artificial nerves on the right side of his face weren't quite calibrated correctly. The delay was as noticeable as the lightspeed lag on their radio link.

"They have indeed," he told her, his voice both more gravelly and less deep than she remembered. "It has been a time for such risks, since you left. Brisingr's tendrils have spread far and deep in this sector, Admiral Demirci, and your flight was wiser than I would have guessed at the time."

"We lost a lot of good people who didn't run, Admiral," Kira observed.

"And many who did, as well," he noted. "I knew then that the

Council of Principals had betrayed us and we were doomed. I did not realize how far our supposed leaders would fall. I did not anticipate where we stand today."

"Apollo's fate could not, I don't think, have been predicted. But it can, I hope, be undone."

Killinger chuckled at her words and inclined his head.

"I hope the same," he agreed. "Our system may have fallen on dark times, but I believe that Brisingr has overreached themselves. They are unstable and we can take advantage of their overextension."

"That is my own reading. I hope, then, Admiral Killinger, that we are unlikely to need our fighters and jammers today?"

"Forgive my paranoia, Admiral Demirci, but under these mines and asteroids seems the only place in the galaxy my little band of rebels are safe," he told her. "Let us meet in person, I think, but we will need to be very careful.

"Do not take this wrong way, Admiral—Jay Moranis would be proud of all you have done!—but you left. And now you have returned, and while that brings hope...it is also not without question.

"I hope we can stand together against what Brisingr has created, but I cannot know for certain that you are not Reinhardt's tools." He spread his hands. "You do, after all, appear aboard ships of his Navy, whatever beacons you fly today."

"Spoils of war, Admiral. These seemed more likely to pass unnoticed in the Security Zone—and, with everyone *except* the BKN, it seems to have worked as we hoped."

Killinger chuckled.

"I am sending you coordinates for a dome on the surface of V-Six," he told her. "Bring your ships into orbit of the moon and come down by shuttle. We will speak in person and see what lies before us."

19

Kira recognized the style of dome from above as the shuttle stooped in. It was a standard ASDF prefabricated design, intended to provide medium-term residence and protection from the elements for ground forces.

Given that V-Six had no atmosphere whatsoever, it would be an absolute requirement for any survival on the moon's surface at all. The rock had enough gravity—about thirty percent of a standard gee —to not require additional gravity systems, but the only air on V-Six had been brought with the humans.

"I see lasers and hyper-velocity missile positions," Milani told her as they entered final approach. "What did you call the thing we found on Bennet? A 'Hall Pass'?"

"Hall Pass is human-portable," Kira replied. H-PAAS stood for Human-Portable Anti-Aircraft System, before soldiers had taken their usual cutting knife to it. "Those are Nemean-Fives, capable of putting beams into the thermosphere of an inhabitable planet."

There, they'd be able to reach into orbit, where her capital ships waited. The Nemean-Five Self-Mobile Antiaircraft System didn't have the power density to actually *threaten* anything bigger than a fighter or pinnace, but it could *reach* her ships. The HVM batteries could, in theory, hurt the capital ships, but their range was inherently limited to a dozen kilometers or so.

Deadly against inbound aircraft and shuttles but useless against starships in orbit.

Still, the dome had an impressive array of defenses around it. Like the dome itself, they were deployable prefabricated assets intended for use by the Hoplite space-to-ground deployments.

"None of the defenses are targeting us," the pilot reported. "They're *online*, but they're very carefully *not* pointed at us."

"Best we can hope for," Milani muttered. "You realize this could be a trap, right?"

"*Everything* can be a trap," Kira told them. "And I've been led to understand that Killinger has a fleet carrier, which means he's hiding at least one ship from us. But we have to meet with him if we're going to get anywhere."

"Pirates who claim patriotism are dangerous, ser," the mercenary commando warned. "Whatever they started as, Killinger and his people have been pirates for a while now. With that type, you never know which side is going to win out on a given day."

"I know Killinger," she said. "I think, if nothing else, we'll be able to get out of here alive."

"You *knew* Killinger," Milani replied. "But that was a long time ago, I'm guessing when he still had both eyes."

Kira was silent. There wasn't really an answer to that.

MILANI DIDN'T LET Kira lead the way into the dome. She wouldn't have come unaccompanied even without their insistence, though she probably wouldn't have brought *quite* so many guards as her dragon-armored commander had insisted.

The tunnel into the main dome was swept by half a dozen fully armored mercenaries before Kira set foot in it—and another half dozen mercenaries accompanied her down it, including Milani themselves.

Killinger was no less paranoid, Kira swiftly realized. Her mercenaries, their armor currently set to the same dark teal as her dress uniform, were matched by an even larger number of rebel Hoplites as she entered the main courtyard of the dome.

Three-quarters of the dome was taken up by barracks, armories and administration buildings. But since it was supposed to be a prefabricated military base, it also had a drill field. Between Kira's mercenaries and Killinger's Hoplites, that drill field was practically lined with armored soldiers doing their best to out-loom each other.

A folding table had been set up in the middle of the courtyard, with a chair on either side of it. Killinger stood behind the table, his hands laced behind his back as he watched Kira approach.

The two Admirals were the only bareheaded people visible. Their escorts were wrapped in power armor from head to toe, but Kira wore her Memorial Force dress uniform—over a shipsuit that contained an extending helmet bubble if necessary—and Killinger wore the familiar stark white uniform of an Apollo System Defense Force Officer.

Except that instead of the four stripes and star of a Colonel, as she'd last seen him, he now wore the star, crossed sabers and four multi-petaled flowers of an ASDF Fleet Admiral.

"Welcome to the end of nowhere and the last bastion of hope, Admiral Demirci," Killinger greeted her, offering his hand.

She took it and shook firmly.

"I don't know about the 'last bastion,' but that's why we're here," she told him. And even regarding Faaselesitila as the "end of nowhere" was a rather...self-centered point of view. There was a lot of Rim out past there—and, from what she understood, a material number of star systems out Beyond the Rim.

The Beyond was marked by where the generally available trade-route maps and the Encyclopedia Galactica stopped updating, after all, not by any actual lack of *humans*. Just enough cooperative inter-system traffic to maintain the mapping centers.

"Forgive me, Demirci; it's been a while since I thought anyone else was on our side," Killinger admitted. He gestured her to a seat at the table.

There were no drinks or food present. Just uniforms, armor and guns.

"You came to us," he continued as he sat across from her. "I assume you have heard of the fate of our homeworld, but beyond that... Well. Tell me what you seek, Demirci, and we shall see if there can be a meeting of minds."

Kira smiled thinly. Milani was right to say she had *known* Killinger—but she still knew the other officer well enough to know that he was considering whether he was going to let Kira and the Recon Group leave at all.

She knew a lot more about his base than he likely wanted, after all.

"I have assembled a significant fleet since leaving Apollo," she told him. "Five capital ships and a dozen escorts. Some Brisingr captures, some Outer Rim-built, one carrier from the Navy of the Royal Crest.

"I have made contact with our diplomatic offices outside Apollo, and they have agreed to fund operations on the part of Memorial Force against Brisingr in the attempt to liberate Apollo. At a significant discount, of course."

Kira had left the exact details of the cost arrangement to her purser, Yanis Vaduva, who remained aboard *Fortitude* in the Samuels System. She had the funds to pay her people and buy whatever she needed from the systems they passed through.

Vaduva would let her know if there was going to be a problem well before there was. He was *very* good at his job.

"Patriotism and money combine to make a powerful motivator, I suppose," Killinger murmured.

"I am no patriot, Killinger," Kira warned carefully. "But I love my homeworld and I will free her. I am no patriot of our government. It betrayed a lot of us."

"It did. Some of us stayed and fought, though," he pointed out. "You ran."

"I retired and went into exile," she corrected. "I did not desert the ASDF, and I did not expect that one retired pilot was going to be able to fight off assassins operating with the clear authorization of our government."

She shrugged.

"You may call that running. I call it surviving."

It was a point she'd expected to cause friction between them. She didn't like that Killinger had turned to piracy, and *he* didn't like that she'd left Apollo behind.

"And now, rich and powerful, you come back to save us all?" he asked. He shook his head and sighed. "I knew Major Kira Demirci. She was a brave pilot and a loyal soldier. *Admiral* Kira Demirci, Outer Rim mercenary...you, I am not so sure of."

"I can say the same for Admiral Henry Killinger, wanted pirate," Kira murmured.

He made a vague *touché* gesture.

"I suppose I come back to my first point, Demirci," he said. "Why are you here and what do you want?"

"I am back in the Apollo-Brisingr Sector to fight Brisingr and free Apollo," Kira reiterated. "But I can't take a star system with less than twenty ships. I need allies. I need to bring together everyone who has a stake in this fight—which is *everyone*.

"But I'm starting with you."

Killinger nodded and sighed.

"You will find many bitter disappointments down this route, Demirci," he warned. "I have spent the years since the war trying to build a coalition of the willing to oppose Brisingr, but all I have ever been offered is help under the table, obsolete ships, and the occasional 'misdirected' wire transfer."

"The situation changed when Apollo was invaded," she told him.

"For the first time, we face a universe in which not only the diplo-macy and trade of star systems but their very sovereign independence is now in danger."

"I have heard little more willingness to act in the last few months than I did in the previous years," Killinger said. "Our former allies have abandoned us, in the main, and now kneel to Kaiser Reinhardt.

"If you think you will find friends to stand against the Kaiser in the Apollo-Brisingr Sector, I fear you will find the cupboard rather bare."

"Perhaps," Kira conceded. "But you, Admiral Killinger, are the boy who cried wolf." And a pirate, as Milani had pointed out, but she wouldn't throw that in his face.

"They have heard these warnings and calls to action from you for over half a decade. Back channels and shadows and fear. I will use none of these things," she told him. "I have returned from the Outer Rim, the prodigal daughter with a war fleet to stand for the freedom of my home.

"They will hear me for the first time, where they have dismissed you for years. The labels they hang on you to dismiss you cannot be hung on me. They *will* listen."

Kira held out her hand palm up.

"And I am making contact with Admiral Michelakis," she noted. "Even if the Friends remain cowed, Apollo's scattered fleets can be gathered once more. We were betrayed and taken by surprise, but they cannot rebuild what they destroyed.

"Apollo's fleets will retake our world, alone or with allies by our side, whatever it takes."

Killinger nodded and leaned back, interlacing his fingers as he studied her.

"You have passion, I see that," he told her. "I don't know if it will convince our former friends, but it might. If you are prepared to place your ships under my command, we can begin to change the course of fate."

And there was the catch, the one thing Kira could *not* give up.

There were no circumstances in which she'd place her fleet under the command of a pirate.

"I do not think that is the right answer," she said, choosing her words carefully. "We share a common cause, Admiral, but my fleet remains a private mercenary company. We are under contract already to the exiled bureaucracy of Apollo's diplomatic corps.

"Part of my contract is to seek allies, and I would be delighted to count you among those allies. But I cannot place my fleet under your command."

She also suspected that being visibly subordinate to Killinger would destroy any chance she had of bringing the systems of the Security Zone into the fight. The former Friends of Apollo had been betrayed by Apollo before, which would make them hard to convince in the first place—and she doubted his preying on merchant shipping had made him fans.

The ships in question might have belonged to Brisingr, after all, but they'd been carrying cargos to the other systems of the Sector.

"You are not choosing courses that make you easy to trust, Admiral Demirci," Killinger told her mildly. "I have walked this path for six years now. I have sacrificed and fought and *bled*. You left. You have wandered far from our home, and now you come back and claim to know the needs of our people as well as I do.

"I am not convinced." He fell silent for a moment, but Kira simply waited. He clearly wasn't done.

"I *know* what principles, values and cause I fight for, Admiral," he finally said. "I knew, once, what Kira Demirci fought for. Today, though... so far as I see, you fight for money and to preserve your own power.

"I am not convinced that you fight for our cause."

She nodded, waiting for another few moments to see what else he had to say.

"You can trust me or not as you wish," she told him. "I know what I fight for. I did not need to come home, Killinger. I did not think I ever would, in fact, and I had made myself wealthy and powerful in the Outer Rim.

"I will ally with you against our mutual enemy. But I will not surrender command to *anyone*. I owe it to my people to retain full control of our actions and preserve their lives."

One of the biggest adjustments Kira had faced was the *very* different risk-assessment criteria mercenaries operated with. Mercenaries were prepared to die to complete their missions, but it was the last resort.

And no mercenary would—or *should*, in her opinion—die for the honor of any flag. She didn't trust Killinger not to expend her people. She wouldn't, in truth, trust *anyone* that much.

"So, your first loyalty is to your people, then?" he demanded.

"Yes," she said frankly. "Whatever else I may be, whatever cause I have taken up, I remain the commander of a private military corporation. That comes with responsibilities to my employees and my shareholders, of a type a regular military officer does not share."

"I doubt you have found leading a...*rebel* fleet to follow the same lines as regular service, either."

She'd almost called Killinger's fleet pirates to his face, and she *knew* he'd caught her momentary hesitation.

"Nothing is as it was," he slowly conceded, reaching up to run fingers along the sunken edge of his facial reconstruction. "The universe is, perhaps, not as we would wish it.

"I will not turn aside a willing friend, Admiral Demirci, but I feel that we must find a way for you to prove your trustworthiness as an *ally*."

Kira had expected that. No matter what the form of their alliance, she hadn't expected Killinger to trust her without finding some hoop for her to jump through.

She smiled and leaned back in her own chair, returning Killinger's assessing gaze.

"Name your terms, then, Admiral Killinger," she told him.

"Let us not be *quite* so crass, shall we?" he asked with a chuckle, but he nodded his understanding as he spoke. "There is a mission we can use additional support on. Your ships would be a welcome augment to our forces."

"If we are allies, then we fight by each other's sides," Kira conceded. "I will need more information, of course. I will not enter any fight blindly."

"The Shenandoah System," Killinger told her. "You can look it up in the EG later, but for now, the *politics* are more important than the astrography."

The astrography wasn't irrelevant, she knew. Roughly aligned with Corosec and Apollo, Shenandoah was central to the Sector and could easily serve as a central logistics base for Brisingr forces across the region.

It had two gas giants and three asteroid belts to fuel industry, but while Shenandoah also had two habitable planets, Potomac and Meadows, they were tiny low-gravity planets that were difficult for humans to live on. Despite the system's mineral wealth, less than a billion people lived in the system.

"And what are those politics?" she asked.

"Shenandoah's leaders have hitched their cart to Brisingr's," Killinger told her. "Like Syndulla and some others, they have made themselves lickspittles to the conqueror. They have been providing logistical support and a safe discharge harbor for the BKN since shortly after the war ended.

"Now, however, they are going a step further. The BKN is building a major fleet base around Dickey, the outer gas giant."

He flicked her a datafile, casually enough to make it clear that he'd had this plan in mind from the beginning of the meeting. Kira opened it, looking at the layout of the Shenandoah System and comparing it to both her memories and her headware's database.

"That puts them pretty far away from the locals," she observed. "There's a reason Shenandoah has never made much use of Dickey. With Skyline close to hand, they've never really needed it."

Skyline, the inner gas giant, was bigger and denser than Dickey.

It was more convenient to the two inhabited planets, and with two asteroid belts inside Skyline's orbit, Kira couldn't see any reason for *anybody* to wander out to the third asteroid belt, let alone Dickey.

"The purpose, from what I've been able to discover, was to keep the base secret," Killinger told her. "They've been using Dickey as a covert discharge point for a while, allowing them to keep more ships in motion through the Sector than anyone was seeing.

"Now they're installing logistics bases and fabrication infrastructure on the moons. I know they've installed planetary defense systems, but they *haven't* put in the usual in-system defenses.

"If they're resupplying at Skyline, Shenandoah Star Command has a defensive constellation in place that I don't want to tangle with. But, so far as I can tell, Dickey has a couple of prefab transportable forts and a few nova-fighter squadrons."

Kira zoomed in on the base information. He'd given her quite a bit, including the details the rebel fleet had on the forts in question.

"Those forts are nasty pieces of work," she noted. "Sixty thousand kilocubics, no nova drive, light Harrington coils. They're slow, but they've got a battlecruiser's turrets."

"And they've put five of them in the system, plus moon-based nova-fighter squadrons," he agreed. "I don't have a solid number on the nova fighters, but intel suggests either a single squadron of bombers or no bombers at all.

"The rest are interceptors and heavy fighters. At any given moment, there is at least a destroyer squadron present as well," Killinger warned. "Naval Base Gretchen might not be fully complete or as defended as I'd want it to be in their shoes, but it's still a nasty nut to crack.

"But if we take it down, we cripple their logistics through the Shenandoah System *and* make them look vulnerable."

Kira shook her head.

"We'll make them look vulnerable, yes," she conceded. "But you already said they were using Shenandoah as a stopover long before they started building Naval Base Gretchen. We'll slow their logistics pipeline, but they're probably already starting to ramp up facilities in Apollo.

"Why use a vassal system like Shenandoah as a base and fabrication center when you have *full* control of Apollo, which has thirty times the gross system product?"

"That's part of what's slowed the development of Gretchen, I'm sure," Killinger conceded. "But that has only made the base more vulnerable. We can use those supplies, and denying them to Brisingr forward units has value, Admiral Demirci."

"It does," she agreed. Hitting the base for supplies was legitimate, though she'd admit that it felt a bit too piratical for her liking. The BKN was far from dependent on Gretchen at this point—and the prefabricated forts were less of a strategic target than an equivalent cubage of cruisers.

But removing the logistics capacity and whatever ships they could drag in to defend it had a value all of its own. And given that her new allies hadn't had access to a planetary industrial base for five or six years, she suspected that Killinger was playing down how much he needed those supplies.

"The operation makes sense to me," she told him. "I just want to make sure we're not overestimating what the results are going to be. We'll give Brisingr a black eye, yes, but we're not cutting them off at the knees.

"Forward my people whatever communications protocols you're using and the details of your plan," Kira concluded. "Then we shall see what we allies can find to discomfort our enemies with."

"Believe me, Admiral Demirci, I suspect we *both* have surprises for Brisingr!"

20

THE FIRST SURPRISE Killinger had for them was clear as they reached Faaselesitila V-Four. The larger moon, as they expected, was anchoring the main rebel fleet. While most of the fleet was what Kira had expected, the big ship around which the small cruisers and destroyers orbited was very, *very* familiar to her.

"Identify beacon says that's the ASDF *Victorious*," Soler said.

"I didn't need the beacon," Kira told her ops officer. "I'd recognize that ship in my sleep."

"Ser?"

"*Benediction*-class fleet carrier. Class of six, commissioned from six months before to a year into the war with Brisingr," Kira reeled off. "One hundred twenty-two thousand cubic meters, twenty six-ship nova-fighter squadrons, ten heavy and twenty-five light plasma cannon."

She shook her head.

"Except she's *Victorious*, which means she's short three of the light plasma cannon because there were parts shortages when she was finishing up and it was more critical to get her into the fight," she continued. "That left a minor blind spot on one of her flanks. It gave most of us nightmares, but I don't think Brisingr ever realized it was there!"

Kira grinned at Soler's confusion.

"The Three-Oh-Three was based on *Victorious* for the last two years of the war," she told her junior. "I know that carrier from stem to stern."

She considered the ship.

"I don't know how Killinger got his hands on her," she admitted. "His nova combat group flew off an escort carrier that we worked with on and off. *Victorious* was never his base, never his ship."

"Not during the war," Soler noted. "That might have changed afterward?"

"It's possible." Kira took one last long look at her old ship. "He wouldn't have been the first ASDF Colonel to go from commanding a nova combat group to commanding a carrier."

It wasn't universal, but since carrier captains were either Colonels or Commodores, it happened often enough. There was a general sense that Apollo's high command preferred officers with both nova-fighter and starship-command experience for the highest ranks, too—which meant that most ambitious officers would *try* to make that transfer.

Which...also fit with her impression of Killinger.

"What about the rest of our new allies?" she asked Soler. "I'm only seeing two major capital ships, right?"

"*Oceanic Trident* and *Victorious* are the only hundred-kilocubic-plus ships," Soler agreed. "They've got fourteen cruisers of assorted weights, ranging from fifty kilocubics to ninety. Ten are ex-ASDF, four are other systems' design."

"And odds are half of the ASDF ships are from the Friends," Kira said. "We did a lot of selling our older ships to our allies. It made sure they were both not falling too far behind us and also not catching up too closely."

She shook her head.

"Politics." Soler sighed. "There's a reason I joined Memorial Force, ser. Taking money seemed easier without the politics."

Kira chuckled.

"So long as you're on a warship, Soler, politics will define your life and your work," she told the younger woman. "So, carrier, battle-cruiser, fourteen cruisers..."

"Twelve destroyers. Again, a mix of sizes, mix of ASDF and non-ASDF ships," the ops officer concluded. "Twenty-eight ships all told. More than we have, but..."

"We have the same number of destroyers, and all of ours are *Parakeets*," Kira noted. The Redward-built destroyers weren't up to full ASDF standards, but they were bigger than a lot of the ships Killinger had. "And our cruisers are up to weight with his heaviest ships except *Trident*...and *Fortitude* outclasses anything he has."

"Just the one carrier, too," Soler said.

"Oh, their problem is bigger than that," Kira murmured as the pieces fell into place. "Look at the number of nova fighters."

"There's too few of them," Bueller said, the engineer stepping up to stand by her shoulder. "We saw eighteen with *Oceanic Trident*—but we're now seeing their standard CAP, and they're down to six."

"A fleet carrier like *Victorious* should have multiple *squadrons* of six on CAP," Kira told Soler. "Generally, you can keep a quarter of your planes in space—and when they're covering this many ships, they probably *should*, just for safety and vision."

"So, if they only have six out..." Soler considered. "They might only have twenty-four nova fighters? *Total?*"

"Exactly," Kira murmured. "Konrad, you've looked at the intel on Naval Base Gretchen?"

"They're building class two drives," Bueller confirmed, clearly following her thoughts. "I suspect they might be all the way to building replacement fighters on site, potentially with a plan to recruit or conscript pilots from Shenandoah.

"Potomac's government has made dangerous sacrifices," he

concluded. "I don't think they—or Syndulla, for that matter—are that far from ending up as integrated territories."

Technically, Konrad Bueller had been hired by a Syndulla System-based exploration company. In reality, he'd been a knowing recruit to the Equilibrium Institute, which had a solid hold on the system.

But at least part of that hold had come through the Brisingr Kaiserreich's alliance with the system. If Reinhardt was leaning toward flexing his muscles to *annex* systems, something very few powers had ever successfully managed to do, close "allies" who were in reality cooperative vassals...

Well, they were going to be the low-hanging fruit. And the Kaiser had already snapped off the hardest-to-reach fruit by seizing Apollo. The fear that invasion had created would be a powerful weapon in his arsenal.

Until and unless Kira took her homeworld back. For which she needed Killinger...and if Killinger had as few fighters as she suspected, she needed more fighters for *Victorious*.

"So, Killinger needs planes," she said aloud. "*Victorious* can build them, but she'd have issues trying to assemble the necessary tools for building class two nova drives.

"But if we steal an intact and operating fabrication plant from Gretchen, he definitely has the flexibility here in Faaselesitila to set it up in the right gravity well. He can talk supplies and undermining Brisingr's logistics chain, but..."

"He's after nova fighters," Bueller agreed. "Because he's got the escorts of half a dozen carrier groups and only one, mostly *empty* carrier."

Kira chuckled. "I'm half-surprised he didn't try to make us give him fighters," she told her boyfriend.

"In what universe would you have agreed to that?" Bueller asked. "Killinger has his own goals, but he's not *stupid*."

"True." She sighed. "We'll go over his intelligence with a fine-toothed comb, and I want you to tell me if anything looks off to your finely tuned sense of Brisingr-isms.

"I don't know what his goals are. Right now, he's trying to conceal weaknesses because he doesn't trust us—and while that's expected and reasonable, it means I'm not comfortable guessing what *else* he is hiding from us."

"And from what Milani said about your meeting, he's definitely hiding something," Bueller said quietly. "Man's got a few spare hands of cards tucked up his sleeve."

"So long as they're played against *Brisingr*, that's fine."

But something in the conversation with Killinger left Kira wondering if the not-quite-pirate was so *selective* in his targets.

Or if, in Admiral Henry Killinger's mind, everyone who wasn't entirely with him was either an enemy or a competitor.

21

"I'VE BEEN TALKING to our prisoners."

Kira paused her review of the report she was reading—a more detailed analysis of the ships and capabilities of Killinger's fleet—and looked over at her boyfriend. Even though she was working, she'd retreated to the Admiral's suite on *Prodigal* to rest, at least physically.

Jess Koch had left them alone a few minutes earlier, after puttering through the room in a gentle whirlwind that had left the two officers comfortably ensconced with warm drinks and ready-to-hand snacks.

For all of the comfort of the small sitting area, Kira had a continuing feed in her headware of the status of the Recon Group and the space around them. She was comfortable that her ships were safe from anyone *except* Killinger's people deep inside Faaselesitila V's rings and moons—but there was a lot to be suspicious of with the other Apollon exile.

With her focus on Killinger, she hadn't quite *forgotten* that they'd taken prisoners from the BKN carrier's fighters, but it certainly hadn't been top of her mind.

Konrad Bueller, on the other hand, had been staying out of sight and out of mind while she dealt with the rebel leader—and the prisoners were his countryfolk, too.

"Learn anything interesting?" she asked, waving the report closed. There wasn't much in the deeper analysis she hadn't guessed —the rebel ships were decent across the board but had been short-changed on supplies and more-complex maintenance.

"I was really only hoping to get a feel for the mood back home," Bueller admitted. "But I did pick up one...interesting point."

"Oh?"

"They all knew who I was," he said softly.

That took Kira a second to think through. Her partner had left Brisingr as, basically, a nobody. A member of the Alteste Families, yes, there were almost two thousand eligible adults among those bloodlines.

He'd been a retired naval officer who'd only made Kapitänleutnant—equivalent to an ASDF Commander—as a bump on retirement. He'd never been famous and never been, well, important.

Not until he'd joined the Equilibrium Institute and then defected to Kira's mercenaries. Bueller had been a key part of the anti-Equilibrium alliance that had driven the manipulative think tank turned conspiracy out of the Syntactic Cluster, but even there... He'd been a technical advisor and a ship's engineer.

Not the kind of role that made a man famous or infamous a hundred light-years away.

"What did they know?" Kira asked.

"Bits and pieces of what I've been up to," he said. "Through a notably biased lens. I...apparently might be being touted as the greatest traitor in Brisingr history and labeled a merchant of death— one selling Brisingr military technology to the highest bidder in the Outer Rim."

She grunted in surprise.

"I suppose Reinhardt decided he needed somebody to blame for the sudden leap forward in the Syntactic Cluster's military tech," she guessed. "Though I have to wonder just what made the Cluster so important in Kaiserreich politics."

"Questions were getting asked about *Deception*," Bueller said. "And the ships that ended up with the Costar Clans." He shook his head. "I'm working with people's hesitantly admitted memories of things that weren't important to them at the time, remember, but it sounds like ex-BKN ships that should have been demilitarized have been showing up in a few places with all of their guns and fighters intact."

"Places like Colossus," she noted grimly. Those theoretically decommissioned ships had shown up in her troubles a few times.

"And other places, farther out-Rim," he agreed. "It appears that the good Kaiser is laying the blame for all of that on *me*. Publicly, as part of a major propaganda effort."

"Damn. I'm sorry, love." She unsprawled from the couch and crossed to perch on the arm of his chair, leaning on his shoulder. "I know we'd assumed you couldn't go home, but that's a level of problem I hadn't anticipated."

"We have over fifty prisoners aboard and they all recognized me," he said quietly. "Yes, they're military officers and hence more briefed on this kind of situation, but...I suspect most of my homeworld knows who I am right now, and my name has been tarred with..."

"With Reinhardt's own crimes," she concluded, squeezing his shoulder. "We'll do what we can once Apollo is free, love. You've said that his power base will suffer then, right?

"We can use that to undermine his story, bring out the truth and clear your name."

He chuckled and covered her hand with his own.

"Thank you, Kira," he told her. "I...I wouldn't have expected it to bother me this much, but then, I never expected to be this close to home again. Everything here was supposed to be sorted, in its own *equilibrium*, as the Institute likes to say."

"But Kaiser Reinhardt has demonstrated why the Institute's own tools and methods undermine their supposed goal," Kira murmured.

"To create peace, they just keep starting wars and wondering why it never works!"

"It all made so much sense when they made the pitch, you know," he said. "They had the logic, the numbers, the idealism, the plans... It all added up and made sense.

"It was only when the blood price started to become clear that I really questioned the spiel. And for some..."

"For some, the ends justify the means," Kira agreed. "I think everyone has a point that's too far—John Estanza and Jay Moranis were both men I respected and served, but both of them knowingly flew for Equilibrium for years.

"It wasn't until the Institute betrayed one of its partners that they thought it had gone too far. But it opened their eyes."

"I think, for some people, it's hard to open your eyes unless someone else forces you," Bueller admitted. "Which, I suppose, is what we're here to achieve."

"It is."

"Meeting with Killinger in the morning, right?" he asked.

"Yeah. We'll keep you out of the meetings, still," she promised. "I figure he knows we have Brisingr crew aboard, but Killinger was always a...*categorizer*. And I *know* that everyone from Brisingr has been categorized as an enemy in his head."

22

THERE WERE DEFINITELY ships in the rebel fleet that could host the gathering of officers from both allied forces. Kira *knew*, from her own experience, that *Victorious* had been fitted out as a fleet flagship, with both briefing rooms for her fighter groups and conference facilities to handle visiting senior officers for conferences.

But, given her suspicions about the status of the fleet carrier's flight deck, she wasn't entirely surprised that the conference was virtual. She and McCaig were physically in the same room—her office on *Prodigal*'s flag deck—but they were linked in to a virtual environment with Ayodele, Davidović and Colombera.

Killinger and his rebels filled the rest of the virtual space, the captain of each of the ships present on their own, plus Killinger's fleet CNG, Colonel Lin Juan.

Kira knew Lin of old. The graceful Chinese woman had been a Major and a squadron commander aboard *Victorious* at the end of the war. She'd been another of "Heller's Hellions," the officers of the elite battle group under Commodore James Heller that had seen many of the key actions of the war.

But Lin was the only nova-fighter pilot from Killinger's fleet, just as Colombera was the only one from the Recon Group. Like many other things, the invitation of *just* the senior fighter pilot might just be a...*choice*.

Except that Henry Killinger was an ex–fighter pilot himself and would understand that the fighter-group commanders were at *least* as important to the plan as the destroyer skippers. All twelve of the rebel destroyer COs were in the virtual conference, but Kira could have brought four more senior flight officers.

And Henry Killinger should have brought at least that many from *Victorious* alone, let alone the cruisers. *Oceanic Trident* should have had a twenty-four-fighter strike wing. The other eleven cruisers should have had at least another twenty *squadrons* between them, calling for even more senior flight officers to be in the briefing.

Instead, there were only the two Commanders, Nova Group, in the conference that gathered on top of a storm cloud. The virtual meeting space was certainly *impressive*, the black cloud rippling underneath their avatars' feet as Kira mentally catalogued the thirty-plus officers who *were* present.

She preferred simpler spaces herself, usually with a touch of coziness to lower people's hackles as they dealt with high-stress discussions. Killinger, it seemed, was of the type who wanted to *impress* rather than *discuss*.

"Welcome to Olympus, Admiral Demirci," he greeted her as her avatar walked into the center of the cloud. A section of the storm rose up under her feet, lifting her so that everyone could see her—if to a lower level than Killinger himself.

"Admiral Killinger," she replied with a measured nod. "Are we ready to depart Faaselesitila?"

"If anyone has any concerns with their ship, now is the time," the rebel Admiral said, half to Kira but mostly to his own officers. "We've been preparing for this operation for a while now, and our new allies tip the odds thoroughly in our favor."

He paused, surveying the crowd.

"Anyone?" he repeated.

Kira would have been *very* surprised if any of the officers spoke up. Any competent captain would have raised—and *fixed*—issues prior to the big all-officers meeting. Any incompetent captain wasn't going to admit to having screwed up.

It would take a very specific combination of failure and spine to speak up at that point, and none of the starship COs around here appeared to have it.

"Good."

Killinger made a sweeping upward gesture with both hands and lightning *cracked* through the air above everyone's head. As the flash faded, a three-dimensional map of their target appeared, hovering over the cloud.

"Dickey," Killinger said unnecessarily. "Shenandoah Seven. Home to the Brisingr Kaiserreich's Naval Base Gretchen.

"Our target is the central logistics and fabrication facilities in orbit around Dickey-One and Dickey-Two," he told them, highlighting the two moons as he spoke. "On our arrival, their orbits will be far enough apart to prevent their forts from being mutually supportive. Three of said forts orbit Dickey-Two; two orbit Dickey-One."

New icons appeared as he spoke, details of space and ground installations hovering over the icons as Kira focused her attention on them.

The *Rastatt*-class fortresses were her biggest concern. Small enough to be transported in four pieces on nova freighters and lacking both nova drives and nova fighters, they packed in eight dual heavy plasma-gun turrets, plus sixteen defensive cannon.

"On top of the defensive forts, the BKN has installed a novafighter base on Dickey-Three with its own ground-defense plasma-cannon batteries," Killinger continued. "Our best intelligence is that they have ten of their ten-plane squadrons based on Dickey-Three, with another ten squadrons split between surface bases on One and Two.

"Unfortunately, our intelligence doesn't extend to what vessels will be resupplying at Base Gretchen when we arrive," he warned. "There *appears* to be a six-ship destroyer squadron on permanent or near-permanent assignment, and our eyes on the scene have seen everything up to a full two-battlecruiser fleet-carrier-group stop over.

"That was, however, the largest single force ever present at Gretchen, and we have no reason to believe that any major force should be passing through the Shenandoah System on our arrival."

"Where will they be if they are?" Kira asked.

"Here," Killinger replied, highlighting an area of space between Dickey-One and the main planet. "Fabrication facilities are being built on Dickey-Two. Primary logistics facilities are anchoring on Dickey-One, allowing easier access to the cloudscoops on the gas giant itself.

"We can assume any vessel present is either refueling, discharging or restocking. Most likely, they will be doing those three things at One. Our agents tell me that the destroyer squadron carries out patrols through the entire planetary system but keeps a minimum of two ships in orbit of Dickey-One at all times."

Three red targeting carats appeared on the screen.

"That gives us three main targets," Killinger noted. "First is what-ever ships are in place and the logistics supply structure at Dickey-One. Our intel says that Dickey-One will be the most defended, between the two forts assigned there and the starships themselves.

"The second target is Dickey-Two," he continued. "In many ways, Dickey-Two is our primary objective. The fabrication facilities present there can be loaded onto our ships and transported back here, augmenting our own capabilities for self-repair and fleet growth."

With a surface gravity of just under a quarter-gravity, Dickey-Two was the right size to host the fabrication facilities for class two nova drives. Kira figured that was as much confirmation as she was going to get of what Killinger *really* needed from this operation.

"The last target is Dickey-Three, where the main nova-fighter strength of the base is located. We have, thanks to our intelligence assets, nailed down the *exact* location of the surface facilities—which opens up some very useful possibilities with regards to tilting the playing field in our favor."

Kira could see how trying to take advantage of all of the possibilities could set them up for defeat in detail—but surprise could also let them clear the battlespace before their enemies realized what was happening.

Assuming they had up-to-date information on what was going on in Shenandoah, at least.

"Intelligence will be key," Killinger told everyone, as if reading her mind. "We have assets and allies in the Shenandoah System, people who disapprove of their government toadying to Brisingr.

"We will be met at the last trade route by several freighters who will do the lion's share of the transport once we've secured the base. One of them will be coming directly from Shenandoah and will be leaving a nova pinnace behind."

He smiled wickedly.

"That pinnace is scheduled to join us around when the cooldown on our nova drives ends, providing us with detailed gravitational sensor data on the outer regions of the Shenandoah System.

"Using that data, we will nova to a location one light-day out from Dickey. There, we will wait for our drives to cool down before proceeding against Base Gretchen."

A new icon marked the staging point, the image of the system spreading out to make space for it.

"The cooldown from a one-light-day jump is less than half an hour," Killinger noted. "Which is a *hell* of a lot better, if something goes wrong, than the twenty hours if we jump directly from the trade route.

"Inserting that pause into our operations also means that if the BKN is aware of our approach, they will believe that we passed by toward a different target. It also allows us a measure of time to scout Fleet Base Gretchen via our nova fighters and pinnaces prior to the attack. We will know what we are stepping into.

"Assuming that the situation does not materially differ from our expectations—in which case we will adjust our plans at the staging point—we will divide our forces into three task groups."

He indicated Kira.

"Task Force *Prodigal* will consist of Admiral Demirci's three ships plus *Hostess, Onager, Scorpion* and *Defender*," he reeled off.

Kira's headware swiftly updated with the information on those four ships and highlighted their commanding officers. *Hostess* was an eighty-kilocubic older heavy cruiser from the ASDF. *Onager* and *Scorpion* were both Extrayan *Siege*-class cruisers, seventy-kilocubic ships. *Defender* was from Shenandoah herself, a surprisingly modern sixty-kilocubic cruiser.

What all four ships shared was a lack of a fighter complement. They were pure direct-fire combatants—which made sense, when Kira had one of the two carriers in play.

But it also fit the pattern.

"Your target, Admiral Demirci, is Dickey-One, the destroyer squadron, and any ships currently fueling," Killinger told her. "We should have sufficiently accurate data for you to nova in inside weapons range of the fortresses and engage them heavily before you need to bring up your jammers."

"That will depend on what the scouts find," Kira noted. "But it's possible."

Killinger nodded and continued on.

"The second force will be anchored on *Victorious*," he said. "Supported by *Brandenburg* and half of our destroyers under Commodore Leander, Task Group *Victorious* will hit Dickey-Three.

"Like TG *Prodigal*, I expect Vivienne's ships to be able to jump into close orbit and bombard the hangar sites before the BKN can react," he noted, gesturing to a tall woman with night-black hair and ivory-pale skin.

Presumably the statuesque woman was Commodore Vivienne Leander. All Kira really knew about Leander was what was showing up in her headware, which told her that the woman was an Extrayan native—as was her ship, the ninety-kilocubic heavy cruiser *Brandenburg*.

Potentially, the former Extrayan officer was part of why there were more Extrayan ships in the rebel fleet than anything other than ASDF ships.

"The last Task Group will be centered on *Oceanic Trident* and consist of the rest of our cruisers and destroyers under my own command," Killinger concluded. "We will proceed to Dickey-Two, neutralize the defenses and land our Hoplite companies to secure the surface facilities in preparation for the arrival of the transports.

"Dividing our forces *is* a risk," he acknowledged, looking around the virtual gathering. "But, according to our intelligence, we have a significant edge over our enemies here. Using that edge, we may be able to clear the battlespace before anyone can escape or even get off a message.

"Without anyone carrying word, even Shenandoah Star Command won't know what's happening quickly enough to intervene. We will be able to load the fabricators onto our transports and empty as much of the storage depots as we can carry without interference."

"We will have the opportunity to reassess at the staging point," Leander noted. "I am comfortable with that as a fallback, ser."

"Demirci?" Killinger turned his gaze on Kira.

"It's workable," she told him. Her brain was already running through the possibilities and the complications. She didn't expect it to be *that* easy, after all.

"A full download of all of our intelligence on Base Gretchen has been sent to all of you," Killinger told the gathering. "Along with your assignments to the three task groups and your exit routes through the minefields and defenses.

"We move out in one hour. To victory!"

"Victory!"

Kira traded a look with McCaig as the virtual reality faded. Her people had all missed the apparent call-and-response—but not *one* of Killinger's people had.

"The plan can work," her Flag Captain told her. "Our people can do our part, anyway. Do you trust him?"

"Killinger?" Kira snorted. "I knew him as a nova combat group commander, not a fleet commander. Everything sounds right, but he's very dependent on his intel being correct."

"Even with the staging point to cover his ass?" McCaig asked.

"We'll be at the staging point for fourteen hours, Caiden," she murmured. "Divide up into task groups and work up, sure, but I wouldn't be making the main operations plan until we're there.

"Or, if nothing else, I'd have three or four plans." She shook her head. "He's set it up to give the appearance of flexibility because *having* that flexibility is how the ASDF prefers to work.

"And I suppose we shall see whether that flexibility actually exists."

"The proof is in the pudding, as they say," McCaig rumbled softly.

23

AT THE POINT the fleets began to move out of the protected area underneath Faaselesitila V's rings and moons, Kira saw that they'd been given at least *some* maps of the minefields. The one-shot plasma cannon were marked on the tactical feeds with a sickly green color, and she suspected the selection was...*editorial* on the ops teams' part.

"They spent a lot of resources building those mines," Bueller observed from his own station on the flag bridge. "Seems...an interesting choice."

"How so?" Soler asked. The younger officer had the glazed expression of someone living mostly in their headware feeds, but she was still listening to the conversation on the flag bridge.

Such as the conversation was, with Kira's command center generally having less than ten people in it. Four officers—herself, Soler, Ronaldo and Bueller—and then four NCOs and specialists supporting them.

They probably didn't need the full battle-stations crew as they passed through the minefields, but Kira agreed with the apparent opinion of Soler's team.

"Each of those mines could be a torpedo," Bueller explained.

"Except, of course, they don't have Harrington coils, so it's more like... any *two* of those mines is enough resources to be a torpedo.

"*This* many mines?" The engineer shook his head and shared a look with Kira. "There's enough resources out there to build a damn warship. Not a gunship, a proper warship—a destroyer, maybe even a small cruiser."

"But this gives them a fortified base, doesn't it?" the operations officer asked—reminding Kira that the pale woman was from Redward. Apollo and Brisingr were arguably backward by the standard of the entire colonized sphere, but the Outer Rim was a step further back.

Apollo, Brisingr, the Royal Crest...the states Kira had grown up with being her local "great powers" were roughly ninth-tier powers, at best, by the standards of broader humanity. But they were the top dogs in her section of the Mid Rim.

Redward had bootstrapped itself into the bottom rung of the same tier as Kira's homeworld and was rapidly dragging the Syntactic Cluster along with itself. But it had yet to see a real extended war between peers at its new level of military-industrial capacity.

Apollo and Brisingr *had*, which gave Kira and Bueller a more accurate vision of what that kind of conflict looked like.

"It gives them a false sense of security," Kira told her subordinate. "They've got, what, a hundred thousand mines out there? A vast investment out of limited resources, one that has cost them in terms of maintaining their ships and sustaining operations."

Soler's eyes lost much of the glazed expression as she focused on the conversation instead of her headware feed. She looked thoughtful now as she studied the holographic tactical plot around them.

"How false is the sense of security?" she finally asked.

"False enough that I'm surprised Killinger did this," Kira told her. "What *don't* the mines have, Commander Soler?"

Teaching wasn't as explicitly a part of her job as a mercenary commander as it had been when she'd commanded a fighter squadron for the ASDF, but it was also an investment in Memorial Force's most important asset: its people.

"Jammers," Soler said slowly, looking at the icons on the display. "There's no multiphasic jammers on the mines."

"Exactly. I've seen experiments with layering jammer platforms throughout a minefield, but it doesn't help as much as you'd think," Kira noted.

"From what I understand, it boils down to the mines can't move either," Bueller added. "And we have, what, three different designs for long-range Harrington-coil missiles in our fabricator databases now?"

"Brisingr's, Apollo's and the Crest's," Kira confirmed. "Against a maneuvering target with multiphasic jammers, an LRM is basically useless. Against a target that doesn't maneuver or doesn't have jammers?

"We can put a missile into it from halfway across the star system. Against this..." She waved at the screen. "Dragon's Teeth."

She could tell that Soler was looking up the system and saw the younger woman's nod of understanding.

"Cluster nukes," the operations officer said aloud. "You'd get full clearance in a cube a hundred klicks on a side, *plus* radiation and EMP effects at least another fifty klicks out from the bomb zone."

"Mines have a reliable range about seven to eight thousand kilometers—half that of a torpedo," Kira said. "Clearing a fifteen-thousand-kilometer-wide path through the mines would take time and a few thousand tons of raw materials, but the biggest headache would be the Harrington coils."

Those could be made in a starship's fabricators, but it wasn't a fast process. Faced with a minefield like this, Kira would run down her existing stocks of coils and then build them up again over time.

"And there would be nothing they could do to stop you. But they could use the time to run or to sortie, couldn't they?" Soler asked.

"That's the only real value of the minefield except for the initial surprise," Kira agreed. "But if you're trying to hide behind a minefield, it's a safe assumption you don't have the firepower to take on whoever has come after you.

"Might buy you time to run...but I'd rather have that extra cruiser, personally!"

"Though, when was the last time *you* saw anyone actually build a long-range missile?" Bueller asked. "I worked on some of the test firings for the latest generation of the BKN version, but I think that was the only time I've even seen them *built*, let alone used!"

"Somebody in the Syndulla military thought they were very clever and tried to mine a trade-route stop," Kira said with a chuckle. "Though, to be fair, I think their goal was to achieve exactly what they did: they locked down a carrier group for three days, building Dragon's Teeth to clear the minefield so traffic could pass safely."

"Seems like a low return on investment," Soler said.

"Depending on how they'd used those three days, it could have been a very good return on investment," Kira admitted. "Of course, as it turns out, they *didn't* use them at all—they were operating on a BKN-style doctrine of *test to see what happens* and decided that the ROI wasn't there."

"Because they didn't use the window they'd opened," the ops officer suggested, but her gaze was still on the minefields.

"Exactly. You're staring at the mines, Commander; something specific coming to mind?"

"Thinking about what the rebels have for ships, ser, and the weaknesses of their defenses," Soler said slowly. "If we had our full fleet here, we could have run right over them. Memorial Force isn't much more than a reinforced carrier group, but their lack of nova fighters and the belief that the minefield would hold..."

Kira nodded.

"I agree. We need Killinger—his ships and his Hoplites are going to be a key part of retaking Apollo—but this base relied on secrecy for safety, not the minefields."

"I find it hard to believe that the Shadows, the people who

arranged one of the few successful interstellar invasions *ever*, couldn't find his base," Bueller admitted grimly.

"I don't think they tried," Kira told him. "Because I agree. But I also think that having an active pirate force, however politicized that force is, has been damn useful for selling the Security Zone to its involuntary members."

"So...wait." Soler sounded concerned. "Killinger's rebellion has been..."

"A powerful tool in the arsenal of his enemy and of the cause he opposes," Kira said. "With this move against Naval Base Gretchen, that might finally change, but my impression is that the Kaiser and Brisingr have allowed Killinger and his fleet to exist because the value of having a known pirate fleet far outweighs the actual costs of his piracy."

The flag deck was silent for a good minute as Kira's people processed that.

"How do we fix that?" Ronaldo asked, the coms officer speaking for the first time.

"We stop them being pirates," Kira explained. "And we turn them into the liberation force they were always *supposed* to be!"

24

AFTER THREE DAYS of watching the rebel fleet transit through the trade routes toward their destination, Kira wasn't sure salvaging Killinger's reputation was going to be *possible*. The moment any ships in the trade routes saw any of the rebel ships, they were immediately piling on all of the sublight thrust they could manage.

They weren't even *that* recognizable, all things considered.

"While I am *tempted* to say that Killinger's people are the most notorious pirates ever, I'm not sure this is entirely their fault," McCaig told her after their morning briefing at the fourth trade-route stop. "That said, I think your home sector might have the jumpiest merchant ships I've ever seen."

And McCaig had been a mercenary ground officer through a significant chunk of the Rim. When Kira had met him as John Estanza's ground commander, he'd already had two decades of experience.

"It didn't use to be this bad," she said softly, watching the merchant traffic in the nova point flee the fleet of warships. "That said, we *are* running around with a group of thirty warships. Most civilians are going to open up distance from that if they can."

"There isn't even much point," her Flag Captain pointed out. "Between *Victorious* and *Huntress*, we've got the nova fighters to catch anyone who can't nova out."

"It doesn't help *much*," she conceded. "But every light-second they are farther from us, that's a second they have to be somewhere other than where we think they are when our fighters arrive."

She shrugged.

"I swear the civilians were calmer when we were fighting an actual *war*."

"Wars have rules," McCaig reminded her. "Even mercenaries, by and large, fight by those rules. Piracy? Not so much."

War was about trade-route control. The invasion of Apollo was an aberration, an oddity. Outside of unusual circumstances and intra-system conflict, wars were fought over who could provide security and charge tariffs on traffic along the mapped trade routes.

Which also meant that modern war was fundamentally almost entirely *about* merchant shipping, and there were very strict, if often informal, rules about how civilian ships were handled. A freighter caught in the middle of a war could expect to be interned by a hostile warship and dragged back to a home system to be assessed and poten-tially fined.

Cargos were rarely touched and insurance often covered the fines —if the captain had paid enough for their insurance, anyway. So long as the crew didn't do anything to reclassify themselves as active combatants, civilian merchant crew was supposed to be untouchable.

That was how Apollo operated. And while Kira had *many* complaints about how the Kaiserreich had handled the laws and customs of the war, she had to admit that they'd followed that rule without question.

"If we're at the point where civilian ships run at the sight of warships, things may have degraded further than I'd dared fear," Kira told the big captain. "Like you said, I doubt it's all Killinger. But even *that* just suggests that Brisingr is failing to actually *be* the guarantor of trade-route safety."

"And if the Security Zone can't provide security, well, that's a good sign for those of us planning on fighting them," McCaig said.

"This is true," she agreed. "But it also suggests that things have changed a *lot* in the last five years. Because there wasn't enough piracy before—or even during!—the war for this kind of reaction."

"Coming home is always rough," he noted. "Guess we'll have to fix things here before we move on?"

She chuckled sadly.

"If we can."

IN THE SWIRL of scattering freighters, it felt odd to have several of them make short-distance novas to join the fleet. They'd been scheduled, but part of Kira really hadn't been sure if Killinger's plans and contacts were going to work out as expected.

"We're getting information downloads from the transports, ser," Soler reported.

"Make sure all of our ships, including our loaners, get it," Kira ordered. "And that we all have the *same* data, just in case."

For herself, she threw the updated information on the Dickey planetary system up onto the displays around her. Time stamps told her that the most-recent data had been recorded from about thirty light-seconds twenty-four hours earlier.

"Huh."

Soler threw a questioning look at her. There were only the two of them on the flag bridge right now, with the rest of the flag staff resting in preparation for what everyone knew was going to be a very busy few days.

"I was expecting *something* notably different from the intel Killinger supplied in advance," she noted. "But everything is looking about as we expected."

There were five fortresses, distributed as shown in their intel. There was no way to definitely say if the fighter bases on the surface of Dickey-Three were there, not from this distance. But they could see the ships and forts and space stations above Dickey-One and Dickey-Two.

Six destroyers were evenly split between the three inner moons, which strongly suggested the nova-fighter base was where they'd been told it was.

"Few extra ships, but..." Kira haloed each of them individually, focusing in on the half a dozen ships discharging static into Dickey itself. "These five are logistics ships. Military, from the beacons the freighter picked up, but not warships."

"But that *is* a battlecruiser," Soler pointed out. "Against the records we got from our Apollo files...L-One-Fifty. Hundred and fifteen kilocubics, ten starfighters, twenty guns in single turrets."

"One of the few ships in the BKN traditionally carrying just Weltraumfuchs interceptors, because it's too few fighters for a strike package," Kira added. "L-One-Fifties were their main battle-line ship during the war. I think they had *one* B-One-Seventy online then."

The B170 cruisers were ten thousand cubic meters bigger and put it all into defenses and packing an extra twenty fighters. Unlike the L150s, the B170s *did* carry a strike package—including a partial squadron of bombers.

"One battlecruiser isn't going to change the balance of force," Soler suggested aloud. "Though she is in our area of operations. A concern?"

"No." Kira shook her head. Six cruisers and a light carrier could handle three forts, two destroyers, and a battlecruiser. "Changes our focus, yes, but not a concern."

The final form of the ops plan was already falling into place in her head. They'd have more intel once they were in Shenandoah, though.

"Have we confirmed that we have nova pinnaces on watch for us?" she asked.

"According to the data dump from the freighters, they left two of them behind," Soler confirmed. "We should get nearly live data before we make the final jump."

"Everything *sounds* good," Kira murmured.

"Ser?"

"I have rarely seen truly successful surprise attacks like this," she admitted to her junior. "We're trying to get all the data for us to take advantage of the situation, but usually, all the scouts end up doing is warning the enemy you're coming.

"Those merchant ships mean that the BKN knows Killinger's fleet is in the area," she continued. "And moving as a group means we have a big target in mind. So, they're watching all their vulnerable points.

"They might not have a lot of warning, but they'll have some. They'll be *looking* for people scouting out Gretchen Base soon, if they aren't already."

She gestured at the screen.

"Twenty-four hours ago, they didn't know there was a problem, but I suspect someone at the base noted those freighters swinging by on their way out-system. Nine million kilometers isn't *close*, but it's closer than they needed to come.

"Unfortunately, I expect to lose the pinnaces," she said grimly. "And for the BKN to know we're coming. But...so long as they don't manage to come up with a couple of carrier groups, we still have the firepower edge.

"And since the only carrier group in the system belongs to Shenandoah Star Command..." A hand gesture brought up data on that group, updating her on the list strength of the SSC and their flagship's battle group.

Shenandoah herself was a Brisingr-built HC-10 fleet carrier, a hundred-and-ten-thousand-cubic-meter ship with eleven squadrons aboard. They had two eighty-kilocubic homebuilt cruisers to back her up, then filled out their allotment under the Security Zone rules with six thirty-five-kilocubic destroyers and five bog-standard ten-kilocubic gunships.

Most of the destroyers and gunships were elsewhere, according to the freighters, but the fleet carrier and both cruisers were in a high-enough orbit of Potomac to allow them to nova to anywhere in the system.

"*Shenandoah* and her escorts *will* be a concern if the Brisingr commander decides to call them in," she said. "But for them to have anything else available...well..."

She sighed and shook her head.

"Everything *looks* good," she concluded. "We'll make this happen. But keep your eyes open, Commander Soler. The Kaiser-reich Navy are *damned* competent, and the amount of prep work we've done for this op makes it far too likely they know something is coming."

25

THE ARRIVAL at the Shenandoah outer-system staging point was enough of a cluster to make Kira actually feel *better* about their mission. Two of their five new freighter companions overshot the staging point by a full light-minute—thankfully, in the opposite direction from Dickey, leaving the ships farther out in the void.

A minute of earlier warning *shouldn't* have made a difference, but Kira wasn't going to turn down the small mercy of the ships overshooting in the right direction. And while the freighters were the worst of it, they weren't the only ones to muck up their novas.

"Okay, so everybody *did* have the same gravimetric data, yes?" Kira asked, amusement underlying her tone as she studied the catastrophe that was pretending to be their formation.

The *plan* had been for the force to arrive at the staging point split into the three task groups. Kira's three ships had arrived in a perfect formation with each other, and a six-ship CAP was orbiting *Huntress* at a decent distance.

Her four "loaner" cruisers, however, were on the far side of a fleet formation that occupied a full million kilometers more than it should have.

"I thought so," McCaig told her. "But those planned nice, neat groups of ships, separated by fifty thousand klicks, well...we don't have that."

"Ronaldo, get on the coms to our loaners and coordinate meeting them somewhere in the middle," Kira ordered. "Soler, let me know if you can see any of the nova pinnaces."

It would be twenty hours before any of the capital ships could nova again, but that only made the information they were supposed to get from their spies more important. The data from the freighters would be almost three days old when the fleet launched their attack—but the old-light scans that the fleet was getting on their own wouldn't have the detail to confirm the locations of their enemies.

"All I can say for sure is that twenty-four hours ago, that battle-cruiser was still there," Soler reported. "I'll have my people dig in to the lightspeed data, see what we can find when we put it up against the freighter scans and the intelligence."

"Good. Trust but verify," Kira told the ops officer. "We have to trust our allies, but let's validate everything they've given us if we can."

"Like I said, boss, definitely a battlecruiser," Soler replied. "I knew where to look for that one."

"And the pinnaces? I know they're smaller, but we knew where to look for them, too."

There was a pause.

"As of twenty-four hours ago, all four of the scout pinnaces were where they were supposed to be," Soler confirmed. "None of them are as close as I'd like for data-collection purposes or as far as I'd like for stealth purposes."

Kira chuckled.

"That, Commander Soler, is almost always the case."

IT TOOK a full hour to get the three task groups sorted out again. That was about fifteen minutes longer than Kira figured that process *should* have taken—and an hour they wouldn't have been vulnerable if Killinger's fleet had been more practiced in jumping based on new raw data.

"Can you check those numbers for me, Ronaldo?" Kira told her coms officer. "I'm only seeing ten nova fighters up for CAP—and I thought *we* put up a six-ship squadron!"

"We did," Ronaldo replied instantly. "*Victorious* put up four Hoplite-IV interceptors ten minutes after arrival. No further support."

Kira suspected she looked like she was sucking lemons. *Huntress* shouldn't have been carrying the lion's share of the Combat Aerospace Patrol. She had seventy-two fighters aboard to the hundred and twenty *Victorious* should be carrying.

But she'd already realized that Killinger only had somewhere between twenty and thirty nova fighters on his ships, total. *Oceanic Trident* alone could carry every fighter they'd seen so far.

"Get me Scimitar," she told Ronaldo quietly.

"Boss," Colombera greeted her a moment later. "I'm assuming you're watching the large and impressive CAP our friends put into space."

"Have you talked to Colonel Lin about it yet?" she asked.

"Nope. Colonel's busy," her own CNG told her. "I figure fifty-fifty she's either avoiding me or she's *on* one of those fighters."

"Understood." Kira looked at the barely shaken-out formation of capital ships. For the next nineteen hours, they were vulnerable. There shouldn't be anything around for them to be vulnerable *to*, but that didn't make their lack of ability to nova less worrisome.

"Get a second squadron up for CAP," she finally told Colombera. "Pull from the cruisers if you need them to keep the numbers up. We'll watch our back and watch Killinger's while we're at it."

"Permission to prep a deck strike package as well," Scimitar asked.

A two-squadron CAP called for a two-squadron backup crewed and on the deck. Adding a *deck strike package* to that would mean taking those two squadrons of interceptors and adding two squadrons of heavy fighters and a bomber squadron.

All fully fueled and loaded with torpedoes. If something went sideways without the fleet being ready, that would give them a capital-ship-killing punch while the rest of the pilots were woken up and the fighters were armed.

"Do it," Kira ordered. "Despite this chaos, things are going according to plan. And that makes me worry."

"Me too. We'll be ready if something goes sideways, ser."

"I know you will."

KIRA FOUND it impossible to sleep. Eventually, she gave up and used her headware's systems to knock herself out. That type of sleep was never as restful as more-natural slumber, but it was better than nothing and she was relatively easily woken from it—though it wasn't a *good* thing to be so woken.

Fortunately, no one felt the need to interrupt her allocated window, and she woke on schedule. Lying in the bed in her quarters, she ran through the readiness reports on her headware.

All seven of "her" ships were now in formation and giving her full readiness information. None of her loaners had starfighters, which kept their reports simpler—if concerning.

None of the four cruisers were in trouble, but equally, none of them were up to the kind of readiness she'd *like* to see. There were a lot of orange flags on their reports—mostly around nova drives and Harrington coils.

Both of those things required specially grown coils of crystal. The Harrington coils could at least be grown in space—had to be, in fact—but it still took time and equipment that no warship carried in quantity. Fleet-logistics ships were supposed to handle that kind of thing—but Killinger clearly didn't *have* one of those, and his ships had long since run through their stockpiles of spares.

Her own ships didn't even have yellow warnings. The two K-90s had been rebuilt and fully repaired. Everything on them was entirely functional—and *Huntress* was still basically brand-new.

She wasn't worried about her people being the weak link, and the rebel fleet, if nothing else, heavily outgunned their expected opposition.

A timer flickered in her vision, telling her that less than an hour remained until *Prodigal* was ready to jump. Nineteen hours of confusion and chaos and vulnerability were down, without any real trouble.

It was time for her to be on her command deck. Just in case.

<hr>

KIRA WAS the last member of the flag staff to return to the flag bridge. Even Bueller, who had been in their quarters when she'd knocked herself out, was there ahead of her.

"Status report, people," Kira ordered as she took her seat.

"Task Group *Prodigal* is ready for combat, ser," Ronaldo told her. "Davidović, Ayodele and McCaig are all on the network. CNG Colombera reports that arming of the fighter group is proceeding and we are expecting to have all fighters fully armed and fueled in ten minutes."

Most of the fighters would make the journey to Dickey inside *Huntress* and the cruiser's flight decks, preserving their ability to tactically nova. The last two squadrons of the CAP, though, would nova with the fleet—and have an only slightly shorter drive cooldown than the capital ships.

"We are ready," Bueller added to Ronaldo's report. "I've reviewed the readiness and engineering reports from all of our ships. The loaners..."

"Are rusty but alive," Kira finished. "We'll keep them close and under careful watch. Scimitar?"

"Ser?" the CNG replied.

"You've seen the status on our loaners?" she asked.

"Vaguely. Do I need to mother-hen them?"

"It might not be that bad," she told him with a chuckle. "But keep an eye on them. They don't have fighters of their own, which means you'll need to watch their backs."

"That's the pilots' job, isn't it?"

"I'm just reminding you that our friends will need a bit more watching," Kira said. "I'm starting to feel like they haven't had proper fighter support in a while."

"Likely. I'll say this, though..."

"What?" she prodded after a moment.

"*Victorious* is definitely short on fighters, but the people she's got flying them? They know their shit, ser. I'd say most, if not *all*, of them are vets from the war, like you and me."

"Huh." That made sense, but it spoke to further problems in Killinger's organization. If they couldn't even recruit new nova-fighter pilots...

"We're here to get him new nova fighters," Kira told Colombera. "We *know* that. And everything looks like what was promised."

"Isn't that when we're supposed to get nervous?" Bueller asked.

"I know I am," Colombera replied. "Last fighter will be fueled and armed in five minutes, and part of me is wishing I'd started the process half an hour sooner."

"We'd be equally vulnerable now, no matter what," Kira warned. "Forty minutes until we can nova."

"That countdown is probably running on every set of headware in the fleet," Davidović said from *Huntress*'s bridge. "Shouldn't we be seeing Killinger's scouts soon?"

"In theory," Kira agreed, studying the displays. "Scimitar, with the strike prep, do we have space to roll out our pinnaces?"

Each of her ships carried two of the small nova craft, but they were kept in the same hangars and flight decks as the nova fighters. With every fighter in the Recon Group fueled, armed and ready to launch...

"There's no space," Colombera admitted. "Not without putting, say, all of either *Harbinger* or *Prodigal*'s fighters into space to clear the deck."

Twenty-four hours before, the scout pinnaces had been where they should have been, but Kira and the rest of the rebel fleet couldn't be certain where they'd been since then.

"I *think* the plan was to have them cycle in, one at a time, over thirty minutes," Ronaldo said. "I know that Killinger sent a nova pinnace forward to confirm locations with them, but she was supposed to lie doggo and try to go unnoticed in Dickey's trail."

Kira nodded softly and leaned back in her chair to wait. More reports trickled in, including the confirmation that all of their fighters on all three ships were fully armed.

She and her captains had a plan, based on the data they had. They'd update based on whatever the pinnaces brought out, but they had a solid starting point.

"Contact!" Soler barked. "Nova emergence at a hundred thousand klicks. Small contact, one pinnace."

"As expected," Ronaldo confirmed, checking the time. "Thirty minutes to contact. Next pinnace should arrive in ten minutes."

"Get the download and let's be ready," Kira ordered. It was almost time.

"Wait..."

Every eye on the flag bridge—and probably the attention of a few people on the warship bridges—snapped to Soler.

"Commander?" Kira asked.

"I just got an odd energy flare off the pinnace," Soler said. "Like there was something behind her?"

There was enough time to see the nova fighter that had followed Killinger's pinnace through the nova before it opened fire, plasma ripping the pinnace apart as the BKN interceptor dove forward toward the rebel fleet.

"Scimitar," Kira said, her voice surprisingly level. "I don't need to tell you anything, do I?"

"CAP already leaping forward. We'll get it, ser."

For a few moments, Kira hoped they'd got it. Four of her interceptors novaed forward to catch the enemy plane—and that plane would have a twenty-minute cooldown.

"Contact!" Soler suddenly shouted, shock and fear tearing through her voice. "Multiple contacts, multiple vectors."

The fighter had followed the pinnace into its nova—but it had taken the time to inform someone *else* of the course it had traced before jumping.

And now an entire *fleet* of warships emerged from nova, and Kira Demirci knew that Henry Killinger had been played.

26

THE STAGING POINT dissolved into the chaos of multiphasic jamming, and Kira swallowed a curse.

"Soler, I need IDs on those bastards," she told her ops officer. "I don't need to know what *ships*, but what types and how many can make a shit-ton of difference!"

The sensor display was updating as she watched, the computers and operations team matching what limited pre-jamming data they had to the optical scans they were performing now.

"We've lost coms with Killinger's ships," Ronaldo said flatly. "Including our loaners. They broke formation almost immediately."

"The entire *point* of formation is to let us talk to them," Kira growled. It wasn't *her* people's fault that their allies had immediately broken back toward their original flagship.

Killinger's people maintained more than just the appearance of military discipline, but they weren't truly professionals anymore. When push came to shove, they fell back on *Victorious* and *Oceanic Trident*.

"Fighters launching from *Huntress*," Ronaldo reported. "Colombera reports Hedgehog protocols."

"Good. Make sure all three captains know," Kira replied.

Hedgehog protocols meant that Scimitar would be keeping most of the starfighters in close to the capital ships. He wouldn't keep *all* of them there—that would take away the FTL fighters' greatest advantage—but keeping most of them would help protect the Recon Group from enemy starfighters.

"Got rough numbers, ser," Soler said grimly. "It doesn't look good. I make it four carrier groups, all of them anchored on an HC-type ship and at least one similar-sized battlecruiser."

That meant four hundred-kilocubic-plus fleet carriers and four hundred-kilocubic-plus battlecruisers. Those eight ships alone probably outgunned the entire combined rebel fleet—they *definitely* outgunned Killinger's fleet!

But...they'd split their forces, making sure that whichever way the allies broke, they were facing a full heavy-carrier battle group. With the lack of nova fighters on Killinger's ships, that would be enough to pin the man's fleet.

"They didn't expect us," Kira murmured.

"Ser?"

"Each battle group could pin Killinger's fleet, but *we* have the nova fighters to change that balance," Kira told Soler. "Has Killinger picked a direction yet?"

They couldn't hold off four carrier groups for the eighteen minutes left on their drive cooldowns. They *could*, with their combined fleet, punch through *one* and get away from the other three.

Maybe.

"I have his vector," Soler confirmed after a second. "*Victorious* and *Oceanic Trident* are vectoring away from the largest battle group."

"Flag the carrier group along that line and pass it to Colombera via *Huntress*," Kira ordered. "He's to hit them with every bomber he's got, backed by the heavies."

She'd expect Scimitar to keep the interceptors in Hedgehog, but that was the CNG's call. *Her* call was to make the breakout attempt at all.

"Keep the Recon Group together," she told Ronaldo. "The enemy will be here momentarily."

The capital ships were still over a hundred thousand kilometers distant, marking the points of a sphere almost a full light-second across. A swiftly collapsing sphere but one that was still distant from Kira and her allies.

At this distance, she couldn't be *certain* what the enemy fighters were doing. But in their place, she'd have jumped the fighter wings to a staging point about a light-minute away to coordinate the strike.

They'd have to cool down their drives at that staging point, but they'd be able to communicate with each other and make their plan. That minute could make all of the difference, in her experience—and it was just about up.

"*Contact.*"

Soler's single-word report was the one Kira had been expecting, and she managed to *not* hold her breath as the new icons appeared around them. None of those icons were certain. Even friendly capital ships more than a few thousand kilometers distant were hard to localize perfectly, let alone hostile nova fighters twenty thousand kilometers away.

"Enemy bombers commencing their torpedo runs," Soler reported, almost entirely unnecessarily. "We appear to be a target. So does *Harbinger.*"

"Also *Victorious* and *Trident*, almost certainly," Kira noted. "Confirm that."

Each of the four largest ships would receive the full attention of a carrier's bomber group, either twenty or thirty of the ship-killing small craft. It all depended on *which* HC-type fleet carriers were out there.

"Interception runs commenced. Enemy interceptors and heavies deploying to protect the bombers."

Kira could follow her fighters' actions faster than Soler could. She needed the data feed from the operations department to manage it, but she knew what the nova fighters would be doing better than the ops officer would.

She *also* needed to watch the rest of the battle. It was hard to ignore the six-squadron strike hurtling toward the ship she was standing on, but she forced herself to shunt it into her side awareness as she tried to get a grip on the entirety of the chaotic mess.

They couldn't nail down numbers through the jamming, but it appeared her BKN counterpart was thinking much as she would. She could see the strike groups charging toward Killinger's two main capital ships—almost certainly the planned targets.

Her two big cruisers weren't heavy capital ships in the same way, but if anyone knew how much threat priority to put on the stolen K-90s, it was Brisingr.

Thanks to *Huntress*'s Wolverines, Kira could reasonably hope that her ships would survive. Her fighters were about half a generation more advanced than Brisingr's, and she had over fifty interceptors to protect the three ships.

The real question was how bad Killinger's nova-fighter shortage actually was.

There were fighters *there*, swirling out from a patrol formation around the battlecruiser and carrier. At this range, Kira couldn't see how many—though it definitely wasn't the hundred and forty or so the two capital ships should have carried!

Across the battlespace, outnumbered interceptors danced around heavy fighters to target the bombers. Kira couldn't spare fighters to help protect Killinger's ships—but the rebel Admiral at least had destroyers to fill in the gaps in his fighter shield.

She *just* had her interceptors, and she could tell at a glance that these enemies were *not* the green recruits assigned to a backwater posting. The experience and skill of the hardened squadrons assaulting her ships showed in the way the heavy fighters matched off with the interceptors, using their superior numbers and firepower to protect the ship-killers.

But the pilots she and Killinger had brought to the Shenandoah System were just as hardened, just as veteran. Kira lost interceptors, but her people danced around the heavy fighters, drawing them off for just long enough for their own heavies, the handful of remaining Hussars not committed to *their* bomber strike, to charge in.

She grinned wickedly as her heavies got amidst the bombers. Scimitar had only held back the cruiser's Hussar squadrons, which meant they were badly outnumbered by their prey—but bombers weren't built for the dogfight.

Heavy fighters like the Hussar-Seven were slower and less maneuverable than interceptors, but they were still built for close combat. The explosions were clear through the jamming as her people ripped through the bombers, and then nova flashes pierced the jamming as well, as the bomber pilots fell back on the oldest adage of anyone flying a nova fighter:

If you are in trouble, *be somewhere else.*

"Enemy fighter strike breaking off," McCaig reported. "We think most of their bombers got out, but their heavies got mangled and they couldn't hold it together."

"Keep your eyes peeled," Kira told the cruiser captain. "They'll make another pass before the cruisers close."

Killinger had been less lucky, she realized. The bombers coming after *Victorious* and *Oceanic Trident* had held their formation together in the face of the escorting destroyers and the fighter intercept.

Even as she was ordering her people to keep watch for the next wave, the *first* wave struck home on their allied fleet. A series of energy surges marked the launch of the Brisingr torpedoes...and a few seconds later, one of the icons marking Killinger's major capital ships vanished.

"Fuck!" Kira glared at the display as if she could bring the missing ship back by sheer will. She wasn't even sure which ship she would rather have lost! Both were powerful vessels, but while she might find Killinger's death aboard *Oceanic Trident* useful, she was well aware that *Victorious* was low enough on fighters to make her value questionable.

Plus, she wasn't *entirely* okay with hoping that an allied commander had died. And she didn't *know* that there was anyone she knew still aboard the carrier.

Either way, they'd just lost a key part of their allied fleet and the clock was running out on their chance to get out of there in time.

"Contacts on Force Four," Soler barked. "Looks like our bomber strike is going in. With some extras—looked like Killinger's Peltasts made the same call as we did."

At this range, Kira wasn't getting more than a rough estimate of the numbers. As Soler noted, though, that was at least four squadrons more fighters than she'd sent.

Combined with the fighters that had defended *Victorious* and *Oceanic Trident*, it looked like Killinger had still had more fighters than she'd *feared*—though it was more on the order of sixty planes between *Victorious* and *Trident*, not the over two hundred the carrier and the assorted cruisers should have carried.

"Move us through Killinger's formation," Kira ordered. "Get the cruisers out in front and leave *Huntress* in the mix of escorts. If *Oceanic Trident* is still with us, let's get *Prodigal* and *Harbinger* on her flanks.

"Hopefully, the rest of the cruisers will form up on us," she continued. "Because no matter how our fighters do, we're going to have to shoot our way through Force Four."

The best she was really hoping for was that the bombers would punch out the battlecruiser. If they nailed the carrier, too, she'd chalk that up as a win—but either way, she was counting four or five lighter cruisers and six destroyers.

They had the edge versus the single battle group. *If* the battle-cruiser was out of the equation.

It wasn't *all* up to her bombers—but if Swordheart's pilots did their jobs, a lot more of Killinger's people were going to make it out today!

27

KILLINGER'S CREWS were out of practice and unused to facing equal or superior opponents. Still, it was clear by the time *Prodigal* and *Harbinger* took their place at the point of the spear that they *were* military crews and they did know the drill.

The lack of coms in combat was always a pain, with only intermittent laser-com links between capital ships and even more variable communications with the starfighters. Formations, maneuvers, combined-force operations—all of these required captains to know their commander's thought processes and plans.

The allied fleet had prepped for the attack on Base Gretchen. They had *not* prepared for flight from a superior force coming at them from multiple vectors.

But like the starfighter pilots, Killinger's ship captains were veterans of the war. Even as her two cruisers moved through the main body of the fleet, the formation was shaking out around her. Destroyers moved to the outer edge of the formation, integrating with the fighter screen as the three remaining heavy capital ships positioned themselves to prevent individual attacks.

"We've got *Oceanic Trident* on the screen, ser," Soler reported.

"Our own bombers are returning as well and loading aboard *Huntress.*"

"There won't be time for them to rearm," Kira murmured. "Tell Swordheart to keep his people aboard the carrier. Fighters are to fill the defensive sphere, if we can contact them.

"Their job now is to stop the *rest* of the BKN groups ramming a bomber strike up our exhaust as we tangle with Force Four."

She felt a moment of grief for *Victorious*. The carrier had been a good ship, and she'd served on it for two years. There had almost certainly still been crew aboard that she'd known, but there was nothing she could do.

And Kira knew that *Oceanic Trident* was a better companion for the clash about to happen.

"Swordheart reports two kills," Ronaldo told her. "They blew the carrier and wrecked a K-Ninety. There were hits on the B-One-Seventy, but she's still in play."

"Understood." There were only seconds left before the two forces entered range of the heavy guns on both sides. By closing with Force Four, they'd kept the time the *other* three carrier groups would have them in range before they novaed to under ten seconds.

But that also meant that they would be in range of Force Four for roughly four whole *minutes* before they could nova out. Kira didn't expect Force Four's cruisers and destroyers to survive those minutes, but it was possible they'd hurt the rebel fleet along the way.

"Range...*now.*"

Prodigal shivered around Kira as her guns spoke in anger. Fourteen turrets aligned toward the enemy and spat plasma. The wide net of fire she spread across space spoke to why the BKN had gone for single-weapon turrets in their latest designs.

Dual turrets and triple turrets were more powerful, but they also had more problems—and fired along one vector each. *Prodigal* and *Harbinger* each laid out a web of fourteen attack vectors around their target.

They'd land less fire on the first salvo, but they were that much more likely to *hit* and locate their target in the mess of multiphasic jamming in a given salvo—compared to, say, *Oceanic Trident*'s ten dual turrets.

The B170 battlecruiser at the heart of the Brisingr line had just as many heavy cannon as *Trident*, but her guns were in single turrets, allowing her to cast an even wider net than *Prodigal* or *Harbinger*.

Overall, Killinger's cruisers had more dual and triple turrets than single, reducing the breadth of the web of fire they wove across the void compared to their opposition—except that the rebel fleet had over twice as many cruisers as Force Four.

"We have light-up," Soler reported. "Multiple hits on the battle-cruiser. Focusing fire."

They didn't even need to pass orders for that. Three ships of the enemy fleet had been hit in the first two salvos, and the third and fourth salvos focused on those three ships.

A rebel light cruiser unfortunate to have been caught by the BKN fire vanished from the screen as the B170 focused twenty guns on it—but two cruisers in the BKN flotilla came apart in the same moment, and the B170 itself was losing fire density.

The enemy capital ship had started with twenty guns and was down to ten when a squadron of heavy fighters flying ahead of the allied fleet entered torpedo range. In the chaos of the capital-ship engagement, the destroyer escorts hadn't been paying enough attention.

Hussar-Seven heavy fighters only carried two torpedoes apiece, not a bomber's sextet, but a squadron of the fighters put twelve torpedoes into the already-damaged battlecruiser.

An energy surge marked the detonation of something critical on the Brisingr ship, and the battlecruiser's fire stopped. *Oceanic Trident* put a final twenty-round salvo into the enemy capital ship, a final coup de grace that left nothing but dust of the warship.

A second rebel ship died as Kira tried to trace the action around her. Then a third—but Force Four was *gone*, leaving the rebels clear to run for open space.

"Nova contacts! Enemy bomber strike inbound," Soler barked. "It looks like they may have gone for full deck, no CAP. They realized we weren't going to send our bombers back out."

And they were right. The BKN was exposing their carriers to a counterstrike—but it was a counterstrike that Kira hadn't preserved the ability to make, because getting all of her people out was more important.

"Time?" She looked desperately over at Bueller.

"Seventy-two seconds."

"Forces One through Three have cut their thrust," Soler reported. "They will not enter weapons range before we nova. It's down to the bomber strike, ser."

Kira nodded sharply and looked at the swarm of vaguely defined icons.

"It's on you now, Abdullah," she murmured to Scimitar—who couldn't hear her. Either the fighters got through twice their own numbers of their counterparts to neutralize the bombers, or the BKN strike might render the entire breakout futile.

"All ships are opening fire with secondary guns. Fighters are closing."

Kira watched as the enemy strike boiled forward. The loss of Force Four's carrier hadn't limited the Brisingrs' ability to rearm their surviving bombers. They'd lost more than a quarter of the attack ships in the first strike.

Her own losses were going to be more than painful. There wouldn't be any chance to retrieve pilots and escape pods. Anyone who hadn't been easily picked up by passing starships would be left behind, though she had *some* faith that the BKN would treat prisoners decently—more so for her people than Killinger's, if she was being honest!

Everything was down to the bomber strike now. She watched silently as the red icons surged toward her ships. Green icons marked allied destroyers lunging out to meet them, but Scimitar's interceptors got there first—many of them novaing across the twenty-thousand-kilometer gap to cut the time.

Novas of less than a light-minute were inefficient in any possible sense, but, sometimes, they were still worth it. This time, the micronovas put several squadrons of interceptors *behind* the incoming bombers.

Kira wouldn't have thought to pull the stunt herself, but Scimitar *had*—and those interceptors tore into bombers that hadn't expected to be attacked from that vector.

It wasn't enough. It *couldn't* be enough—but then the heavy fighters and destroyers were in *front* of the bomber strike, laying down a wall of fire that tore into the Brisingr interceptors and their own heavy fighters.

For a few moments, it wavered in the balance.

Then the entire Brisingr nova-fighter strike vanished, the pilots' mental risk-benefit calculation concluding they weren't going to get enough torpedoes through to make a difference.

"Eight seconds," Bueller said softly as the fighter strike evaporated. "We don't have time to collect the fighters; those capital ships *are* closing."

"Every damn pilot out there knows the fallback point," Kira replied. "Soler, order to all ships and fighters we can reach. Fallback Alpha."

The fallback point was a full light-month away. That would take the capital ships just over an hour to cool down from—and even the nova fighters would take forty-five minutes.

The Brisingr ships would know the *angle* the allied fleet novaed along, but they shouldn't be able to work out how far they'd gone. Unless someone in Killinger's fleet was *completely* incompetent, anyway.

They'd find out the hard way, she supposed.

"Cooldown complete," Bueller reported.

"Get us the hell out of here, McCaig," Kira snapped.

28

THE NOVA FIGHTERS drifted in over the next thirty seconds, roughly the same amount of time it took for the multiphasic jammers to be slowly stepped down across the fleet.

"Get the fighters aboard, refueled and rearmed, ASAP," Kira ordered. "Worst-case scenario, we should have a few minutes before the BKN shows up."

They didn't even know how far away the BKN battle groups had novaed from. It was possible they had a full twenty-hour cooldown before their enemies could pursue. The downside, though...

"Konrad, how many novas can we make before the static discharge gets dangerous?" she asked.

"Took us four to get to Shenandoah, and you can do the math," the engineer said calmly. "We have two full-range novas left. Then we need to discharge static or risk losing ships when we nova."

"Or sit for *weeks* at a trade route somewhere," Kira finished. "Damn. Soler, what can we get to in two novas?"

"Shenandoah," the ops officer replied drily. "Otherwise...well, if you've got a mapped dark stop in the right spot, we could probably get to Apollo."

Kira brought up an astrographic chart on her optic nerves. They were eleven light-years—give or take a few light-months—from her home system, the closest she'd been in a very, very long time.

"I probably *do*," she admitted. "But I doubt that novaing into Apollo is going to get us a warm welcome."

"This fleet probably came from there," Bueller suggested. "But...I doubt they risked pulling more than a third of the nova fleet out of Apollo right now."

"They had a damn good idea of what Killinger had for ships and fighters," Kira said. "They pulled enough to assemble an overwhelming force. If we hadn't been there..."

"Killinger would be explaining his little cult and fleet to the gods right now," Soler finished. "I'm going to have to run through the uninhabited systems, see if anything within a dozen light-years is quiet enough and has something with a strong-enough magnetosphere for it to be worth the stop."

Kira was loading her map of the ASDF's dark nova points from encrypted cold storage. Her data on them was most of a decade old, but it should be safe to use for a nova. Ish, anyway.

"Ronaldo, I need you to check with Killinger's people," she said slowly as she saw the answer. "See if they have updated mapping for ASDF Covert Transit Point Delta-Seven-Three."

She tossed CTP-D-73 onto the main display.

"Five light-years from here, four and a half from Corosec," she explained to the flag staff. "The only habitation in Corosec was destroyed—most likely by the BKN as a practice run for their invasion of Apollo.

"So, there's nobody there—and the planet's magnetosphere is sufficient to discharge."

Corosec had mostly been of value to Apollo due to the high quantities of transuranics and other heavy metals in the asteroid belt. But the single planet in the system *had* a magnetosphere. It even had an atmosphere, though the only oxygen was tied up in carbon dioxide.

"Two novas from here," Soler noted. "Yeah. We can make that work. Do we travel as a fleet?"

That was an interesting question, Kira reflected. Because what Soler was *asking* was *Are Killinger's people worth sticking with?*

"For now," Kira finally answered. Because right now, that was the plan—but the plan could always change.

KILLINGER'S artificial skin didn't pick up the same degree of color as his natural flesh. The flush of anger spread across his original skin ended sharply where the synthskin began. His expression was dark, his natural eye sharp and glaring, and his shoulders and neck *vibrated* with tension as he appeared in Kira's headware.

"This is a private channel," she told him quietly. "Headware to headware. My people can't hear this, and I presume the same of yours?"

"As private as it can be when I'm on my bridge," he said flatly. "We were betrayed, Demirci. I will find out by whom and there will be *consequences*."

Kira swallowed her initial retort. She had a rather different assessment of how they'd ended up where they were, but it didn't matter right now.

"Unless you're planning on throwing good money after bad, how we got here isn't relevant until we're fully *out* of this mess," she told him. "I'm down over twenty fighters, Killinger, and we only picked up half a dozen escape pods. Two of them are yours."

That cut through whatever he'd been about to say like a hot knife, and he inhaled heavily.

"Thank you for picking up my people," he told her hoarsely. He paused for a moment, checking his own data. "We have four more of your pods scattered through the fleet. Without *Victorious*'s shuttles, we're lucky to have that many."

He didn't, Kira noted, mention how many of his own people they'd pulled out of the dark. Hopefully at least as many as hers.

"I lost a fifth of my fleet, Demirci," he said flatly. "Two destroyers, three cruisers, and *Victorious*. We can assume that some of the crew escaped, but any that did are now Brisingr prisoners. Our next step becomes freeing them!"

There was something to be admired in that being his first thought, Kira supposed, but it was a dangerous impulse. For that matter, she had to admit that *she* hadn't noticed the loss of the destroyers in the midst of the battle.

The fog of war was bad enough *before* humans found technological ways to make it even more opaque.

"Our next step has to be seeing to our own survival, Admiral Killinger," she said. "We will gather intelligence and learn the fate of our people over time, but right now, we need to make certain we complete the extraction of our fleets."

"We're out of Shenandoah; what more do you want?" he growled.

"In thirty-six minutes, we will be able to nova," Kira conceded. "The question, Admiral, is to nova *where*? We can't go back. The presence of my Recon Group was sufficiently unallowed-for on Brisingr's part to get the main strength of your fleet out, but they have more than enough firepower left to run over our combined forces.

"Falling back on Faaselesitila isn't an option. We're too far away and we need time to discharge static." She shook her head. "I'm taking my ships to Corosec, Admiral Killinger. I would prefer—I think we and our homeworld are all best served—if your fleet accompanied us and remained under the protective umbrella of *Huntress*'s fighters."

Replacing the Recon Group's fighter losses would take them a week and every replacement part they had aboard. Kira's mental math said they had *just* enough class two drives to replace their fighters.

She wasn't sure they had enough *pilots*, but that was a different problem. Both of those problems could be solved by rendezvousing with the rest of her fleet.

"Corosec?" Killinger murmured. "I...I suppose there isn't anything there now. And we do need to discharge."

"There's an ASDF dark stop that should get us there," Kira told him. "I hope your people have a more-updated version of the map than I do, but Delta-Seventy-Three is at the right point between here and there.

"And going by a dark stop *should* let us evade BKN pursuit."

"You've thought of everything, I see." His tone was not entirely complimentary.

"None of us are worth anything to our homeworld or our captured friends if we are dead," Kira told him. "We need to move swiftly, carefully and safely."

"From Corosec, we can return to Faaselesitila," Killinger said. "We have further resources there. We will be able to carry out some repairs and rearmament."

But not all. Half of the purpose of the attack on Gretchen had been to restock Killinger's spare parts. Another major battle without that replenishment would wear his fleet down that one tiny step further.

The components that required gravity wells and planet-scale industrial infrastructure to produce were generally minimized in the construction of a starship. What was left was what couldn't be avoided, which meant it was also absolutely critical. They could be jury-rigged around for a time, replaced with civilian versions or otherwise kept limping along.

"We will escort you back to Faaselesitila," Kira promised. "From there, we will have to make arrangements for future contact. I *hope* that we have proven our bona fides, Admiral, because you and I are only two of the many players that we need aligned to free our world."

"Once I have you safely to your base, my ships must move on."

She had to make contact with Michelakis—and hoped that the

remnant of the ASDF main carrier fleet was in better shape than Killinger's pirates!

"We will talk about that in Faaselesitila," Killinger told him calmly. "Once my people are safe and I have had a chance to assess what the hell happened in Shenandoah, Admiral Demirci.

"You are right that we must look to our survival first, but we must also understand who betrayed us and how. If we cannot prevent future betrayals, our entire effort may be pointless."

"And if we destroy the faith of our people in a blind witch hunt, we may render said effort *impossible*," Kira warned.

He grunted and cut the channel. Somehow, Kira didn't think he'd been convinced.

29

Kɪʀᴀ ʜᴀᴅ ʙᴇᴇɴ to Corosec more than once before leaving Apollo and had always found the system...unpleasant. In hindsight, the exploitative nature of the penal-industrial colony there had been a clear warning sign of the flaws of Apollo's oligarchic system.

In Apollo, the oligarchs were limited by the powers of a judiciary that was almost entirely independent of the Council of Principals— beholden more to the municipal governments that appointed the entry-level judges than to the government that wrote the laws they enforced.

In Corosec, there hadn't been any municipal government. The stations and mining platforms had been private property, run by corporations owned by Apollo's wealthy. They'd *started* with contracted workers and a limited penal-labor pool, but over time, the contracts had become so ironclad and punitive that the difference between prisoners and indentured contract laborers had been irrelevant.

Only the desperate had signed a ten-year contract on the Corosec platforms. The ASDF had raised concerns over the situation there, but only silence had answered them—and they'd relied on those same corporations to build the asteroid fort that had guarded the system.

But for all of its flaws and unpleasantness, there had been three million people in Corosec, and the section of the asteroid belt around Fort Mycenae and the space between Mycenae and Corosec Alpha, the solitary planet, had always been busy.

Remembering those traffic lanes and the bustle of the platforms left Kira with a deep sense of foreboding.

"This place feels like a tomb," Bueller told her, watching the wallscreen in her office with her.

"You haven't been here before, have you?" she asked.

"No, but I was briefed on the system as part of a plan to neutralize it as a supply source for the ASDF during the war," he admitted. "We concluded that Mycenae was too much for us to handle without unacceptable losses.

"Command figured we *could* take the station, but she had her own nova fighters and a protective flotilla. When the force quotient exceeded eight heavy-carrier groups to get a *fifty percent* chance of success, they wrote off the plan."

"And then later they found a way," Kira murmured. There was a ghost icon on her screen, a marker where Fort Mycenae *had* been— before a set of fusion demolition charges had torn the battle station apart.

"Everything we have seen since says it had to be my people," he agreed. "Which makes the fact that I haven't heard anything about the *people* from Corosec since disturbing as fuck."

"I can't quite bring myself to believe that even the Shadows murdered three million people as part of a test run for the attack on Apollo," Kira pointed out. "I'm no fan of Reinhardt or his personal killers, but that seems too bloody-handed even for them."

"And yet we haven't heard of *anyone*," Bueller said. "I would agree that I can't see the Shadows murdering that many people, but they sure as hell didn't let them go, either."

"There are no good possibilities, though I find myself hoping that their situation might still have improved," she said. At his surprised look, she smiled bitterly. "Whatever rumors and propaganda Brisingr spread about Corosec, they were probably more accurate than you think."

"Ah."

"In more...current concerns, what's status of the Recon Group?" Kira asked.

"Another fourteen hours to complete the static discharge. Minor damage to all three ships, but nothing we can't repair out of onboard resources before we even make it back to Faaselesitila. Wouldn't mind replacing our raw materials and parts stocks, but..."

He trailed off.

"Parts mean fall back to Samuels, but raw materials should be grabbing a convenient rock in Faaselesitila," Kira said. "Which should be straightforward enough. Something on your mind, love?"

In a private meeting like this, the dividing line between talking to her boyfriend and talking to the senior engineer of her mercenary fleet was...well, completely thrown out, if she was being honest.

"It's nothing I can put a solid finger on," he admitted. "But most of the Brisingr folks in the Recon Group are in the engineering teams." He snorted. "All seven of said engineers—and then we have a pilot and a gunnery noncom who came in via the very long way around."

Kira nodded her partial understanding. The lion's share of the personnel in Memorial Force these days were from the Syntactic Cluster, but they'd picked up a lot of assorted exiles over the years— and Konrad Bueller had brought several dozen defectors with him when he'd helped them take *Deception*.

She'd have to check her numbers to be sure, but it was likely there were more ex-BKN people in Memorial Force than there were ex-ASDF. Given how those folks had ended up under her command, she wasn't worried about their loyalty at all—but most of them were also on the older ships, not on the three *newest* capital ships.

"Thanks to us all getting the shit kicked out of us, we've spent more time talking to Killinger's engineers in the last dozen hours here in Corosec than we did in the buildup to the operation. And I get the feeling they've *definitely* noted the Brisingr accents."

"That shouldn't be a problem," Kira insisted—with a grimace that she knew revealed the truth of her feelings. "Are they causing trouble?"

"Not yet, but I can *hear* the change in tone when I have other people talk to them for me," Konrad said quietly. "Like you say, it shouldn't be a problem. But...well, there's a reason I didn't go over to Killinger's ship with you."

"He'll behave," she told her boyfriend, her tone flat. "He needs us more than we need him. Especially now that he shoved his *fingers* in a meat grinder and lost a fifth of his fleet."

"Shenandoah was...rough," he said. "And Killinger strikes me as the type of man who looks for people to blame."

"Shenandoah was a trap," Kira told him. "And I will make that point very clearly to Admiral Killinger when the time comes. Brisingr had a damn good idea of what he had and a pretty good idea of what he needed.

"So, they dangled the perfect bait out in front of him and set up a trap that should have wiped him out." She shook her head. "I'm not convinced Faaselesitila is as much a secret as he thinks. *We* sure as hell are not staying there once we've got him back to his hidey-hole."

"What happens if he crawls into that hole and doesn't come out?"

"We deal with that then," Kira said. Shaking her head, she rose to her feet. "Come on."

"Where?"

She chuckled and melodramatically leered at him.

"Will you move faster if I say *our quarters* or *our bed*?" she asked. "Because I think we both need to stop thinking about anyone else for a couple of hours."

30

IF ANYONE HAD ASKED, Kira would have told them that she expected *somebody* to challenge them before they made it back to Faaselesitila. The Kaiserreich Navy had to have an idea of the *area* of the trade-route network where Killinger was hiding, after all.

But the only warships they saw on the five-day journey from Corosec to Faaselesitila belonged to the smaller star systems of the Security Zone. Solitary destroyers and corvettes weren't going to pick a fight with the Recon Group, let alone Killinger's fleet—even if they had any reason to try.

And in the place of the Security Zone's systems, many of them former Friends of Apollo, Kira would be keeping her head down and leaving Brisingr's problems to Brisingr. Reinhardt might well have bitten off more than his nation could chew—and most of his involuntary protectorates were likely neither ready to fight him or willing to fight *for* him.

"Well, welcome back to the uninhabited shithole no one cares about," McCaig rumbled. "What's *our* next step, boss?"

"We check the system to see if our contact has left a message somewhere," she told him. "Zamorano should either have been here or be here shortly."

They were running up against the logical timeline for the Terran spy to have found Admiral Michelakis, after all. If he wasn't here or showing up soon, Kira was falling back to Samuels and making her own plans to find the ASDF carriers.

"I'm not picking up any signals or beacons," Ronaldo reported.

"Then we'll set up camp outside Five's rings," Kira ordered. "We're waiting for a courier, one who won't have the codes and vectors to travel through the minefields.

"We got them here safely. That's the end of what I promised Killinger."

Bueller snorted.

"Bets on whether he expects more?" the engineer asked.

"Not taking that," Soler replied. "I think my opinion would qualify as...*prejudicial to the command structure.*"

Soler, after all, had been a Redward Royal Fleet officer before she'd been a mercenary. Some of the habits stuck.

"Fortunately, Commander Soler, Admiral Killinger isn't *in* your command structure," Kira said with a chuckle. "Ronaldo, communicate our intentions to the Admiral. We'll remain here for...forty-eight hours.

"That'll give him a chance to decide how he wants to set up a communications channel."

KIRA RECOGNIZED the problem before it became fully manifest. She didn't fully process what was going on in time to *act*, but she saw the change in Killinger's formation as *Oceanic Trident* and four of the heaviest pirate cruisers separated from the rest of the ships.

Instead of heading into the minefields and the supposedly safe harbor amidst Faaselesitila V's moons and rings, those five ships fell back until they suddenly had Kira's Recon Group surrounded.

"Ser!"

"I see it," Kira told Soler. "Pull the cruisers up on *Huntress*'s flanks. Power to the guns; Scimitar is to start prepping fighters for scramble.

"Ronaldo, get me a damn channel."

It took a few seconds, but then a holographic image of Henry Killinger appeared in the center of Kira's bridge. He was fully dressed up in his dress uniform and what she supposed was an imposing expression as she glared down at her.

"I warned you, Demirci, that there would be consequences for the traitors who sold us out to Brisingr," he told her. "And I have gone over, again and again, the facts before me—and I am left with one glaring sore thumb of a point, standing out.

"We had never been so perfectly ambushed before. Not until we went into operations with *your* fleet—your fleet, I have learned, that is *full* of Brisingr personnel."

Status indicators were turning green in Kira's headware, marking heavy plasma turrets coming online. The five cruisers surrounding her people had an edge in firepower, but she wasn't going to go down without a fight.

"What the actual flying *fuck* are you thinking, Killinger?" Kira snapped.

"I think that you have brought a nest of vipers into my system," Killinger told her. "I don't think *you* betrayed us, Demirci. Your people fought as hard as any. You, too, were betrayed. But the vipers you have taken to your breast, these Brisingr spacers who hide among you...they have betrayed us all."

"You have no idea who the Brisingr people on my ships are," Kira warned. "You have no idea why they are with me. What they have sacrificed. There is not *one* Brisingr on my ship who would not be arrested the moment they set foot on their homeworld.

"They chose the freedom of others over their ability to go home, Admiral Killinger. That sacrifice earned them my trust. It should earn them yours—and I will defend my people, regardless of their birth world, against *any* threat."

She held Killinger's gaze, hoping he could see that she wasn't bluffing. She didn't want to fire the first shot—she *wanted* him to realize he was being an idiot and back down—but she'd be damned if she'd be intimidated into surrendering any of her crew.

"If you're so certain, give me your com logs," he demanded. "If they are as innocent as you think, then you have nothing to fear."

"I am not going to violate the privacy of everyone on my ships who has touched a communicator in the last few weeks because you have decided my people have done the impossible," Kira said. "You are as capable of doing the math as I am, Admiral. No one aboard my ships knew our destination before we left Faaselesitila.

"We *physically could not* have betrayed the mission." She shook her head at him. "And Brisingr didn't need *anyone* to. They dangled the perfect bait in front of you, Admiral, and you took it. They knew what you'd do, they watched your assets and they moved once they were sure we were in place.

"If we'd been *betrayed*, Killinger, we would have been jumped when we had *hours* left for our drives to cool down, not minutes. We were deceived, we were lured and we were ambushed.

"But I do not believe anyone, of my people or yours, betrayed us."

"That is because you are *far* too trusting, Admiral Demirci. I do not know what wonderful tricks of loyalty you have found in the Outer Rim, Admiral, but here? Here the Shadows are *everywhere*, bribing and blackmailing, sowing the seeds of betrayal wherever they go.

"*Someone* sold us out."

"No, Killinger," Kira said, softly but firmly. "No one sold you out. But your enemy knows you far better than you think. Why seek out a traitor when you already know which way the enemy is going to jump?"

He couldn't just grunt and close the channel this time, not unless he was actually prepared to start a fight. For a few eternal-seeming seconds, they held each other's gazes across the electronic link.

"Argue as you like," he finally said, "I will *not* go into battle with anyone from Brisingr on the command decks of the fleet! I *know* who your 'fleet engineer' is now, Demirci, and I will be *damned* if I hand my battle plans over to one of the Kaiser's cousins!"

"Fine," Kira told him. "We'll deal with that bridge when we come to it."

The solution in her mind was that they simply wouldn't use any battle plan of Killinger's in that case! She wasn't exactly impressed with his tactical and strategic acumen anymore.

They glared at each other for a few more seconds, then he nodded sharply and cut the channel.

"I swear, he *is* capable of politely ending a conversation," Kira muttered. "Soler? What are they doing?"

"Cruisers are swinging away from us, heading into formation with the rest of their fleet," her ops officer reported. "He appears to have been convinced."

Kira sighed heavily, watching her allies dive toward the gas giant.

"Can we discharge static from here?" she asked.

"Slowly, but yes," Bueller confirmed. "Forty hours or so."

"Good. Thank you."

"Thank *you*," her fleet engineer said. "I mean, I wasn't worried for *myself*, but I have a somewhat...*special* status. The rest of our Brisingr crew are more...uh..."

"They're not sleeping with the Admiral?" Kira suggested archly. Her direct callout of his prevaricating earned them several chuckles from the rest of her staff.

"I would be very busy if I was sleeping with all of the Brisingr crew in Memorial Force," she continued after a moment. "But as I told Killinger, every last one of your fellow Brisingrs aboard my ships *chose* to be there, knowing that Reinhardt would regard them as criminals.

"I trust you all." She chuckled softly. "More so, I'm realizing, than I trust Killinger."

"From what I have seen, we can trust Killinger to be Killinger," Soler said. "Unfortunately, it appears at least one officer of the BKN has figured out the same trick!"

31

AFTER THE STANDOFF ON ARRIVAL, every minute that the Recon Group remained in Faaselesitila made Kira's back itch. She knew that it was *unlikely* that Killinger was going to change his mind and come boiling out of the minefields to attack her ships—but she would have said it was unlikely that he'd demand she surrender her Brisingr crew, and he'd come within centimeters of doing just that.

Soler's report of "Nova contact!" early on the second day was a relief.

"Do we have an identity?" Kira demanded. "Make sure the CAP has the location."

There were enough questions about her people's safety that they had a full squadron of interceptors in space, the six planes dancing around the cruisers in a carefully calculated pattern.

Now that they had a contact, the formation shifted, with cruisers and interceptors adjusting to put themselves between the stranger and *Huntress*.

"Contact is small, sub-twenty-kilocubics," Soler told her. "McCaig's people are running her metrics."

"We have a beacon," Ronaldo reported. "Listed as *Ghost Dance*, out of Attaca."

"Ah, yes," Kira replied with a chuckle. "Let's give our friend a few minutes to confirm our beacons and come say hello."

"Ser?"

"*Baile Fantasma* means *Ghost Dance*," Kira pointed out to her coms officer. "Captain Zamorano is a bit later than I expected but entirely within the window. Once he reaches out, make sure he is clear all the way in to *Prodigal* and invited to send a shuttle over.

"If he is planning on something other than coming over to talk in person, let me know."

KIRA HADN'T NEEDED to worry. She and Konrad Bueller met Tomas Zamorano in a small meeting room just off *Prodigal*'s landing bay, well away from prying eyes. Most of her people only knew that Zamorano was an intelligence agent they were working with.

Only her most senior officers knew who the Terran agent actually was.

"Welcome aboard *Prodigal*, Captain," Kira told him as Jess Koch withdrew, leaving a tray of pastries and coffee behind. "I hope your journey was fruitful."

"Long, messy, annoying...but fruitful, yes," Zamorano confirmed, snagging one of Koch's handmade danishes.

He took several appreciative bites and sighed.

"Em Koch is, from what I understand, an even better bodyguard than she is a cook," he noted. "And *that*, to anyone who has tasted her pastries, is utterly terrifying."

"I will pass that somewhat-roundabout compliment on to her," Kira promised. "Fruitful, you say? Did you find Michelakis?"

"I did."

Kira waited patiently for a moment before gesturing for him to continue.

"Before I get into that, how have you found *Admiral* Killinger?" Zamorano asked.

"He's a pain in the ass with a cult of personality and a severe case of paranoia," Kira replied. "He'll be useful, but I'm worried he's going to take managing."

"He's an exiled warlord who has assembled a privateer fleet over half a decade that started with faking his own death. I'd be surprised if he wasn't a paranoid pain in the ass," the spy said. "That fits what I was expecting.

"Which brings me to my discussion with Admiral Michelakis."

"You actually managed to speak to her?" Kira asked.

"Via heavily anonymized radio on both of our sides," he admitted. "She doesn't know who I am, and I don't know where she was. But we traded enough key pieces to know we were at least moving against the same enemy."

"Thank gods. Is she willing to meet us?"

"She's willing to meet *you*," Zamorano said quietly. "And, most absolutely explicitly, *not* to meet Killinger."

Kira blinked.

"That is not what I expected," she admitted.

"Reading between what she did and did not say, ASDF Intelligence thinks Killinger was laying the groundwork for a coup d'état. Contacts on the ground, combined with his existing fleet..."

Zamorano shrugged.

"I don't think he could have pulled it off, not without the level of infiltration that the Shadows managed and some spectacular breaks of luck, but no ASDF officer is going to trust him, even in this mess."

"We're going to need him, too. Even if he's a pain, he's a pain with a fleet."

"That is a conversation that *you* will have to have with the good Admiral," Zamorano replied. "Your contact point is in Extraya. If I may make a suggestion?"

"Of course."

"I understand the logic in having you move around with a battle group," he told her. "But it's drawing attention. I have acquired a set of BKN identification codes for a K-Ninety-class cruiser. So long as you don't end up in the same system as *K-Ninety-Three-D*, you should pass without question even by BKN forces.

"But I only have one such set of codes," he admitted. "You'll be better served moving in just one ship."

Kira sighed, considering the situation.

"Killinger is basically out of nova fighters," she told Zamorano. "Leaving *Huntress* here to watch his back is a gesture of good faith that might help soothe some ruffled feathers. I do need someone to carry messages to Memorial Force in Samuels, too."

"I can't," Zamorano warned. "I have other places to be."

"Then I guess I only have *Prodigal* to go meet Admiral Michelakis with," she said grimly. "We'll send Ayodele back to the main fleet to coordinate a rendezvous. *Huntress* will remain here to act as support to Killinger for the moment, and you'll go wherever you go."

The spy chuckled grimly and eyed Bueller.

"I suspect that Commander Bueller is partly the cause of those ruffled feathers?" he asked. "Not through any action of your own, of course, but I cannot see Killinger's paranoia welcoming senior officers who were born on Brisingr."

"Got it in one," Bueller said grimly. "I was *planning* on going through the status of Killinger's ships with his engineers and seeing if we could use our parts to get them more up to speed, but...I'm not feeling warm and fuzzy toward the Admiral right now."

"I have a possible solution there," Zamorano told them. "Because a few of my contacts have finally pulled together enough pieces that my next stop is Brisingr itself. And I could use a native guide."

"Given what we are hearing from our prisoners and the news sources we're acquiring, I'm not sure letting Konrad, specifically, go to Brisingr is a good plan," Kira said. "He appears to be very high on Reinhardt's target lists."

"*Officially*," the spy replied. "But part of that, from what I understand, is that Reinhardt thought Commander Bueller was happily settled in the ass end of nowhere. If a man has made something of a name for himself in the Outer Rim, then it's easy to hang a pile of crimes on him without having to worry about being challenged."

"That isn't going to make him any *safer*," Kira objected. She glanced over at Konrad, who didn't *quite* roll his eyes at her. "Konrad?"

"Let's hear him out, Kira," her boyfriend said softly. "I've heard everything you've heard, but so has Captain Zamorano. So, what are you thinking?"

"First and foremost, please, Admiral, do you really think I can't get the Commander onto Brisingr undetected and unidentified?" Zamorano asked. "I am confident that our insertion into the Kaiserreich will go without attention.

"Secondly, as a member of the Alteste Families, the breadth and type of charges Reinhardt has leveled against Commander Bueller work to his advantage. I can make certain that the Commander doesn't merely 'disappear'—and Reinhardt can't justify leveling any charges less than treason if you fall into the hands of the Kaiserreich's law enforcement."

Kira could tell that meant something useful to Konrad, and she gave him a gentle glare.

"I'm not sure how exactly that *helps*," she asked acidly.

"Theoretically, as a member of the Alteste Families between the age of forty and sixty-five, I am a potential heir and, arguably, competitor to Kaiser Reinhardt," her boyfriend explained. "To prevent the Kaiser from abusing their judicial powers to limit the pool of potential successors and hence take the choice *away* from the people, any charges of significant severity have to be confirmed by the Diet.

"And any member of the Alteste Families has the right to demand that their *trial* be before a jury of the Diet itself. If Reinhardt has me arrested for treason, we can make it very public and very messy." He shook his head and eyed Zamorano. "So, if there are any small slips in whatever cloak of deception our friend here weaves, Reinhardt may be tempted to *ignore* them."

"Which helps keep us all safe," the Terran spy confirmed. "And gives us some potential weapons. I am in distant contact with several factions in the Diet, but *I* can't be the face of the discussions with them. Commander Bueller can."

"Politics are not your forte, love," Kira warned Bueller.

"Much as I dislike pandering to assholes, remaining here might put our entire cause at risk," he told her. "Killinger will not accept a senior officer on your staff being from Brisingr—and that's assuming he *doesn't* discover our relationship, which could destroy his trust of *you*."

"I am not overly concerned about Killinger," Kira replied.

"Bullshit," he snapped. "He might be an ass with a chip on his shoulder, but he still has twenty nova warships. He is a powerful player in the alliance you're constructing and the game you're playing, Kira. You need him.

"And, frankly, we should have considered that the presence of someone from Brisingr among our senior officers was going to be a problem." Bueller shrugged. "I can do a lot of good with you or with the main fleet, but doing my job requires me to be visible enough to grate on our allies.

"If I can help with the cause *without* causing friction, it might be worth it."

"I believe you can be of great value as we build alliances on Brisingr," Zamorano promised. "My involvement in building an alliance that can retake Apollo is complete, I think. I have made the connections I know I can make, and I have, I believe, used other connections to put fertile soil in place for future ties.

"The liberation of Apollo I leave in your capable hands, Admiral Demirci, along with the information on how to reach Admiral Michelakis. I must now target *my* true enemy here: the Equilibrium Institute.

"The majority of their operations in my area of authority have been coordinated through Brisingr. Where they have brought money, schematics, ships, systems...all of that has been funneled through Brisingr, because Kaiser Reinhardt is their agent.

"My task is to neutralize the Institute in my AO. Liberating Apollo is a solid first step to neutralizing Kaiser Reinhardt as an asset, but there are follow-up movements that will need to be in place on Brisingr."

The Hispanic Terran spy grinned.

"I have a plan, but it depends on what my contacts on Brisingr are willing and able to do. The Alteste Families have their own etiquette and rules—and researching etiquette and culture will never work as well as bringing a native guide."

"All right, Captain," Bueller said. "I'll be your 'native guide.'" He met Kira's gaze. "I think he's right, Kira. I can do more good laying the groundwork on Brisingr for what happens after you win in Apollo than I can aggravating your allies by my mere existence."

"I don't like sending you alone into the lion's den," Kira admitted. "But I trust your judgment."

"Thank you," Zamorano told them both. "I can't promise absolute success—if nothing else, my impression is that the Diet and the Alteste Families are going to stick with Reinhardt until something goes wrong.

"But between my contacts, myself and Commander Bueller, I think we can get a few people *looking* for him to misstep."

"And I will make certain that something goes *very* wrong for the Kaiser," Kira promised. "And very right for my homeworld."

32

"So swift to run when things go wrong, I see."

Henry Killinger was not, so far as Kira could tell, even *trying* to stay on her good side.

"You are one part of the alliance we are trying to build," she reminded him. "Admiral Michelakis has asked to meet with me, specifically—much as *you* did."

The gaunt Admiral grunted his acknowledgement and allowed a surprisingly honest grimace to cross his face.

"Apologies, Admiral Demirci," he forced out. "My people..." He sighed. "My people's morale is in rough shape. We got our asses handed to us, and while I *still* think that your Brisingr people are far from innocent, our evidence suggests that the BKN knew exactly what to bait us with."

"Your losses were more than painful, Admiral," Kira told him. "We lost less than thirty people all told on my side, and *that* hurt. Your people lost hundreds of their friends."

He nodded sharply.

"I...apologize for my manner since Shenandoah," he told her, the words still sounding like he was gritting his teeth. "It has been a long time since I lost officers and crew under my command—and I have *never* lost this many."

He'd been a nova combat group commander during the war. Kira had confirmed that he'd been promoted to command *Oceanic Trident* after that—an odd choice for a fighter officer, but given that *Trident* had been joined at the thrusters to *Victorious*, she could see the logic.

And then that entire battle group had been "lost in an accident," giving him the foundation of his rebel fleet.

He'd lost more people at Shenandoah than he had ever *commanded* before he'd talked an entire battle group into mutiny. She still wondered how he'd done that—and just *what* had happened to Rear Admiral Eden Sosa, the highly decorated officer who'd commanded Carrier Group *Victorious*.

"We did all we could," she told him. "Our enemies knew your weaknesses. Even the ones you *hadn't* told us."

"I have more concerns than mere pique over your departure, yes," he allowed. "With the loss of *Victorious* and the fighting at Shenandoah, we have less than three squadrons of nova fighters left. Two bombers. Six heavy fighters. Eight interceptors. *Trident*'s hangar holds them all and still feels half-empty."

A third empty, in truth. The battlecruiser alone should have carried four squadrons, twenty-four planes.

"I am..." He grimaced and glanced past Kira. Presumably, the office he was sitting in had some kind of display on the wall behind her hologram. "I am not as convinced of the safety of the Faaselesitila base as some of my captains."

"Minefields can be overcome. They buy you time," she told him.

"I know." He nodded. "I know. But they were a defense we could produce without consuming any resource we couldn't find in Faaselesitila. And they have been our shield for long enough that even I was falling into the trap of thinking here was invulnerable.

"But after Shenandoah..." He sighed. "I reassessed and realized we had slipped into complacency. I think I will need to move the fleet, but we will complete what repairs we can here before we move on."

"The logic follows," Kira told him. "My intent, Admiral, is to detach Captain Davidović and *Huntress* to guard your back. Davidović will still not be under your command, but we are your allies and she will help get your people to safety.

"If you let us know where you are going to take your fleet afterward, we will arrange a further rendezvous there."

"I...thank you, Admiral," Killinger said. "When you said you were leaving...I feared we would be left to our own devices."

Killinger was either hot or cold. The man didn't seem to have a *middle* setting. That was probably part of why he'd ended up a pirate warlord.

"I need both of my cruisers, but *Huntress* will stick with you for now," she promised. "In the worst case, she should be able to send a pinnace with a message."

Nova pinnaces, like nova fighters, had class two nova drives. That meant a full six-light-year jump was a thirty-plus-hour cooldown, which made the shuttles inefficient couriers. But they'd draw less attention than an actual warship.

Killinger nodded and seemed to come to a decision.

"Corosec," he told her. "Either I will take the entire fleet there, or I will send a ship to act as a relay. We won't be here for more than a few days."

He sighed.

"If they knew enough to realize we were short of fighters, it seems wise to assume they know where we're hiding. I have to take *some* time, but the sooner we have all moved on, the better we will be, I think."

Given that Kira had been hoping to convince him of just that, she certainly had no objections!

"WHAT DID I do to deserve *this*?"

Davidović's response to the orders for *Huntress* was not, Kira hoped, entirely serious. Certainly, the rest of the Recon Group's senior officers certainly took it as a joke, from the chuckles and smiles surrounding her.

"Blame Scimitar," Kira told *Huntress*'s Captain, gesturing at the other Apollon veteran pilot. "We need fighters to make sure that Killinger's fleet is still around when we need it—and Colombera is the only other person in the Recon Group who met Killinger before this!"

Though given that Abdullah Colombera had been a brand-spanking-new flight-school graduate at the time, Kira doubted that he'd made much of an impression on the then-Colonel.

"We'll watch his back," Scimitar promised in turn, a thoughtful expression on his face that had usually entailed some kind of prank in the past. "But we'll watch *Huntress*'s back first."

"Exactly," Kira told him. "We each have our own roles to play," she continued, looking at the officers around her. "Konrad is going with our intelligence-operative friend. I'm not going to say where, for everyone's safety."

Bueller nodded his acknowledgement. Kira knew she was going to miss his solid presence, both personally and professionally, but they needed that groundwork on Brisingr.

"Davidović, Colombera and *Huntress* will remain here to watch Killinger...and to watch Killinger's back."

Her careful phrasing of their mission got her more knowing chuckles. Henry Killinger was definitely on their side—but just because he was on their side didn't mean he wasn't an asshole.

"Ayodele." Kira turned to *Harbinger*'s commander. "You're heading back to Samuels and joining Zoric's battle group."

Fleet, really. The Recon Group was a carrier group, but *Fortitude* was almost a fleet on her own. Add on *Deception*—an older cruiser but still a powerful ship—and the dozen brand-new *Parakeet*-class destroyers, and Kira's second-in-command easily had most of Memorial Force's firepower to hand.

And once *Harbinger* joined that force, it would be a force that even the BKN would have to respect.

"And what about *Prodigal?*" McCaig asked.

"Your people and Ronaldo have gone through the software and files we were given?" she replied. "Because if that toy doesn't work…"

"It'll work," McCaig promised. "It might not if we weren't basically the same class. But our beacon hardware is the same. Creating a new beacon, to be *Prodigal*, was easy.

"Rigging it to fake a specific *other* beacon? That's hard. My understanding is that the software our friend gave us is up to the task. Once we leave Faaselesitila, we will be *K-Ninety-Three-D* to all and sundry."

"Which will make our task much easier," she said. "*Prodigal* is heading to Attaca. There, I will be making an appointment with a retirement-finance advisor."

"How many millions are they going to take care of for you?" McCaig asked with a chuckle.

"Hopefully, none," Kira said. "I'm not expecting to have to bribe the advisor in question to give me the instructions I need, but they're our point of contact on Paraeus.

"Now, Zamorano had a reasonably live conversation with Admiral Michelakis while discharging static at Megaras, the gas giant, which means she can't be far away," she continued. "My suspicion is that the Admiral is holding her fleet at one of the dark stops within six light-years of Attaca, using friendly assets both political and industrial in the system to provide a point of contact.

"Most likely, her call with Captain Zamorano was from a nova pinnace."

Kira smiled.

"I intend to duplicate that plan. I have, thanks to our friend Killinger, a reasonably updated map for a dark stop six light-months out from Attaca. *Prodigal* will stop there initially while I go ahead in a pinnace and see what the good Admiral has waiting for us."

"Attaca is a long damn way from here," McCaig pointed out. "More than we can make in one run."

"I know. We'll discharge in Corosec again," Kira said. "The system seemed quiet enough last time, and we'll see trouble coming before it's on top of us."

She surveyed her officers.

"Once I've made contact with Michelakis, I'm hoping to bring *Prodigal* back to Samuels to rendezvous with the fleet," she told them. "If *Prodigal* hasn't made it back to Samuels in twenty days, though, the orders Ayodele is carrying for Zoric instruct her to bring the fleet to Corosec.

"Killinger is also planning on moving to Corosec once his repairs are complete. My current expectation is that in one month, we will all be in Corosec."

She shook her head.

"The reminder of what happened there, I think, will be motivating for us all."

33

STOPPING over in Corosec was just as depressing the second time as the first. Nothing about the system had changed. There was an occasional spark of energy in the asteroid belt as *Prodigal* discharged static, but none of them had been more than long-dead systems releasing their last ergs of power.

Or, in the current case, an unexploded torpedo that was drawing more attention than the weapon honestly deserved.

"How the hell does a *torpedo* fail to detonate?" Kira asked. "It's a handful of seconds from launch to conversion."

Two Wolverine interceptors hung in space a thousand kilometers from the potentially still-dangerous weapon, while one of their non-nova-capable shuttles slowly approached the munition.

"It can happen," Soler said. "Obviously. More common with cruder weapons, though. Like, uh..."

She coughed.

"The first generation of Redward torpedoes, for example," she admitted. "We'd got past them by the time you arrived, but I saw some of the trials as a cadet. We'd have as many as a quarter fail to ignite."

"I'm surprised it's live enough to detect," Shigeru Lévêque, the shuttle pilot said on the open channel. Lévêque was a search-and-rescue pilot, mainly, which meant he had more exposure to munitions than most of the shuttle pilots available to them. "It's got to be, what, nine months old?"

"Closer to a year," Kira replied. "Forty-eight weeks. I'd have thought the security sweep would have found this."

"Remember that the BKN was part of that force," Soler noted. "Yeah, it was mostly ASDF and a few of the former Friends, but the BKN had cruisers there. It's part of the Security Zone."

"True. I suppose that made everyone a little too twitchy to see anything small."

"From what I'm seeing, there might not have been much *to* see," Lévêque reported. "The signal is still intermittent, but it's accelerating."

"Accelerating?" Kira asked.

"When we picked it up, it was pinging about once a minute. It's up to once every fifty-eight seconds now.

"Assuming that it's kept about that pace, it might have started with a once-a-month ping. Some kind of disconnected wire—which would explain why it didn't fire."

"Is there a point in us picking it up rather than vaporizing it?" Lasso, the senior of the covering pilots, asked.

Kira considered the question for a few seconds, then sighed.

"Yes," she told her people. "If we can prove that the attack at Corosec was Brisingr, those three million missing civilians become a *hell* of a stick to wave to get people onside.

"But only if you think we can disable it safely, Lévêque," she concluded.

"I've got three demo techs in the back who are all but drooling at the chance to disarm a torpedo," the shuttle pilot replied. "*They* think they can do it, and I'm not arguing with Milani's people."

The ground-forces commander wasn't even *on* the bridge, but Kira heard them chuckle on the main network.

"All right. It's down to them. If they say bail, you bail, Lévêque," she ordered. "It might be *useful* to have that torpedo, but I want my people back!"

THE SHUTTLE WAS FAR ENOUGH AWAY to make a full video channel a touch unreliable. *Prodigal* couldn't venture too far from the solitary planet without slowing down the discharge that was their main purpose in the system.

Still, Kira was able to watch the space-suited demolition technicians float around the torpedo. They presumably had *some* idea what they were doing, but Kira didn't have the background to understand what was going on.

They spent almost ten minutes just floating there, running scanners over the weapon from a few meters away, before they even touched it.

When the first panel came off the torpedo—easily half again as large as any of the techs—even Kira was holding her breath.

"Well, that tells a story, doesn't it?" one of the techs said on the channel. "Exterior panel identifiers and serial numbers, etcetera, were burned clean. Someone took a plasma torch on low and melted them away.

"But they didn't think anyone was going to be *inside* the torp. Don't have the bandwidth for live video, but I'm sending a pic."

Kira had suspected—*everyone* had suspected, after the Fall of Apollo—but it was still something else to see it. The circuit board the tech had sent her was the torpedo's "brain"—not even smart enough to qualify as an artificial stupid, since it mostly just received instructions from the launching fighter.

It was a piece of printed circuitry any system could build. No one would use someone else's circuit boards for that—and *this* particular circuit board had the flaming sword and gauntlet of the Brisingr Kaiserreich burned into its surface.

"Disarm it and bring it back aboard, people," Kira ordered quietly. "Pics are well and good, but I have the distinct feeling I'm going to have an opportunity to drop that fucking torpedo on someone's desk before this is over.

"And I want to see their face before they realize *why*."

"CONTACT—NEW CONTACT, NOVA EMERGENCE!"

Kira swallowed a curse as the report echoed across *Prodigal*'s flag bridge.

"Report," she ordered. "What are we looking at?"

"The timing cannot be worse," Soler warned. "The techs have the torpedo wide open, but if they try to back off now, it *will* detonate."

"Nova emergence is on the other side of Alpha, about a light-minute distant," McCaig passed on from the bridge. "We're scanning for beacons and details on the emergence signature now."

"They see us," Soler noted. "Contact is heading *away* from Alpha, which only makes sense if they're avoiding us."

"They might be patrolling the asteroid belt?" Kira suggested.

"Maybe, but I'd still expect them to discharge static at Alpha," her ops officer replied.

Kira nodded. She'd thought much the same, which made the contact's clear course *away* from Alpha—and the apparent Brisingr cruiser orbiting the planet—interesting to her.

"Signature puts her around twenty-five kilocubics," Soler said after a few more moments. "Heavy corvette or lighter destroyer."

"About the type of ship I'd expect to be seeing doing an occasional check-in on the system," Kira said. "Whoever she is, she isn't a threat to the demo techs, but let's keep a careful eye on her."

"Her beacon is live, but she hasn't challenged us," Ronaldo reported. "Beacon says she's the Extrayan corvette *Leviathan*. Nothing in our databases on that particular ship, but an Extrayan vessel shouldn't be an issue."

"No," Kira agreed. Extraya had been one of the wealthier Friends of Apollo, and she doubted the system was being any more cooperative to their new overlords than they had been to their old ones.

"Do we challenge *them*?" Ronaldo asked. "I'm pretty sure that's what a BKN ship would do."

"Maybe, but I feel no need to live down to BKN doctrine," Kira replied. She studied *Leviathan*'s icon. "Even if *Leviathan*'s CO decides we're suspicious, she's not going to *do* anything about it. We're still a heavy cruiser and she's still a corvette.

"Tell our techs not to worry about the stranger," she continued. "I still want that torpedo and I still want them back intact. No rushing."

"What do we do if *Leviathan* does challenge us?" Soler asked as Ronaldo turned his attention back to the coms.

"Depending on what she says? Probably ignore her," Kira admitted. "She's not going to pick a fight. Right now, she's already decided to keep her distance and do her patrol before discharging so as to avoid us.

"So long as she doesn't do anything to threaten us or the demo team, I see no reason to bother her in turn."

EVERYONE ABOARD *PRODIGAL* breathed a shared sigh of relief when the demolition team confirmed they'd safely disarmed the torpedo. Now split into three pieces—initiator, payload and chassis— the torpedo was loaded onto Lévêque's shuttle.

"Our new friend has noticed the shuttle," Soler reported. "She's trying to be subtle about it, but she's definitely keeping a clear line of sight to the nova fighters and the shuttle."

"I would too," Kira said. "How long until everyone's back aboard?"

"A bit over two hours," Soler replied. "I mean, Lasso and Ricochet's nova fighters could be back right now, but that would leave Lévêque and our new bit of evidence hanging on their own."

"And while I doubt *Leviathan* would be so brave or so foolish as to try to steal our shuttle while we're *right here*, why expose our people we don't have to?" Kira agreed. "Time to finish discharging static?"

"Thirty minutes. We'll be ready to leave well before Lévêque is back."

"Good. Good." Kira smiled. "I'll want our techs to go over that torpedo in fine detail. Match her up against the old-light data we have from Zamorano of the attack. I have a pretty good idea of what went down here, at least in terms of the battle, but having an example of the weapons in play can't hurt."

"Wasn't our old-light scan data from Extraya?" Soler murmured.

"Attaca," Kira corrected. "Our next stop." She shook her head. "It won't be our last. There are too many conversations we need to have before we're ready."

34

AFTER WORKING with the commando for years now, Kira was completely unsurprised to find Milani waiting for her in the nova pinnace. She shook her head at her officer as the holographic red dragon flickered across their armor, a childish grin on the fantastic creature's face.

"You *are* on the passenger list," she pointed out. "We weren't going to leave without you or Jess."

Two more commandos trooped into the shuttle as she was speaking, one of them hauling a black box that she recognized from a trip to Bennet that had gone very sideways.

"Why, exactly, are we bringing an HVM?" she asked.

"Because we needed it once, and that means I feel it's a good idea going forward," Milani replied. "Blaster rifles, power armor, an HVM. Most of my people have limited soldier boosts and need the gear."

"That's part of what makes people like me effective," Koch said, the Redward-born bodyguard following the commandos aboard. "I mean, who expects the hundred-and-sixty-centimeter blonde in a dress to pack more muscle than most two-meter thugs in armor?"

"Anyone with a brain who watches you move," Milani told her.

Kira had to agree with that assessment—Koch wasn't exactly *one of a set*, per se, but she'd been trained and augmented with the personal bodyguards of the Queen of Redward. If Kira understood it correctly, she had been intended to *be* one of Queen Sonia's bodyguards, until Sonia had asked for a volunteer to enter Kira's service.

She'd never asked her steward slash bodyguard *why* the younger woman had decided to make guarding Kira her life, but she appreciated the woman's presence.

And as Milani had said, *she* wasn't surprised to realize how augmented and trained Jess Koch was. Even outside of armor—today in a frilly pink sundress that was approximately four times as feminine as *Kira* would ever wear—the bodyguard moved like a stalking panther.

"I should work on that, then," Koch murmured. "Spend some time watching a couple of your more drunken troopers wandering the ship's halls."

"Sadly, while my drunkards might act like stoned aurochs, they still move like someone trained them to be walking killing machines," Milani noted. "That someone being *me*, in case you were wondering."

"Is everyone aboard?" Kira asked. "Or am I showing up to my theoretically civilian appointment with an entire platoon of armor?"

"Just the four of us," Milani replied.

"You realize you are far too senior to be watching my back directly, yes?" she asked them.

"Serves two purposes, ser," the dragon-armored mercenary replied. "One, I make absolutely certain that the woman who signs the paychecks can still sign the paychecks. Two, it means I am generally fully informed of what you're planning, where you're going and what you're going to ask us to do next.

"I may not have the level of soldier boosts that Em Koch does, but I have significantly more headware than most. I can do my job from anywhere close enough to establish an encrypted radio link to the ship."

"And we've all made sure we have subordinates who can fill in for us," Kira noted. "Including on the paycheck-signing, you know."

Milani chuckled and the dragon made a rude gesture.

"And in Marjukka Altamura, I hung an anchor around Captain Zoric's neck that's almost as clingy as I am," they observed. "*Fortitude* has the largest chunk of our people and needed a good officer. Commander Altamura *also* knows that her job is to keep Zoric alive while I bounce between ships, keeping *you* alive and staying on top of our plans."

"Right." Kira chuckled. "You assume, Milani, that *I* know what our plans are."

"I don't, ser. That's why I live in your back pocket."

PARAEUS WAS AN ABSOLUTELY beautiful and notably *chilly* planet. Named for the port city of ancient Athens—but with the same slight romanization adjustment as the system itself—there was a stark contrast between its immense, pure-white icecaps and the brilliant green of an aggressive plant ecosystem determined to drink up every scrap of sunlight and water it could.

The planet's relatively minor inclination meant that the unfrozen belt of the planet stayed relatively constant. With an average planetwide temperature below freezing, though, even the "habitable zone" was a chilly place, rarely above the low teens Celsius.

The local plant life had adapted to their situation with some of the highest-efficiency and greenest chlorophyll equivalents Kira had ever encountered. That, genetically mixed with Terran plant stocks, had also created some of the most *fascinating* beers and breads she'd ever consumed.

From Koch's expression as they finished their lunch in the pub

Kira had picked, the Redward native found *fascinating* to mean something other than *tasty*.

"From Em Koch's expression, I see that my decision to stick to the protein mix I brought with me was a wise one," Milani murmured.

Paraeus's second-largest city, the sarcastically named Gloomhaven, had fewer restrictions on armor and firearms than most cities of ten million–plus people Kira had seen. Milani and the two mercenary commandos were actually wearing full power armor, though the junior troopers had taken their helmets off to eat.

Koch was still wearing the frilly sundress but had added thermal tights and a long crimson faux leather jacket that Kira suspected contained the same kind of anti-blaster armor as her own bomber jacket.

And despite her grimace of displeasure at the single beer she'd been drinking, Koch had seated herself to watch the entrance to the pub.

"Our destination is in the office across the street," Kira told her escorts as she took another sip of her beer. *She*, at least, liked Paraeus's beer. "I booked an appointment as the pilot was bringing us into the shuttleport.

"Everything is aboveboard and clean so far."

"I'm honestly surprised we're not getting more hassle than we are," Milani murmured. "Just because the laws say we can move around in power armor doesn't always mean that people don't have a problem with it."

"Look up the Gloomhaven wolverine," Kira suggested. "Also, the Gloomhaven orc-pig, the Gloomhaven owlbear, and the Gloomhaven roc."

There was a silence as her people ran through the notes on those four particularly difficult-to-eradicate, capable-of-eating-humans local predator and omnivore species.

"Why did anyone *ever* settle here?" Milani finally asked.

"Elevated region, minimal cloud cover, four hundred and

seventy-five out of four hundred-eighty days sunshine a year," Kira reeled off. "You saw the solar farms on the way in. Plus, while a few interesting critters were first IDed around Gloomhaven, the wildlife around most of the planet is pretty similar."

"So, everywhere on this planet is going to make me want antiair-craft defenses?" Koch asked.

"I mean, they're pretty good at keeping the rocs out of the cities," Kira told her. "And there's generally at least one Attacan Ranger aircraft watching over most cities. Gloomhaven is almost certainly perfectly safe, but cultural habits born of smaller centers still hold true.

"So, armor and weapons are not as rare as they would be other-wise." She shrugged. "I am *reasonably* sure the people who were telling me about orc-pig problems in cities were exaggerating."

Before the war with Brisingr, Kira had served on a cruiser posted on "diplomatic duty" in the Attaca System. She'd heard a *lot* of stories about orc-pigs.

"I'd be more worried about the *two-hundred-kilo bird of prey* than the ground-feeding omnivore, I have to admit," Milani admitted. "But that might be foolish of me."

"Every roc on the planet is tagged and tracked, I think," Kira replied. "Orc-pigs, on the other hand, are extreme omnivores and starting hunting for their adult ranges when they're roughly the size of a medium dog.

"As it was explained to me, they get into cities, looking for garbage, and are small enough to avoid notice until they become full-size boars and sows." She shrugged. "And then you have a colony of three-hundred-kilo extreme omnivores who have replaced any fight-or-flight instinct with kill-then-eat instincts."

Everyone processed that—and were likely looking at the informa-tion on wolverines—best described as "angry carnivorous badger meets living buzz saw"—and owlbears—best described as "flightless bird meets living buzz saw."

Living buzz saw occurred a bunch in the description of larger animal life from Attaca.

"What an interesting planet," Koch finally concluded. "When are we leaving?"

"Meeting is in twenty minutes. Hopefully, nothing will eat us before we get to it."

35

Five-M Personal Finance Consulting was a small and unimpressive office with an extraordinarily impressive view. On the sixtieth floor of an office tower on the higher end of the plateau holding Gloomhaven's downtown district, it looked to the north, away from the rest of the office and residence towers, and out over the highlands surrounding the city.

Large swathes of the moors were now marked with a checkerboard pattern of open space and elevated solar-panel farms, but the open spaces still showed the brilliant green of Paraeus's plant life— and where the moors rolled up to the mountains in the distance, the solar panels gave way to a towering arboreal forest.

The *office* might not have been much, but the company was making a point about what did and *didn't* have value.

It fit with the schema that there was a human receptionist, a pale and soft-voiced young man who served them excellent espresso as he introduced himself.

"I am Alan Millicent," he told them. "I'm not one of the five Ms— but my uncle is. You're on my list, Admiral Demirci, but we didn't realize you were bringing companions..."

"If you know roughly who I am, you can imagine that I don't travel unescorted as a rule," Kira replied. "We can leave...*some* of my escort out here if necessary."

"Absolutely not," Millicent said cheerfully. "I've already checked with Em Michelakis and the Grand Conference Room is available, so we've moved the meeting from Em Michelakis's personal office to the conference room. It will have plenty of space for you all.

"I believe we have a power connection that should suffice to recharge the armor, if you wish?"

"That won't be necessary," Kira told him. It was entirely possible, if unusual, that the office tower could support the charging systems for her people's powered armor. What wasn't possible was that Milani would allow their people to plug in to a power source they didn't fully control.

"Of course." Millicent paused, tilting his head to listen to a voice no one else could hear. "Em Michelakis is ready for you. If you will follow me?"

"I'm afraid my appointment didn't say who I would be meeting," Kira noted as she laid the shined aluminum espresso cup down on the young man's desk.

"Oh, our mistake," the receptionist said breezily—in a manner that told Kira that it hadn't been a mistake at all. "Your appointment is with Em Stephanos Michelakis. I hope that's acceptable?"

Kira smiled.

"That will be just fine," she told the youth.

Because if Em Stephanos Michelakis wasn't related to Admiral Fevronia Michelakis, however distantly, she'd eat her armored sheep-skin jacket.

STEPHANOS MICHELAKIS WAS a tall man with dark features and a broad, white-toothed smile. He gestured them all into the

Grand Conference Room—a space whose only claim to grandness *was* its name.

It was large enough for Michelakis, Kira, her escorts and Millicent and not much more. No one was particularly squeezed or crowded, but it was clear that any larger number of occupants would have been a real issue.

"Welcome to Five-M Financial Consulting, Em Demirci," Michelakis greeted her as he gestured everyone to seats. "Em Millicent will be joining us, if that's all right? His role here is as much an apprenticeship as it is administration and greetings."

"That depends on which part of your business he's apprenticing in," Kira noted calmly. "And, I suppose, how secure this room is."

"Straight to the chase, I see." The consultant was still smiling as he gestured the door closed behind them. "If this room is *not* secure, there are several very expensive consultants and a security firm that will be in very real trouble.

"I am delighted if your Em Milani or Em Koch wish to double-check the security."

Kira hadn't introduced *any* of her escorts, which told her that Michelakis was quite well informed.

"Jess, Milani," she said quietly. Both of those worthies stood and walked careful circuits of the room. Neither did anything so obtrusive as to pull out a sensor. Milani's were concealed in their armor—and Koch's were a series of implants positioned throughout her body.

"Clear," Koch declared. Milani nodded their confirmation.

"Good to hear," Michelakis said, leaning back in his chair. "And to answer your question, Admiral, Alan is apprenticing in the *full* scope of Five-M's operations. Both in terms of investment and political activity.

"While our firm is rarely *very* active, we take certain interests and, with the permission of our investors, use the influence available to us through our assets under management to pursue certain goals."

He shrugged and gestured out the window.

"This is, admittedly, mostly supporting environmental protections for Paraeus's native wildlife and forests in normal times. But these are not normal times, and some of the same skills apply."

"I would hope that environmental activism would be safer than this," Kira said.

"This is Paraeus, Admiral Demirci," Michelakis said grimly. "Only thirty-two percent of the planet's surface is inhabitable by human beings, and there are almost three billion people here.

"The conflict over preservation of our extraordinary ecosystem versus making space for our citizens is of long standing and of some...*fire*, let us say. Not helped, of course, by just how energetic some of said ecosystem can become."

"Hard to sell people on preserving orc-pigs?" Milani suggested.

"They're one of the harder sells on preservation, yes," Michelakis agreed. "But the Attacan Rangers know their job and have management programs in place. They are professionals—but professionals sometimes require political support to keep being able to do their jobs."

"Like what's left of the ASDF, I take it?" Kira asked.

"More complicated, of course," the consultant told her. "You had the right codes and connections to get this meeting, and I know who you are. That helps. But just being *related* to Admiral Michelakis is risky right now."

"And yet you're in communication with her and were given to me as my point of contact."

"I am and I was. Yours is a name to conjure with, Admiral Demirci. These are strange times with dark tidings, but the news from the Syntactic Cluster has been a ray of hope for those who want *everyone* to prosper.

"And it is news, Admiral, that your name has been woven through—one of Apollo's exiled daughters, making a name for herself forging safe worlds in the Outer Rim."

"We do what we can," Kira said quietly. "And, given what Memorial Force *is*, what we're paid to. Little of the credit belongs to me, in truth."

"Perhaps not, but here? Where, one way or another, Apollo's reputation and culture has great influence? Here, it is your name that those stories carry."

"I suppose I can't complain too loudly," she admitted. "Especially if it opens the doors I need to pass through. I have to speak to Admiral Michelakis."

Stephanos Michelakis spread his hands.

"Why?" he asked. "I'm not sure what value the last Admiral of a fallen state has to you."

She studied him suspiciously.

"Do you think I'm here to convince the Admiral to come back to the Rim with me?" she asked. "To turn the last carriers of the ASDF into a new mercenary fleet, one to win entire wars on its own? Even taking Mid Rim carriers to the Outer Rim, a dozen of them will not suffice to conquer star systems, though they could paralyze an entire sector's worth of traffic."

"In honesty, Admiral, I have no idea what you want with my cousin," Michelakis told her. "I am not sure what *she* wants with you—or with anything. I don't know her as well as I would like, but I suspect that even she doesn't know what to do with herself or the fleet that has followed her.

"The ties of blood keep me in contact with her, acting as a point of contact for you and others. The chain of duty binds her—but the question is: duty to what?"

He met Kira's gaze.

"I don't believe you are intentionally here to lead Fevronia into a trap," he conceded. "But I wonder if you might do so by accident. So, tell me, Admiral Kira Demirci. I can pass on a message with ease, but if you want me to put you in direct contact with my cousin, I have to know *why*."

"Because..." Kira exhaled a sigh, considering how transparent she should be with this man. There was very little he could do to *harm* her cause, even if he handed everything she said over to the Shadows.

If he was going to hand *her* over to the Shadows, she was already in trouble. The worst thing that Stephanos Michelakis could do to her was refuse to connect her to his cousin.

"Because Reinhardt did something few others have done in all of history, but he overextended Brisingr's resources to do it," she told him. "I am pulling together the loose strings around the edges of Brisingr's 'Security Zone,' and I am building an alliance to retake my homeworld.

"But if I am to succeed, I need two things, Em Michelakis: I need to know *exactly* what happened the day Apollo fell—and I need every damn warship and carrier that's left of the ASDF.

"Fevronia Michelakis can give me both of those things."

The Grand Conference Room was silent for a good ten seconds, then Michelakis rose to his feet and crossed to the window, looking out over the highland moors with their scattered greenery and solar panels.

"I believe you are correct," he finally said, still facing away from her. "She can deliver you both of those things. I don't know if that will be enough. It's not my skillset. All I have truly done, so far, is arrange supplies for my cousin's fleet.

"I am afraid, Admiral Demirci, of the war to come if my cousin thinks she can win. She has enough warships left to get a lot of people killed, but I don't know enough to know if she can truly fight the Kaiserreich."

Kira waited in silence, then smiled as a file-transfer request appeared in her headware.

"Go to these coordinates," the consultant told her. "*Not* in a warship. I imagine you have one, but none have entered orbit that could have carried you. I hope you have some level of discretion in play here.

"You will be met."

"Thank you, Em Michelakis."

"Don't thank me. *End* this fucking Security Zone. Apollo was bad enough for Attaca, but the burden of being a 'Friend' could be borne. The costs Brisingr imposes... I am a financial analyst, first and foremost, Admiral.

"Brisingr's tariffs and fees will slow every economy in the sector—and the money flowing into Brisingr won't be enough to speed *their* economy to a level that would offset it. This level of trade tolls will slow the entire *Sector's* path to prosperity—in exchange for making a few hundred people on Brisingr richer and more powerful.

"Even the Kaiserreich will not benefit in the end from the regime they have created."

36

THE COORDINATES they were given weren't where Kira was expecting. By and large, most traffic, industry and population in a star system focused on three areas: the habitable planet, the most profitably harvested asteroid belt and the gas giant most easily used for static discharge.

The gas giant Megaras was a good six billion kilometers out from the Attaca Belt and over seven billion from Paraeus. Six light-hours was distant enough that even Harrington coils couldn't get ships out to the gas giant in less than days, which meant a lot of even the in-system traffic used nova drives.

Not that anyone would have been surprised by a nova pinnace making a jump out to the gas giant if it was closer in. The whole *point* of something like their pinnace was to travel swiftly around a solar system.

Their coordinates didn't take them to Megaras, though. The cluster of loose debris they emerged "above" orbited sixty degrees behind the massive gas giant, at the trailing Lagrange point. Like the Trojans of Earth's Jupiter, the cluster forever followed Megaras in its orbit, drawn by the points of gravitational stability between the gas giant and its star.

In systems where the gas giants were closer in, trojan clusters were sometimes nearly as heavily exploited as inner asteroid belts. Megaras's two clusters, after all, contained over two-thirds the mass of the Attaca Belt between them.

But the trip to the Attaca Belt from Paraeus with Harrington coils would be a day or so, versus closer to a week to get out to the Megaran Trojans.

"We're not *entirely* alone out here," the pilot told them. "If you look there"—the woman highlighted an energy signature on one of the larger asteroids—"that looks like a listening and patrol base for the Attacan Fleet."

"Probably a nova or sub-fighter squadron, plus logistics and minor repair support for a monitor patrol," Kira guessed. "I imagine there's some civilian traffic out here, too. Just enough to make this a terrible place for Michelakis to hide her fleet."

"If the Attacans are supporting her, it could be done," Milani said. "But I wasn't under the impression that the Attacans liked your old homeworld."

"Attacans were fine with Apollo right up until the Council of Principals sold them out and Brisingr made them scrap two basically complete hundred-and-thirty-kilocubic battle carriers," Kira said grimly. "The government and military are likely to put the blame on the Principals, not on my people.

"But, no, I don't think that—"

"Nova emergence!"

There might have been someone hiding in the asteroid cluster. The listening post might have had a deal to warn the remnant ASDF fleet if anyone showed up. Kira didn't know *how* the contact had known when to arrive—but they'd put the pinnace exactly where they'd been told to.

And now a carrier emerged from nova, her flight deck wide open, and scooped up the pinnace like a whale swallowing krill.

"Activate station-keeping!" Kira snapped. The pilot had already beaten her to it, the nova pinnace's systems working to hold the small craft steady in the middle of a large hangar.

"Nova pinnace, this is Deck Control," a sardonic voice greeted them over the radio. "We have the ball. Surrender flight control."

"Not much choice," Kira murmured. "Give them the link, Harriet."

The pilot nodded, exhaling a sigh as she activated the commands to give the carrier deck control of the shuttle's systems.

"There are politer ways to do this," she muttered.

"I agree," Kira said, then turned to escorts. "Lock and load, Milani. Koch. Let's leave the HVM behind, though."

"Sidearms and armor," Milani told their people. "Sound right, Admiral? Show respect by not bringing big guns; show concern by arriving in full armor."

"Sounds right," she agreed. She felt the pinnace touch down on the deck, a soft vibration shivering through the vessel.

"Did anyone get a look at what the *hell* just scooped us up?" she finally asked.

AFTER ABOUT A MINUTE OF SILENCE, a clear deck party assembled around the nova pinnace, and Kira led her party down the ramp. She was surprised to hear an Apollon bosun's panpipes trill through the deck, in the very specific and formal sequence of notes acknowledging an Admiral's arrival.

"Memorial Force, arriving!"

A shuttle-load of memories came crashing in on Kira as she stepped forward and returned the salute of the crisply turned-out Captain (Senior Grade) standing at the head of the deck party.

"Welcome aboard *Medusa*, Admiral Demirci," the officer told her. His duty identification beacon was active, information flowing into Kira's headware with the ease of long practice and good system architecture.

Captain (SG) Behar Prifti was fifty-nine years old, a native of the Prásinoi Lófoi District on the opposite side of Apollo from where Kira had grown up. She hadn't known him during the war, though, so she didn't have any information, and Prifti's was quite limited. He'd *intentionally* added his district of birth to assure her he was Apollon.

"Thank you for the welcome, Captain Prifti, though I will admit that the, ah, *method* of our arrival was a shock."

"The extent of our informal agreement with the Attacan Fleet is that so long as we don't cause trouble, they don't see us," Prifti noted. "While there is a hard minimum of how short a time period we can be here, we wanted to stick to that minimum."

As the Captain was speaking, a ten-minute timer Kira had started almost automatically ticked the zero—and the gentle sensation of a nova rippled through the carrier's flight deck.

"*Medusa* is merely your taxi today, Admiral," he noted. "But, bluntly, I wanted to avoid conversation that might cause delays. By scooping you up, we are asking forgiveness—but we did not have time to ask permission."

"Where am I being taxied to, if I may ask?" Kira said drily. "I understand the logic, even if my nerves may take some time to recover."

Prifti chuckled.

"We're at a dark stop a...*number* of light-years from Attaca," he told her. "*Medusa* is approaching the main fleet." He coughed delicately. "We would prefer to transship you to *Salaminia* on one of our own shuttles, ser. You are welcome to bring your escorts, of course, but the Admiral wishes to maintain our operational security until she has been able to speak with you in person."

"Captain, my options are limited," Kira pointed out with a chuckle. *Medusa* wasn't even a fleet carrier, but at ninety kilocubics, the *Mythology*-class carriers had formed a solid back line during the war.

Her pinnace and four protectors weren't going to stand up to the carrier's arms and Hoplites.

"I am here to meet with Fevronia Michelakis," she concluded. "I am prepared, within a flexible definition of reason, to accommodate her requirements for that.

"So long as I meet her."

"We're about twenty-five minutes out," Prifti told her. "I have a pilot and shuttle standing by to take you over to the flagship then, but the windows will be blacked out."

"That is fine, Captain," Kira repeated. "Assuming that the Admiral is waiting for me?"

"With bated breath, I suspect, Admiral Demirci. You may be the first sign of hope the Last Fleet has seen in six months."

37

THOUGH KIRA HAD NEVER ACTUALLY SEEN a *Trireme*-class carrier in person, she still didn't need the sensors and windows to be shared with her on approach to *Salaminia*. The first ships in Apollon service to be built with a twelve-kilocubic 12X class one nova drive, their capabilities and lines had been the talk of the fleet for the last months of the war.

Salaminia would be a squashed cylinder, thirty-five meters wide and twenty-two high, almost a quarter of a kilometer long. Her central core would consist of the open space for her flight deck, much of which would be taken up with her twenty-four six-ship nova-fighter squadrons.

If she'd been armed exactly as per the designs Kira had seen, she had six heavy plasma cannon in solo turrets along both her dorsal and ventral keels, each matched with a lighter anti-fighter cannon, and then another nine light guns along each "broadside."

Her plasma cannon were a distinctly secondary weapon system, of course, with her main killing power resting in her fighter wings and bombers.

A killing power that Kira realized was severely lacking within *seconds* of walking down the ramp of the sublight shuttle that had carried her to Michelakis's flagship.

Deck Control had parked the shuttlecraft off to one side, in a sheltered landing area meant for exactly that purpose, where she had a minimal view of the stacked storage bays that should have held *Salaminia*'s starfighters.

Even as the panpipes were once again playing the proper salute to an Apollon Admiral—a courtesy Kira had never expected and hence never noticed Killinger denying her—she was counting the cubicles she could see.

Less than three squadrons' worth of fighter bays were visible—fifteen of the cubicles. Six held Hoplite interceptors. The other nine were empty.

Kira was still processing that as she drew up sharply in front of the tall and graying woman in the stark white Admiral's uniform of the Apollo System Defense Force. Where even *Kira* had felt odd at seeing Killinger wearing the star, sabers and four flowers of an ASDF Fleet Admiral, there was no question in her mind that Michelakis deserved the same insignia.

"Admiral Demirci," the ASDF Admiral greeted her, returning Kira's automatic salute. "Welcome home."

That...had not been how Kira had expected the conversation to begin, and the rush of emotion at those words, coming from an officer she knew by reputation if not in person, surprised her. She had to pause and take a long, deep breath.

"Thank you, Admiral Michelakis," she finally said. "Commodore Heller always spoke well of you. I regret that he isn't with us today."

"I'd like to think that James would have stopped this mess in its tracks before it got this bad," Michelakis replied. "But then, from what I now understand, that's part of why he is no longer with us."

"Can we speak in private, Admiral?" Kira asked, glancing around the shuttle bay. "I will need to bring at least one of my people."

"Bring two," the Admiral said with a chuckle. "I'm bringing my chief of staff and Flag Captain."

SALAMINIA HAD BEEN BUILT to impress. Only six of the *Trireme* class had been completed before the Fall of Apollo, and they were a full twelve thousand cubic meters larger than the biggest ships the BKN had constructed.

While Kira suspected that Apollo's occupiers had already sent enough information back to their home system to update the BKN's next wave of construction, for now *Salaminia* was one of the largest nova ships in the Apollo-Brisingr Sector.

There was space for a private meeting room just off of the flight deck, though Kira's practiced eye could see where the bulkheads would move to open the space up. *Victorious* had been built with the same system: an array of spaces that could be combined into multiple sizes, ranging from intimate meeting rooms like this to fighter-squadron briefing spaces all the way up to a full-scale ballroom for major diplomatic functions.

But she could tell there was a reason they were in the closest space Michelakis could find and that there'd been some planning put into place to make sure she didn't see the state of most of the flight deck.

Kira waited quietly until everyone had been seated—her, Milani and Koch on one side of the table, Michelakis and two gentlemen of Kira's own age. Presumably, Commodore Aldéric Lister was the chief of staff and Captain (Senior Grade) Chand MacCàba was *Salaminia*'s Captain.

As the Admiral was about to speak, though, Kira smiled and opened with her own question.

"So, tell me, Admiral, how bad is your fighter shortage?"

The room was dead silent for several seconds, and the graying Admiral chuckled sadly.

"Forgive us our attempt at concealing our weakness, Admiral Demirci," she told Kira. "Our situation, as you can imagine, is difficult. We only know each other by reputation and, well, you went to Killinger first.

"That's not exactly a recommendation."

"I'd guessed," Kira said mildly. "But the truth is that the individual who arranged our contacts was already in touch with Killinger. It was easier to establish the connection with him and, well, if we are to succeed, we will need him."

"Succeed at what, Admiral Demirci?" Commodore Lister asked bluntly. "The Last Fleet are not yet prepared to become pirates like Killinger. We may not have struck great victories, but we are still at war with Brisingr."

"Good," Kira replied. "Because I didn't come all the way home to throw a damn party, Commodore. Let's start with the question, though: how bad is your fighter shortage?"

"I am not yet prepared to hand over the full details of my force, Admiral Demirci," Michelakis said calmly. "But you have judged correctly. We have spent most of the months since our retreat repairing our damages and attempting to source class two nova drives.

"The vast majority of Home Fleet's fighters and escorts were lost, either before we conceded the battle or in covering the carriers' retreat."

"And then we discovered that someone had fucked us," MacCàba growled. He had a gravelly voice that lent itself quite well to growling —something Kira suspected had been a boon to his career.

"Beyond everything else that had happened?" Kira asked.

"Seventy-two percent of the stored transition-coil units for our spare class two drives were either missing or defective," Michelakis said flatly. "Stolen, sold, made too cheaply..."

She shook her head.

"*Pilots* should have been our problem, not fighters. *Salaminia*, for example, was issued one hundred and twenty spare class two drives. We successfully retrieved twenty-one fighters—not all ours, given the fate of most of Home Fleet—and then discovered that ninety-one of our spare drive units were either garbage or had literally been replaced with rocks."

The math was easy enough. Assuming *Salaminia* hadn't found any more fighters or sent fighters over to the other carriers, that meant she was carrying fifty nova fighters. Barely more than a third of her designed flight group.

"How?" Kira asked.

"I don't know if the answer to that will ever be truly known," MacCàba said. "I have Chiefs who swear, on their mother's honor, that they'd checked every coil, exactly on schedule—which would have had every coil in the ship inspected over the previous six months.

"But aboard *my* ship, with Chiefs I would trust *without question*, we were short ninety-one class two nova drives."

"Whether it was corruption or another attack by the Shadows is, I suppose, irrelevant now," Michelakis observed.

"Unless there remain Shadow operatives aboard your ships," Kira countered. "You say you don't trust me, but I am wondering whether I can trust you."

"There may be rot on our ships," Michelakis conceded. "I have to admit that possibility. I would suspect, though, that any agents on my ships would have shown themselves by now—or found a way to betray our location to the BKN.

"I have not, after all, kept my people locked up like prisoners. About fifteen percent of our people have left. The rest...look to our command staff for some kind of hope."

"And do you have a plan for that hope?" Kira asked.

"Again, Admiral Demirci, we find ourselves at the impasse of trust," the older Admiral told her. "I know you by reputation, and that reputation is solid. I knew Heller and Moranis and others I know *would* have trusted you.

"But they are all dead, and you have spent half a decade running around the Outer Rim as a mercenary. So, I have no idea why you've come home now, and I fear what you want from us."

"All right." Kira exhaled a sigh and marshaled her thoughts and purposes. "I have a one-hundred-and-fifty-kilocubic Crest-built supercarrier, two ninety-five-kilocubic and one ninety-six-kilocubic Brisingr-built cruisers, a seventy-kilocubic Redward-built light carrier, and a dozen Redward-built destroyers.

"All of my ships are carrying the latest generation of starfighters from the Navy of the Royal Crest—thanks to fabricator schematics we acquired along with the carrier."

That was the kind of information she was trying to *get* out of Michelakis, but sometimes the only way to get trust was to extend it.

"I am in communication with a loose collection of former diplomats and trade attachés from the Apollo diplomatic service, who have coordinated the financial assets made available to their offices to support the operating costs of my mercenary fleet—a fleet currently effectively under a costs-only contract with said exiles.

"We have the committed support of the Samuels System, which is in a state of war with Brisingr thanks to the Kaiser's meddling in their conflict with Colossus. They have offered safe harbor to any Apollon force still in being."

She met Michelakis's gaze and smiled.

"*I*, Admiral Michelakis, am here to gather allies and assemble a combined fleet with which to retake Apollo from Brisingr. Admiral Killinger and his ships are committed. Memorial Force is committed.

"I need intelligence on what exactly Brisingr *did* to take the system in the first place. I am hoping to source intelligence on their current positions and forces. And I am hoping that you, Admiral Michelakis, will join in this undertaking."

There was a long silence, then Commodore Lister chuckled.

"She's got your number, ser," he said aloud. "I don't know if either of you can pull this off, but you're both definitely thinking in the same direction."

"So we are," Michelakis confirmed. "You'll forgive me, Admiral Demirci, for wondering if that is too much of a coincidence. I have my suspicions about the weaknesses of Brisingr's position in Apollo, but I lack the strength with my current fleet to...close the deal, let us say."

"I've come a long damn way, Admiral Michelakis, to shove a foot up Kaiser Reinhardt's ass," Kira told the Apollon officers. "Left to my own devices, I probably wouldn't have come as far as Samuels—but Reinhardt and certain allies of his arranged for Samuels to hire us.

"They tried to lure my entire fleet into an ambush. They started a goddamn *war* between Samuels and Colossus. Killed thousands. All to try to kill me."

Kira smiled thinly.

"Kaiser Reinhardt apparently sees me as a very dangerous enemy. I intend to prove him oh-so-very correct in that belief."

Michelakis sighed, then nodded.

"Brief her, Lister," she ordered, leaning back in her chair.

There was a momentary hesitation, and then a three-dimensional fleet-status display appeared in the middle of the room.

"The Last Fleet is not as powerful as I imagine any of us would like," Lister said quietly. "I imagine you are not familiar with Home Fleet's final strength?"

"No," Kira conceded, her gaze flickering across the holographic ships and counting.

"Home Fleet had eighteen fleet carriers of assorted classes and twenty-two lighter carriers," Lister told her. "This was supported by twenty-four battlecruisers of assorted classes, thirty cruisers of assorted classes, and eighty destroyers. There were also the fortresses, monitors, nova gunships and corvettes of the Apollo Defense Command.

"The core of the fleet was the six *Trireme*-class ships like *Salaminia*, with Admiral Serkan Küçük flying his flag aboard *Olympias*."

Kira's count only had four of the big supercarriers and, well, Admiral Küçük wasn't in command there.

"*Olympias* was destroyed before the battle even truly started," Lister continued. "Of the sixty-four primary fortresses of Apollo

Defense Command, the battle opened with the destruction of twenty-eight. Twenty-three of the remainder turned their guns on the mobile vessels of ADC and Home Fleet.

"Only thirteen of the fortresses that should have guarded Apollo against any enemy remained loyal. All were destroyed in the first five minutes," the chief of staff said grimly. "With Admiral Küçük dead, communication was in flux."

"*Chaos* is the term Lister is avoiding," Michelakis interrupted. "I was second-in-command of the fleet, but only half of our ships had jammers up and we had laser coms with maybe a quarter."

"Chaos or not, we got most of Home Fleet's fighters into space," Lister continued with a sigh. "What we weren't sure of was who to shoot at—until the BKN arrived with a nova fleet anchored on *twenty-two* fleet carriers.

"It was the traditional balance. Our ships were individually bigger and generally more capable on a cubic-to-cubic basis, but they had more of them. In this case, a *lot* more of them—and our own key fortresses had just turned on us, shattering our morale and cohesion."

The room was quiet for a moment.

"We fought. Our nova fighters did everything they could—but we lost most of the *carriers* we lost before we even got out of weapons range of our own battle stations."

"At which point, we needed to run, to get far enough out to use the class one drives," Michelakis said softly. "The decision was and could only ever have been mine, Admiral Demirci. It was the only decision that could have been made, but I abandoned our homeworld in the face of the enemy."

"But you got a fleet out," Kira replied. "That is worth something."

The other Admiral nodded sadly and gestured at the display.

"Lister?"

"We have four of the *Trireme*-class ships left," the chief of staff noted. "*Salaminia, Parthenos, Naiad* and *Delphis*. We also have two *Benediction*-class ships, four *Mythology*-class ships, and nine light carriers of assorted older classes."

Kira nodded slowly as she processed. Six modern fleet carriers—the *Benediction*s were *Victorious*'s sisters, and they weren't brand-new, but they were big enough and new enough to deserve the name. The *Mythology*-class ships like *Medusa* were older but almost up to fleet-carrier size on their own.

Light carriers could be in the fifty-to-seventy-kilocubic range. Most of the ships she could see were closer to the upper end of that range, giving Admiral Michelakis a damn solid fleet of carriers.

And not much else.

"Extracting the carriers became the priority at the end of the battle," Michelakis noted softly. "Not one of our battlecruisers survived. We have eight lighter cruisers and ten destroyers. We have *more* carriers than we have escorts—and *Salaminia* has the highest number of fighters aboard."

Lister waved a hand vaguely in the air.

"We spread the fighters and bombers out, just in case," he noted. "But overall, we're running at an average of twenty-five percent capacity with no spares. We have limited reserves of pilots, but we have more backup pilots than we have backup fighters."

It was supposed to be the other way around. The "backup fighters" might be components and raw materials, usually, but a carrier was supposed to be able to replace most to all of its fighter complement, given access to the average asteroid. The expectation was that you could retrieve many, if not most, of your pilots.

In victory, at least.

"I suppose it helps, in terms of force balance at least, that Admiral Killinger doesn't have any carriers," Kira noted. "He has nine cruisers, ten destroyers, and a *Sun Arrow*–class battlecruiser. Combined with my own cruisers and destroyers, along with your own escorts... we have something that is closer to a balanced fleet."

It would still be heavily carrier-focused, but that was fine in Kira's books. The *last* thing she was planning on doing was taking nova warships into the weapons range of asteroid fortresses! Nova fighters had a half-decent chance of getting in and out, and she had some ideas rattling around the back of her head, but even the largest nova warship was a toy against the scale of an asteroid fortress.

And warships couldn't dodge nearly as well as starfighters could.

"I am hesitantly prepared to trust you, Kira Demirci," Michelakis told her. "I do not and *can*not trust Henry Killinger. He didn't fake his death, desert and go into hiding to fight Brisingr. That may have been the story he told, but our intelligence was clear.

"He was building his fleet to fight the *Council of Principals*. He was laying the groundwork for a coup d'état in Apollo. Groundwork I can't help but suspect that Shadows used as part of their own plans."

"Admiral...do you know why I left Apollo?" Kira asked. "Because believe me, I have very little sympathy left for the Council of Principals."

"I am now aware of the Shadow Détente," Michelakis said levelly. "I was not so aware prior to becoming the commander of the Last Fleet. Certain codes that became automatically available to me on Admiral Küçük's death gave me access to classified items and orders that were concealed even from full Admirals.

"So, yes, Admiral, I can guess why you left Apollo. ASDF Intelligence was aware of *something*, but, of course, their investigations were overridden and short-stopped.

"We do not even know, for certain, how many of our officers and pilots were murdered under the authorization given by the Détente. It should not have happened."

"And the Council of Principals signed off on it," Kira replied. "Knowing the levels of *their* treason, can you really blame Killinger for scheming against them?"

"He swore a sacred oath, as did we all," Michelakis replied. "I do not blame those who fled, deserted, retired or otherwise entered exile to avoid the Shadow Détente. I cannot, however, ignore a man who actively committed treason against the state we serve."

"A state that betrayed him. And his friends. And *us*." Kira shook her head. "And, bluntly, a man we need. I don't ask you to *trust*

Killinger—gods know, I won't object to any eyes you want to keep on him!—but we do need to work *with* him.

"We need every ally we can get."

"I..." Michelakis glanced over at her chief of staff. "At this point, do I admit to being outvoted, Lister?"

"This isn't a democracy, ser."

"No, but when the only *other* ally we've really seen as an option makes the same argument you do, Commodore, I have to admit to being wrong."

Michelakis flashed Kira a small smile.

"It is all too easy, as the fleet commander, to forget that you can be wrong," she warned. "But we have to keep that lesson in mind.

"I am prepared to work with Killinger. As an *ally*. Not yet a comrade."

"That's all I ask." Kira shrugged. "That's all I offered him. That's all I'm really offering you."

"An alliance against the people who overran our homeworld." Michelakis nodded firmly. "Then done and done. Do you have a plan? Most of mine, I will admit, have been focused on trying to source new fighters."

"I confess I had expected that *you* would have excess nova fighters we could use to fill the flight decks of Killinger's cruisers," Kira warned. "But...if we fall back to Samuels and the safe haven they've promised, all of our forces should be able to restock and repair. Killinger is short of more parts than just fighter drives—but Samuels makes everything we will need."

"The problem is time, Demirci," the older Admiral warned. "Only eight fortresses survived the battle, but Brisingr knows the vulnerability they have created. Prefabricated stations only go so far, but they have delivered dozens of them—and our own facilities for the production of asteroid forts were taken intact."

"So, they're back up to twelve asteroid forts, most likely," Kira murmured. "And only a few months until they have more."

Twelve was already the most she figured they could take with fighter strikes. Another eight fortresses...

"When we fled Apollo, we had no friends, and Brisingr's enemies were too terrified to help us," Michelakis said. "Now enemies like Samuels have begun to challenge the Kaiserreich. But I fear that whatever window of opportunity we might have is closing."

"We need support," Lister told Kira. "More ships, more fighters, more pilots. Pilots and, at the very least, class two drives that *exist*."

"We can fabricate fighters relatively quickly," MacCàba noted. "Hell, I have the chassises and such for most of the gaps in my groups fabricated already. We'd need a bit more in terms of parts than *just* the class two drives, but given the proper support, we could rearm the entire Last Fleet in two, maybe three weeks."

"That you're telling me this makes me think you *have* an idea of where to get those," Kira murmured. "And that you think I can help you."

"I do, on both counts," Michelakis told her. "Tell me, Admiral. How far do you think Samuels will go to support you?"

"Quite a ways," Kira said. "They don't have the ships to fight Brisingr on their own—or even to really push outside the Corridor—but they owe me."

"Then we may have our window, if you can convince Samuels to give it to you," the Admiral noted. "The former Friends of Apollo are...a difficult bunch for us to deal with right now.

"We took advantage of them and maintained a hugely unequal relationship on both an economic and political basis." Michelakis shrugged. "Facing the truth of what it meant to be a *Friend* of Apollo is critical now.

"With the evidence of the Shadow Détente in front of me, I am forced to admit, now, that our betrayal of our supposed Friends was a warning sign of the flaws of our government. But that betrayal under-mined any effort I can make today to build new relationships.

"Our informal agreement with Attaca to be ignored if we don't cause trouble is about as good a relationship as the Last Fleet has with any of our former allies." The Admiral sighed. "And I cannot blame any of them. We sold them out. We cannot really expect them to trust us now."

"But?" Kira prodded.

"We do have a few contacts who are willing to provide us with information. Personal friends, family connections like my cousin on Paraeus, folks who absolutely despise the Kaiserreich.... Those kinds of people.

"And through them, we have learned that some of the key former Friends and current protectorates of the Brisingr Security Zone are... considering their options, let us say. The failure of the BKN to maintain the promised security has certainly been a factor, especially given the restrictions they've imposed on everyone *else's* fleets."

"They're planning to fight?" Kira asked.

"I don't think they're at planning yet," Michelakis admitted. "But they're...talking about thinking about planning, if that makes sense?"

"I don't know how helpful that can be, but I follow."

"In eleven days, senior military and political officials from the Attaca, Extraya, Prasináda and Luxum Systems will be meeting in the Exarch System," the Last Fleet's commander told Kira. "There is no way in hell or fresh void they will allow *me* to openly attend. But I *do* know that the Samuels System was, very quietly, invited to send a representative."

Attaca, Extraya, Prasináda, Luxum and Exarch were all names Kira recognized instantly. By the standards of, say, the Syntactic Cluster, any of them would be powerful wealthy systems. By the standards of the Mid Rim, they were second-tier systems. Individually, even if they built up their fleets to the maximum their economies could allow, none of them could have faced down the ASDF or the BKN.

Combined, though...

"I suspect at least part of their goals will be to never have masters again," Kira murmured. "If they help liberate Apollo, there will be prices to be paid."

"Apollo will never dominate this region as it once did," Michelakis said flatly. "Too much of our spaceborne industry was destroyed in the invasion. Too much of our shipping was slowly degraded over the course of a decade. Too much of our interstellar goodwill was burned to ash.

"To be one among equals is the best we can hope for now. And we will need to convince that meeting of that—and since, without their help, Apollo is doomed, I think we can.

"But first, we need to get into that meeting. I think that the Samuels delegation *can* get us in."

Kira nodded, considering. From Attaca to Exarch was a full six-nova trek. It *could* be done, but it was pushing the limits of the nova drive. From Attaca to Samuels was impossible. But...

"Assuming that the delegation is leaving Samuels to arrive on time, they'll go through Prasináda," she noted aloud. "To go directly would require dark nova points that Samuels doesn't have.

"Whereas we can make it from here to Exarch in one discharge cycle, if there's at least one conveniently located dark stop?" Given the age of her data, she was hesitant to rely on any map she hadn't had updated.

But she was *reasonably* sure there was a stop along the way.

"There is," Lister confirmed. "We were plotting out the course, but...we can't take the Last Fleet. We will *not* be welcome."

"You seem very certain of that," Kira observed.

"We asked our contacts in Attaca," Michelakis said. "They were...quite honest. To be fair, there are few places in the *galaxy* I think the Last Fleet would be welcome as an entity."

"So, we need Samuels." Kira considered the map and the routes. "If we headed to Exarch now, we'd be there in six days, give or take, given that we need to pick up *my* ship."

McCaig would be using *Prodigal*'s new BKN codes to not-quite-bully his way into discharging static at Megaras. That would make him easy for the nova pinnace to find, once Kira was truly on her way.

"And if the Samuels delegation is expecting to be there in eleven days, we can discharge in Exarch and then head back along the route to Prasináda," she said softly. "We can intercept them at least two novas short of Exarch.

"I'll talk to them. I think I can get them on side."

Especially because Kira had a *damn* good idea who First Minister Buxton would send to represent their government at that kind of delegation. Doretta Macey had been the envoy they'd sent to recruit *Kira*, after all.

"And we're supposed to put all of our faith in you?" MacCàba asked.

"That's up to you," she told them, spreading her hands. "My people and I are going to return to *Prodigal* and set out to find the Samuels envoy. Given my plans, I *need* to be at that meeting.

"I am willing to bring anyone Admiral Michelakis wants to send —within reason, of course!—with us. But as for you…"

Kira considered. There was the closest thing to an actual rebel battle fleet around them, according to the fleet-status display they'd shown her. It was *possible* Michelakis and her people were running some kind of long con, but none of the four people she'd spoken to seemed the type.

"Killinger's fleet is going to be rendezvousing with mine in the Corosec System," she told them. "I would suggest that we use Corosec as a gathering point and staging position for our operations against Apollo.

"It certainly doesn't seem like anyone is doing more than sending an occasional scout through." Kira chuckled. "Scouts, I suspect, that belong to the very people we want to get on our side at Exarch."

Michelakis glanced at her two senior officers then leaned forward.

"We need fighters, pilots, ships…and while I'm not sure I *believe* that our once-betrayed allies will give them to us, I see no other sources," she admitted. "Which means all of this makes sense to me."

The Admiral smiled.

"Commodore Lister and I will accompany you—plus some escorts, I'm sure, as I believe my Hoplites will have a collective heart attack if I tried to go without them!"

"I don't think they would be so polite as to have a heart attack as opposed to just tying you up and sitting on you," Lister said calmly. "Leaving Vice Admiral Munroe in command?"

"Branimir will survive," Michelakis agreed. She arched an eyebrow at Kira. "Did you ever meet Captain Branimir Munroe during the war, Demirci?"

"He was *Sun Arrow*'s CO when we pulled them out of the fire," Kira replied. "I met him briefly, but there was a lot on everyone's mind that day!"

The ambush of *Sun Arrow*'s battle group had been the last battle of the war, a slim tactical victory for the ASDF thanks to the fortuitous arrival of Task Force *Victorious*. The peace treaty had already been signed, but news of the cease-fire hadn't reached the carrier groups that ambushed Apollo's most advanced battlecruiser.

"He's a good man, but he's a cruiser commander through and through," Michelakis said. "He was the commander of Home Fleet's cruiser wings. Temporary command of the full force will be good for him."

"Munroe only made it out of Apollo because his staff dragged his unconscious ass off *Torment* between the flag bridge getting hit and *Torment* taking a torpedo barrage meant for *Salaminia*," Lister observed. "None of us had a good day that day, but his was rough even for the members of the Last Fleet."

"Like I said, it will be good for him," Michelakis concluded firmly. "Do you have space aboard *Prodigal* for a second nova pinnace, Admiral Demirci? I think catching up to you at the nova point may work best for us all.

"I would prefer not to just up and wander off on my fleet without warning, after all."

38

WITHOUT KONRAD BUELLER, Kira's quarters on *Prodigal* felt vaguely too large. Thankfully, there was plenty for the mercenary Admiral to do as they made their trip to Exarch—mostly going over the details of the Last Fleet with Admiral Michelakis to know what they needed to ask their potential allies for.

At the heart of it were fighters and pilots, as she'd expected. There were other parts and supplies that could help take the ASDF's survivors from ninety-five percent efficiency to ninety-eight percent, but they'd need the fighters to get the fleet up to that ninety-five.

For her own part, Kira had gone through the numbers she had for Killinger's ships. The privateer fleet needed a lot more in terms of parts and supplies, but they, too, mostly needed nova fighters and pilots.

Not that any member of the still-fledgling alliance to retake Apollo was going to say no if the members of the conference decided to put up actual *warships*. Even restricted by the Agreement on Nova Lane Security and the rules of the Brisingr Trade Route Security Zone, the five nations expected to have representatives in Exarch could field a full carrier group apiece.

And *that* was assuming that they'd obeyed the letter of the rules imposed on them by an external power and a treaty they hadn't signed themselves. Kira would be surprised if it turned out that those five firsts-among-equals of the second-tier powers didn't have at least a couple hundred kilocubics of capital ships hidden away somewhere.

Each.

For now, though, *Prodigal* was alone. Fifteen billion kilometers even from Patriarch, Exarch's seventh planet and sole gas giant—and outermost outpost of civilization—Exarch X was a ball of ice, iron, and helium that drew very little attention from everyone.

It was the perfect place for a covert static discharge, which was why the Exarch Templars maintained a listening post in orbit of the planet. They'd flashed their BKN codes at the automated Exarch military station and settled in to clear *Prodigal*'s drive core.

"So, where is our deep and mysterious meeting taking place?" Kira asked Michelakis as she stepped into the flag bridge to find the other Admiral sitting in the observer's seat, staring at the holographic illusion of the void outside.

"Patriarch Doce," the Admiral replied after a moment, gesturing at a slightly larger star on the display—a point of light that was actually the distant gas giant. "Twelfth orbital of Patriarch, a frozen ball of waste with enough water and native oxygen to make producing breathable air on site easy."

A headware command brought the moon into the room, rotating at the center of the flag bridge as Kira considered it.

"A luxury resort?" she asked, processing the information her implants popped up.

"As I understand it, it's the view," Michelakis replied.

They weren't alone on the flag bridge. Soler and a few of her techs were holding down assorted posts—and Michelakis went nowhere without a Hoplite in low-profile combat armor. Said armor wasn't up to the same level of augmentation as proper battle armor, but it still gave the Hoplite a boost.

That young woman was standing next to the main door, doing her best to imitate a statue.

"The view, huh?" Kira studied the planet for a moment. "Of Patriarch itself, mostly?"

"Patriarch, its rings, its other moons. I'm told it's quite impressive —and that the designers and builders spared no expense in building one of the most luxurious getaways for a hundred light-years in any direction."

The Admiral chuckled bitterly.

"Something like forty percent of their customers were people with full franchise on Apollo," she observed. "I suspect our particular system helped the whole place exist in the first place."

"Full franchise" meant that they were paying taxes in the highest income-tax bracket—which meant they could vote for the Council of Principals and other planetary offices. It was a category that had never included Kira but had permanently shaped Apollon politics and interstellar relations.

That class using their political power to get a luxury resort built in another star system definitely sounded all too likely to Kira.

"Soler, are we seeing any sign of unusual activity at Patriarch Doce?" Kira asked.

"Well, I don't know where the Templars usually keep their battle-cruiser," the operations officer replied. "But she's currently in a high orbit of Patriarch, outside Doce, with a pair of lighter cruisers as escorts.

"Dozen or so monitors scattered through the planetary system, looks like six forts at key positions... Except for the battlecruiser, all of that looks normal enough."

"I imagine it is," Michelakis replied. "We're still five days from when the conference is supposed to take place, and they won't want to draw *that* much attention to it."

"Wait. It's hard to tell at this range, but I *think* I'm seeing beacons for a restricted flight zone around Doce?" Soler said.

"Byzantium Hills—the resort we're looking at—is one of the

preferred vacation getaways for the rich and influential of half a dozen star systems," Michelakis pointed out. "And there's *nothing* else on the moon."

"If I was running it, I'd always have a restricted flight zone up," Kira said. "Otherwise, people would start wondering who was there when I *did* put up a restricted zone."

"We weren't planning on trying to show up in a cruiser flying a Brisingr beacon, anyway. Somehow, I don't think *Prodigal* would be welcome under *any* of her identities."

39

ONCE THE SENSOR team knew what to look for, Samuels' fast consular ships were surprisingly easy to pick out of the general background noise. There were a *lot* of twenty-kilocubic fast packets and couriers in the Apollo-Brisingr Sector, but very few of them were built around two-and-a-half-kilocubic 12X nova drives capable of taking *thirty* kilocubics into nova.

Springtime Chorus was also a particular ship that Kira and her people had spent a lot of time with over the last year or so, since it acted as Doretta Macey's personal transport.

"They are...not pretending about why *Chorus* has that extra nova cubage anymore," Soler observed a couple of moments after they identified the consular ship. Multiple nova fighters were latched on to the extra airlock docking systems *Springtime Chorus* carried for that purpose.

"I see them," Kira murmured. "Guardian-Threes?"

Based on an older model of Apollo's standard heavy fighter and then evolved in Samuels' own starship industry, the Guardian-Three was typical of the heavy fighter type: designed to be able to do *every* role a nova fighter could handle, it cost more than a specialized plane and was generally less capable than a specialist in any particular role.

There was a four-plane flight group currently attached to the consular ship, with a second flight group currently flying escort on the courier.

"Any idea how long until she has to nova?" Kira asked. "I'd *like* to get closer before I try to talk to our friends over there. Without drawing attention to why a Brisingr ship is talking to a Samuels ship."

"There's plenty of strangers here who can carry tales," Soler agreed. "No Brisingr warships, though, so that limits the likelihood of someone starting..."

Kira waited a few seconds for Soler to resume speaking before making a questioning noise.

"Sorry, ser. I just spotted the rest of *Chorus*'s escort and wanted to triple-check what I was looking at."

Before Kira could say anything, the sensor display expanded and adjusting, bringing a second—much larger—nova ship into view. Kira had to blink a couple of times to be sure of what she was looking at, because she had no reason to expect a *Baron*-class light cruiser to be this far away from Redward.

"That's new," she murmured.

"Beacon says she's *Teal Circlet*...of Memorial Force, ser," Soler reported. "Did we have an order for ships in that I missed, ser?"

"Not that *I* know of," Kira said. "I can think of a few ways that we might have ended up with a Redward cruiser I wasn't expecting, but I still didn't know she was coming."

She shook her head.

"And if she *wasn't* flying in company with Doretta Macey, I'd question her existence a lot more," she admitted. "As it is...pulse her with a laser com for encrypted challenge-and-response.

"We're going to play *inspection party*, as the BKN claims the right to inspect mercenary ships in their territory," she continued. "But hopefully, whoever is aboard *Circlet* actually works for me, because that could make this whole chunk of things much easier."

THE *BARON*-CLASS SHIPS HAD, originally, been the emergency-build cruisers assembled to break the blockade of Redward. Designed from the keel out by Konrad Bueller, they'd been the product of a thousand and one compromises.

At least, the Flight One *Baron*s had been. The *second* flight of the ships, built after the Equilibrium Institute's patsies had been defeated and Redward had been reestablishing themselves as the first among equals and favored neutral arbiter in the region, had seen many of the compromises smoothed away.

Teal Circlet was a seventy-five-thousand-cubic-meter light cruiser, designed to fight her peers and smaller vessels rather than battlecruisers or even heavy cruisers. She carried eight dual turrets, each packing lighter guns than, say, *Prodigal* but more than a match for any destroyer's main battery.

Captain Gala Negri had been aboard the destroyer *Passion* last time Kira had seen her, but Kira at least knew the woman by sight. That was the last piece she needed to be certain that, yes, *Teal Circlet* was actually a Memorial Force ship.

Somehow.

"We'll all play along, grouchily, in public, ser," the recording of the cruiser CO told her. "I'll let Mrs. Macey know you're coming. Bit of a surprise for us all, but a welcome one, ser." She grinned. "We won't jump away before you get here, in any case. Which I might have managed if you *hadn't* told us who you were by direct link!"

The recording ended, and Kira shook her head as Negri's pale brown face vanished.

"Are *all* of my ship captains turning into snarky wretches?" she asked with exaggerated patience.

"You do encourage a certain degree of lèse-majesté, ser," McCaig replied. "Are we good to go say hello?"

"Apparently, Captain Negri upgraded while we've been out wandering around," Kira told him. "I want your coms department hailing *Teal Circlet* with standard BKN protocols—not tightbeam, the kind where everyone else is eavesdropping with the effort we know they're putting in.

"We're demanding inspection rights and Captain Negri is going to, begrudgingly, allow that."

"And Mrs. Macey?"

Kira had spent enough time working with the Samuels people to use their gendered honorifics for married people, even if the whole cultural logic made very little sense to her. Calling people what they wanted to be called was easy enough, though.

Especially when they were paying her.

"Negri said she'd be in touch with Macey—probably with Hennessy, too," Kira noted. Hennessy had been *Springtime Chorus*'s Captain last time she'd seen them.

"I'm sure between all of the very clever people who seem to end up working with me, we'll find a way for Admiral Michelakis and me to talk to Mrs. Macey and see what we can manage."

There were definitely questions about how far Doretta Macey would go for them. Kira figured Macey would let *Kira* hide behind her skirts. Michelakis, though...

Well, that was why they had to talk to the woman.

40

KIRA HAD NEVER SPENT a great deal of time on any of the *Baron*-class cruisers. Thanks to her boyfriend, though, she knew *everything* about the class, and the shuttle bay felt entirely familiar as she disembarked.

Looking around the bay, she spotted a handful of indicators to make clear that *Teal Circlet* was, as she'd presumed, a Flight Two ship. Possibly even Flight Three—though the differences between the second and third batches were smaller. She had been reasonably sure that Redward wouldn't have sent any of the emergency war builds to the Apollo-Brisingr Sector, but it was good to see the confirmation.

What she could *also* see, however, was several places where the logo of the Redward Royal Fleet had been painted over with the eagle-topped obelisk of Memorial Force. Whatever flag the cruiser flew today, she'd been *built* for the RRF.

"Welcome aboard *Teal Circlet*, Admiral," Negri greeted them. "And, um. Admiral?"

"Captain Gala Negri, meet Admiral Fevronia Michelakis and Commodore Aldéric Lister of the Apollo System Defense Force," Kira introduced her companions. "And Hoplite escort."

Kira had theoretically come on her own. *Theoretically*, in that she was the only person from *Prodigal* who was there to work. Milani and the three commandos with them were her escorts.

Michelakis and Lister had their own trio of Hoplites as well, bringing the total party from *Prodigal* up to ten, plus the shuttle's three-person crew. Everywhere Kira went, she brought a crowd.

"Admiral Michelakis, Commodore, meet Captain Negri," Kira continued. The conversation about where Negri had found the cruiser would take place later, away from her Apollon allies.

"A pleasure, Captain," Michelakis said with a firm nod. "The ship is Redward-built, I understand? Not quite what I would expect from the Outer Rim, but I suppose Redward has made great strides."

"Captain Negri was originally a loaner from the RRF," Kira noted mildly. "She decided to stick with us since, but she is *intimately* familiar with the limitations of the RRF prior to the last few years."

"Home is bootstrapping themselves into a state where they can keep everyone around safe, one piece of tech at a time," Negri said cheerfully. "And a lot of that is due to Admiral Demirci."

The cruiser captain smiled sweetly.

"Thank you so much for driving her off; we'd have been in real trouble if you'd kept her."

Michelakis put her hand over her heart.

"I intended no insult to Redward, Captain, but I still very much deserved that," she conceded. "We need to meet with the Samuels delegation. Can you arrange that?"

"I already did," Negri replied. "Mrs. Macey is waiting in the main briefing room. Shall we?"

DORETTA MACEY WAS a broad woman clad in a simple-seeming frock, her blond hair clearly going silver but her blue eyes utterly piercing as she studied Kira's companions.

"Admiral Michelakis, Admiral Demirci," she greeted them brightly. "I am not familiar with the Commodore, but given your companions, ser, you come well referenced."

"Thank you for making this meeting, Doretta," Kira told the diplomat. "I recognize we are putting you in a difficult spot."

"No more so than certain others I could name," Macey replied. "It is not, after all, the preference of a member of the Society of Friends to be negotiating military alliances. Let alone *secret* military alliances."

The Society of Friends—the Quakers—were still one of the dominant religions on Samuels, and their pacifism shaped many things about the planet. The mistake Kira had learned not to make and Brisingr apparently *hadn't* was assuming that *pacifist* meant *helpless* or *pushover*.

Samuels' people would defend themselves.

"I appreciate that we're not playing games about why we're all here," Michelakis said. "I have reason to believe, Em—apologies, *Mrs.* —Macey, that you have been invited to a conference of key systems in the Apollo-Brisingr Sector. A conference on, for lack of a better easy description, what to do about Brisingr."

"A correct-enough summary," Macey confirmed. She was now studying Michelakis, and Kira concealed a small smirk.

She didn't think the Apollon Admiral was going to misjudge the woman she was dealing with. Macey was in her element and knew it.

"On the other hand," Macey continued, "while I know *of* you, Admiral Michelakis, I don't *know* you. Your name has been bandied about in these discussions, and unfortunately, I can confirm that you are most definitely and specifically *not* invited."

"And yet I think I need to be there," Michelakis replied. "Those discussions...if they happen fast enough and with enough *conviction*...We can undo much of the damage that has been done."

One of *Teal Circlet*'s stewards entered with a tray of coffees—and a water for Macey, who avoided stimulants and intoxicants of any kind.

Everyone took a beverage, and Kira smiled at the familiar scent of the Redward Royal Reserve. That was the private blend of the Redward royal family and the fact that Kira had an ongoing supply of it was a clear sign of King Larry and Queen Sonia's opinion of their one-time mercenary contractor.

"I do not necessarily disagree," the Samuels diplomat told Michelakis. "But I am not the organizer of this event. We have made commitments with regards to secrecy that I have probably already broken the spirit of this evening.

"I am sorry, Admiral Michelakis. I believe we share a cause and I *know* we share an enemy—and I believe the same is true of the other attendees at this little get-together I am headed to.

"But they have already resolved that you will not be included. It is not my place, as a guest who is arguably *not* a true part of the discussion, to oppose that decision."

Kira didn't know Michelakis well enough to know how the woman was taking that, but she could practically *hear* the gears grinding as the other Admiral considered her response.

"What about me?" she asked Macey. "Can you get *me* into that meeting?"

"That, my friend, is a very different question," the diplomat replied with a knowing smile.

"And?" Michelakis prodded.

"I can't get you in, Admiral Michelakis, because they have by *name* said they won't invite you," Macey said bluntly. "Kira hasn't been mentioned at all. Even if Kira *had* been mentioned, though, Kira is both a personal friend and someone the Ministries and Quorum of Samuels are heavily indebted to.

"I will bend rules and instructions for Admiral Demirci that I will not bend for you. That is why we are having this conversation at all."

"I understand that, Mrs. Macey," the Apollon Admiral said softly. "And if it is necessary, I can and will trust Admiral Demirci to speak on my behalf. But there are tens of thousands of spacers, soldiers and officers who look to me for leadership and to make the best of the situation we have found ourselves in.

"I would be doing them and my cause a disservice not to argue that only I can truly speak to our situation and our mission."

Macey spread her hands.

"I understand what you believe," she conceded. "But I am bound by the promises I have made. I will take Kira Demirci to this meeting. Leave her whatever information and instructions you can."

There was a long silence. Kira wasn't going to argue with Macey —as the Samuels diplomat had told them already, she was going out on a limb to bring Kira in.

"May I make an alternate suggestion that may serve all of our conditions?" Commodore Lister said.

Macey smoothed the front of her frock and regarded the Apollon officer like she was considering which chicken to *harvest* for supper.

"Speak, Commodore."

"Rather than introducing Admiral Michelakis into the mix at Byzantium Hills without permission or notice, allow the Admiral and myself to travel to Exarch with you," Lister suggested. "We will remain on your ship and out of the way of the conference but stay in contact with Admiral Demirci.

"If, after speaking with Admiral Demirci, the conference representatives are willing to meet with Admiral Michelakis, we can then join as invited guests. We make ourselves *available* to the conference without inserting ourselves into it."

Macey continued to study Lister for a few more moments, then smiled.

"Why do I have the sudden feeling that the military is also familiar with the type of middle management without which the entire corporation suddenly collapses?" she asked.

"We call them staff officers, Mrs. Macey," Michelakis replied. "Or senior noncommissioned officers, depending on the exact role and individual."

"Whatever you are paying this man, it isn't enough," Macey told the ASDF Admiral. "I like your plan, Commodore. I think we will execute it."

She made a dismissive gesture.

"For now, though, Admiral Demirci and I must speak in private. I'm sure Captain Negri can find you and your escort some food while we prepare to return to *Springtime Chorus*."

―――――

"THANK YOU," Kira said softly.

Macey shrugged.

"Lister's idea is good," she admitted. "I would prefer not to involve Michelakis at all, but I see the value in having her available. Your mission has been successful, I take it?"

"I've made contact with both anti-Kaiserreich forces that I know of, and we have some levers moving to potentially undermine Reinhardt at home," Kira said. "I don't know how reliable those levers *are*, but they are in motion.

"But everything on Brisingr needs Reinhardt to lose and lose badly. We *need* to retake Apollo."

"I don't pretend to know enough about the realities of warfare to judge the likelihood of that," Macey said. "I trust you if you say it can be done, but everything else I have ever heard says your homeworld should never have fallen in the first place."

"It shouldn't have," Kira agreed. "And that's *why* we might be able to take it back—enough damage was done in the invasion that Apollo is vulnerable.

"For a while. Not forever. And that's why we need Brisingr's enemies. I am *told* that some of the paths have been smoothed for us."

"Not, I see, Apollo's old friends," Macey noted. "From the messages I have exchanged with the other parties to this meeting, a wise distinction to draw—but if anyone has been clearing the way for you, I have heard nothing of it."

"No one in this Sector owes Apollo anything," Kira said flatly.

She wasn't surprised that Zamorano's efforts had gone unmentioned, though she was still counting on them. "The Council of Principals burned our goodwill to the ground a long time ago. If we are to get their help, I need to sell them on how it serves *their* needs."

The diplomat in the room chuckled. "You understand the task before you, then," Macey conceded. "I wasn't sure. There is a harsh limit, Kira, on how much I can support you in Exarch.

"Once I introduce you to the conference, *my* influence and good-will there are almost certainly spent. You will start from zero."

"I'm going to the people Apollo betrayed, asking them to fight for the people who screwed them over. I'm starting a *lot* lower than zero."

"Yes. I can get you into the room. I believe I can make certain you are allowed to speak." Macey shook her head. "I cannot guarantee that they will listen."

"No one could. You have already promised everything I can reasonably ask for, Doretta," Kira said. "And more, honestly. I appreciate it."

"I was fooled into luring you into a trap once," the Samuels woman said softly. "I hope you recognize that this could easily be another one. The Institute and the Kaiserreich are very old hands at the games of deception and betrayal."

"I know. But without some immediate support from Brisingr's other enemies, none of the allies I have found have the strength needed for the task before us," Kira admitted. "So, we must take the risk and hope that fear of the Brisingr Kaiserreich is sufficient to bind us all together."

41

THERE WERE a thousand things that Kira should, probably, have made time for before transferring to *Springtime Chorus*. Among the few things she managed to arrange, though, was a quick meeting with Gala Negri.

"I can guess what your questions are," the mercenary Captain told Kira as the Admiral took a seat in Negri's office.

"Just one question, really," Kira said with a chuckle. "Where did you get the cruiser?"

"Redward?" Negri grinned at Kira's dirty look. "They showed up shortly after you left Samuels. Dirix had worked with the RRF at the King's order to sort out the transfer and skeleton passage crews to get them out to us."

That...fit. Stipan Dirix headed up Kira's "ground office" back on Redward and the ex-Redward Army officer knew what she'd want. More, King Larry *knew* Dirix would be able to sort out those kinds of details!

"They'd filled out the crews with recruits here and there along the way, but Zoric reshuffled everyone to get solid cadres of older hands on every ship."

"'Crews,'" Kira echoed. "Plural. How many ships?"

"Two *Barons*, a *Bastion*, and six more *Parakeets*," Negri laid out instantly. "A decent light carrier group. All newer ships, though I think *Shillelagh*, the *Bastion*, served for a year in the RRF before the transfer."

Kira slowly nodded. That was a significant boost to Memorial Force's strength—if somewhat less than it would have been before they'd acquired *Prodigal* and *Harbinger*. It wasn't an immense boost to the strength of the alliance she was putting together to retake Apollo, but everything counted.

"Who's paying for these ships?" she finally asked. All of *her* money was tied up in the multi-client contract funding Memorial Force's operations right now.

"There's a message from King Larry and Queen Sonia explaining that," Negri told her, flicking a file over to Kira's headware. "I believe Zoric has viewed it, and Vaduva went over the paperwork and seemed fine with it, but no one briefed *me*."

Kira chuckled. "Anything *else* I should know?" she asked.

"Commodore Michel did a tour of the Rimward end of the corridor with a checking account the Apollons underwrote," Negri said. "Picked up *another* six destroyers, though they're a bit more of a mixed bag.

"Zoric was tearing her hair out, trying to find enough crew for everything, when Samuels asked if we could hire out to escort a consular mission for them," Negri concluded. "Since *Teal Circlet* wasn't stolen from the BKN, we figured that she was one of the better bets for the mission."

She coughed.

"The only fighters in my bays are SDC," she observed. "We've got twenty planes between us, enough for a decent CAP. We're running three flight groups through my maintenance team at a time, keeping the whole group as optimized as possible."

Kira wasn't entirely sure *how* they were fitting three flight groups in a *Baron*'s fighter bays, given that the Flight One ships hadn't been designed for fighters *at all*, which hadn't left much space to squeeze in Flight Two's single six-ship squadron of nova fighters.

"Aren't you designed for six *interceptors*?" she asked aloud.

"I'm going to say that I have good deck chiefs and stay the stars-loving *fuck* out of their way," Negri replied. "Because I'm pretty sure there is some space-time warping going on in my fighter bays to make it happen, yes."

Kira chuckled.

"Okay. So, Memorial Force picked up two cruisers, a carrier, and a dozen destroyers while I wasn't looking," she concluded. "If Em Vaduva thinks we can pay the crews, I don't argue with the purser on that point!"

Negri nodded with a smile, then paused as she received a head-ware message.

"Your shuttle is ready," she told Kira. "I'm assuming you'll want to check the King's message before you fully put yourself in Macey's hands, regardless of how much Samuels is on our side right now."

"Thank you. Do you have a private space I can use?" Kira asked.

"I'm going to step outside and leave my office to you," Negri said. "Let me know when you're ready to head out—or can you find your way on your own?"

"Konrad designed these ships from the keel out while living in my back pocket," Kira told her subordinate. "I can find my way to the shuttle bay on my own."

Negri nodded and saluted before slipping out of her office, leaving Kira alone with her thoughts and a message from the monarchs who'd become her friends.

HIS ROYAL MAJESTY Lawrence Bartholomew Stewart, First Magistrate and Honored King of the Kingdom of Redward, looked *exactly* like what people envisaged when they heard the words "King Larry."

He was a red-faced jolly-looking man with an exceptional girth—only accentuated when he was sitting next to his wife, Sonia. Putting them next to each other drew slightly more attention to the fact that the King shared Sonia's two-meter height, but her elegant slimness was a sharp contrast to his bulk.

The image of the pair was frozen as Kira's headware and the software envelope containing the video played a back-and-forth game of "Are you who you say you are?" for a few seconds, then the message finally started.

"Kira, I hope you are receiving this message in good health and that events in your home sector have not overrun you just yet," Larry told her. "Sonia's sources that far Coreward are not what we would like them to be, but I don't think *anyone* is blind enough to miss the fall of a major star system to its enemies."

"I can only begin to imagine the kind of groundwork and effort that went into arranging Brisingr's invasion," Sonia added. "What information I have suggests that covert operations and infiltration were absolutely key to the endeavor. Considering how much effort it took us just to find people willing to *talk* to us in some systems around here..."

Sonia shook her head.

"I am both impressed and horrified," she admitted.

The irony, to Kira's mind, was that Larry and Sonia ran one of the few multi-system states she knew of—including a second habitable planet, Wilhelm. They'd even taken the four Costar Clans systems by force.

But the Costar Clans had been desperately poor, a harsh techno-poverty that had driven them to become pirates across the Syntactic Cluster. The Kingdom of Redward had absorbed those systems, and from what Kira could tell, the four Costar Systems had benefited more from the process than Redward had.

The fall of the KSR-92RR System *technically* qualified as the same kind of interstellar invasion as had taken down Apollo—but no one was counting it in the very short list of interstellar assaults. That list was generally limited to systems with proper defenses, like Apollo had very much had.

"As you can imagine, we are not in a position to do much of anything about Apollo from here," Larry warned. "Our logistics infrastructure is not up to force projection outside the Syntactic Cluster. Presence missions by single cruisers are the limits of our distant military presence right now."

"But we owe you," Sonia said, picking up where her husband left off. "Not least for not stepping hard enough on our shipyard complex when they started yanking you around. Unfortunately, we simply don't have a hundred-and-twenty-kilocubic ship to spare. Were you still here, we'd be attempting to contract you for bench strength."

"The Cluster is at peace," Larry observed. "This, of course, has drawn attention from outside. Things are under control, and the rapid growth of the rest of the Free Trade Zone's fleets will hold the line in the long term, but in the short term, we can't give up our mainline capital ships."

The problem with getting shafted for good reason was that you were still getting shafted. Kira had needed the hundred-and-twenty-kilocubic carrier she'd been promised *years* before. Now it was basically too late—and from Larry and Sonia's expressions, they realized that.

"We promised you a fleet carrier at cost to make up for the loss of *Conviction*," Larry admitted. "As our yards and military procurement teams have ramped up and sidestepped that promise, we've leaned on them to sell you a lot of other ships at cost, but that was targeted at maintaining the relationship, not honoring the debt.

"And we are now out of time."

"No one has *officially* told us that you're taking your fleet up against Brisingr," Sonia murmured. "But the situation seems clear. The fate of your homeworld hangs in the balance. It is a time for all debts to come due, and we have failed to meet ours."

"So. This message will accompany the arrival of Carrier Group *Shillelagh*," King Larry told her. "A *Bastion*-class carrier, two of the

Flight Three *Barons*, and six of the Flight Seven *Parakeets*. There was some...*commentary* when we told the RRF what was happening."

"He means screaming, Kira," Sonia said blithely. "We took *Shillelagh* out of active service. Her escorts are brand-new but were in the process of working through their trials for RRF service."

"The ships are yours," Larry concluded. "No costs. No strings. Paperwork is included and Em Vaduva is likely reviewing it already. Sonia has spoken to Stipan Dirix to acquire personnel for the passage crews, but I recognize that you'll be receiving them with minimum crews aboard."

"We also did not load them with nova fighters," Sonia said. "They are carrying about three times their standard allotment of class two drives, parts and materials, but we know that the fighter designs you acquired from Crest are superior to anything in our arsenal.

"Using those drives and materials should enable you to manufacture new fighters from your schematics to fill their bays."

The two monarchs paused and looked over at each other.

"I..." Larry swallowed. "I don't necessarily feel that this is best way to honor the debt we owe, Kira, and I do not think that it fully clears it. But it is what we can send you now. As others have said, ask us for anything but time.

"You did not ask, but *time* I cannot give you. A light carrier group, on the other hand, I can."

He chuckled.

"Whatever happens, Kira Demirci, know that you always have a home for both yourself and Memorial Force here in Redward. We hope that *Shillelagh* and her escorts will help you with your cause."

There was a long pause, and Kira realized that Sonia's hand was hovering protectively over her stomach. As she started to wonder, though, the Queen smiled.

"In more personal news, I'm pregnant again," Sonia told her. "We've confirmed it's a girl and we're going to name her Kira. So, at some point in the future, young lady, you will need to come back to meet your namesake if nothing else."

Kira laughed. "Young lady" was priceless coming from Sonia, the Queen being almost a decade younger than Kira.

"Good luck, Kira," Larry said. "May God and the stars watch over you and guide you home."

"Wherever home may be," Sonia finished.

The message ended and Kira smiled at their frozen images. They weren't wrong in that *Shillelagh* and her escorts weren't, really, a clear payment of the promise they'd made.

Yet, on the other hand, an entire carrier group was a grand gift indeed. Apollo might be her homeworld, but Redward would always have part of her heart.

And if home was where the heart was, Kira Demirci didn't think she'd ever have just *one* home again.

42

VERY FEW THINGS manage to be monuments to both technological achievements and the selfish arrogance of the unimaginably wealthy. Byzantium Hills pulled off that duality with a grace that made it easy to forget that just the *landing fee* for a shuttle was more than the price tag of the average home.

To actually refuel was another invoice again. Just breathing at the Hills cost more than the average annual salary on Apollo.

And standing on a stone veranda, looking out over a lake and up at the gas giant above her head, Kira saw no real sign that she was living on an uninhabitable rock with a toxic atmosphere, with the temperature outside the dome hovering around one hundred and twenty Kelvin.

There were *fish* in the lake, a painstakingly balanced ecology drawing on species from six systems. Wildlife scampered through the bushes beneath the balcony, though Kira suspected that every one of the raccoon-like creatures was tagged and tracked.

Like the fish, the wildlife had been drawn from multiple systems and painstakingly designed. None of the animal life was dangerous to humans, and all of it was adorable.

The space she was standing on was attached to her room, paid for by the Samuels government—at a heavily discounted rate, from what Kira had seen of the costs of just *existing* in Patriarch Doce's sole habitable dome.

"Either this place is always this empty, or the organizers of this meeting bought out the entire dome," Milani said behind her.

She turned to eye her bodyguard. Byzantium Hills banned weapons and powered armor, but Milani's medical notes had once again cleared them to wear a full-body powered suit. *Theoretically*, the outfit was demilitarized and only provided regular human-level musculature while anonymizing Milani's physicality.

Kira wasn't going to test the theory that Milani's *medical* body suit wasn't capable of duplicating most soldier boosts if they wanted.

"I suspect the answer, Milani, is both," she told her companion. "My quick check says that there are only a few hundred guest units. About five thousand staff."

Of course, that number included all of the engineering and maintenance crew required to run an entirely enclosed artificial environment. But given that the Hills appeared to be determined to keep the majority of its automation away from the eyes of its guests, there had to be more customer-facing staff there than in a similar-sized more-normal resort.

"Five core star systems, plus a couple of extras like Samuels," Milani muttered. "Every high muckety-muck brought at least one grunt like me, even if we're all wandering around pretending that we're harmless valets."

Kira snorted at the mental image of Milani helping her dress—still clad in minimalist powered not-quite-armor.

Given that Kira was wearing an armored uniform jacket over a shipsuit, she suspected her dress uniform was going to come up short against expectations in Byzantium Hills, but there was a limit to what she was prepared to do.

There was a chime in her head, and she accepted the call.

"Demirci."

"It's Macey. I've had the discussions; I've cleared the board. You're up in twenty-three minutes."

The diplomat paused thoughtfully.

"I was going to make a point of how much political capital I've expended to set this up, but frankly, my First Minister would be *very* disappointed in me if I hadn't. So, it's done, and we've spent that capital for what it was meant for.

"Knock 'em dead."

DORETTA MACEY HAD UPGRADED the fabrics of her intentionally simplistic frock, but the style remained. Somehow, despite its intentional homespun appearance, the garment still managed to look perfectly at home in a crowd of people in an assortment of dress fashions from half a dozen star systems.

Two of those people were in a very familiar, extremely geometric style. It appeared that, as usual, the Bank of the Royal Crest had been drawn into the mess. Whatever else the Crest might be—and it had been almost as in bed with Equilibrium as Brisingr was, before Kira had helped enable a coup—it remained the largest financier and the source of the interstellar currency of choice for their segment of the Rim.

The larger of the two individuals from the Crest was wearing a suit whose shoulders had clearly been extended artificially to turn the entire jacket into a sharp triangle. They were a shaven-headed enby with delicate makeup woven over strongly defined features.

Familiar ones. General Voski of the Dinastik Pahak commanded the personal bodyguard of the Crown Zharang of the Kingdom of Crest. They were not normally sent out without Jade themselves, but Kira didn't recognize the other person with Voski.

Voski had spotted her as well. The Crest soldier met her eyes and inclined their head. Whatever game the Crest was playing, Voski, especially, would be an ally. Kira was officially persona non grata in the Crest Sector but had earned that working *for* the royal family.

They just hadn't really expected her to keep the supercarrier she'd hijacked for them.

Macey was ignoring the mutters and surprised gazes as she led Kira through the crowd to the main stage. The current main meeting of the conference was taking place on a platform suspended above the lake, with a buffet table along the left side and a stage at the far end, with the water and the slowly rising gas giant as a backdrop to the speakers.

"Delegates, envoys," Macey said loudly as she stepped up onto the stage. There was no visible pickup, but it was clear that Macey's voice was being spread by more than just acoustics.

"I have imposed on the goodwill of many of you here to create this opening today, on the first day of what I suspect will be many meetings and discussions. Some of you know who I am introducing, because I told you.

"Some of you know Admiral Kira Demirci from other times and other places."

Kira stepped up beside Macey as the diplomat spoke, scanning the crowd to see if she *did* recognize anyone other than Voski. There was one Attacan officer she was reasonably sure she knew, if not well.

And there was... Oh. One Luxum officer she definitely knew. *Intimately*.

Mason Andrewson wore a Vice Admiral's uniform now, but he'd been *just* a Flight Commander when they'd met during the war. Broad-shouldered, muscular, and entirely outside of her chain of command, the infatuation had been mutual and the fling explicitly short-lived.

She wasn't entirely sure if having an ex-boyfriend in the audience was going to help or not, but she stepped into the center of the platform and nodded to Macey.

"Thank you all for hearing me out," she told them. "This is an extraordinary time for your systems, and I know you are feeling threatened. For all that I have been away from our Sector for over half a decade now, I know most of you look at me and see an Apollon.

"You see the world who, before Brisingr humbled them, demanded much of you and gave little in return. You, I know, are all too aware of the truth of what it meant to be a Friend of Apollo." She smiled grimly.

"So, I assure you, am I. While I wore Apollo's uniform and served my homeworld, I supported that structure and fought for it. Even then, though, I honestly believed our system was better than what Brisingr would impose."

Kira spread her hands and gave her audience a small shrug.

"I did not expect to be proven correct so thoroughly and brutally," she admitted. "Nor did I expect that my own government would just...give up."

She let that hang.

"We knew we were losing the war," she told them. "But aboard *Victorious* and the other task groups still in space, still fighting? We also knew we could turn it around—in concert with our allies.

"But given the choice between protecting themselves and rebalancing the agreements with the Friends of Apollo to something more equal, something that would give everyone a cause to fight for, the Council of Principals instead chose to protect their personal power.

"They betrayed you. But they also betrayed *me*—not just in abandoning the fight I and others were willing to keep up, but more directly and immediately."

She surveyed them. From the expressions, at least a quarter of her audience knew what she was talking about.

"The Shadow Détente, delegates, is the name they gave to the classified, secret agreement between Apollo and Brisingr. An agreement that was even more of an abject surrender than the Agreement on Nova Lane Security.

"The Shadow Détente authorized the Brisingr Shadows to operate in Apollon space to murder Apollon officers on a list—key ace

pilots, ship commanders, and flag officers. And they used that authorization to cover a lot of other things, too.

"We all saw how that ended. That's why you're here."

Kira was honestly surprised no one had challenged her yet. She
wasn't sure if that was what Macey's "political capital" had bought
her—or if her audience just honestly wanted to hear what she had
to say.

"That's why *I'm* here," she told them. "The Rim made me
wealthy. The mercenary fleet I gathered around myself made me
powerful. But I went into exile because the Council of Principals
betrayed me.

"As they betrayed you. As, in the end, they betrayed Apollo
itself."

She smiled sadly.

"You can guess why I'm here," she said. "I have spoken with
Admiral Henry Killinger and Admiral Fevronia Michelakis. I have
brought my own fleet home, and I have forged alliances with what is
left of Apollo's fleets.

"But we cannot retake our home alone. We need your help." She
held up a hand. "And we *understand* that what was cannot be again.
There will be no return to the status quo ante. What Apollo was is dead.

"We look for true allies now, not 'friends' who are junior partners
at best, exploited protectorates at worst. To stand and build a future
for this sector *together*. Not at the whim of Brisingr and not at the
whim of a collection of oligarchs from my own homeworld."

She fell silent, waiting for the inevitable challenge.

"If the rumors are correct, Admiral Michelakis's so-called Last
Fleet outnumbers and outmatches any force available to any of us," a
stranger Kira didn't know told her. The man's faux-clerical vestments
presumably meant he was from Exarch, but there were no active
identity beacons on the gathering platform.

"Why would we send our spacers to join a fleet more capable
than anything we have?"

"Someone once said that in war, the moral is to the physical as three is to one," Kira replied. "But in my experience, *logistics* are more important than anything else. Neither the Last Fleet nor Killinger's privateers have the logistical capacity to make good the damage they have already taken.

"But yes: the alliance we have assembled *can* take the fight to Brisingr," she told them. "I won't turn aside anyone who wants to fight alongside us, but what we need from you isn't your ships.

"We need *supplies*. Spare parts, food, fuel—but most of all, nova fighters."

Kira didn't really *want* to tell this gathering what the key weakness of both the Last Fleet and Killinger's rebels was. But she needed their help to make it up.

"Fighters and pilots, delegates," she repeated. "Volunteers, I would hope, for the pilots. We don't have the resources to refill the flight decks of the Last Fleet's carriers. We don't have the parts to undo the better part of a decade of wear and tear on Killinger's privateers.

"We could source all of these things outside this sector, given time. We have never had that time. We have even less of it now— there is a window of vulnerability around Apollo. A time period in which her fortress network remains uneven and understrength.

"It will not last much longer. We must rearm the Apollon fleet. We must strike." She shrugged. "Or this meeting here will rapidly become irrelevant, because Brisingr will merge the two largest economies in the sector into a single industrial engine, producing a fleet that will lock bands of iron around your worlds."

"Our systems remain inviolate," another delegate told her. "If we play by Brisingr's rules, or at least pretend to, we are safe. Why should we risk anything for Apollo?"

"Do you truly believe that what Reinhardt did to Apollo could not be done to Extraya?" Admiral Andrewson told the delegate. He glanced up at Kira. "We know that the Shadows undermined all of

Apollo's defenses and even bought members of the Council of Principals.

"Can you be so certain that a professional fifth column isn't at work on your world? I am not so certain about my own Luxum!"

"That is why we are all here," the Extrayan delegate snapped. "It does not mean we must put our necks on the chopping block next to Apollo's!"

"Apollo as it was is gone, envoy," Kira told the man. "The Council of Principals will not be restored. I do not know what form the future of my homeworld will take—that is for her citizens to decide.

"I only know that I am prepared to fight for her. So are Michelakis and Killinger and the spacers and Hoplites who follow them both."

She gestured to the Extrayan delegate.

"I'm not asking you to put your necks on the block at all," she reminded him. "Volunteers and fighters and a freighter or six full of spare parts. None of these can be definitely traced back to anyone. I *understand* your fears. I understand that you do not owe Apollo anything—and I remind you, that if you help us, the future Apollo will owe *you*."

"Speaking of 'owe.'"

Every eye on the floating platform turned toward the speaker, a softly feminine voice that shouldn't have cut through the hubbub as cleanly as it had.

The woman standing next to Voski smiled gently, like a schoolteacher studying her class.

"For those of you unfamiliar with me, I am Senior Finance Director Loretta Baghdasaryan of the Bank of the Royal Crest," the small dark-haired woman introduced herself. "I was, I presume, invited here to see if you could convince me—and, through me, the Bank of the Royal Crest—to advance loans to help fund a counter-Brisingr buildup."

She glanced around the gathering, the gentle smile still somehow holding them all silent.

"I was close to the Apollo-Brisingr Sector for reasons of our own, so when you asked for a BRC representative, I decided to insert myself. I am glad I did."

Baghdasaryan gestured toward Kira.

"For those of you who are unaware, Kira Demirci stole a fleet carrier from the Navy of the Royal Crest. She is officially and formally banned from ever entering the Crest System or from directly receiving any financing from the Bank of the Royal Crest for herself or her mercenary company."

Kira hadn't actually been *aware* of the bank ban, though it made sense. One of the key power levers the royal family had maintained, prior to their recent seizure of power, was ownership of the sovereign shares in the BRC.

Of course, she also knew that *Voski* knew the truth behind Kira's relationship with the Panosyans. And the name Loretta rang a bell...

"Given Admiral Demirci's interactions with my partner's family and their father's government, I feel that I have a key and critical perspective on the Admiral's suggestion," Baghdasaryan continued.

Oh. *Oh.* She was *that* Loretta—the wife of the Crown Zharang, the mother of Jade Panosyan's children. Kira hadn't met Jade's wife during her whirlwind visit to the Crest Sector. On the other hand, she was also certain that Loretta Baghdasaryan knew *everything* about her mission for the Panosyans.

"I make no excuses for my activities in the Crest Sector," Kira told Baghdasaryan with a smile of her own. "Some long-standing enemies of mine had got themselves involved."

"Indeed." Baghdasaryan met Kira's gaze—and the Crester's dark blue eyes sparkled with unconcealed amusement. "I cannot, of course, tell the representatives of the sovereign governments of these systems what to do.

"However, the Bank of the Royal Crest is prepared to advance below-prime loans to underwrite the provision of the supplies and support Admiral Demirci has asked. We cannot, as I have said, advance any funds to Admiral Demirci herself, but we are prepared to assist in financing these sovereign stars in aiding her mission."

"Somehow, that seems very like a bank," Kira told the Crest executive. "Your offer is appreciated, Director."

She looked around the crowd, most of whom were looking thoughtful now.

"I believe we are now at the point where I should withdraw and allow you all to consider the information and suggestions that have been made," she suggested. "I am, of course, at the full disposal of this conference for the next few days.

"I also note that Admiral Michelakis herself is in this system, available to meet with the conference if invited."

She extended a hand, palm upward.

"We will fight for Apollo," she told them. "In fighting for Apollo, we fight for you. I believe that you and your nations will be well served by standing with us."

43

BYZANTIUM HILLS HAD SEVERAL DIFFERENT "ZONES," though the only two Kira had seen were the titular ski hills and the artificial lake. After her speech, she followed a clearly marked path that wrapped around the lake to the east, putting some distance between herself and the platform to let the delegates talk.

She'd spotted a few stone benches along the way, and by the time she'd walked about two kilometers along the side of the lake, she stopped at one. Brushing her hand over the plain-seeming white stone, she found it warm, as if it had been under sunlight for most of a day.

Given that Byzantium Hills was primarily lit by a diffuse illumination produced by the dome itself, the light didn't carry enough warmth to heat the stone. The bench was warming itself, but the feeling was nice, and Kira dropped onto it with a concealed sigh, looking out over the rippling water.

The entire place was artificial in ways that the human brain found hard to process, but she had to admit it had been well done. A vast amount of effort and money had been poured into this place, and only a tiny percentage of people in the Exarch System would ever see it.

It was impressive and wasteful—but she supposed there was also a value to having a perfectly secure *moon* for secret meetings like this.

A fish leapt out of the water in the gleaming light from Patriarch, and as she was trying to source the splash, a disgruntled *meow* informed her that she'd apparently stolen someone's afternoon nap spot.

Kira turned to find the source of the sound, but the massive orange tabby cat wasn't particularly hard to find. He leaped up onto the bench, meowing at her again as he checked if there was enough room left for him.

To her own amusement, Kira shifted over to make space for the animal. With a final, almost *smug* meow, the cat curled up on the warm spot next to her. After a few moments, she reached out and scratched behind the cat's ears.

She was rewarded with a rumbling purr that she could *feel* rippling up her arms and soothing her muscles. Kira wasn't much of a cat person, but this particular tabby had picked a good time to demand pets from her perspective!

"Does the cat secretly work for your bodyguard, or is this a good time to say hello?" Andrewson's familiar voice asked.

She'd heard him approaching, but as he'd observed, she knew that Milani was shadowing her. Anyone the mercenary commando let near her was probably safe.

"Well, I know they do like cats," Kira replied. "And I'm not sure you'd win the arm-wrestling match for the other half of the bench."

Andrewson stepped around the seat and fell into a much-practiced parade rest next to her, studying the tabby.

"No, I'm not sure I would," he conceded. "Plus, he looks *far* too comfortable for me to want to disturb him."

"And I don't?" Kira asked.

"Well, I hope *my* disturbance is at least somewhat welcome,"

Andrewson told her with a chuckle. "You made quite the impression, Kira. Both today and, well, a long time ago for me.

"My diplomatic half—Vice Director of Luxum Special Projects Olivera Alan—is thinking over what we're going to do and arguing with everyone else," he noted. "And yes, Em Alan's title is as much bullshit as you think it is. Her job is to be the person who negotiates for Luxum in places Luxum can't officially be."

"Sounds like a shitty deal," Kira considered aloud.

"Ninety-nine percent of the time, someone like Olivera speaks with the full authority of our government," he said. "The other one percent of the time, they are being completely written off, everything they said and did disavowed—as they take the fall for the government's scheming becoming public.

"So, yeah. It's not a great deal. As I understand it, it pays well, though."

"And you?" she asked.

"I know my position on all of this and have told Olivera," he said. "Personal isn't the same as professional, but it does mean I have a solid sense of your judgment, Kira. If you think you can do this, I believe you."

"I appreciate that."

He was *very* close, she realized. Close enough that she could smell the high-end cologne he was wearing. Close enough that it would take almost no movement for her to lean against him.

Andrewson shifted slightly, putting his hip softly in contact with her shoulder.

"I was wondering if you wanted to catch up over dinner?" he asked. "I, for one, am unlikely to ever spend time in a place quite so luxurious again."

Given their past...Kira could only read one thing into that invitation, and while she was disinclined to celibacy, she was *also* in a committed monogamous relationship.

She shifted her shoulder away from him and looked up at him flatly.

"Are you planning on making Luxum's support conditional on my sleeping with you?" she asked acidly.

Andrewson recoiled as if struck, his entire body language shifting as he took a long stride away from her with a horrified expression on his face.

"No, that wasn't— *Fuck*— I mean— I didn't— I kind of— I— *Void take it.*"

Now he was standing close to the edge of the water, well outside of any personal bubble as he locked into a very stiff parade rest.

"I apologize, Admiral Demirci," he said formally. "While the thought of temporarily rekindling our former relationship had certainly crossed my mind, I did not intend to imply the slightest amount of pressure. In no way is Luxum's support for the operation against Apollo contingent in any way upon anything between us."

The tabby lifted his head at the upset tones and made a very clear *stop interrupting my nap, humans* meow.

Kira chuckled and nodded—at either the cat or Andrewson, she wasn't sure.

"Apology accepted, Mason," she told him. "My partner isn't here, but that doesn't change the promises I've made and the intentions I have."

"That is entirely fair and correct," Andrewson told her. He paused, then coughed. "Mine *is*, but Olivera and I are very clear on the limits of our claims upon each other."

Kira arched an eyebrow.

"Not just your *political* partner, then," she said.

"No. We worked together before we fell into bed together," he explained. He shook his head. "You left after the war, Kira; I don't think you really get how bad it got for the Friends."

"From what I understand, messy."

"We never agreed to the terms Apollo set with Brisingr," he reminded her. "But, at least in Luxum's case, our fleet had been all but wiped out by then. We wanted to rebuild the entire fleet, but Brisingr informed us that if we built more than five hundred kilocubics of ships, they'd blockade us until they'd either wrecked enough cubage to get us inside that limit or we scrapped it ourselves."

He shrugged.

"We never agreed to anything," he concluded. "But we *obeyed*. On the surface, anyway."

"Mason, I am assuming that absolutely *none* of the member systems of the Security Zone have observed the spirit, let alone the *letter*, of the Agreement on Nova Lane Security," Kira told him.

Andrewson chuckled, turning away from her to look over the water—and, not accidentally, she was sure—to minimize any threat profile.

"We had no carriers left at the end," he said. "We were down to three eighty-kay cruisers. No escorts. No carriers. No battlecruisers. Just three nova cruisers.

"I got my first star, Kira, basically by still being *alive*." He tapped the two six-pointed gold stars on the left side of his high tunic collar. There were no epaulets or wrist-cuffs on the uniform, and only the stars marked his rank.

"I was the fifth-most senior member of the Luxum Nova Fighter Corps alive at the end of the war," he explained. "Two of the more senior officers resigned. Whether out of protest at our concession to Brisingr or sheer exhaustion, I don't actually know.

"A year after the war ended, we were finally in a place where we *had* the half-million-cubic-meter force we were allowed. One fleet carrier, those three cruisers, and six destroyers we'll swear until the stars die are twenty-three kilocubics apiece."

Kira chuckled.

"And how big are they?" she asked.

"Twenty-three kilocubics," he assured her, turning around to flash her a brilliant smile. "And the new cruisers are *definitely* only eighty thousand cubics, too."

"Somehow, I have the sneaking suspicion that *cubic meter* doesn't mean quite the same thing around here anymore."

"We ask that no one inspect our measuring tapes *too* closely," he agreed archly, then chuckled again.

"But after that year of rebuilding, we realized that Brisingr was keeping a very close eye on our yards. We expected them to turn a reasonably blind eye to us pushing the definition of a meter, but we knew that if we started building extra cruisers, they were going to call us out on it."

"So?" Kira prodded.

"I got a second star; Olivera got a fancy-schmancy job title and a black-as-vanta budget," he told her. "Our job for the last few years has been to create something exactly like this conference. Us and Exarch are the reason everyone is here, Kira, though I suspect there is at least one hidden hand at play."

Zamorano was subtle, Kira knew, but if Andrewson had been working on arranging a conference for the last few years, he'd likely noticed the extra push the SolFed agent had exerted.

"Attaca probably has the most to throw at any given problem, but like Extraya and Prasináda, they were willing to go along to get along until Brisingr pulled a fast one and took control of Apollo," the Luxum officer concluded.

"Now everyone is getting twitchy—but whatever games we've all played, we still have fundamentally limited fleets."

"Except for the remnants of Apollo and a certain prodigal daughter and her mercenaries," Kira said grimly.

"Hiring mercenaries from out of the sector was high on my list of likely options," he told her. "Which resulted in part of my job being mapping dark nova points and arranging secret logistics caches."

"Oh?" Kira's mental ears perked up, and she reached over to pet the cat to conceal her interest.

"I can't promise pilots and nova fighters," Andrewson admitted. "If we get the rest of the system delegates on board, we'll go home and *ask*—and there are a few things that Olivera and I will be able to do out of said black budget no matter what.

"But those logistics caches should include all the spare parts you need to revamp any damage the Apollon ships have taken," he concluded. A file-transfer request pinged up on Kira's headware.

"I believe there's even class two drive units in them, but not enough to fill the Last Fleet's decks."

"Thank you, Mason," Kira murmured. "I apologize for snapping."

"No," he told her calmly. "You were correct to yank me up short. Rekindling a friendship is one thing, but part of me was not thinking with my brain."

He smiled.

"Would you care to join Em Alan and me for dinner tonight?" he asked. "With your officers, of course. A working meal."

44

ENTERING the room she'd been sent to for brunch the next morning, Kira found herself in a surprisingly intimate space. Centered on a single round table sized for eight people, the room had tinted glass walls on all sides except the one she'd entered from—and as she took her seat, the room vibrated around them and lifted into the air, lifting away from the hall she'd come through.

As the dining room rose until it stood at least fifty meters above the resort's main buildings, a meal-ordering interface appeared on Kira's headware. She glanced around the table with a questioning look.

"There's an automatic elevator connection in the support pillar," Olivera Alan told her with a chuckle. "No human enters this space who isn't one of the invited guests, and there's an additional layer of signal-blocking built into the glass.

"Even for Byzantium Hills, this is secure."

"I see." Kira gave the interface her order and assessed her brunch companions.

She knew Doretta Macey, of course, and her dinner with Andrewson's partner had been interesting. Olivera Alan was intelligent, dedicated and silver-tongued. Even if Kira hadn't *known* the woman had come up through Luxum's intelligence bureaucracy, she'd have figured it out quickly enough.

Kira wasn't as familiar with the other four occupants of the room, but given the bona fides of the people she was certain of, she knew what was going on. These were the six actual *delegates* to the conference, the officials with the power to bind their governments.

"I don't imagine you all dragged me up here for the view," she observed. "There is no one in this room who shouldn't have a bodyguard." She chuckled at a thought. "How many of our bodyguards do you think are set up in spots that give them clear lines of sight on this pod, with collections of *tools* that definitely can*not* be assembled into an impromptu sniper rifle?"

"Most if not all," replied a white-haired woman in the faux-clerical cassock of Exarch's upper class and government. "While the Templars have guaranteed the security of the Hills for this meeting and we have asked everyone to refrain from bringing weapons, I have no illusions about the type of guardians people like us have brought."

A small gesture from the Exarch woman sent Kira her details. Nata Viktorov held the always-illuminating title of Minister Without Portfolio in the Presidential Cabinet of the Orthodox Republic of Exarch.

"There was a larger conversation on the dock yesterday, and the six of us spoke at length afterward as well," Viktorov noted smoothly. "We do not agree on all things, Admiral Demirci. But what we *have* all agreed to is that no one is telling tales to Brisingr."

"I would have hoped that was the base cost of entry to a meeting like this," Kira murmured.

"It was," Alan agreed. "But certain of our subordinates felt that an active plan to attack Apollo was somewhat beyond the scope of what we had promised to keep concealed."

"And the lack of enthusiasm of certain parties for Henry Killinger and Fevronia Michelakis cannot be understated," the Extrayan delegate said flatly. The Black woman was looking at Kira like she might burst into snakes at any moment—and had *not* provided a digital contact card.

"You have made your bed with a pirate who would be king and a woman who has sat on a battle fleet for six months," the Extrayan concluded. "This will culminate only in further disaster. But, yes, I have agreed that neither I nor my people will expose your conspiring."

"We know, Choe," the delegate in the uniform of the Attacan Star Navy said flatly. Their identity beacon flickered into existence as they spoke, introducing them as Admiral Mtendere Payton. Like Iris Choe—whose name Kira had finally pulled from the earlier introductions—their skin was pitch-black.

Unlike Choe, Payton wore a military uniform like they'd been born to it and had removed all of their visible hair. Still, they flashed Kira a brilliantly white smile.

"Attaca has our own problems with Apollo," they observed. "But I have to appreciate your willingness to concede what must change. And despite what Minister Choe thinks, I think that the worse disaster will come from doing nothing.

"If one of our systems were to act unilaterally, even working with Michelakis, we would expose ourselves to our utter destruction," Payton continued. "This, Michelakis failed to understand. It was in her hands to bring together a grouping such as this and build the support needed for the task before us.

"She did not fail—she did not even try. Her tactical skill cannot be doubted, but I question her strategic acumen. But *you* are here. You have brought Apollo's rogue and Apollo's remnants to the same table, as well as forces of your own."

Payton gestured to Macey.

"You have preserved Samuels' sovereignty in the face of Brisingr's attempts to impose influence on the Samuels-Colossus Corridor. Your name and company are known across the Rim these days. And the Crest has made it clear that they will financially support your operations, if indirectly."

They shrugged.

"I do not believe, and I have assured all of my companions of this, that there is a better horse in this race to bet on. I cannot speak to the full scale of the resources that Attaca will be able to muster, but I can promise that Attaca *will* support you, Admiral Demirci.

"If all I can send when I return home is a single transport full of fighters and volunteers, trust that you will receive at *least* that."

"I can commit the same for Luxum," Alan said. "As Admiral Payton says, the details will need to be hashed out with my government at home, but we will send *something*."

That was the problem, Kira knew. There was only one person in the room who could *know*, with any degree of certainty, that their government would back them entirely.

"Extraya declines to participate in this endeavor," Choe said calmly. "But we will also refrain from betraying your efforts to Brisingr. If you are successful in liberating Apollo, we are willing to come to the table to discuss the future of this sector and the conflict against Brisingr, but at this moment, the situation appears clear, and we are unwilling to risk our sovereignty or the safety of our citizens in pursuit of some vague ideal of liberty."

"Prasináda has limited resources to commit," the final representative said softly. "Thanks to the conflict in the Corridor, we are unwillingly playing host to a Brisingr Kaiserreich Navy battle group. The eyes of the Kaiser are close upon us.

"We do not oppose this operation and we will provide what support we can manage, but understand our limitations," the woman concluded. "Until the BKN withdraws their forces from our system—or we are given sufficient confidence to engage that nova force with our sublight defenses—we must tread carefully."

Viktorov had not yet committed to anything beyond secrecy, and the sudden smooth arrival of their plates in the middle of the table interrupted further conversation for a moment.

"Exarch is in," she finally said, eyeing a heap of mixed egg and potatoes that, Kira presumed, had been fried up in a skillet of some kind. "I have confirmation from the rest of the Presidential Cabinet of our intentions. Some details, you and I will speak of in private, Admiral Demirci.

"But first, I realize we have all made grand promises of potential resources," Viktorov continued. "But I have heard few details. We know that you need pilots and nova fighters. We know that none of us can provide warships.

"Outside of those limits, Admiral Demirci, what do you need? You plan to achieve the impossible. I do not expect you to *share* that plan, but we must know enough to help."

Kira nodded, taking a moment to carefully assemble her toast and eggs into something easily edible while she marshalled her thoughts.

She *did* have a plan—or, at least, the beginnings of one.

"Brisingr took Apollo by stealth and deception," she observed. "We don't have that option. While I am certain we could build contacts with troops and factions on the ground who would help us, I doubt that the BKN is allowing *any* locals on the fortresses.

"They recognize their vulnerabilities, just as we do. We must take the system by a coup de main, an open assault with nova fighters and warships with the sole true advantage of surprise."

She smiled thinly.

"And the fact that no one expects it."

"A disaster, as I said," Choe interrupted.

"I have a plan," Kira replied. "Forgive me, but I'm not going to lay it out with you in the room, Minister Choe."

That shut the Extrayan woman up—though, Kira at least had to concede, she didn't seem *upset* by the statement. Choe might think that the whole operation was doomed, but she didn't appear to be out to sabotage it.

Just to keep her own system out of it.

"In terms of resources, first and foremost, we need nova fighters," she reiterated. "Then pilots. Fully informed volunteers if at all possible. Third, Harrington coils. In any quantity you can provide—as many as you can provide.

"Fourth, I need freighters and transports. I don't intend to risk them, but what I need them to do will not be safe."

Kira wasn't one hundred percent certain what that was going to *be*, but she was about...ninety percent of the way there.

"Taking a star system isn't going to be easy, painless or quick," she warned. "But given fighters, pilots, engines and freighters, I think I may just be able to pull it off."

45

"ARE you familiar with the original Knights Templar of Old Earth, Admiral?"

Kira took a careful sip of the beer she'd been handed and barely managed to not side-eye Minister Viktorov.

The two women were seated in a gazebo on a cliff, overlooking the lake and well away from any of the other members of the meeting. The server who'd passed them their beers wore the uniform of the Byzantium Hills staff, but Kira could see the reality in the way the man moved.

Uniform or not, the soldier-boosted man was the Minister Without Portfolio's bodyguard.

"Not in any great deal, I have to admit," she conceded. "A few bits of half-remembered Crusade history."

"From what I can tell, that might be *more* than my ancestors remembered when they set up Exarch and named our military the Templars," Viktorov told her. "With the haze of some two centuries of history between them and me, I cannot be certain what they were thinking or even why the mythology of the Third Nicaean Council

Orthodox Church was so interwoven into our planet's traditions and naming."

At Kira's expression, the local chuckled.

"Even *I*, who am a good Orthodox girl in my spare time, cannot explain the full array of history, legend, propaganda and truth that has led to the modern panoply of Orthodox Christian subbranches," Viktorov admitted. "Roughly twenty-eight percent of Exarch's people are members of some form of the Church, with another twenty percent in other related faiths of the Abrahamic umbrella.

"But all the names and games we play have very little connection to the reality of the past." She shrugged. "The Templars of Exarch are not a religious order, though they are known to occasionally ape the stylings of one. Knightly chivalry and similar propaganda lends itself well to the auras and attitudes needed for novafighter pilots."

"It definitely does," Kira agreed. "What about the historical Templars is relevant, then?"

"That I bloody well wish my ancestors had picked up a history textbook," Viktorov said. "The Templars died messily, in controversy and conspiracy and lies. Their inheritors were everything from nurses to the Italian air force under false pretenses.

"An interesting history to draw on, one with many flaws and warts and issues." She shook her head. "Irrelevant, as you say, but also a worrying trend. The Knights Templar were destroyed by a conspiracy. Whether that conspiracy was founded in truth or lies, history does leave to us. Only that a king immensely in their debt turned on them."

Kira sighed and took another sip of her beer.

"I'm not sure I follow your point, Minister."

"The Equilibrium Institute is my point, Admiral," Viktorov said. "A conspiracy with tendrils that run through our entire section of the Rim—except, it seems, where you have passed. One wonders if the woman across from me is the enemy of the knife I see in my shadows or just a different tool."

That was not an accusation Kira had run into before, and she swallowed her initial response as she studied the other woman.

"I did not know what the Equilibrium Institute was when I went to the Syntactic Cluster," she told Viktorov. "Through John Estanza, who had deserted them, I learned. And when the Institute came to the Cluster, we fought them.

"I have not, necessarily, wholly chosen to make fighting them my purpose in life, but they keep showing up and being obnoxious." Kira grimaced. "Kaiser Reinhardt and the Institute appear to be inseparable out here. Their influence through him is dangerous—as are the resources they make available to him."

"You do know your full enemy, then," Viktorov conceded. "I fear the knife in the shadows, Demirci. I fear what kind of enemy will attempt to stop us rebuilding once we defeat Brisingr."

The Exarch woman shook her head.

"But I fear the world Kaiser Reinhardt is already building more. I swore an oath to serve the people of Exarch. I would betray that oath if I stood by and allowed Brisingr to turn us all into good little tributaries.

"Uneven trade deals and enforced junior partnerships were Apollo's crimes, yes, but they were still deals and partnerships. The world the Equilibrium Institute would impose upon us, the world Brisingr works toward... It is no such thing."

"I know," Kira said. "They have determined that they know the right path. And any price is acceptable in pursuit of that path, anything can be destroyed. They cast aside working structures that have kept entire sectors at peace for a generation in favor of their perfect model."

"I am no psychohistorian, and Seldonian analysis is beyond me," Viktorov noted. "But I *am* a historian, a student of the past of mankind all the way back to Old Earth and into the mists of time. And I can assure you, Admiral Demirci, that *every time* someone has become convinced that they know the *one true way* for humanity to function, they are wrong.

"And they are usually proven wrong in the blood of millions of innocents, one way or another."

"I don't think I know a good way for humanity to exist," Kira replied. "I'm only somewhat convinced I know a good way to run a mercenary fleet. The only thing I'm sure of, if I'm being honest, is that almost everyone who claims the ends justifies the means is one misstep at most from evil—and that I will fight to keep either of my homes free."

"Your honesty does you credit," Viktorov said. "Some would try to twist their views and words to match what they think I want."

"I have no idea what you want, Minister. I'm here because you promised me support and I want to get the details before I leave."

The old woman chuckled.

"The promise of fighters and pilots is sufficient for you to listen to the ramblings of an old woman who is convinced that history may not repeat...but it sure as all stars *rhymes*?"

"For a while, at least," Kira said with a smile.

"First." Viktorov paused to finish the beer. "This is damn good beer. Everything here is. It's fucking grotesque, really, but it tastes good and looks good, doesn't it?"

Kira wasn't sure how that related to her promised supplies and pilots, but she couldn't *disagree* with Viktorov's assessment of Byzantium Hills.

"Sorry; when you reach my age, even cybernetics have problems keeping you focused," Viktorov replied. "First and foremost, you benefit neatly from the Templars liking to pretend they are a knightly order.

"Volunteer for a potential suicide mission for justice, chivalry and glory? The young fools are lapping it up." She chuckled. "So are some older, not-so-foolish officers who have axes to grind or are aligned with ideologies that say a world should not be conquered by force.

"The current estimate I am getting is about four hundred pilots and four thousand fighter support and spacers."

Kira considered that.

"I'm...not sure I need four thousand spacers, Minister," she pointed out carefully.

"Likely not, but they seem to have volunteered anyway," Viktorov said brightly. "So, before you leave the system, I will need you to do me a favor, Admiral Demirci."

"A favor?" Kira suspected she was being led down a very specific path. She didn't think she was going to mind where it ended up, but four thousand spacers were easily the crew for a solid *squadron*.

Between her extras, Killinger's fleet and Michelakis's fleet, she wasn't sure they were in need of four *hundred* extra spacers.

"From here, I need you to go to Ravenna's trailing asteroid cluster," Viktorov told her. She waved a hand delicately. "It's some twenty-five light-minutes; you may wish to nova, I don't know."

Ravenna was the system's inner gas giant. As Viktorov said, its trailing Trojan cluster was a long way away.

"Once there, find Albrecht's Antioch Asteroid Assets," she continued. "A-Four's founder and owner, the titular Albrecht, is very fond of alliteration. More importantly, however, he is quite fond of both his home star system and his government's money.

"You will speak to Albrecht himself and tell him that you are there to collect the contents of raw materials bins eighteen through twenty-two," Viktorov concluded. "I will arrange for your volunteers to meet you at Albrecht's facility."

Kira had to raise a questioning eyebrow at that. The pieces fit a pattern and she could *guess* at the pattern—but from Viktorov's expression, the Exarch minister wasn't *just* playing games.

Even there, amidst delegates sworn to secrecy, in a place far from any prying eyes...Viktorov wasn't going to admit what was in those five raw materials bins.

46

"I HAVE TO ADMIT, I appreciate that four of the delegates actually *spoke* to me," Fevronia Michelakis observed as *Teal Circlet* drifted apart from *Springtime Chorus*. "Having come all this way to just sit in orbit was rather...humiliating."

"I think the fact that you were here at all made a difference," Kira told the Apollon officer. "Especially since you *were* willing to speak to them. Putting your pride aside to accept that they weren't willing to risk being seen with you? That meant something to them."

"I hope so," Michelakis said. "But then, after the last year or so, I'm not sure what pride I'm supposed to have. I abandoned a lot of good people."

Teal Circlet didn't have an Admiral's bridge, so the two flag officers had taken over a conference room more normally used by the senior tactical chiefs. It had the right connections to give the two women a decent display of the system and kept them from getting in Captain Negri's hair *too* much.

At that moment, it was focused on the light cruiser pulling away from the consular ship she'd escorted. *Chorus* was heading back to

Patriarch Doce, as Macey and the rest of the delegates were going to stay there a while longer.

Not long enough, Kira hoped, to still be there when they needed to convene new discussions on the post-liberation world. Messages had been sent, quietly, back to all of the home systems with the agreements that had been made.

A lot of people, ships and matériel would be converging on the Corosec System in about three weeks. Kira was mentally allowing about three weeks after that to exercise and prepare the fleet—and lay the groundwork for her plan.

Six weeks.

After everything she had done and everything they had faced, in six weeks she would be going home at the head of a battle fleet. Kira Demirci was going to kick the BKN all the way back to Brisingr, where Konrad Bueller would be waiting for them, ready to finish putting the boot in.

"Sers, we are standing by to nova to the designated trojan cluster," Negri's voice said over their headware. "Anything we should be watching for?"

"Brisingr ships," Kira warned. "Even civilian ones. Whatever Exarch has tucked away, we won't want any friends of the Kaiser running home with tales to tell."

"Nothing in our area of Patriarch," Negri replied. "Only other warship around here is the Templars' battlecruiser. We are clear."

"Nova when you are ready, Captain," Kira ordered.

The world rippled around them in answer to the command, informing Kira that her captain had *already* been ready.

"We have the cluster on screens and are locating our alliterative asteroid-refining friend," Negri told her with a chuckle. "I'll forward contact info to the conference room as soon as we have him nailed down.

"Should I have my coms team talk to his coms team to get Em Albrecht himself on the channel?"

"Please," Kira asked. "That should save everyone some time."

MICHELAKIS WAS STILL in the conference room with Kira when they finally linked to Lavrentios Albrecht. The beefy olive-skinned man who appeared above the table could have been one of the shepherds in her home village overlooking New Athens—he might not be from Apollo, but there was definitely Greek stock in Exarch.

"Admiral Demirci," he greeted her jovially. "I am not sure what brings a warship to my little asteroid-mining operation here in the boonies of Exarch, but if you are looking to purchase raw materials, I think I can definitely cut a deal. I've got a second cousin you pulled out of the fire during the war, still speaks highly of you!"

Kira, if she was being honest, didn't even have a list of everyone who would qualify as "pulled out of the fire" by her during the war. It had been a busy three years.

"I may take you up on that," she told him. "We're supposed to be having a few freighters meeting us here by midnight Constantinople Central. But I also have quite specific instructions for what I'm supposed to tell *you*, Em Albrecht."

It was a subtle change. Some of the joviality and ease in Albrecht's posture dissolved. The dancing spark in his eye suggested that this was a more-honest amusement now but also a more serious one.

"Instructions, I hear?" he replied. "Well, Admiral, lay them on me."

"I am to tell you that I am here to 'collect the contents of raw materials bins eighteen through twenty-two,'" Kira told him, carefully repeating the words Viktorov had used.

The joviality was completely gone now. Albrecht wasn't *upset* or anything of the sort, but he was now deathly serious.

"Time and past time, I suppose," he told her. "I don't suppose you know what you're getting out of that?"

"I was told to tell you exactly that," Kira replied. "By a member of the Cabinet, though I don't think I should be more specific. I'm assuming it's a code of some kind?"

Albrecht chuckled, a touch of the joviality returning to his face as his eyes started to sparkle again.

"Oh, no, Admiral Demirci. It is *exactly* what you just said. There are a few validations I need to run, but I suggest you take your ship to the coordinates I'm transmitting you.

"Once I've completed my validations, we'll send you the access codes for those bins. I hope those freighters you mentioned are bringing some people, Admiral. You're going to need them."

RAW MATERIALS BIN TWENTY, the center of the five Kira had been sent codes to, was identical to the *other* roughly fifty such storage containers around Albrecht's Antioch Asteroid Assets. The main purpose was to hold asteroid material in the stage between "blasting the asteroid into pieces" and "feeding the pieces into a massive blast furnace for refining and separation."

Each bin was a cube of roughly cast asteroid iron two hundred meters on a side. Two opposing sides were hinged, creating access hatches so massive, they were opened with Harrington coils.

The bin itself could use the same coils to move around the refinery, if very, *very* slowly.

"Transmitting the code," Negri reported. "Starting with just bin twenty. Let's see what Em Albrecht has for us."

The two-hundred-meter-wide hatch pivoted outward to reveal that raw materials bin twenty, by the standards of a bin supposed to be full of chopped-up asteroids, was empty.

The sole occupant of the bin was a wedge-shaped starship, a hundred and seventy meters long and built to a familiar-looking design.

"That's a *Hero*-class heavy cruiser," Kira noted. "Ninety thousand cubic meters. Eight dual turrets armed with heavy cannon. She's...a hell of a ship."

"Visual markings call her *Coyote*, no hull number," Negri reported. "What's an Apollon cruiser doing in an asteroid-refining facility's materials bin?"

"She's not an Apollon cruiser," Michelakis said. "We built twenty-two *Hero*-class ships. None of them were called *Coyote*. She's an Apollon *design*, but I suspect Exarch built her themselves."

"Hence named for a trickster hero," Kira guessed. "Do I want to guess what's in the other four bins? Dare I hope for more heavy cruisers?"

"It would make a lot of sense for Exarch to have built themselves a squadron of cruisers that would fly under an Apollon flag and stir up trouble," the Last Fleet's commander murmured. "I admire the concept, even though I suspect *I've* borne the blame for anything they've got up to."

"I don't care what they've *been* up to," Kira said with a chuckle. "Negri, please tell me what's in the other four bins?"

"Looking much the same, sir. Names...*Loki, Odysseus, Hermes, Mercury*."

"Tricksters one and all," Michelakis concluded. "Bastards."

"Maybe. But *useful* bastards, because we have volunteer crews coming out to handle those ships," Kira reminded the other Admiral. "And they're coming to Corosec with us."

Regardless of what plans Exarch had built their squadron of trickster *Hero*es for, they'd decided to at least *lend* them to Kira and Michelakis.

And she wasn't going to look a gift squadron in the plasma guns!

47

RETURNING to Corosec was a stark reminder of what they were fighting for. Kira hadn't had to drop the Brisingr torpedo on anyone's desk, though she'd kept it in her back pocket, just in case.

No information had arisen yet to prove that the Kaiser's people had done anything other than murder the entire population of the system. The original old-light data from the rescue ships suggested that Corosec's residents had been loaded onto the fleet of armed transports that had launched the attack—along with everything else of value that wasn't nailed down.

But no one had seen those people since, and Corosec remained a graveyard.

It was not, however, an *empty* graveyard. Kira arrived with seven cruisers, but her "escort" was a fraction of the firepower assembled in the star system. Admiral Michelakis's fleet was waiting for her, nineteen carriers and their sparse escorts arrayed in an onion-like layered sphere in a trailing orbit of Corosec's solitary planet.

In a leading orbit of Corosec Alpha, distinctly and likely specifically out of heavy-cannon range, Admiral Killinger's privateers were assembled. He'd found replacements for two of the three cruisers he'd lost at Shenandoah, leaving that rebel fleet with a battlecruiser, thirteen cruisers and ten destroyers.

Above Corosec Alpha and positioned exactly midway between the two Apollon forces were Kira's own ships. *Fortitude* held the center of her own layered sphere, with *Huntress* and *Shillelagh* positioned on her flanks.

Deception hung "above" the supercarrier, with *Harbinger* on the opposite side to complete a four-ship box around *Fortitude*. *Marchioness*, the other *Baron*-class cruiser, was ahead of the wall of heavier starships, and then twenty-four destroyers formed a near-perfect sphere around the cruisers and carriers.

Each of the three fleets had their own, clearly distinct CAPs up. Memorial Force had two squadrons, twelve planes. The Last Fleet had one squadron. Killinger's privateers had two interceptors.

Twenty nova fighters were in space, all told, which was about what the combined fleet *should* have had...if it were actually a combined fleet instead of three separate contingents who didn't quite trust each other.

"Ronaldo, instruct Knight-Admiral Cullen to bring his ships in behind us," Kira told Ronaldo. The rendezvous with *Prodigal* had returned her to a proper flag bridge—though she'd be heading over to *Fortitude* once they were fully "home."

"We'll keep Trickster Squadron under our wing for the moment. Soler"—she turned to her ops officer—"make sure Admiral Michelakis has everything she needs to get aboard *Salaminia*."

"On it, ser."

Kira nodded to her staff and leaned back in her chair.

"Both of you get integrated with your teams on *Fortitude* ASAP," she continued. "Once we're aboard, I figure we're going to need to hold a big fancy get-together to make sure everyone is on the same page."

"What happens if people aren't willing to talk to each other?" Ronaldo asked.

"Then they can refuse to talk to each other in *Fortitude*'s main theater," Kira replied drily. "Over the course of the next ten days, a hopefully immense amount of supplies, fighters, pilots and war matériel is going to be arriving in this system.

"Those resources are not going to any particular segment of this fleet. They have been put up for the *mission*, and they are going to be assigned as best to return the *entire* fleet to full warfighting capability."

She smiled.

"And if that means I need to play kindergarten teacher to some Admirals who should damn well know better, so be it."

48

FORTITUDE's main theater was a multipurpose subdividable space, designed to act as everything from a ballroom to a conference center to an operational briefing space for all twenty-five squadrons' worth of pilots and copilots.

Opening the whole space up for a meeting of less than twenty officers was overkill, but Kira agreed with the plan. Now, with Kavitha Zoric one step behind and to her left, she strode into the open space and took her place at the head of the table.

Knight-Admiral Cullen—equivalent to an ASDF Vice Admiral, as she understood it—was seated at the far end, the solitary representative of the Exarch Templars. He was a squat blond man with severe features and sunken eyes, seeming to take in much more than he ever said so far.

Around the rest of the table were Kira's own key officers, the mercenary Commodores Mwangi, Patel and Michel now joined by Zoric. They now led her cruisers, fighters, destroyers and carriers, respectively, and the Apollons.

Killinger had brought *Oceanic Trident*'s captain and his destroyer flotilla commander. The three men sat stiffly, glaring at the other Apollon contingent.

That was Admiral Michelakis, Commodore Lister, Vice Admiral Branimir Munroe, and Rear Admirals Spring Kristiansen and Oda Annevelink.

Michelakis had kept most of the carriers from Home Fleet, which meant she had a disproportionate number of the flagships and hence Admirals. Each of the four Admirals flew their flag from one of the *Trireme*-class carriers now.

Cullen was silently watching everyone else at the table. Kira's people were doing the same, though she knew her subordinates well enough to *feel* the impatience rippling off of them.

It was the two Apollon contingents that were radiating daggers drawn as they faced each other across the table forged from *Conviction*'s broken hull. Kira knew that the source of the conference table was only meaningful to her mercenaries—but she could also tell that at least a couple of the other officers recognized what it was!

"Officers," she greeted them all. "We have a lot of work ahead of us before we're ready to go. Nonetheless, I think it is absolutely essential that we make sure we are all on the same page."

Kira paused, studying the dynamic in the room before smiling sadly.

"And, it seems, to clear the air," she noted. "I could *cut* the tension in this room's air, people, and that will not do."

She rapped her knuckles on the metal table.

"All of you, look at this table," she told them. "At least some of you have already realized what it is. For those of you haven't: this is hull metal. The largest retrieved piece of the carrier *Conviction*, the original home for many of my officers and crew.

"Faced with an overwhelming attempt by an outside enemy to impose their will on the Syntactic Cluster, Captain John Estanza chose to risk his ship to protect the people who'd hired him," she continued. "In the end, that risk culminated in a collision between *Conviction* and a hostile carrier.

"Both ships were destroyed and the Syntactic Cluster was kept free." She was silent for a moment, then shrugged.

"Understand, then, that Estanza is the standard I hold people who want me to follow them to. It is the standard I hold *myself* to. I have come a long damn way because I learned my homeworld was in trouble and because Kaiser Reinhardt chose to make me his own damn personal enemy.

"Now we are all sitting at this table on this ship. We share a goal. We share an enemy. So, tell me, what is the damn problem?"

There was a long, somewhat shameful silence.

"They let hundreds of our people be murdered by Brisingr and did *nothing*," Killinger finally said, gesturing toward the officers of the Last Fleet. "*Nothing.*"

"No one in this room knew the Shadow Détente existed until Apollo fell," Michelakis countered. "Our government betrayed us, yes, but how the hell were we supposed to know?

"As opposed to, say, knowing that *piracy* is a crime?"

"We at least were fighting back against Brisingr!" Killinger growled.

"By giving them an excuse to tighten their rules, tighten their patrols?" Michelakis demanded. "Every time the Security Zone had new rules, every time they twisted the agreements to impose new standards and restrictions, it was *your* name and *your* pirates who were given as the reason!"

"As you sat, fat on your ass, collecting a paycheck from the very bastards who sold us out!"

Kira leaned back and let the two tear into each other for a few more rounds, then slapped her hand on the deck. The metal rang like a gunshot, and both Admirals shut up and glared at her.

"None of us did everything right," she reminded them. If she had to pick, she would have picked Michelakis's deception-bought loyalty over Killinger's thinly justified piracy, but that wasn't a conversation for today.

"I fled into exile. Michelakis served, without knowing what our government was doing. Killinger faked his death and assembled a fleet of, let's be generous here, *privateers*."

She met each of their gazes in turn.

"What matters here and now is this: *Apollo. Has. Fallen.*" She accentuated each word with another smack of her fist against the metal table. "Our home has been invaded and occupied by our enemy. Members of our highest governments conspired with a fifth column of our enemy's covert operators to undermine and shatter our defenses."

Officers on both sides were now looking sheepishly down at the table.

"There will be a discussion of the future once the dust settles, but right now, the key thing is that we *must* retake our homeworld," Kira told them. "Knight-Admiral Cullen and his people—and even my own Memorial Force—are outsiders who have agreed to help. Others have committed to send us fighters, volunteers and supplies.

"Those will start arriving very shortly. We need a plan, to make sure that we get every ship in this new combined fleet up to full capacity and that we fight in a coordinated fashion.

"I will not fail in the mission before us because the officers involved cannot put aside their pride and their anger for long enough to fight as one fleet."

She glared down the table.

"Am I understood? If any of your officers want out, let them go. But I must have buy-in from you two, Fevronia and Henry. Or our home may be doomed."

Killinger looked like he'd eaten a lemon, but he slowly nodded.

"You are correct, of course," he conceded. "I apologize, Admiral Michelakis. I understand that the Council of Principals played all too many people for fools."

Michelakis nodded silently, holding her tongue until Kira met her gaze and arched an eyebrow.

"Thank you, Admiral," she told Killinger at last. "I understand, too, that the lines are fuzzy when running a fleet of rebels in a time when no one is sure who is on whose side."

She looked over at Kira and nodded again.

"But I know that everyone here is on the same side," she said levelly. "We face a common foe and stand in common cause. I will not see Apollo remain occupied for the sake of my pride. I have failed our people once.

"I won't do so again."

"Good." Kira smiled thinly. "Now, we aren't entirely sure what resources we *are* going to get, so we'll need to sort out our priorities now..."

49

When the war had ended, the ASDF's 303 Nova Combat Group had nineteen living pilots left. Among those pilots were two of Apollo's top ten aces and eleven of their top hundred aces of the war. The 303 had been involved in key actions throughout the war, making a name for themselves as individuals, as a formation and as part of Heller's Hellions, the task group that had *almost* turned things around in the final year.

For those achievements, Kira's government had sentenced them to death through the Shadow Détente.

By the time she'd fled Apollo herself, seven of those nineteen pilots were dead. Only six, other than her, had made it to Redward. One had used his share of the safety net their commander had set up for them to buy a ship and keep going.

The others had stayed with Kira and become Memorial Squadron. Then, later, with the acquisition of *Deception* and the loss of John Estanza, they'd become key officers of Memorial Force.

Several of their friends had died *in* Redward, when local thugs had cashed in on a death-mark bounty Brisingr had put out. Joseph

Hoffman had died in the battles to save the Syntactic Cluster—and Evgenia Michel had lost her legs in the same fights.

But there were five survivors left of Kira's old fighter wing, and for one precious day as the final pieces of the plan came together, all of them were aboard *Fortitude* and able to join her for dinner.

Kira leaned against a wall with a drink in her hand as Koch's minions cleared away the last plates, smiling as her subordinates and friends appeared to actually *relax* for once.

The bodyguard-slash-steward did one final circuit of the room, checking on drinks, then popped open a fresh bottle of wine and vanished out the door.

"People," Kira said, drawing their attention to herself and raising her glass. "A toast, if you'll indulge me: to us! The people Brisingr tried to kill and are damn well going to shove a fleet down their throats!"

"To us!"

Kira sipped her wine. She didn't have any intentions of a speech —it was too small of a group. Still, Cartman moved up to occupy the wall next to the Admiral, the woman now in charge of *Shillelagh*'s starfighters grinning at her old boss.

"You could have any position in this organization you wanted, you know," Kira murmured. "Any of you could. I'm glad you agreed to take on *Shillelagh*'s group. Third time's the charm, I guess?"

"If we want to count *ships* you offered me as well, I think you might actually be at fifth or sixth time," Cartman replied, equally quietly. "But there was a very specific reason I was on *Deception*, boss, and I'm still a bit hurt you fucked off across the galaxy without me."

Kira took a moment to digest that before nodding her understanding. Cartman had been leading *Deception*'s starfighters because *Deception* was the ship Kira tended to operate from. And then Kira had moved aboard *Prodigal* and headed off without her best friend.

"There was so much else going on at the time," she admitted. "I should have asked. Though I *will* point out that you turned down command of *Prodigal*."

"Evgenia didn't have a choice about giving up the cockpit," Cartman noted, gesturing toward the youngest and most injured of the 303's survivors. Michel had turned out to have problems with most forms of cybernetics and regeneration—at least as available in the Syntactic Cluster—which had resulted in her having oversized and heavily built cybernetic legs that would have been dangerous in a cockpit.

"She's taken to starship command like peanut butter to jelly, but I'm with the rest of us in wanting to stay in a starfighter." She shrugged. "I don't mind taking orders from Dawnlord, if you're worried—and as a shareholder, what job I do for Memorial doesn't really impact how much you pay me."

"Part of why I kept offering was because *I* needed you to take on more," Kira confessed. "Outside of a few of the old *Conviction* hands, there's nobody I trust as much as our Three-Oh-Three crew."

She smiled.

"And even inside that circle, I trust you."

"I know. But I wanted to have your back." Cartman shrugged. "Now you've got Dinesha and Kavitha watching your back on *Fortitude*—and Dawnlord is, frankly, better at full-strike-group command than I am. I've got five years of experience on the little shit, too!"

Kira shared Cartman's chuckle. Dinesha Patel had proven to have an absolute gift for the needs of higher-order starfighter command.

"It's a bit scary, isn't it?" she agreed, then sighed. "He probably learned it from Joseph."

Both women were silent, taking sips of their wine. Joseph Hoffman had been Patel's boyfriend before his death—and also the most senior of the ex-303 after Kira herself.

"He was a good man and a good friend," Cartman said quietly. "He is missed."

"A lot of people are. Gods. What I'd give to have Moranis,

Estanza and Heller to hand this mess over to," Kira admitted. "Ninety-plus warships and a hundred transports? I was a *squadron leader*."

"And now you're the woman who convinced the last, best hopes of Apollo to sit down and come up with a plan," her friend observed.

"Wait, are we supposed to pretend the plan was a group effort?" Colombera joined them in their corner with the kind of ease that had Kira looking for a prank. Scimitar had grown up over the years...but not *that* much.

"It's generally politic to say that the other Admirals had their part to play," Kira told him mildly.

"Funny." It was *impossible* to miss Michel clanging up these days, which drew Kira's attention to the fact that her old friends had clearly decided that she and Cartman had taken enough time moping in a corner.

The other old hands were approaching as one now, but it was Evgenia Michel who, as usual, delivered the second punch of the one-two combo.

"It's funny you say that, because *I* understand that you had the plan in mind before you ever talked to them about it," Michel continued, echoing herself once she had Kira's attention. "And I have to admit, given how perfectly the supplies everyone sent us lined up with what your plan needs..."

"Honestly, I think the idea was in her head from the moment we saw the minefields at Faaselesitila," Colombera observed.

"Surely, the final scheme to smash down Brisingr's iron hold on our homeworld and liberate our people from oppression was not forged from idle speculation over how to destroy an ally's defenses," Dawnlord Patel said with a chuckle, the tanned man lifting his wine glass in salute to Kira.

"No, that's exactly where it came from," Kira conceded. "Because while asteroid forts have a lot of things going for them, they share one fundamental weakness with mines: they don't move very quickly at all."

"They just take a *lot* more killing," Cartman murmured. "It's a hell of a plan, ser. And what's the backup if it turns out we need *more* than twenty thousand missiles?"

Kira grimaced.

"We almost certainly will," she warned her people. "The missiles have two purposes, after all, and only one of them is actually to take out Brisingr's version of the ADC."

Long-range missiles had clear weaknesses in an age of multiphasic jammers. The missiles being loaded onto their freighters could literally be fired from the other side of a star system, but they had no magical ability to penetrate multiphasic jamming.

On the other hand, a jamming bubble was only a light-second in diameter. The missiles could get *to* the bubble; they just couldn't find their targets once they were there. A purely AI-driven optical-recognition system had an effective range of twenty thousand kilometers in a jamming field.

So, to hit, the missile had to know, within a twenty-thousand-kilometer radius, roughly where its target was going to be before it entered the jamming zone. Against anything with proper sublight drives, that was extraordinarily unlikely.

Even against forts, Kira figured they were going to lose half their missiles in that stage. Plus, the forts had defenses designed against at least the possibility of this kind of attack. *Plus*, the forts were, well, built out of asteroids averaging eight to ten kilometers across.

"Twenty thousand missiles against twelve forts," Scimitar murmured. "And we don't expect it to be *enough*?"

"I'm also aiming at the prefabricated forts, to be fair," Kira replied.

"And for every missile we get in, between jamming and defenses, we're going to lose ten along the way," Cartman noted. "So, each thousand missiles launched is going to put a hundred thirty-megaton warheads on target. A target that is protected by a layer of nickel-iron thirty to forty meters thick, fronted and backed by twenty to fifty centimeters of modern ferroceramics and energy-dispersal webbing."

"You put it that way, why aren't we bringing more missiles?" Scimitar asked.

"Space," his usual partner in crime, Michel, reminded him. "That's a *hundred* freaking transports. Each LRM takes up a standard TMU."

"If we could bring more, we would," Kira conceded. "But I'm surprised and gratified that our not-quite-allies put up a hundred ships. Five million cubic meters of cargo capacity, people. *Seven* million cubic meters of shipping and over ten thousand civilian volunteers.

"Hopefully, none of them will ever even be seen, let alone identified, but this isn't risk-free for them."

They'd been fabricating long-range missiles for three weeks, and they finally had enough. The repairs were done. The flight decks were full—Hoplites and Phalanxes and Peltasts, Apollon-design fighters to avoid anything being traced back to the systems supporting them—and the pilots had been trained on their new ships.

"We're ready," Kira said. "One last meeting in the morning with the Admirals, then I believe we're kicking off.

"We're going home, my friends," she told them. "We are going home—and there is no power in the stars or void that's going to stop us!"

50

THERE WERE several ways by which Kira could have argued that Knight-Admiral Cullen shouldn't have been part of the senior officers' meeting. While he was the senior representative of the Templars, his command was smaller than the forces available to Kira's Commodores or Michelakis's Rear Admirals.

Still, he was the senior officer of one of the force contingents present, so Kira had invited him. She'd used that as an excuse to include Vice Admiral Munroe, Michelakis's second, and Kavitha Zoric.

It was probably a positive sign that Henry Killinger *hadn't* taken advantage of the option to invite a subordinate of his own. That left them with five Admirals and a "Commodore" who commanded as much firepower as most of said Admirals.

"We have produced as many missiles as are going to fit in our transports," Kira told them. "Same with starfighters, torpedoes and every other expendable part or munition we can manufacture in the void.

"Memorial Force wasn't short nearly as much as the Last Fleet or our privateers, so we are at one hundred percent combat readiness."

By fighters and hulls, Kira commanded the second-largest force present. Killinger edged her out *slightly* on cubage, due to having thirteen cruisers to her five, even if his destroyers were smaller and he didn't have carriers.

"The Last Fleet isn't in as good a shape as Memorial Force," Michelakis admitted. "But we have made good the attrition of months without proper facilities and supplies. Despite everything, though, some of my ships still have damage from the last battle of Apollo that is irreparable without a proper shipyard."

She shrugged.

"Overall, I'd say we're at ninety-five to ninety-six percent combat capability."

There was a pause as they waited for Killinger, but it was Cullen who spoke after a moment's silence.

"My squadron lacked fighters and had some inevitable decay from being laid up, even in vacuum," he told them. "We now carry proper nova combat groups of Phalanxes and have smoothed our rough edges. I have some concerns about my people's lack of experience working as crews, but mechanically, we are at one hundred percent readiness."

Kira had similar concerns about many of her own people and almost all of the other forces' fighters. They'd done what training and exercises they could, but the fleet was still very much a haphazard and unbalanced group.

Now, though, she turned her attention to Killinger. It was funny, she thought. He'd had no chance to update his surgery or anything of the sort, but he looked much better than he had when she'd arrived at his base in Faaselesitila.

He'd put on weight, she judged, and suspected it was a combination of reduced stress from no longer standing alone against Brisingr and somewhat-steadier access to supplies since his privateers had joined up with the rest of the forces in Corosec.

"We have made great strides," Killinger noted, sounding almost pained, "but the truth is my ships have gone far longer without proper repair, support or spares than anyone else here."

He grimaced.

"Destroyers, thankfully, are easily fixed. All of my tin cans are as good as they can get. Even shipyards would do them no good—there are few repairs for a destroyer than can't be managed with some scaffolding, some spare parts and some can-do.

"My cruisers are not so lucky," he continued grimly. "There are things we simply do not have the spare parts to replace. I have several ships that are straight-up missing turrets. We'd left them in place before, where intimidation was as relevant as combat power, but we've stripped them off now.

"Overall, my light and heavy cruisers are probably around eighty-five percent combat-ready."

There was one ship that hadn't been included in his rundown so far, and Kira could tell that everybody knew it.

"And *Trident*?" Michelakis finally asked.

Oceanic Trident was their only battlecruiser. Between Memorial Force, Trickster Squadron and the privateers, they had nine heavy cruisers, but even heavy cruisers could only fight battlecruisers with a cubage advantage. The Last Fleet didn't even have heavy cruisers!

"*Oceanic Trident* has basically been everyone's first target when they've clashed with my fleet," Killinger reminded them. "She was also the most capable of *taking* fire...and, bluntly, a ship that we rarely needed to actually fight. A battlecruiser showing up generally convinces anything that *isn't* a battlecruiser to surrender or run."

"I saw her take fire at Shenandoah," Kira murmured. "How bad is it, Killinger?"

"We have managed to get every one of her main guns back online," he told them. "We have most of her dispersal net operating but only at around sixty percent."

It had been a major achievement of the military upgrade project to get Redward-built ships *up* to sixty percent dispersal—but a *Sun*

Arrow–class battlecruiser should have been operating at *eighty* percent.

"Worse, the armor over the dispersal net is basic nickel-iron plating rather than reactive plating," he continued. "Between the parts provided over the last few weeks and moving around our own plates over the years, we maintained modern battle armor over key points, but it is very limited.

"*Oceanic Trident* is, at this point, a glass cannon. Worse, she has structural damage that prevents us from powering more than about half of her rated Harrington coils, and we have a power-distribution problem that keeps burning out our multiphasic jammers."

Killinger did *not* sound happy to admit that.

"Bluntly, *Trident* cannot hold her place in the primary battle line. I suggest, much as it pains me, that we keep her in reserve or hold her in defense of the carriers."

His unhappiness was clear and the conclusion was reasonable... and yet...Kira had to doubt a collection of problems that very clearly put the man's flagship well out of the main line of fire.

It wasn't that having *Oceanic Trident* playing guard dog over the carriers was a bad thing—if nothing else, that would let them free up two heavy or three light cruisers to do something else—but she knew damn well that Henry Killinger's plan was to put himself in control of Apollo when the dust settled.

They were going to *need* the political infrastructure he'd spent the last few years building on the surface, too. She knew that. Michelakis knew that. They were just hoping they could hold things together without having to put a crown on Killinger's head.

All of that meant that a situation that would clearly keep Killinger's head *intact* for said crown was suspicious as all hell.

"We'll have to deal," was all she said aloud, though. "That will require some rejiggering of the task forces. Shall we go over it?"

"Of course," Killinger allowed, gesturing for her to proceed.

Kira took a moment to reassess her plans before gesturing a set of models of the fleet's ships into the middle of their shared virtual space.

She suspected Killinger might still be standing in his Olympus setup, but she'd set the system to let everyone see their own preferred virtual reality. In her case, that meant everyone else was just sitting in her office.

"The Liberation Fleet, people," she introduced their assembled force. "There were a few larger formations during the war, but we're definitely up in the reaches of larger forces ever deployed in this region of space."

It was a *lot* of ships and a lot of firepower. Hopefully, it was going to be an ugly surprise for Kaiser Reinhardt's people.

"We will operate in three distinct task forces," she continued. Everyone had been involved in the planning, but it was still useful to lay out the final organization and steps before kicking off the second-largest battle to ever sweep her home system.

"Task Force Liberty One was going to be anchored on *Trident*," Kira noted, glancing at Killinger. He'd also been intended to *command* Liberty One, but now...

She made a sweeping gesture and the battlecruiser slipped sideways as ships moved around to organize by their new task forces.

"Instead, Liberty One will include all nine of our heavy cruisers," she told them. "I will transfer my own flag back aboard *Prodigal* and take command of Liberty One."

She waited to see if anyone argued—the other logical option, in her mind, was for her to stay aboard *Fortitude* and put Knight-Admiral Cullen in command of Liberty One, but he seemed content to stay subordinate.

"Liberty One will be the first and most obvious part of our operation," she continued. "We will also attach nine light cruisers and twelve destroyers."

The destroyers were an even split—four Memorial Force, four Last Fleet, four privateers—but the light cruisers were mostly privateer ships, with Kira's two *Baron*s included.

"They will initially arrive in system as escorts for Liberty Four," she continued. "Liberty Four will consist of our civilian volunteers. We will stage the novas to keep the drive cooldown to minimum for everyone, but it is most critical for Liberty Four.

"We will be bringing them into the system at least ten light-minutes from New Athens. They will drop their cargos and then they will run for the damn hills," Kira said. "I'm hoping to keep Liberty Four's time in system to a ten-minute minimum cooldown so that the BKN forces never have a chance to engage them.

"Once the missiles are in play, Liberty One will accompany them toward the fortress cluster at New Athens. Around this point, Liberty Two will enter the system to provide distant carrier support."

More ships moved around.

"Liberty Two consists of the carriers we figure Brisingr *knows* we're bringing to the party," Kira said. "That means *Fortitude* and all four *Triremes*. They'll also have five light carriers, eight light cruisers and twelve destroyers for escorts."

Again, the destroyers were an even split, but this time, all of the light cruisers and light carriers were from the Last Fleet.

"We were going to keep *Hostess* and *Prodigal* as part of Liberty Two," Kira noted. "But with the need to hold *Trident* back, I've moved them to Liberty One and put *Trident* in Two. Questions?"

"Who will command Liberty Two?" Killinger asked.

"Admiral Michelakis is bringing four of the five supercarriers to the party," she replied. "I think she has the flag."

Liberty Two was mostly a Last Fleet force—but if *Oceanic Trident* needed to be there...

"Admiral." Killinger inclined his head to Michelakis. "May I request the honor of serving as your second and taking command of the carrier screen?"

That could be a problem, given that the screen was mostly anchored on Last Fleet's light cruisers...but it also made a lot of sense and was more reasonable than she'd feared Killinger would be.

"Of course, Admiral," Michelakis agreed. She was looking at the display. "That division puts a lot of our fighter strength in Liberty Three still," she observed.

"Nine hundred and sixty to Liberty Two's thousand and fifty," Kira confirmed. "Liberty Three will have limited direct combat capability and is overall made up of relatively light ships.

"Ships that I suspect Brisingr may not have been keeping as close track of."

"You're hoping they forget we exist?" Vice Admiral Munroe asked.

"Exactly, Admiral Munroe," Kira told him. "We're giving you a whole fleet of ships that fit in someone's back pocket. You'll have the most hulls of any of the three task forces but the least cubage or firepower.

"But when push comes to shove, your hundred and sixty nova squadrons are going to be the key to all of this."

She looked at the four-part division of their fleet.

"The BKN will see the LRM salvo ten minutes after it's launched," she reminded them. "There's no way we're hiding twenty thousand high-powered Harrington coils. They'll have roughly eight hours to run the numbers and come to the same conclusion we did: the forts are positioned in a constellation that expects there to be a *lot* more stations.

"They don't have the mutual coverage to protect each other against this kind of attack—and this level of saturation bombardment is...*impractical* by most standards."

Kira suspected that she would never have received enough Harrington coils to pull it off without the Crest agreeing to finance the whole operation. She wasn't entirely clear on the price tag of the stunt she was about to launch—but she *did* suspect that she was about to burn up several percentage points of a planetary GDP in a single salvo of expendable munitions.

"The usual defense against this kind of attack is nova ships," Michelakis observed.

"Exactly," Kira confirmed. "We know, with a reasonably degree of certainty, what the BKN's Battle Fleet Apollo looks like. Whoever is in command over there is going to almost certainly figure that ten battlecruisers with ten fleet carriers' worth of fighter support are going to run right over Liberty One.

"At which point, Liberty *Two* convinces them of the error of their ways," Killinger said. "With Three in our back pocket in case Brisingr has a surprise we're not expecting."

"I'm expecting a surprise," Kira warned. "Nobody in the BKN is stupid. They've got roughly fifty percent of their nova capital ships in Apollo right now. They know they've got a limited monitor force, and they know their fortress constellation is understrength for a top-tier Mid Rim system.

"They're going to be expecting us to have tricks up our sleeve, and *they're* going to have tricks up their sleeve." She shrugged. "We don't have a fifth column to take out the forts; we're limited to a relatively direct operation."

"So, we hold back a third of our strength?" Michelakis asked. "That seems...risky."

"We all agreed that Liberty One and Two should have enough strength to take down Battle Fleet Apollo in a straight-up duel between nova ships," Kira said. "We'll lose more than we would if we had Liberty Three in support, yes. And if it looks like BF Apollo is *all* we're facing, we'll call them in.

"But this is a battle, I suspect, that is going to be won by the last person to commit their secret reserve. And we very much want to *win* this battle."

51

THE ENTIRE PLAN had been built around the idea of keeping Battle Fleet Apollo from realizing that things were happening in time to prevent the earliest stages.

It still felt worrying as the first stages went entirely according to plan. Kira stood on *Prodigal*'s flag bridge again, watching silently as the transport fleet dumped their cargo into the void.

Eleven light-minutes away from New Athens put them outside Crete's—Apollo III—orbital path. The distance meant that their missiles would take hours upon hours to reach their targets, but the asteroid forts couldn't move very far or very fast.

Even the prefabricated forts, assembled from flat packs of hull and parts brought in on freighters, didn't have a great deal of maneuverability. They needed nova ships to be absolutely certain they could stop this kind of attack.

But then, the BKN had nova ships. Twenty capital ships, fifteen cruisers and forty destroyers were layered through the defensive constellation. Once they recognized the threat, Kira expected to see Battle Fleet Apollo's battlecruisers in short order.

For the moment, though, standard ten-meter units spilled out from her freighter fleet like autumn snow. It wasn't that the TMUs—five meters wide and tall by ten meters long—contained palletized versions of the LRMs.

The TMUs *were* the LRMs. Streamlining was irrelevant in space, and the freighters' cargo-handling systems were designed for the containers. So, they'd co-opted the containers the supplies had arrived in—and manufactured more of the standard cargo pods—to contain Harrington coils, power sources and thermonuclear warheads.

There were more Harrington coils in the missiles than in the entire Liberation Fleet, including starfighters, shuttles and the transports hauling the missiles. Even if her plan worked, this wasn't going to go down in history as a particularly practical or cost-effective way to take a star system.

"That's the last of the missiles deployed," Soler reported. "Control-link tests are firing green so far; we have links with fifty-two percent of the weapons and rising."

"Get the transports out of here, Ronaldo," Kira ordered. "And everyone on their toes. The transports are leaving about when the enemy is going to see that we've arrived."

It was strange to be home. She knew the orbital layout and mechanics of the Apollo System like the back of her hand, even now. To incorporate all of that knowledge and training to *attack* Apollo felt wrong, but here she was.

And there the Brisingrs were.

"Sixty seconds to transport nova," Ronaldo reported. "All ships are reported full drive cooldown at that point across the board. Sixty seconds after that, BF Apollo should see us."

Assuming there hadn't been any unfortunately positioned nova fighters that had reported in without being seen by TF Liberty One. It would have been a lucky positioning, but Kira wasn't going to assume all of the luck was on her side.

"Ninety-nine-point-two percent of missiles linked in," Soler reported. "We have a few troublemakers, of course. I have teams going through the last hundred and fifty individually. We should be ready to fire within a few minutes."

Kira nodded, and part of her shivered as a hundred transports vanished in a moderately synchronized maneuver. They'd been committed, in many ways, at least since they'd left Corosec. Somehow, though, the exit of the transports brought the whole thing crashing home.

She had thirty warships with her and was staring down the defenses of an entire star system. By every paradigm she'd ever studied or been involved in, that wasn't even a particularly *extended* form of suicide.

"BF Apollo will have delayed light in thirty seconds," Ronaldo said. "Tactical network online; tightbeams connected. All ships report standing by fighter decks and multiphasic jammers.

"CAP?"

"First squadrons up," he confirmed for Kira. "Thirty interceptors. Remaining squadrons are prepped on all cruisers."

Liberty One might not have had a carrier, but between nine heavy and nine light cruisers, Kira had forty-two squadrons of nova fighters. No bombers, but half of them were Phalanx heavy fighters carrying three torpedoes apiece.

Icons on the main display and Kira's headware implant went green at the same time.

"All missile links established," Soler reported. "We have four duds. I'm passing targeting orders to the fighters to destroy them once the rest of the salvo is clear."

"Four out of twenty thousand," Kira said. "I can live with that. Any other issues?"

"No, ser. Awaiting your order."

"New Athens has seen us," Ronaldo warned.

"It's a damned expensive order," Kira told Soler, forcing a chuckle. "You have the targeting data?"

"We've dialed in fifteen asteroid forts and sixty-two prefabricated box forts," the ops officer replied. "A few more than expected but within what I think the salvo can handle."

Kira exhaled, looking at the display showing her homeworld and marked with the red icons of dozens of hostile space stations and nova warships.

"Fire."

FOR A SINGLE AWE-INSPIRING MOMENT, Kira's sensor screens and data feeds were overwhelmed. Twenty thousand missiles threw off immense quantities of heat, Jianhong radiation, gravimetric disturbances... Every scanner her ship had was almost as badly swamped as if they'd just fired off a thousand multiphasic jammers.

Unlike the jammers, though, the missile drives had predictable patterns and frequencies. The sensors quickly adapted, even as the missiles opened the distance from *Prodigal.*

"Lancer reports dud missiles destroyed," Ronaldo passed on a few moments later.

Commander Jowita "Lancer" Janda had been one of the first pilots recruited by Kira in Redward. Once a gunship pilot for the RRF, she now commanded the four-squadron combat group flying off *Prodigal.*

"Pass on my thanks," Kira replied. "Any sign of response from our friends at New Athens?"

"Won't see anything for another nine minutes or so, unless they decided to move *real* fast," Soler reminded her.

"They won't," Kira told her staff. "They're going to at least half-expect us to nova closer. Plus, until the transports leave, we probably look like the landing force of an attack fleet that misjudged our timing."

She grinned.

"Let them have their illusions. Either way, they won't rush out to meet us. Their first priority is securing New Athens itself. It's only once they see the missiles and realize what we're doing that they'll send fire in our direction. Probably starting with fighters to get a closer look."

"Speaking of fighters, the first courier from Liberty Two just popped through," Ronaldo told her. "Their drives are cooled off and they are standing by to deploy nova-fighter strikes upon request."

Picking the fallback locations for the other two task forces had been a game of risk versus reward. Liberty Two was over a light-hour away, hiding in a quiet portion of the Apollo Belt. The pinnaces tasked to run a courier cycle keeping the two fleets in communication would have a seven-minute cooldown after their jump.

Fortunately, they *had* enough of the nova-capable small craft to spare to run seven of them on that route, meaning that Admirals Michelakis and Killinger shouldn't be more than a minute out of date at any time.

Liberty *Three*, on the other hand, was a full light-week out. They were *hoping* Liberty Two would go undetected and be able to send off fighter strikes with the advantage of surprise. They *needed* Liberty Three to remain hidden, which meant that the updates to Admiral Munroe were cycling much more slowly.

They had to make sure there was either a pinnace or a fighter with a ready drive to nova to the third task force when they were needed. Once they'd done so, however, Munroe could bring his ships in wherever they were needed—and his *fighters* would have ready drives when they arrived.

Kira had kept the plan as simple as possible—but she was still using Liberty One as bait, and that meant she had to be in contact with the jaws of her trap.

"Nova flare at thirty seconds," Soler barked. "No—three small flares. Nova fighters."

"Taking a look to see what we're up to," Kira said. "And they won't be able to see anything through the missile drives—but the missiles themselves are what they need to see."

She smiled.

"For both their purposes...and ours."

52

War is vast swathes of waiting divided by moments of utter terror. Space battles only expanded the waiting and accentuated the terror. Kira could have put her entire task force in New Athens orbit, but that would have ended in their annihilation.

So, she waited, watching her missile storm sweep toward her home. At least she didn't need to worry about accidentally *hitting* the planet, even once the multiphasic jammers came online. Optical-recognition algorithms intended to detect a target a few hundred meters across from twenty thousand kilometers away were easily capable of seeing *planets*.

There were multiple layers of safeguards to make sure the missiles didn't hit a planet. Kira had gone over the LRMs' designs herself to be sure of it.

They were, after all, shooting at her homeworld. Somewhere on the green-and-blue orb in the distance were her brother and his sheep. And, she supposed, his wife, but Kira would freely admit she ranked the sheep over the shepherdess in this case.

The Brisingr nova fighters vanished after a minute, scampering home before Kira's intercepts could take out the prying eyes. They'd been expecting that, so Lancer hadn't even sent planes after them.

"How long?" Soler asked aloud.

"Depends," Kira admitted. "We have good intelligence but not perfect. I know Battle Fleet Apollo's strength but not who's in command.

"I can assume it's a close ally of Kaiser Reinhardt's. They've got basically *all* of the B-One-Seventies and HC-Thirties that the BKN has in commission."

Thanks to her allies throughout the Security Zone, Kira's intelligence was better than she had any right to expect. They'd missed an asteroid fort, though, so she couldn't trust it completely.

But her information said that after the Fall of Apollo, the BKN only had twelve of their most modern battlecruisers and ten of their most modern fleet carriers *left*. And there were ten of each class in orbit of Apollo.

"One way or another, Battle Fleet Apollo is currently the BKN's plum command," she concluded. "Whoever is over there is from the Alteste Families and, quite possibly, the person Reinhardt is grooming to replace him.

"But I don't know who that is, which worries me," she admitted. "I can't predict which way someone I know nothing about is going to jump.

"That said, I'm *expecting* a closer fighter sweep once they've had a chance to warm up the carrier decks. Let's get the rest of the squadrons into space."

Ronaldo started passing the orders, and new green icons began to sparkle across Kira's displays. Her cruisers and destroyers were concealed from New Athens by the massive wall of noise that was the missile storm, but she didn't expect that to buy her much time.

It created uncertainty, though. Her counterpart on Battle Fleet Apollo knew she was there. They could see the *missiles* from New Athens orbit now—but the very thing that had made Liberty One's presence unmistakable rendered it difficult for the enemy to resolve details.

"Ask me for anything but time," she murmured.

"Ser?" Soler eyed her.

"It's a quote," Kira replied. "Our friend over there has a lot of options. They've even got time to play with. But sooner or later, they have to act."

Because if they did nothing, in a little under eight hours, the entire defensive constellation over New Athens would cease to exist.

───────

"CONTACTS, multiple contacts! Estimate two hundred–plus inbound!"

"Jammers up," Kira snapped.

Her people were well ahead of her, the storms of radiation and visual distortion sweeping across her displays as the systems came online.

"Tightbeam links solid," Ronaldo replied. "Fighters are...out of touch."

"As usual," Kira agreed. "Keep an eye on them for me. Soler, what are we looking at?"

"Jammers are mucking with everything now, but we got a decent look at the enemy before we fired them up," the ops officer replied. "Twenty-six squadrons, two-hundred-sixty bogies. At least five squadrons of Weltraumdachs bombers, with Weltraumpanzer and Weltraumfuchs escorts."

"Orders to the ships: layered testudo."

That formation put the destroyers a critical ten thousand kilometers closer to the incoming bombers. The Brisingr pilots would be forced to choose between firing at the destroyers—who could dodge the torpedo blasts but were also unfortunately more expendable—or flying into the destroyers' range to attack the cruisers.

Twenty-six squadrons was the full complement of two of the

HC-30 carriers in orbit. A fifth of the enemy carrier-based fighter strength, which meant...

"It'll be six bomber squadrons," Kira told Soler. "Ten each of interceptors and heavy fighters. It's the strike groups from two carriers. They're testing us."

It was a test Brisingr was going to fail. Liberty One had twelve fewer fighters than their attackers—and that was only because Kira's two K-90s were carrying a pair of bombers each that they were holding back.

Worse for the BKN, the three Memorial Force cruisers carried next-generation *Crest* fighters, with a small but measurable edge over Brisingr and Apollo's current design. And while the BKN might have more nova fighters in the scramble about to happen, sixty of theirs were bombers that they needed to get through.

Plus, her people had the destroyers and the cruisers behind them. The hail of fire from the main guns was inefficient—but *inefficient* wasn't the same as *ineffectual*.

The first clash was between the Brisingr interceptors and their Apollon counterparts. Kira swiftly realized that Janda had held back all of the Memorial Force fighters, using their allies' fighters to tie up the BKN planes.

Then, as the BKN heavy fighters swooped in to keep Liberty One's fighters away from the bombers, the Memorial Force fighters novaed. It was a tiny nova, only a few dozen thousand kilometers— dangerous inside a jamming sphere, but it put almost sixty next-generation fighters on top of the bombers.

And while bombers were not *defenseless*, they weren't designed for dogfighting.

It was a massacre, one that less than a tenth of the Brisingr nova fighters escaped—without firing a single torpedo.

"Cycle the jammers; get me a headcount," Kira ordered as the last enemy ship vanished into FTL. "We hurt them, but what did it cost us?"

The last thing she wanted to do was fight a battle of attrition.

Liberation Fleet had a *lot* of fighters—but each of the asteroid forts had based twenty Apollon six-ship squadrons under ADC command.

She doubted they were hosting less now that Brisingr was in control of them.

"Search and rescue are up," Soler reported. "We're down... twenty-three Hoplites, twelve Phalanxes, eight Wolverines and four Hussars."

Thirty-seven fighters. Against over two hundred losses for the BKN.

It wasn't a bad start. Depending on how many people they pulled from the escape pods, it might not even haunt Kira's nightmares later.

There was no way the battle wasn't going to, though.

"Estimated time to impact?" she asked.

"Seven hours, forty-six minutes," Soler replied. "What happens now?"

"Well, if our opponent is an *idiot*, they'll try that again with twice as many fighters," Kira murmured. "But most likely..."

She shook her head.

"Get every fighter cycled through the bays as fast as we can," she ordered. "I want torps on every bird and full fuel tanks.

"I figure we have about twenty minutes and then we're going to get introduced to Battle Fleet Apollo's main battle line."

Because one test was plenty in her mind—and if *she* had ten battlecruisers to an enemy's nine heavy cruisers, she wasn't going to play many games.

Sometimes, you had a hammer, and the problem really *was* a nail.

53

"ALL FIGHTERS ARE BACK OUT," Ronaldo reported. "We are running a one-in-three jamming cycle."

"Sensor drones are on the edge of the jamming bubble now, transmitting in on the bounce," Soler added. "Data from New Athens is still pretty old. As of about ten minutes ago, though, the carriers had started to launch fighters like party favors."

Kira acknowledged her officers with a nod. Her focus remained on the planet with its hovering red icons. She'd intentionally created a Sword of Damocles to test her enemy's patience.

She hadn't quite realized how much it was going to test her *own* patience.

"Courier is standing by?"

"Yes, ser," Ronaldo confirmed. "She's outside the jamming bubble, linked in to the sensor drones. She'll have as much information as humanly possible when she jumps out to Michelakis."

The BKN commander was slower than Kira had expected, but everything she was seeing on the data feeds said they were preparing for exactly what she was expecting. In a few more minutes, the entire nova-capable strength of Battle Fleet Apollo was going to descend on her command.

Her last update from Michelakis said that Liberty Two had their fighters in space. On Kira's order, another thousand starfighters would descend on the Brisingr ships. She just needed to separate them from the forts.

"What is taking you so long?" she muttered at her enemy. "You've got to be suspicious, sure, but you also can't let twenty thousand missiles hit the forts. You have to act."

It was almost a relief when a rash of red icons flared into existence on her display.

"Contacts at one-point-five light-seconds," Soler snapped. "I make fifty-plus starships, thousand-plus nova fighters. That has to be just about everything they've got ready to move."

"Keep us in testudo and get us between them and the missiles," Kira ordered. The LRMs had endurance, but they were no faster than her warships in this stage of their attack. Maneuvering around them was surprisingly straightforward.

"Get me numbers on types of ships and fighters. Let them come to us."

Data filtered in slowly now. Both sides had multiphasic jamming bubbles up, bubbles that overlapped and were slowly moving closer together.

"Confirm on ten battlecruisers and ten fleet carriers," Soler finally reported. "I make it fifteen light cruisers and fifteen destroyers as well. Lot of fighters. Didn't get a clear scan, but we're estimating at least two thousand."

Kira smiled thinly as she heard at least one tech in the room make a surprised choking sound.

"They had to have fighters on the forts," she reminded people. "All of this was planned for."

"Fighters are *definitely* coming our way. Haven't nailed any of them down, but they're at around two fifty and closing."

"Understood."

"Do we call in Liberty Two?" Ronaldo asked.

Kira hesitated. They were only going to get one pure-surprise alpha strike. She needed to get the timing *perfect*.

"Have they held back a CAP?" she said to Soler.

"Looks like around ten squadrons, a hundred interceptors."

"Okay." Kira took a breath and nodded, glancing at the estimated distance to the enemy forces. Battle Fleet Apollo was still over three hundred and fifty thousand kilometers away, but their fighters were approaching two hundred thousand.

"Release our fighters to attack at will," she ordered. "Then send the courier to Liberty Two. They'll have everything we have."

And much as Kira was *tempted*, she wasn't going to backseat-manage Admiral Michelakis or her fighter-group commanders. Dinesha Patel was in charge over there, commanding the largest fighter strike he'd ever *seen*—but Kira trusted the younger officer's unexpected talent for his craft.

"Courier is off," Ronaldo said.

One more die cast. Kira held her breath for a few seconds, then forced herself to breathe. She couldn't guarantee that Dawnlord and the fighter strike would arrive before that became unhealthy.

"Our fighters are engaging their lead elements."

She could see that. Her people were outnumbered seven to one. Even her mercenaries didn't have the experience and skill to offset that kind of disadvantage. There was no way Liberty One could win this battle.

Liberty One wasn't supposed to *have* to win this battle.

"We're the bait," Kira murmured. "Where the hell is the trap?"

Michelakis was late. They'd talked about this. The courier had been sent almost a full minute earlier, and the nova-fighter strike had been supposed to arrive within thirty seconds of the final call.

"Contact! Multiple contacts. *Holy shit!*"

Soler's curse tore through the bridge as Kira was processing what the ops officer had seen. The delay, it turned out, had been for the nova-fighter pilots to recalculate their jumps. A hundred squadrons of interceptors and heavy fighters emerged on top of the ongoing dogfight, emerging from novas directly into firing passes on the Brisingr pilots.

At the same time, ten squadrons of interceptors and thirty squadrons of bombers emerged *inside torpedo range* of Battle Fleet Apollo. The Brisingr commander had held back their carriers under the protection of their battle cruisers—and now nine bombers blazed in on each of the Brisingr capital ships.

And there were sixty Wolverine interceptors in the hands of hardened mercenary veterans to clear the way through the fighters the BKN had held back to protect themselves.

The Brisingr CAP never stood a chance. Kira recognized Patel's hand in the slicing attack that separated them from their supposed wards, divided them up and then wiped entire squadrons out in lightning-fast circles of plasma fire.

With the fighters gone, the bombers descended on the Brisingr ships like an avenging god. A hundred and eighty bombers launched over a thousand torpedoes, hurtling fifty-plus weapons at each of the battlecruisers and fleet carriers.

For a single heady minute, it looked like Kira's plan had worked out beyond her wildest hopes. Focused on Liberty One, Battle Fleet Apollo had taken the bait, and the nova fighters had slammed the trap closed with consummate skill.

It wasn't bloodless. It wasn't cheap—but it was *victory* and Kira could taste it on her tongue as the last of the BKN battlecruisers blew apart.

Then a new wave of nova signatures flared across her screen.

"New contacts, twenty-five-plus contacts," Soler barked. "Wait... that's *Fortitude*. The *Triremes*. What the hell is Liberty Two doing *here*?!"

Liberty Two had been supposed to remain in the asteroid belt, well out of sight from everyone. Except that it was possible, if you were determined enough, to track nova jumps. Not backward...but if someone had put eyes on the nova pinnace they'd left in open space to allow her to track the course of the battle, they would have known where she jumped to.

And Liberty Two was missing ships. One of the *Triremes*. Several destroyers. Three of the cruisers...

"Someone jumped them," Kira snarled. "Get me coordinating links! We need to combine the fleets and ping the courier for Liberty Three."

She'd always known this battle would be decided by who had the last reserve. If she was very, *very* lucky, Liberty Three would be it.

But as a new series of nova flares faded from the screens and new data filtered in, she realized that Liberty Three wasn't going to be enough.

An entire second battle fleet emerged on the far side of Liberty Two. Another half dozen carriers—and four capital ships unlike anything she'd ever seen.

"What the *hell* are those?" someone asked. It might have been Kira. She'd never seen a three-hundred-thousand-cubic-meter warship before.

"Star Kingdom of Griffon *Fearless*-class battlecruisers," McCaig said softly.

Kira's attention snapped to her link to the Flag Captain—native of a world in the Fringe who'd followed John Estanza into the Rim.

"*What?*"

"Fringe battlecruisers, ser," he repeated. "Which, in this context, I suspect means *Institute* battlecruisers."

54

THE BKN NOVA fighters had scattered to the winds, but they'd taken far too many of the Liberation Fleet's nova fighters with them. As more starfighters spilled out of the carriers accompanying the monster battlecruisers, Kira was grimly aware that even Liberty Three's fighters might not be enough.

Most of the fleet anchored on the *Fearless*es was older Brisingr ships, half a dozen HC-10 and HC-20 carriers escorted by a matching set of L150 and L140 battlecruisers. Their lighter cruisers were more modern, but Kira was barely paying attention to the escorts at this point.

Those carriers had just put another eight hundred nova fighters into space, and she had *nothing* that could stand up to the Griffon-built starships. The only thing that might have even have *tried* out of Liberty Two was *Oceanic Trident*, and she was all too aware of the supposed weaknesses of Killinger's flagship.

Even as she was processing the situation, the closest *Fearless* drew into range of Liberty Two's screen and opened fire. Two destroyers simply...vanished. The Fringe battlecruisers outranged the escorts' light guns by ten thousand kilometers at least.

"All cruisers are to form on *Prodigal*," Kira ordered, without even being wholly aware of the words leaving her mouth. "Echelon formation and advance. Inverse testudo. Destroyers will fall in between us and the carriers, and the carriers will fall back as rapidly as possible.

"And get a damn message to Munroe," she snapped. "We need Liberty Three's fighters *now*."

Most of the new Brisingr force's nova fighters had vanished, likely converging on a distant rendezvous point with the survivors of the prior strike. Two hundred fighters remained in position around the new battlecruisers, but if the pilots from Bogey Two managed to find and organize the survivors of the last wave...

Despite the losses Liberty Two had inflicted, there were still at least a thousand starfighters left of that force. Without Munroe's fighters, they were outnumbered in *every* class—and the *Fearless*es were bearing down on the supercarriers at speed.

"Get a link to Michelakis and Zoric," Kira said grimly. "I don't care *what* it takes, but they have *got* to fall back toward us. We need to get between them and Bogey Two."

Ask me for anything but time, indeed.

It was a three-way race now—between the fighters and pinnaces sent out to Liberty Three and Admiral Munroe's reaction time, the reorganization and return of the Brisingr fighters, and how long it would take the four monster Griffon ships to tear apart Kira's people.

All she could do now was buy time—by putting the heavy cruisers between the carriers and the enemy.

EVEN AS THE heavy cruisers assembled on *Prodigal* and charged through the jamming toward the enemy, the Brisingr super-battle-cruisers drew into range of *Naiad*. A *Trireme*-class carrier wasn't defenseless by any means, with a suite of plasma guns to rival most heavy cruisers.

But against the *Fearless*es, *Naiad* might as well have been unarmed. Plasma fire washed over her like a falling avalanche, and while Kira had to believe the carrier had got some licks in, she vanished from the screens a moment later—taking over a thousand ASDF and volunteer personnel with her.

Kira didn't even have the communications to order a full retreat—and even if she did, Michelakis had just novaed her ships. They were stuck far too close to the Fringe battlecruisers for at least five more minutes.

Nine Rim heavy cruisers and a scattering of light cruisers had no business fighting four Fringe battlecruisers, and Kira knew it. The four *Fearless*es had her cruisers outmassed, outgunned and outclassed.

In the quiet of her own mind, Kira knew she'd committed her cruisers to a death ride. Not one of the captains had argued. Even Knight-Admiral Cullen, a volunteer from a star system that wouldn't suffer for the loss of this battle, was in formation and charging with her.

They would die. But in the dying, they would cover the carriers. That would allow the carriers to rearm the bombers, and *that* would give the Liberation Fleet their one chance against the—

"Ser, *Trident*!"

Kira's attention was yanked away from her own intentions to watch *Oceanic Trident* suddenly move at full speed—the speed Killinger had said she *couldn't* move at.

Multiphasic jamming snarled her view, but even through it she could see the pulse of debris as pieces of Killinger's ship literally fell off under the motion. It looked very much like he'd told the truth —*Trident* shouldn't have been moving at that pace.

But moving at that pace swung the worn-out battlecruiser in between the four *Fearless*es and their prey, and while *Oceanic Trident*'s engines were falling apart underneath her and her armor was a joke, her *guns* were intact.

Kira's breath caught in her throat as she saw Killinger's ship charge into the teeth of eight times his volume, *ten* times his firepower, and hammer the second-closest enemy battlecruiser with every gun *Oceanic Trident* possessed.

Even the light anti-fighter cannon hammered the *Fearless*, and for the first time since Liberty Two had novaed into the main battle-space, the four massive battlecruisers shared one single target.

"He must have faked being mission-killed," Soler said aloud. "They ignored *Trident* until she was inside weapons range."

Whatever reasoning had led the enemy ships to dismiss Killinger's flagship had betrayed them, and Kira swallowed a shout as the impossible happened:

One of the massive three-hundred-thousand-cubic-meter battle-cruisers died. *Oceanic Trident* might not have matched her opponents in size or firepower, but Killinger and his crew brought enough ferocity to make up the difference.

In that moment, Kira finally understood why Henry Killinger's spacers would follow him into hell—and had been prepared to break all of their oaths to make the man king.

And she also understood it would never matter. *Oceanic Trident* had claimed her prey, but her hull was coming apart under the strain of her full-power engines and the overwhelming firepower being thrown at her.

It was only at the last moment that Kira realized why Killinger had focused his fire on the *second*-closest battlecruiser—as the *closest* battlecruiser's icon merged with that of *Oceanic Trident*, only for both ships to be replaced by the blinking radioactivity icon of a fusion-core overload.

When the fireball faded, both ships were gone.

THERE WAS NO TIME. Not to mourn. Not to question whether the judgment everyone had leveled at Henry Killinger and his people had been unfair. Not even to plan the next few seconds.

The destruction of two of the battlecruisers at Killinger's hands brought a momentary respite in the hail of fire, the two *Fearless*es seeming to take a moment to reassess and pause their headlong charge.

Their commanders had clearly assumed their ships' defenses and weapons made them invulnerable, and the loss of half their number in a few shocking moments brought visible hesitation.

"Past the carriers," Soler reported. "Liberty Two's remaining cruisers are forming up."

Kira hadn't given orders for that. She wasn't surprised, though. At that moment, every remaining cruiser of their first two task forces was steering for the flash of the guns, forming a terrifyingly fragile wall between the two Fringe battlecruisers and the carriers.

Any destroyer her people had been able to reach was supposed to be forming a defensive layer between the cruisers and the carriers, to buy the only ships that could rearm the bombers space. Technically, they were obeying.

Technically meant that the growing skirmish line of destroyers was barely a thousand kilometers behind the cruisers.

"Brisingr battlecruisers are moving up to support the *Fearless*es," Soler reported. "That brings them up to eight ships."

Eight ships that more than matched the cruiser flotilla Kira was leading out to meet them.

"Where are my fighters?" she asked. The problem was that even if she had Liberty One and Liberty Two's fighters, they didn't have torpedoes. They'd used up their torpedoes on Bogey One—annihilating the BKN warships as a fighting force—and had no ammunition left for this new enemy.

But then, *where was Liberty Three?*

"If we have been betrayed by one of our own again, I will condemn Branimir Munroe from hell for all eternity," Kira said, surprised by the sheer icy calm in her voice.

"Soler, designations on our targets, please."

New data tags attached to the eight battlecruisers now advancing steadily toward her. Their fighters were being held back for defense now, she noted. The fate of Bogey One was clearly stuck in Bogey Two's commander's mind.

The first plasma shots flared out from the Fringe battlecruisers, and *Prodigal* shook.

"McCaig?" Kira asked.

"Solid hit," her Flag Captain told her, his tone equally icy calm. "We lost turret twelve and her entire crew. Main armor belt held."

That left *Prodigal* still with thirteen main guns. It also meant that Caiden McCaig had just lost eighteen of the spacers under his command—and that was assuming none of the plasma had burned into the portions of the turret inside the main armor belt.

"Hold her together, Captain," Kira said. It wasn't an order. It was *phrased* as an order, but her subordinate knew her calm words for what they were: a prayer more than even a request.

Plasma fire washed back across her fleet and her very soul. For a critical few seconds, Kira's people *couldn't* fire back. The *Fearlesses'* Brisingr-built companions had the same limitation, though, which meant only the two most powerful ships in the battle could engage.

Killinger had shaken their assumption of invulnerability but not destroyed it. The *Fearlesses* clearly missed too many shots for their commanders at full range and advanced with their smaller sisters.

The shots they *did* land were harsh but not crippling.

"They're focusing fire on the K-Nineties," Kira said aloud. "They *know* how capable *Prodigal* and *Harbinger* are, so..."

They also knew the limitations of the class, though *Kira* wasn't aware of any key vulnerabilities to her new ships. As she watched, though, *Harbinger* lost three of her turrets, forcing the cruiser to rotate in space to present undamaged armor to their enemy.

"Where are my fighters?" Kira demanded again, the words ashy ice on her tongue. Even Patel's wings should have been back by now. Everything she was doing was to buy time to get the bombers from Liberty One and Liberty Two back to *Fortitude* and the two remaining *Triremes*.

"We don't know, ser," Ronaldo admitted. "We have the CAP on the carriers. No contact with *any* of the fighters from the strikes."

Something was wrong. Or...was being done.

"We have to have faith," she told her flag staff. "Our people are doing *something*—and I *don't* think it's getting ambushed by the Kaiserreich!"

As she spoke, her cruisers finally entered range of their own guns. Despite the hammering the *Fearless*es had given her ships—mostly *Harbinger*, if she was being honest—Kira still had nine heavy cruisers and ten light cruisers in the rough wall she was bringing to bear.

"Target Four," Kira ordered silently via her headware, pinging one of the older BKN battlecruisers. "Then work our way through the L-One-Forties. They'll die fastest, and every one that dies is a ship not shooting at us."

Whatever was going on, Kira's people needed time. Asked for or not, she was going to buy it for them.

55

It was in the moment that *Harbinger* and Ionut Ayodele died that Kira realized they were all doomed. Whatever had drawn away her fighters and Admiral Munroe's Liberty Three was going to kill them all.

The K-90 cruiser died hard, her guns raining hellfire across space toward the target that Kira had flagged. Across her ships, they were producing over two hundred distinct vectors for their fire, and they'd spiraled in on the L140 battlecruiser in record time. *Harbinger* put at least two full salvos into her cousin before the fire from the battle-cruisers hit something critical.

Target Four didn't long survive the Memorial Force heavy cruiser —but neither did *Hostess*, the one heavy cruiser from the privateer fleet having slipped a few dozen kilometers ahead of the main body and drawn the full attention of one of the massive Fringe warships.

One of the Templars' *Hero*-class ships—Kira couldn't tell which one through the jamming—blew apart, bringing her down to six heavy cruisers. A second L140 died. Then a second Templar ship, followed by the last of the L140s.

Only the most modern of the BKN's battlecruisers remained,

between the L150s and the *Fearless*es, and Kira *knew*, in her bones, that five heavy cruisers, even backed by ten light cruisers, couldn't take on five battlecruisers.

Even if they'd only been the hundred-and-fifty-thousand-cubic-meter L150s, let alone the *three-hundred-thousand*-cubic-meter Kingdom of Griffon ships.

"What ships have cool drives?" Kira asked Soler.

"All of the ships from Liberty One," the operations officer answered instantly. "Liberty Two still has ten minutes left, minimum."

Michelakis had jumped across half the star system. The carriers couldn't retreat. Kira could pull the five heavy cruisers to safety, plus about half of the light cruisers and destroyers...but only by sacrificing the three surviving supercarriers, including *Fortitude*.

Or *Prodigal* and the rest of the heavy cruisers could die to buy the carriers enough time to get out.

"Plot a tactical nova," Kira ordered, surprised again at the calmness of her own voice as she made the decision. "I want to put all remaining cruisers behind and within two thousand kilometers of the *Fearless*es. We won't leave the jamming, and we will focus *all* of our firepower on those two ships."

A moment later, McCaig linked to her headware, a conversation flashing past at the speed of thought.

That's suicide.

I know, she conceded. *But we have to cover the carriers.*

There's a better option.

I'm listening, but we don't have much time. Kira wasn't sure what the better option was, but the conversation was taking place over the blinks of an eye, as more plasma fire hammered into *Deception* and she watched her last flagship begin to die.

Their carriers. They've kept their fighters around the battlecruisers, but I think their carriers might have been left uncovered—and undefended.

Kira's attention followed McCaig's thought. The six modern fleet carriers that had arrived with Bogey Two weren't defenseless in themselves, but they lacked the firepower of the battlecruisers.

And they were guarded by a handful of escorts. Bogey Two had been far from a balanced fleet.

"Soler, change that order," Kira said.

"Ser?"

"New target. The Brisingr carriers—and pass the course to *everyone* who can nova. The cruisers and destroyers that can't are to fall back on the carriers at maximum sublight speed."

Plotting the new course took critical seconds—seconds only bought for *Deception* by one of Killinger's privateers, *Onager*, diving in front of the stricken heavy cruiser and taking a full salvo from one of the *Fearless*es.

Onager survived, but she was crippled. Her engines failed in a flare of energy and she began to drift out of the battlespace, left behind by everyone.

"Ready!" Soler snapped.

"All ships," Kira replied. "Nova!"

THE UNIVERSE FLICKERED FOR A MOMENT, then reality converged back on them. With it came the chaos of the jammers, augmented a moment later by the jammers on the cruisers and destroyers Kira had brought with her.

At ten thousand kilometers, they were *inside* weapons range of the BKN ships. The power of the tactical nova was what gave nova fighters their *purpose*.

But the ten-minute timer now ticking down in the corner of Kira's eye was a stark reminder of why *starships* didn't do it. A nova fighter needed a minute, minimum, to reset their drive. A nova *ship*, using a class one drive, had a minimum of ten minutes.

Kira had bought a powerful tactical advantage by trapping her entire fleet in the battlespace with the Fringe battlecruisers—but as

Prodigal's guns tore into one of the Brisingr fleet carriers, she knew McCaig's suggestion had been the right plan.

Two carriers blew apart almost simultaneously—and their escorts were dying faster. The fighter CAP pilots had clearly thought the battle was all but over. They were *not* ready for a dozen destroyers to suddenly appear amidst their formation.

A hundred fighters attacking a dozen destroyers was usually a rough time for the destroyers. This time, every one of the advantages normally held by the nova fighters was in the hands of the larger vessels.

Less than half of the fighters survived to nova away. Their own destroyers were still in drive cooldown, and Kira's light cruisers went after them. Equal numbers of cruisers of *any* kind versus destroyers wasn't a winnable situation.

Thirty seconds after their jump, the carriers, escorts and fighters were crippled, destroyed or fled into nova.

But Kira's focus was on the battered hulk of *Deception*.

"Do we have any contact with Captain Mwangi?" she asked softly. The only people aboard Memorial Force's first cruiser she didn't know by name and face were newcomers, replacing people that had moved aboard *Prodigal* or *Harbinger*.

"No signal from *Deception*," Ronaldo admitted.

"Her jammers are down; her engines are down," Soler said. "Sensors indicate that hull integrity is intact in some sections."

"Let's get search-and-rescue into space," Kira ordered. "All combat-capable ships are to come about. It looks like the *Fearless*es are sending their fighter escort on ahead, but *everybody* is coming for us now!"

The *right* thing to do would have been to send the fighters after the cruiser force and pursue the carriers with the capital ships.

What the BKN had done instead... Kira ran the numbers and smiled.

"Ser?" Soler asked, seeing her expression.

"*Ask me for anything but time,*" Kira quoted again. "But it turns out, if you're prepared to pay enough, you can buy time.

"Liberty Two will be clear to nova before the Brisingr group can get near to them now."

There were still hundreds of starfighters and five battlecruisers heading toward the remains of Liberty One, but the carriers could get clear. Find the bombers. Rearm for another strike. Cover the missiles.

"I do believe, people, that we just saved Apollo," Kira said loudly. "Because *now* Michelakis can go get our bombers. They can't risk going after the missiles now—and without a nova interception, those missiles are going to shred their orbital forts."

She was right. She *knew* she was right.

But she was also trying to convince both herself and her people it had been worth it. Because she also knew that *they* weren't going to be around to see it.

At least she was going to die for her homeworld. She wouldn't have regretted it to have died for Redward or Samuels, but there had definitely been a job or two along the way where she'd have been dying for her own bottom line. Which just felt...strange.

"Estimate forty-five seconds until enemy fighters are in range," Soler reported in a near-whisper. "Estimate two minutes to range from the *Fearless*-class battlecruisers, two minutes ten seconds until range for our and Brisingr's heavy guns."

Kira nodded acknowledgement. Now that the BKN had finally unleashed their fighters, it was going to be over soon. There didn't seem to be any bombers in the fighter wings coming toward her now, but there were enough Weltraumpanzer heavy fighters that it wasn't going to matter.

"Thank you," she told her flag staff. She wasn't thanking Soler for the estimated time to range and everybody knew it.

"Wait!"

Every gaze in the room snapped to the sensor tech who'd spoke, who was staring at their screen in shock.

"Nova flares," they finally snapped, looking up at the rest of the flag bridge as the new contacts appeared on the screen, the computers doing their best to resolve them out of the multiphasic jamming.

"Multiple nova flares, estimate *two thousand–plus* nova fighters!" the tech continued. "They're..."

The tech fell silent as *everyone* saw the torpedoes launch, and Kira *finally* understood what Dinesha Patel and Branimir Munroe had done.

Out of the almost twenty-three hundred nova fighters of the entire Liberation Fleet, roughly six hundred had been bombers. Over three hundred of those had expended their torpedoes shattering Bogey One. Kira's entire sacrifice play had been to get the carriers free to rearm those bombers.

Except that Liberty Three had *twelve* carriers. Half of them had been light carriers, but all of them had been capable of rearming bombers.

Given time.

And Kira's people had bought her fighter pilots and Admiral Munroe's carrier that time.

Now *six hundred bombers* swept in on the battlecruiser formation like an avenging murder of ravens. Even the three L150 BKN battle-cruisers found themselves the target of five hundred missiles apiece—and that left over a *thousand* for each of the *Fearless*es.

None of the five ships survived. And over a thousand interceptors and heavy fighters were now screaming at the surviving BKN fighters charging Kira's line.

To a one, those pilots chose the ancient truism of nova-fighter crew: when the going gets tough, *be somewhere else.*

And for the first time since Bogey One had come out to attack Liberty One, Kira's screens were clear of hostiles.

"Tightbeam incoming from Commodore Patel, ser," Ronaldo reported.

"Put him through," Kira told him—and her voice was no longer calm. She couldn't even be ashamed of the waver. Thirty seconds earlier, she'd known she was going to die.

"I have to apologize for the delay, ser," Dawnlord said immediately. "We had to rearm the bombers and, well, I wanted to make sure the survivors of that first strike made sensible life choices."

He grinned.

"I also found some friends," he continued. "It turns out there were a few ASDF squadrons lurking around, making friends with the space workers. And since, well, we were making a big show of things, we, uh, picked up an extra fifty squadrons or so of backup."

"Thank you, Dinesha," Kira finally managed to say. "For a few minutes, well...I didn't know what had happened to you."

"We needed time, ser," he told her. "And we couldn't think of a way to ask for it without tipping our hand. We..." He swallowed, and for the first time, Kira could see the shadows of a recent terror in his eyes.

"We had to have faith," he whispered. "And hope that you would have faith with us."

56

"ADMIRAL, you may evacuate the stations, or you may die aboard them. Either way, in eleven minutes, the orbital fortresses will be destroyed."

"You have won a great victory today, Admiral Demirci, but I believe you overestimate what you have achieved."

Vizeadmiral Athaulf Kempf was a tall man with massively bushy white hair and mustache. Some long-ago injury traced a scar from the bottom of his left cheek all the way back across his skull, leaving a strip of bare skin through his scalp.

"Vizeadmiral," Kira said with a cold smile. "You are welcome to raise your jammers and fight it out with the missiles. To be completely honest, I can't turn them off at this point, anyway."

The long-range missiles were in final targeting mode. That had activated almost ten minutes earlier and would last until they were about to enter the multiphasic jamming field around the fortresses.

Kira could have *stopped* the missiles—given all of the information her people had on the weapons, her two thousand-odd fighters could shred the salvo well before it became a threat to the forts.

She wasn't going to.

"Either way, in just over ten and a half minutes, your forts are going to be overwhelmed. Anything that survives the salvo will then be reduced by nova fighters while we prepare Admiral Michelakis's Hoplites for their assault landings."

She was tired. She was grieving—for ships, in a way, as much as people. Only a third of *Deception*'s crew had been saved, and the heavy cruiser was unsalvageable. Between lost ships and lost fighters, Kira had led roughly twenty thousand people to their deaths today.

And killed about ten times that.

She was *angry*.

"If you evacuate the fortresses and order the surrender of the Weltraumsoldats and other ground forces on the surface, no one else will die today," she told Kempf. "But no matter what *you* choose, Apollo will be liberated today."

"I cannot give those orders, Admiral Demirci," the Vizeadmiral told her. "I have no authority over the surface forces." The bushy mustache twitched in what might have been a sad smile.

"And I have been denied permission to land even nonessential personnel." He shook his head. "The orders from the Governor of Apollo and my Kaiser are clear. You will not retake Apollo today, Admiral."

The channel cut and Kira glared at the screen.

"People, I believe there is an irredeemable bastard who needs to die in the next ten minutes, and it's *not* Vizeadmiral Kempf," she said loudly. "Please tell me we are contact with people on the ground."

"For now," Ronaldo said. "I don't know if we have anyone with major resources, though. We have contact info for Killinger's assets, but they're all a bit concerned over his fate.

"Michelakis is hitting old contingency-plan contact nets, but..."

"It's not like anyone on Apollo took those plans seriously," Kira said grimly. She studied the displays. "Tell them—all of them, hell, tell anyone who will listen!—that Governor Patrick Kurz has ordered all Brisingr personnel to stand and die.

"And that said personnel have *no* chance."

Kira didn't know if that was going to do anyone any good. She *did* know that if no one did anything in the next nine minutes—less, really, given the time required to evacuate the forts—Vizeadmiral Kempf and his people would die for nothing except the honor of a flag she'd already soaked in blood today.

"Message is going out on omnidirectional broadband transmission," Ronaldo told her. "Plugged it into every Brisingr net with every code we have for them, too."

He grinned.

"The codes left from *Prodigal*'s days as *K-Ninety-Two-E* are old codes but still valid enough for this," he observed.

"Let's hope someone was listening," Kira replied. "For now, we wait."

There wasn't long *to* wait. The reassembled Liberation Fleet was in position about ten light-seconds behind their missiles, watching the Harrington-coil weapons head toward their destination. The nova fighters had been rearmed, and if they were down three super-carriers, the three hundred ASDF pilots who'd somehow managed to go dark and survive until Kira arrived were *more* than willing to rough it.

That was a story Kira wanted to hear someday. Preferably over the many, many, *many* rounds of drinks those pilots and their civilian supporters had earned.

"Two minutes to impact," Soler reported softly.

"Tell Dawnlord to get his people into space for the follow-up," Kira ordered. The last of the bombers should have been finishing rearming. They needed to send the follow-up strikes in *immediately* after the missiles were done.

"Wait," Soler said. "I have evac craft and escape pods firing from several of the Apollo-built forts. No contact, no information. I think at least some of the crew have decided they don't *care* what the orders are."

Kira wasn't sure what she'd have done in the place of the general crew and officers aboard those stations. Their duty post was *supposed* to be invulnerable, but the vulnerability of asteroid fortresses had been demonstrated *right there*.

And most of the officers, at least, had enough data to do the math.

She knew that, in *Kempf's* place, she would have ignored the governor.

"Last of the bombers are deploying," Soler said, shaking her head. "All of the asteroid forts have seen at least *some* evacuation. Nothing that looks organi—"

She stopped in mid-word as *every* remaining station, from the big asteroid forts to the smaller prefabricated stations, suddenly exploded in evacuation craft.

"Full evac plans appear to have been activated, ser," Soler finally reported.

"Recorded burst transmission from Vizeadmiral Kempf, ser," Ronaldo told her.

"Play it."

It was a pure audio message, likely generated from the Vizeadmiral's headware without him ever speaking aloud.

"I do believe, Admiral Demirci, that I am never playing poker with you. Assistant Governor Mayer's sister serves as XO on one of the prefabricated forts. It appears that Aloisia may have decided that Kristine was more important than her boss.

"We won't know, however, as both Mayer and Kurz are dead. They may have shot each other. They may have been killed by their bodyguards. I don't know.

"All I know is that makes *me* Governor of Apollo. I am evacuating the orbital fortresses and, presuming I make it to the surface alive, am prepared to discuss the terms of surrender for the occupation garrison.

"I am prepared to die for Kaiser Reinhardt Wernher. I am *not* prepared to get half a million good soldiers and spacers killed for nothing more than his pride."

The message ended and Kira turned back to watch the icons tracking across her screen.

"Get word to Dawnlord," she ordered quietly. "The missiles *should* be able to avoid the evacuation craft, but if it looks like any of the escape ships are in danger, his people are to shoot the threat down."

"And the stations, ser?" Soler asked.

"As I told Kempf. We can't stop the missiles now. With his jammers inactive, we shouldn't even need to worry about missing or anything else. The stations are going to be destroyed.

"And then, I think, I'm leaving Kempf to Michelakis. No matter what, I do believe negotiations will be *short*."

After everything it had taken to get there, the actual destruction of the fortresses by the fires of twenty thousand thermonuclear bombs was...anticlimactic.

57

Kira didn't, as a rule, have to consciously think about things like gravity and oxygen levels when visiting habitable planets. Asteroid stations and other non-planet bodies required more thought, but when traveling between planets in the habitable range, ships were set to slowly adjust gravity and oxygen levels along the way.

Still, the moment she walked out of the shuttle onto New Athens's landing pad, there was a half-mental, half-physical *click* as everything slotted into the zone she'd grown up with. The ocean breeze carried just the right mix of just the right salts. The air had the right trace gasses. The star had the right wavelengths.

This was *home*. In her earlier career, she'd been back to Apollo often enough that she'd never experienced it quite as heavily as this, and she froze on the concrete.

"Keep moving, ser," Milani's voice murmured in her ear. "Landing home hits hard, I know, but the security cordon is up for a reason."

She glanced over at her ground commander and bodyguard. The red dragon on their armor was watchfully alert, whipping around its projectors and sweeping for potential threats.

Milani gestured forward and Kira nodded with a deep inhalation.

Memorial Force had taken over responsibility for this spaceport under contract with, well, Admiral Michelakis. There was no real planetwide government at the moment. Admiral Kempf was being held in a very nice house in one of New Athens's wealthier districts, under guard by Hoplites who'd been aboard the Last Fleet rather than living through the Brisingr occupation.

"There is a crowd gathered," Milani warned as they approached the edge of the pad. "We have a secured corridor to the vehicle, but I felt that it was wisest to keep an eye on them and let them see you."

The dragon made a displeased expression.

"You're right," Kira agreed. "These are my people, Milani. This is home."

"That's the only reason I'm taking the risk," they confirmed.

Power-armored mercenaries formed a cordon around the landing, and a gap emerged as Kira and her two escorts—Milani and Jess Koch —reached the edge. Kira could hear voices as they approached the security wall, and, considering Milani's warning, inhaled a fortifying breath.

Then she passed through the gate and into the space between two files of her mercenary commandos. Only one in four of the visible commandos were in full armor, the rest in formal dress uniforms with their blaster rifles held over their chests.

Beyond the two files of mercenaries, there was a packed crowd of people. Civilians, mostly, though she saw at least some uniformed police trying to direct traffic.

At the sight of Kira and her companies, a massive cheer broke out, and Kira stopped at the sheer force of the shouting.

"Keep moving," Milani murmured. "We're not seeing a threat, but this is vulnerable."

Kira's headware had flashing icons for the concealed layers of security. A dozen snipers held positions scattered around the path the commandos held open. A nearby hangar concealed the Hoplites' contribution to the security—a five-vehicle platoon of medium tanks.

A full *company*, over two hundred mercenaries strong and roughly a quarter of the entire ground-forces portion of Memorial Force, was in position to protect Kira.

She waved cautiously to the crowd but kept moving at Milani's urging.

She made it almost three-quarters of the way to the waiting aircar before a message request popped up on her headware. With the security protocols running, only a handful of people would have the ability to get through the filters stockpiling her messages for later.

Kira only read the name of the sender before she stopped on the spot, sweeping the entire crowd for the face she knew had to be there. And there he was.

Alistair Demirci had put on weight in the last five years and it looked good on him. He looked even more like their father than he had before—and his small wave as he saw her looking at him was *very* much their father.

"Milani, tagging my brother," Kira told her bodyguard. "Can we get him in the car easily?"

"*Easily* might be an ask, but probably," Milani replied.

"Oh, ye of little faith," Koch said. "Hold the car until we get there. Shouldn't be more than a minute extra."

Kira barely even saw where Koch *went*, but she was somehow through the cordon of mercenaries and into the crowd.

"I believe we leave that to Jessica," she told Milani. "And I'll warn my brother she's coming!"

ALISTAIR DEMIRCI LOOKED a bit taken aback and bemused when the aircar door opened and Koch ushered him in.

"I'm not quite sure that was necessary, sis," he told Kira in his slow, not-quite-slurred accent. "But it is good to see you."

"I was worried," Kira admitted. "How's Sophia?"

"Watching the sheep and your nephews," the younger Demirci replied with a slow grin.

Kira knew better than most that her brother wasn't stupid. He was, though, a very considered man who did everything at about two-thirds of the pace *she* would prefer.

"I didn't know you'd managed to carry on the family name," she told him.

"I..." He paused thoughtfully, considering in his usual way. "I knew enough of why you left, sis, that I figured sending you mail wouldn't be good for either of us."

"And I'm sure Sophia didn't mind not trying," Kira said.

"Sadly, no," he admitted. He glanced around at Kira's companions. "She's...reconsidering right now, but I figured it would be better if she stayed with the boys. We've three now."

He chuckled.

"I swear the neighbors think we're going to keep trying until we get a daughter. I'd have liked one—so would Soph—but I think we're done putting ourselves through that. Exowombs or not."

"I didn't come back for you and Sophia," Kira admitted. "If I had...well...I'd have been loading you and yours onto a transport, sheep and all, and hauling you out to Redward, where I could keep you safe."

"Sis, I have never in my adult life doubted that you loved me," Alistair said quietly. "Soph has her issues with you, but we all three knew, in our hearts of hearts, that all she needed was for you to spend some time in the village."

He snorted.

"And that Sophia's attitude was *why* you didn't spend time in the village." He shook his head. "I married a mighty woman but a stubborn one."

Kira's little brother, she realized, would have made an excellent therapist or spy. But he'd *wanted* to be a shepherd.

"You did, on both counts," she told him.

"ETA five minutes," Milani murmured. "Not to interrupt the family catch-up time."

"I'll make time for dinner later," Kira promised. "But I need to get to this meeting."

"The major Mayors," her brother said with a nod. "I don't want to interrupt. But I did need to see you, confirm that the news was true and it *was* you."

Everyone in the room stared at him.

"How did you know that?" Koch finally asked. "We thought we were keeping that pretty quiet."

"Oh, you are," he confirmed. "But even us little mayors have our ears and our networks."

"*Mayor*, huh?" Kira replied, eyeing her brother. That was out of character with her brother as she remembered him, but...five years was a long time. "I see we really do need to catch up."

"Give Soph a day or two, then we'll have you up for dinner," he told her. "I needed to see you, but I don't need to slow you down! Your work is important. *I* need you to make this meeting, from what I understand!"

58

Stepping out of the aircar, Kira caught a distinct smell on the wind that made her shiver. Blood and ash, the aftermath of hard fighting. One of the reasons New Athens the city was named that was because of the rock outcrop it was built around. Like the original Acropolis on Old Earth, it was naturally flat.

While the colonists hadn't needed a defensible location in the way their Greek ancestors had, the hard elevated site had made for an excellent landing site for the initial colony ship. While much of the ship had been dismantled to build the original city, a specific section around her main computers had been intended to remain intact.

That section was now surrounded by transparent armor at the heart of the Archive of Apollo on the south edge of the Acropolis, the greatest museum and library in the star system. Past the Archive was the Council Halls, a series of administrative centers that had served the planetary government.

Despite the successful assassination of the military governor, not all of the Brisingr troops had surrendered on Kempf's command. The largest core of resistance had been there, and the damage told.

"Milani, can you see my brother back to his home with the

aircar?" Kira asked. "Things are still shaken up and I want to know he's safe."

"Of course."

The dragon-armored mercenary gestured the shepherd into the aircraft.

"If you want us to give you a lift, that is, Em Demirci?"

Kira nodded to her brother, took a deep breath of the air and headed toward a set of buildings she'd only ever entered on tour.

THERE WERE HOPLITES *EVERYWHERE.* All of them wore the flashes of ships Kira recognized, though. These weren't troops from the brigades they'd found still holding out in the bunkers of the fall-back networks and dug into New Athens's mountains.

Kira suspected that the use of Last Fleet Hoplites concerned people on Athens, but she understood why Michelakis was doing it—and *she,* unlike the locals, recognized the difference between Last Fleet Hoplites and Hoplites from Killinger's privateers.

That there were almost as many of the latter as the former reassured Kira against the Apollon Admiral making her own play for tyrant.

Two of the Hoplites slipped in around her and Koch as they headed toward the central dome.

"Admiral," the one next to Kira greeted her. "Long time. Master Sergeant Nikolaos Rot, from *Victorious.*"

"You weren't a Master Sergeant then, but I remember you," Kira said with a smile. "Everything secure here, Nikolaos?"

"Yes and no," the Hoplite replied. "The Council Halls were intact when we landed, Admiral. We and the holdouts made a damn mess of things, but there was no fighting here when Brisingr took over."

Kira nodded grimly.

"No surprise, even if I'd prefer it had gone another way," she said. "So, we're not sure about..."

"We're tearing the original security system out," Rot said bluntly. "At this point, it's pretty clear some of the Council sold us out, so we can't trust anything they controlled.

"And it's possible there are ways in we don't know about."

Kira hoped Rot was being paranoid...but she saw his concerns as well.

"If we can get the rebuilding moving, some of those concerns slow down," she observed. "Which is what we're here for."

"The Thólos awaits you, ser. The last of the Mayors landed just before you did. Everyone should already be there."

There was probably an argument that should make Kira walk faster—but as she walked down the laser-smoothed promenade of her government's central buildings, she also just wanted to take in the realities of home.

The Council of Principals would not rise again, but they'd built some incredible buildings as monuments to their power along the way.

KIRA HAD BEEN in the Thólos of the New Athens Acropolis twice in her life. Once, as a thirteen-year-old student on a guided tour, and then a second time as a twenty-one-year-old officer when she'd taken her oath of service.

Now she walked into the Thólos as one of the people who were going to decide the fate of their planet.

The Council of Principals had varied in size over the years, from a peak of forty members just before Kira was born to a minimum of eight in the first century after landing. It had been twenty strong for most of her adult life.

The *space* its meetings had officially occupied, though, was immense. The Thólos was a white stone dome a hundred meters across that contained a single room. There were spaces underneath the building for security and the systems that ran a world government, but the Council met in a space reserved for them. One intentionally only slightly smaller and noticeably grander than the space set aside for the much larger Apollon Legislative Assembly.

The table at the center of the room was carved from the same white stone as the Thólos itself, though Kira knew that there were multiple matching copies of the furniture to allow for various sizes of meeting.

Michelakis had chosen the arrangement with intent. The massive circular stone slab could have seated sixty. The two dozen major Mayors around the table looked like they were missing people who should have been there.

"Admiral Demirci," Michelakis greeted Kira clearly. "Please, join us."

The acoustics of the room and the table were incredible. Even with a table sized for sixty, any attempt at side conversation would still be carried to everyone.

Kira took a seat directly across from the other Admiral and surveyed the room. She didn't know any of the twenty-four politicians around the table, though her headware readily added their names and the locations they governed above their heads.

There was a long silence as stewards in ASDF uniforms went around the table with coffee and water. No alcohol there today.

"Well?" the Mayor of New Athens finally asked. "We seem to be missing some of our counterparts, but you gathered us here for a reason, Admiral."

"The Mayor of Hansonberg apparently died here," Michelakis told the politicians softly. "We are not sure if she was with the holdouts voluntarily—or whether she was murdered by them or killed by our own troops.

"The Mayors of Vergeville, Neothebes and Macedonia, however, have been detained by our forces. Along with eleven of our formerly

honored Councilors, they were key public supporters of the occupation and acted as the face of Brisingr.

"Whether or not they have been involved in any actual crimes
beyond collaboration will be established in a proper trial," Michelakis
concluded. "But we cannot include them in this gathering just yet."

"And what *is* this gathering?" another Mayor asked.

"This table holds the senior surviving officer of the Apollo System
Defense Force, the Apollo-born mercenary officer who was key to the
existence of Liberation Fleet, and twenty-four of the Mayors of the
twenty-eight largest cities on Apollo," Michelakis reminded them all.

They were, in fact, the capital-M-Mayors of the only twenty-
eight municipalities that the government *gave* the name *polis*—a title
that gave the Mayors and municipal governments specifically
augmented powers and clear roles in the planetary system.

"You twenty-four are the most qualified and appropriate people
to establish the initial Provisional Government."

The tension in the room changed at those words. It didn't necessarily relax, but it shifted from being afraid *of* Admiral Michelakis.
An improvement, Kira hoped.

"Would not the members of the Council of Principals be more
suited?" a gold-haired woman from the southern-continent city of
Roanoke asked.

"Would *you* trust anyone from the Council now?" Michelakis
asked. "We need to find a path forward, but I do not think that
restoring the Council of Principals will be an acceptable option to the
people of Apollo—let alone our allies!"

"While it was not explicitly promised," Kira noted, "we strongly
implied that the Council would not be restored as part of the price of
the aid that liberated Apollo.

"We *did* promise that the days of the Friends of Apollo and one-
sided trade treaties and protectorates were over," she added.

"We would lack the strength to enforce any such thing for a while
yet, regardless," Michelakis added. "We must hold our fleet to defend

Apollo until we can rebuild the defense constellations and shipyards. Our one-time Friends have fewer ships than remain of our fleet, but they will be rebuilding more quickly."

"What, then, do you envisage the role of this 'provisional government' being?"

"Rebuilding those constellations and shipyards," Michelakis said. "We will need to coordinate resources and funding for those operations. I would, of course, be prepared to take on the duties of coordinating the military side of things, but I am not qualified to *lead* Apollo."

"Our protection must be the highest priority," the Mayor of New Athens observed. "Would we not be well served by...well, a dictator, in the classic Roman sense?"

"One of you two Admirals could take up the role," the woman from Roanoke suggested. "For a specified term—say, two years?—while we arrange a constitutional convention and new elections."

Kira suspected she now knew at least *two* people Killinger had groomed for his planned ascension to power. The concept of a term-limited single executive had *some* credence, but she certainly didn't want the job!

Neither, from her expression, did Michelakis.

"We must begin as we intend to go on," Michelakis told the politicians. "If we create a temporary dictator, it would be too easy for us to justify turning ourselves into a constitutional monarchy like Brisingr.

"I do not believe that suits us. My inclination is more toward a presidential republic with clear division of powers—but I, Mayors, am a soldier. It was my job to keep our world free. Failing at that, as I did, it became my job to *liberate* our world.

"Thanks to Admiral Demirci, I succeeded at that. Now, I look to you, the highest-level officials elected by a universal franchise on our planet, to guide our people into our new era."

"First, we must deal with the traitors and collaborators you have already detained," a hawk-faced Mayor from the western continent growled. "A few public executions will make the price of treason clear!"

"Unless our judiciary has been wiped out or lost some of its traditional independence and fractiousness, that would be murder," Kira said. "And I would happily place Memorial Force at the service of said judges to deliver people to trial."

It was a very subtle threat, she hoped—but she also knew that no one in the room was stupid.

The Apollon judiciary was appointed by the municipal governments, but they were not beholden to them. The Mayors—and the other elected members of Apollo's government—had a *say* in who was appointed to the higher roles, but it would be, for example, the municipal judges who would select from their own to fill the regional court.

Then the regional-court judges would select from their numbers to appoint the continental judges, and the continental judges selected the supreme court from their numbers.

The most the politicians could do was force a recall vote where every citizen in that judge's area of responsibility voted on whether they were removed. It *happened*, but it wasn't at the whim of the day-to-day government of Apollo.

Kira would have to check, but she suspected that the Apollo Supreme Court either still existed—or that the Continental Courts had already selected who was going to *fill* it.

The Apollon judiciary wouldn't be slowed or impeded by something so minor as a planetary occupation, and they would *not* stand for the new government executing people without justification.

"We must think to the future," Kira continued. "We must show that *crimes* will be punished, yes. And our court system can handle that. But I feel that, outside of the *highest* levels, the people who ran the planet for Brisingr did what they had to do.

"Some will have abused their power. They will face charges for their crimes. But merely serving what looked like it was going to be the long-term government?"

Kira smiled coldly.

"By that standard, *all of you* are collaborators, aren't you? There can be no mass executions. There *will* be trials, I hope, but we cannot become monsters—or we will undermine the very state we are trying to preserve."

That got her some sheepish looks. She figured her point was made.

"We can't operate with no planetary government, but the leadership of our previous government has completely discredited not only themselves but, I suspect, the entire concept of constitutional oligarchy," Kira told them. "You were all elected with broader franchises, which gives you a popular authority we need.

"We cannot have a Provisional Government imposed from outside, not if we want to maintain our people's pride and approval. We can no longer be the first among all in our stars, but I do not believe our citizens will accept being the begging pauper, either.

"But unless we *are* ready and have people in position to speak for our world when Brisingr sends people to negotiate..."

She let that image sink in.

"I do not think anyone in this room is opposed to stepping up in Apollo's time of need," the Mayor of New Athens said. "We will act as suggested, in coordination with you two. A constitutional convention will take time to organize. What happens until then?"

"For now, the municipal governments can manage their own affairs," Michelakis suggested. "Much of the apparatus of the planetary government still exists, especially if we offer a blanket amnesty for anyone who merely participated in the occupation as a bureaucrat, for example.

"If they look to a council of the *polis* Mayors for the next year or so instead of a Council of Principals, I think they will be fine."

"What about Brisingr?" the Roanoke woman asked. "They will be back."

"If we are lucky, they will talk before diving in fleet-first," Kira said. "If not, we will fight. The yards are intact enough to repair the ships of our fleet. It will take time for us to regain the traditional invulnerability of an inhabited star system—but we received enough covert aid to be confident that if we ask for *overt* help, we can forge new alliances."

"Of equals," Michelakis said calmly. "Time is not on our side, and it will only be two weeks before Brisingr can get a fleet here. Anything they send quickly, we can probably handle. The longer they take, the more powerful the force the BKN will muster against us.

"We will want to get accredited diplomats chosen and sent out as quickly as possible. Even in the best-case scenarios, we may need a third party to negotiate the prisoner exchange."

Apollo had a *lot* of prisoners right now. They were under control, but it was taking up a lot of police and ASDF personnel that could be better used elsewhere.

"If we are to take on this role as the Provisional Government, then I think we are going to need more information," the Mayor of New Athens observed. "I think we should..."

Kira leaned back, concealing a smile as the brains around the table engaged.

No one became the Mayor of a *polis*—inherently a city of millions—without having the instincts and skills for this, after all.

59

"So. When does Memorial Force move on?"

Zoric's question struck at the core of Kira's current dilemma.

"And when we do, are you coming with us?"

Kira winced and held her hand to her breast. "That strikes right to the heart, doesn't it?" she replied.

The two women were in Kira's office aboard *Fortitude*. The carrier had stood down from full battle stations only a few minutes earlier, trading off the main watch with *Delphis*.

They'd expected the Kaiserreich Navy a full two weeks earlier. After twenty-eight days without a word from the enemy, everyone was getting nervous. An "International Squadron," anchored on an Attacan battle carrier that Kira was eighty percent sure hadn't been on any lists a month ago, was working up in the asteroid belt, but the ASDF and Memorial Force were still carrying the main chunk of the guard.

"We have been *well* compensated for our service in retaking Apollo," Zoric observed, gesturing at the task force status display—now including three *Hero*-class cruisers. Knight-Admiral Cullen, as it turned out, had been given two orders for the long-term fate of his ships: they couldn't come back to Exarch, and Apollo couldn't have them.

The solution had been obvious to everyone as soon as he'd explained the situation.

"The Provisional Government was delighted to sign the new contract as well," Kira noted.

"Yes, because they're still angling to get you into the election for the transitional President!"

"*I* suggested Mel." Kira grinned. Nightmare had *not* been impressed with the idea.

"It sounds like Michelakis is kicking and screaming as she's being dragged to the nomination, but I have the feeling she will actually stand," Zoric told Kira. "But..."

"A bunch of the Mayors would rather the transitional President was me," Kira conceded with a sigh.

The Council of Mayors had decided that, to get popular buy-in for the Provisional Government and the Constitutional Convention they were convening, they needed an executive figurehead.

The situation was such that no one was entirely sure what powers the transitional President would *have*, beyond being first among equals of the Provisional Government's leading council, but the system-wide election would be a useful dry run of making the infrastructure work.

But neither Kira Demirci or Fevronia Michelakis wanted the job of leading the Provisional Government.

"I don't know if I can really *leave* at this point," she admitted. "We're going to lose at least two of the old Three-Oh-Three hands as well."

Unfortunately, the ones she *knew* were Dawnlord and Scimitar. Patel had lost his boyfriend in the Rim, and Colombera still had a massive clan spread across New Athens.

Cartman was thinking about it, but Kira... Well, if she was being honest, Mel Cartman was going to go where Kira went.

Evgenia Michel, on the other hand, suited the mercenary life too well to leave.

"That's fair," Zoric replied. "I'm not necessarily planning on buying people out, either. If we've got shareholders settling in this sector, we'll end up homeporting here. Transporting everything from Redward will be sad and we'll lose some of the folks *from* Redward, but I am *not* dealing with the banking issues of paying dividends from a Redward-ported mercenary fleet to shareholders in Apollo!"

"You're already assuming I'm leaving, aren't you?" Kira realized aloud. "Thinking like an Admiral already."

Zoric flushed, her skin going surprisingly dark with the color change.

"I have to contingency-plan," she said quietly. "I have a responsibility."

"So do I, Kavitha," Kira told her. "And I appreciate it. We have to take care of our people, one way or another."

She sighed.

"*If* I leave—and I have *not* decided yet—you and I will need to make an exchange," she continued. "Thirty-one percent of the company for some monetary value and certain contractual promises. If I'm making you Admiral, you need to be the majority shareholder."

Kira held fifty-one percent of Memorial Force's shares to Zoric's twenty. She wasn't at all sure how to *value* shares of the mercenary fleet for a buyout, but she knew that she couldn't retain fifty-plus percent of a mercenary fleet she didn't actively command.

"I see the logic," Zoric agreed. "We'll want to involve Vaduva in that conversation. If anyone can evaluate what a third of this fleet is worth, it's him."

"Like I said, I haven't decided yet."

"But Michelakis offered you a job, yes?"

Kira arched an eyebrow at her second-in-command.

"*That* is entirely unofficial. Milani is telling tales out of school?" That was...unusual for the dragon-armored mercenary.

"They felt it was important that I know about it, though they told me I had to tell *you* they told me," Zoric said with a chuckle. "They're right, too. As I understand it, Fleet Admiral and command of the primary battle fleet? Basically the second-ranked officer of the entire ASDF or whatever it ends up called?"

"And her replacement as *commanding* officer if she takes the transitional presidency," Kira said quietly. "Nothing in writing, nothing committed. Just Michelakis's word. Which is..."

"Enough," Zoric concluded. "Gods, Kira, with everything that's gone down in the last decade, either of us could retire and live like queens anywhere in the Rim. We funded most of this operation out of pocket, knowing that the diplomatic corps had money chasing us, and the Provisional Government has more than made up our lost revenue, let alone our costs."

"And that was before the cruisers."

"Exactly," Zoric confirmed. "The new contract to help in system defense is less...aggressively generous, but it's certainly fair enough. But much as I like your world, I'm a mercenary for a reason.

"For me, and for a lot of the folks in Memorial Force, we have to move on eventually."

"We will," Kira promised. "I'm *thinking* when the second set of forts comes online. Eight months, give or take."

Brisingr had expanded the asteroid-fort construction facilities dramatically. With one set of fortresses already under construction and a second to start as soon as they were done, Apollo would have twenty-four asteroid fortresses in eight months.

Kira wouldn't truly breathe easy until they were back up to sixty-odd, each with a hundred nova fighters aboard, but twenty-four would secure against anyone less willing to spend five percent of a system's GDP on a single salvo than she had been.

"All right." Zoric raised a hand. "I'm going to—"

"ALERT ALERT—NOVA CONTACT! MULTIPLE NOVA CONTACTS!"

The message slammed into both of their heads and the displays around them. Kira met Zoric's gaze and smiled grimly.

"I'm not expecting anyone from our allies, which means that's almost certainly Brisingr."

"RESOLVING the contacts in more detail; we're looking at fewer ships than we thought," Soler reported as Kira arrived on the flag bridge. "It's just that one of them is another *Fearless*."

"Wonderful. Run me through them?" Kira asked, dropping into her chair.

Datafeeds and icons flickered around her.

"They are roughly one light-minute out and holding position," the ops officer replied. "Appears to be a light task group anchored on the battlecruiser. Pair of fleet carriers, six destroyers. That..."

"Is not a fleet that's planning on retaking Apollo," Kira murmured. "Nova fighters?"

"Two hundred up in CAP formation," Soler told her. "They *appear* to be heavy fighters and interceptors, but..."

"I don't like the way you said 'appear,' Soler." Kira was studying the planes as her ops officer spoke, though, and she could see the problem.

"Energy signatures are too dense," her subordinate said. "Last time we saw anything like this, it was the Manticores in Cobra Squadron's hands. But these are..."

"Even more modern," Kira guessed.

"Yeah. Those were obsolete by Fringe standards, even though they were terrifying in the Syntactic Cluster. *These* are...last-generation birds, I think. Not front-line starfighters for Griffon but definitely on par with the *Fearless*es for tech."

"Someone is making a *point*, I see," Kira said drily. "Fleet status?"

"Battle stations across the board. Admiral Michelakis has asked us to hold our fighter strike, though."

Kira nodded.

"I was going to suggest the same. They've brought enough to

demonstrate that continuing this fight is a bad idea but not enough to actually threaten us.

"They're here to talk."

60

A NOVA PINNACE marked with the flaming sword and gauntlet of the Brisingr Kaiserreich was among the last things Kira would have expected to see on the flight deck of a *Trireme*-class supercarrier.

The small craft's presence, slowly settling to the deck aboard *Salaminia*, was a good sign, though. Its path had been precleared by long-range messages, negotiated over lightspeed coms with a minute's flight each way.

Now, with defensive guns blatantly trained on it, the pinnace settled to the deck. A company of ASDF Hoplites executed a swift evolution, encircling the pinnace and forming a path between the ramp and where Kira and Michelakis stood.

The "plug" in that bottle, to stop any suicidal attempt by the BKN to attack the two Admirals, was formed by Milani and five Memorial Force commandos. Past her dragon-armored subordinate, Kira watched the pinnace's ramp descend and a pair of power-armored soldiers march out.

Like Milani, these soldiers had holographic iconography flickering over their armor. Instead of Milani's red dragon, the Brisingr soldiers' armor carried a black-armored knight apiece, the chest of both real and virtual knight emblazoned with the Kaiserreich's sword and gauntlet.

"Reichsgarde," Michelakis said softly. "It appears they *are* serious."

The Reichsgarde were not, as Kira understood it, the Kaiser's security. They were the *Diet's* security—and Brisingr's legislature would have needed to empower the Kaiserreich's representative.

So would the Kaiser, of course, but the presence of the Diet's security officers was a promising sign. Whoever they had sent was hopefully accredited by the Diet, which should theoretically save time.

The two Reichsgarde swept the room with their gazes and sensors, then stood aside as a second pair of armored soldiers advanced. The four of them, ostentatiously unarmed, formed a semi-circle in front of the ramp while their charge advanced down it.

It took Kira several seconds longer than it should have to recognize the man behind the soldiers. He had shaven his head and wore a long formal tunic, black on black, with no insignia or blazons.

But Konrad Bueller's presence aboard the Kaiserreich shuttle meant things had either gone very right...or very, very wrong.

BUELLER ADVANCED along the path the Hoplites had left open for him, stopping and allowing Milani to scan him before he advanced to stand in front of the two Admirals.

"Admiral Michelakis," he greeted Kira's companion, then inclined his head to Kira herself. "Admiral Demirci. Kira."

Kira could *feel* Michelakis's questions at Bueller's use of her first name, but the commander of Apollo's defenses took one step forward and turned a wintry gaze on Kira's boyfriend.

"And you are?"

"I am Konrad Bueller, and I am the accredited ambassador of the Diet of the Kaiserreich of Brisingr," Bueller responded calmly. He drew a black leather folio from his tunic, his motions slow and clear to keep the bodyguards calm, and offered it to Michelakis.

"My documents and credentials, Admiral. I am here to offer a cease-fire between our nations and to speak as Brisingr's representative in discussions between us."

There was a long silence before Michelakis took the folio. She didn't open it—though Kira knew her headware would be scanning the electronic copy of the credentials included.

"I do not see Kaiser Reinhardt's authorization on these documents," Michelakis finally said. "Do you think we are so foolish as to be lured into missteps by the Diet?"

"If you review the final document, you will see that a supermajority of the Diet has overridden the necessity of the Kaiser's approval," Bueller said instantly. He raised his hand before Michelakis could say anything more.

"There are two things, I think, that I should explain before you say anything else, Admiral," he told her. His gaze flicked to Kira.

She hoped that her gaze was providing whatever support he needed—assuming, of course, that her love had not become her enemy while he was gone.

"First and foremost, Kaiser Reinhardt Wernher is dead."

Five words, plainly and clearly stated, cut the worst of Kira's fears off at the knees. They seemed to echo around the ship and she could *see* the realization ripple through the Hoplites and naval crew on *Salaminia* slowly and surely.

"Kaiser Reinhardt committed suicide the night after the news of the liberation of Apollo reached us," Bueller continued. "Enough questions had already been raised that his Kaisership was considered unlikely to last out the next day, and he appears to have chosen to... leave office on his own terms."

Kira knew Konrad Bueller well enough to know he wasn't saying everything. For now, though, she waited.

"And your second piece of explanation, Em Bueller?" Michelakis asked.

"Thanks to the questions already raised prior to the news of the liberation reaching us and the events that followed, the Shadows of Brisingr have been officially dissolved," he told her.

"I am tasked by the Diet of the Kaiserreich of Brisingr to *end* this war. Kaiser Reinhardt's foolishness has brought both our nations to the brink of collapse.

"There are discussions to be had with other star systems, about the fate of the sector and the Trade Route Security Zone, but all of those, in the minds of the Diet, hinge upon peace, Admiral Michelakis.

"So, I must ask: are you empowered to negotiate on behalf of the Apollon Provisional Government or to deliver me to people who are?"

"I am empowered to negotiate," Michelakis told him. "Come, Em Bueller. A space has been prepared, and it seems we have much to talk about."

61

"To peace."

"To peace," Kira replied to Konrad's toast, clinking her wineglass against his.

There were a lot of details to sort out. Konrad had swiftly conceded the *concept* of reparations, but the exact amounts would take time to calculate and negotiate. It was very clear the Diet had sent him out with a blank check and a *lot* of both authority and trust.

She wasn't sure how he'd ended up in *that* position from infiltrating the planet with a Terran spy.

Still. The cease-fire was signed. A draft structure of a peace treaty had been agreed. Twenty-four hours after Kira had seen her boyfriend for the first time in over a month, there was peace.

Now she sat on the couch in the sizeable guest quarters put at Bueller's disposal and eyed him across the wineglasses.

"You were the last person I expected to see walk off that pinnace," she finally told him. "You have some explaining to do. Where's Zamorano?"

"He left Brisingr a couple of days before I did, off to some new crisis somewhere, I think," Konrad admitted. "The bugger set me up, you know."

"I was guessing," she said dryly. "What *happened?*"

"Turned out that some of his contacts on Brisingr were senior members of my own family," he told her. "Between what they knew and the direction I was able to provide with what *I* knew, plus some documents Zamorano helped me find, we had enough to put together a case against Reinhardt in the Diet.

"And the easiest way to be able to *present* that case was to force him to prosecute his accusations against me on the Diet floor." Konrad shrugged. "So, we arranged for me to be arrested by a friendly police agent, who started the process running on my claiming Alteste Family privilege.

"My family turned the whole thing into a media spectacle that was making Reinhardt look guilty as sin—but success covers a lot of sin," he reminded her grimly. "It was looking pretty clear that I was going to walk without any of the charges sticking.

"Then the news arrived about Apollo and, well..."

"Reinhardt killed himself."

In private, Konrad didn't even bother hiding his opinion of that.

"Someone killed him?" she asked.

"Nothing we can prove," he admitted. "But there was no suicide note, and a *lot* of Shadows and identified Institute agents were gone by the time we started rolling up those networks a week later.

"I think whatever's left of the Brisingr Shadows now belongs to the Equilibrium Institute," he concluded. "Which...isn't great, but they no longer control Brisingr."

Kira eyed him carefully. There was still something he wasn't telling her. *Something* had consumed two extra weeks before he'd come to Apollo.

"What aren't you telling me?" she asked flatly.

Konrad swallowed and nodded slowly.

"We move quickly to elect new Kaisers," he observed. "Generally, the nominees are established within five days of the Kaiser's death, and the election, by law, cannot be more than twenty-eight days after the death.

"It hadn't happened yet when I left, but the polling and evidence were pretty clear. We know who the new Kaiser is going to be."

Kira stared at him uncomprehendingly for a good ten seconds before it finally sank in.

"Your family and Zamorano put you on every screen and the top of everyone's mind," she murmured. "The man who stood up to Reinhardt, exposed his crimes. I'm guessing the timeline after impeachment is pretty similar?"

"Yeah."

"It's you, isn't it?"

"Yeah." He met her gaze and shrugged helplessly. "Brisingr needs me, Kira. They *need* someone who wasn't in the heart of this mess to take charge of cleaning it up. Reinhardt spent his entire reign shifting the ground rules around himself, creating a new power base in the Shadows, laying the groundwork to take over the Sector.

"Now all of that has come crashing down, with the lies and the crimes exposed. They need a symbol of a new era, someone they *know* stood against all of Reinhardt's shit."

He sighed.

"So, yeah. I let my family nominate me. One other candidate withdrew. Reinhardt's first-choice candidate is dead here. His faction's second-choice candidate *surrendered the fleet* here."

Kira chuckled. She knew who both of *those* were.

"So, I was running against two other Alteste Family members, only one of whom had any public profile, and polling and analysis were expecting a seventy-plus percent landslide."

Her chuckle faded as she considered what that meant.

"You're not rejoining Memorial Force," she observed.

"I can't." He paused, swallowing. "I also..."

He trailed off, but Kira waited patiently. She'd have her own plans to make, but she wasn't sure how her boyfriend ruling Brisingr would impact them. Or ex-boyfriend? She wasn't sure how that would work, and the thought made her hide a wince.

"I can't do this on my own, Kira," Konrad whispered. "I'm an *engineer*. I can...see the system, find the problem, but the solutions are beyond me. I'm not sure I can lead—but the Kaiser can't follow, either.

"And I can't be Reinhardt Wernher, either. But I have to be Kaiser, because Brisingr needs it."

He swallowed.

"I can't do it alone, which makes this a shitty deal to offer you," he admitted. "You're already wealthy, already powerful, so all I can really offer is one of the crappiest, hardest, most thankless jobs in the universe. But I *know* that with you at my side, we can redeem Brisingr. Restore Apollo. Turn this entire sector into a beacon of hope.

"But I can't do it alone," he repeated for the third time. "So..."

He was on one knee, holding out a ring he'd clearly made himself, before she fully caught up.

"Kira Demirci, will you marry me and be my Kaiserin?"

JOIN THE MAILING LIST

Love Glynn Stewart's books? Join the mailing list at

GLYNNSTEWART.COM/MAILING-LIST/

Be the first to find out when new books are released!

ABOUT THE AUTHOR

Glynn Stewart is the author of *Starship's Mage*, a bestselling science fiction and fantasy series where faster-than-light travel is possible–but only because of magic. His other works include science fiction series *Duchy of Terra, Castle Federation* and *Vigilante,* as well as the urban fantasy series *ONSET* and *Changeling Blood.*

Writing managed to liberate Glynn from a bleak future as an accountant. With his personality and hope for a high-tech future intact, he lives in Southern Ontario with his partner, their cats, and an unstoppable writing habit.

VISIT GLYNNSTEWART.COM FOR NEW RELEASE UPDATES

CREDITS

The following people were involved in making this book:
  Copyeditor: Richard Shealy
  Proofreader: M Parker Editing
  Cover art: Jeff Brown Graphics
  Typo Hunter Team
  Faolan's Pen Publishing team: Jack, Kate, and Robin.

 facebook.com/glynnstewartauthor

OTHER BOOKS BY GLYNN STEWART

For release announcements join the
mailing list or visit **GlynnStewart.com**

STARSHIP'S MAGE
Starship's Mage
Hand of Mars
Voice of Mars
Alien Arcana
Judgment of Mars
UnArcana Stars
Sword of Mars
Mountain of Mars
The Service of Mars
A Darker Magic
Mage-Commander
Beyond the Eyes of Mars
Nemesis of Mars
Chimera's Star *(upcoming)*

Starship's Mage: Red Falcon
Interstellar Mage
Mage-Provocateur
Agents of Mars

Starship's Mage Novellas
Pulsar Race
Mage-Queen's Thief *(upcoming)*

DUCHY OF TERRA
The Terran Privateer
Duchess of Terra
Terra and Imperium
Darkness Beyond
Shield of Terra
Imperium Defiant
Relics of Eternity
Shadows of the Fall
Eyes of Tomorrow

SCATTERED STARS

Scattered Stars: Conviction

Conviction
Deception
Equilibrium
Fortitude
Huntress
Prodigal

Scattered Stars: Evasion

Evasion
Discretion
Absolution *(upcoming)*

PEACEKEEPERS OF SOL

Raven's Peace
The Peacekeeper Initiative
Raven's Course
Drifter's Folly
Remnant Faction
Raven's Flag *(upcoming)*

EXILE

Exile
Refuge
Crusade
Ashen Stars: An Exile Novella

CASTLE FEDERATION

Space Carrier Avalon
Stellar Fox
Battle Group Avalon
Q-Ship Chameleon
Rimward Stars
Operation Medusa
A Question of Faith: A Castle Federation Novella

Dakotan Confederacy

Admiral's Oath
To Stand Defiant
Unbroken Faith *(upcoming)*

AETHER SPHERES
Nine Sailed Star
Void Spheres *(upcoming)*

VIGILANTE
(WITH TERRY MIXON)
Heart of Vengeance
Oath of Vengeance

**Bound By Stars: A Vigilante Series
(With Terry Mixon)**
Bound By Law
Bound by Honor
Bound by Blood

TEER AND KARD
Wardtown
Blood Ward
Blood Adept *(upcoming)*

CHANGELING BLOOD
Changeling's Fealty
Hunter's Oath
Noble's Honor
Fae, Flames & Fedoras: A Changeling Blood Novella

ONSET
ONSET: To Serve and Protect
ONSET: My Enemy's Enemy
ONSET: Blood of the Innocent
ONSET: Stay of Execution
Murder by Magic: An ONSET Novella

STAND ALONE NOVELS & NOVELLAS
Children of Prophecy
City in the Sky
Excalibur Lost: A Space Opera Novella
Balefire: A Dark Fantasy Novella
Icebreaker: A Fantasy Naval Thriller

Made in the USA
Middletown, DE
29 April 2023

29695749R00257